Copyright © 2025 by Hillary Bowen

All rights reserved.

No part of this book may be reproduced in any form or by any electronic or mechanical means, including information storage and retrieval systems, without written permission from the author, except for the use of brief quotations in a book review.

Cover art by Tina Carbone @palesile. 2025

❈ Formatted with Vellum

OUT WITH LANTERNS

HILLARY BOWEN

For Raph. It has always been you.

CONTENT INFORMATION

Out with Lanterns contains themes that some readers may find difficult. These include:

- multiple explicit sex scenes on page,
- mentions of familial neglect (some on page, in present),
- death of a parent (off page, in the past),
- traumatic memories of war, death, and injury (on page),
- recovery from injuries,
- mentions of bigotry and misogyny (past and present),
- food scarcity,
- colic in a horse (detailed, on page),
- threat of blackmail,
- threat of unhousing

Please take care of yourself and make your reading decisions with your own mental health in mind.

"The power of a glance has been so much abused in love stories, that it has come to be disbelieved in. Few people dare now to say that two beings have fallen in love because they have looked at each other. Yet it is in this way that love begins, and in this way only."
    Victor Hugo, *Les Miserables*

PROLOGUE

January 1917
  Wood Grange Estate, Somerset, England

It was dark by the late afternoon, dreary and damp in the way that cold January days almost always are, and Ophelia hurried to collect the last of the items laid out on her bed before she completely lost the light. In a neat row on her counterpane lay a packet of her favourite biscuits the housekeeper, Mrs. Greene, had carefully wrapped in waxed paper along with a note of encouragement, her journal and pen, and a small portrait of her mother in a chased-silver frame. Tucking them into the side pocket of the carpetbag, she ran her hands over the items inside. Chemise, blouse, skirt, stockings, nightdress, cardigan. Everything was accounted for, but once she closed the clasp on the worn bag, she was admitting to herself that she was actually going to go through with the plan. A noise in the hall caught her attention; she listened to catch a hint of the walker's gait, the telltale click of her father's walking stick on the hardwood floors. Nothing. *Thank God*. Then a small scratch at the bedroom door. She opened it a crack to the housekeeper's serious round face.

"A minute, Miss Ophelia?" she whispered.

Ophelia opened the door and hurried the woman inside. She came only to Ophelia's shoulder, her strawberry-blonde hair streaked with grey and escaping in soft tufts from her top knot, her blue eyes serious in her wide intelligent face.

"I had a thought and brought ye one more thing for the road," she said, pressing a small flask into Ophelia's hands. "It was my mam's. She kept it in her knitting basket for when she needed a little extra courage or calm, as it may be." The housekeeper smiled up at Ophelia, who was turning the small silver container over in her hands, wondering whether at the ripe old age of twenty-two drinking on the run was going to become part of her new life. Mrs. Greene patted her hand gently, saying, "It's no bad thing to have a nip to warm you or when you need a little fortitude."

Ophelia returned the press of the woman's hand with hers. "Thank you so much, Mrs. Greene. I'm sure I'll need all the courage I can get, but oughtn't you keep it?"

Mrs. Greene waved her hand. "I'm glad for you to have it. Mam approved of women finding their own way in life, even in the bad old days. She'd be happy to know it was going with you on your adventure." The housekeeper clutched Ophelia's hand, eyes teary, nose a little pink. "I'm so proud of you, miss, doing your bit for the war. You're going to have such an adventure in that Women's Land Army, I just know it. But you ought to get going now. The longer you tarry, the better the chance of your father noticing something's afoot."

Ophelia nodded, pressing the clasp on her carpetbag home, the click feeling as heavy as the beating of her heart.

Down the stairs and out through the kitchen entrance, she made her way carefully in the dark, past the long beds of the kitchen garden toward the gate in the brick wall. The warmth spilling around Mrs. Greene in the kitchen doorway disappeared quickly when the housekeeper doused the light. There being no moon, Ophelia had to rely on her memory of the estate to make her way out of the garden, through the gate, and across the gravel drive. She clutched the leather handle of her bag tightly, listening intently for any sign of disturbance behind her. It seemed unlikely that her father would notice her absence before the next day; he rarely sought her out unless he required her presence for one or another of his schemes, but she couldn't shake the feeling that he would suddenly acquire some parental awareness after a lifetime of ignoring her.

Reaching the rise of the drive and breaking out of the shadow of the Atlas cedars that lined the long entrance to the house, Ophelia stood for a moment to catch her breath. She could hardly believe she was going through with this. She turned to look back at the house, only one or two windows visible from this vantage. Its warm stone walls had been the scene of her entire life, had witnessed every quiet day, every lonely night, every conversation that had gradually brought her to this moment. Her chest felt tight, but her head was clear. She nodded to herself and stepped up onto the road.

"Thought you might've changed your mind," came a voice from the gloom. The owner, a tall red-haired woman, stepped forward, her face a delicate collision of angles and shadows in the low light. Ophelia started, then moved toward her.

"Hannah?"

"Said I'd meet you, didn't I?"

"Yes, it's true, you did." Ophelia felt flustered, the determination of just a minute ago fading a little in the face of her terse companion. She shifted her weight from foot to foot uncertainly. She felt the same flush of naiveté she had upon meeting Hannah at the Women's Land Army recruitment event months before. The other woman had a directness of speech and action that made Ophelia feel like an awkward schoolgirl.

"Let's be on our way then. The wagon will take us a good way to the station. We'll walk the rest." She turned, and Ophelia trotted to catch up with her. A small cart waited a little ways up the lane, the dark horse at its head standing quietly. "Let me get you up, then I'll pass your bag," Hannah said.

Ophelia dropped her bag and grasped Hannah's hand, stepping on the wheel to get a foot onto the footboard of the cart. Seated, she settled her bag at her feet and waited for Hannah to clamber up the other side. They started off down the lane, the horse's hooves hollow and loud on the packed earth of the road.

"I wasn't going to change my mind," Ophelia said into the silence. She didn't know why she needed Hannah to know that she hadn't hesitated, but it felt important to her that the woman know she was committed to her decision, to this choice. "Only I got to the edge of the property and it hit me all at once that I was really leaving."

"Ah, I know. I was only cheeking you," Hannah said, a hint of the North in her voice. "'Tisn't easy for anyone to leave a place they know, even when it's not been good to them. I know that well enough myself."

Ophelia nodded and squeezed her hands together on her lap.

"Were you able to get away without interference from your father?" Hannah asked. "It was he you were worried about, wasn't it?"

She thought of her father's diatribes at the dinner table over the last year, venting his spleen about the termagants set on rending the very fabric of England. "Ideas above their station, no matter they've husbands and families waiting at home for them," he'd fumed, poking his kidney pie viciously, as though it, too, had demanded the right to vote.

"Yes, he doesn't support women, me, working—" she began, but that wasn't true. She began again. "He thinks I should be accepting the suitors he's arranged for me, that I am useful only as a means to refill the estate coffers." Her face felt hot in the dark, like she had revealed too much.

"Huh." Hannah huffed a quiet sound, half laugh, half acknowledgement. "It's often the way men think. Can't tell you how many of the women I've recruited for the WLA that have some version of that story. Husbands, fathers, and brothers who want to keep us silent, chained to our homes by history and ridiculous notions of what women are capable of."

"I think Father would have been just as ghastly to a son—"

"Unlikely," Hannah interrupted.

"I only meant that he is not a good man, not to anyone," Ophelia said. "I wanted to leave because of what he wanted from me, but it wasn't only that."

"No?"

"No. I want something different . . . for my life." She faltered a little. "I'm not sure what, really . . . but when I heard you speak at the village hall, I thought perhaps the WLA could be it."

"You didn't seem so sure that night," Hannah countered.

"No, but what you said stayed with me and . . . well, when I decided to leave, this felt like the right choice."

"And you've nothing keeping you here? No beau waiting in the wings?" Hannah said this with a slight edge to her voice.

Ophelia shook her head. "No one."

"An eligible lady such as yourself, I'm surprised."

Ophelia wasn't sure if Hannah was teasing or insulting her, and before she could stop herself, she said, "I did share something with someone, once, but it's been two years since he left for the war." Ophelia thought of Silas, hands moving quickly as he spoke, green eyes crinkled with mirth. Hannah was silent, and Ophelia felt awkward and embarrassed to have blurted out such a silly confession. "Never mind, it was nothing, ancient history. As I said, I'm sure this is the right choice."

"I think 'twill be. You'll be billeted at Mrs. Darling's. She's a good woman who could use the help. Bess is to join us from Bristol, and I'll be there, as well. To keep an eye on all of ye," Hannah said, and Ophelia was relieved to feel the sound of a smile in her voice.

They travelled on in silence for a while, Hannah clicking to the horse every now and then, Ophelia's head nodding as they passed along the winding lane toward the village. She wondered where she would sleep on the farm and had a quick pang of nerves thinking of her soft bed at home. But soft beds were nothing compared to a life of one's own, she reminded herself. And she thought, perhaps one day, a woman mightn't have to choose between the two.

CHAPTER 1

January 1918
 Hartwood House Estate, convalescent hospital, Somerset, England

EYES CLOSED, just on the verge of waking, echoes of gunfire and screams fading with his dream, Silas held himself still waiting for the pain to appear, for its blistering pokers to push up from his shattered foot into the muscles and bone of his calf. It was like a sly dog, lying just out of sight, ready to pounce. He felt tired, older than his twenty-six years, weary from the memories, pain, and the effort of recovery. To distract himself from his leg and the dregs of the awful dream, he let his mind be pulled into the room by the now familiar sounds: the soft tap of the nurses' sensible shoes on the parquet floors, the creak of narrow metal beds under the weight of men, some still sleeping, some so broken they made no noise at all.

The pain hadn't appeared yet, so Silas let his mind travel further into the room, hearing the glide of ancient, well-cared-for wood on ornate hinges as the door opened to admit the breakfast trollies. They rolled forward on institutional wheels, pushed by women scarcely out of girlhood, made adults by the litany of horrors they tended to each day, by the tears and weeping of grown men, limbs pitted and pocked by shrapnel, or entirely absent in some cases. Silas opened his eyes, found instead of hot ribbons of pain, only a steady background hum of discomfort, and pushed himself to sit against the headboard. A nurse, dark-haired and efficient, slid his breakfast onto a tray in front of him, swiped her wrist across his forehead to check for fever, then ducking her head in acknowledgement of his gruff "good morning" moved on to the next patient.

Pulling the bowl of watery oats forward, Silas brought a spoonful to his lips, and despite a lifelong hatred of them, swallowed methodically. He knew the nurses would fuss if he didn't eat, which reminded him of his mother, and that all still felt too painful, so he made his way through the plain breakfast, saving the cup of dark, sweet tea to savour last. Sipping it, he let his eyes roam the room.

Tall windows soared the length of the space, offering views over manicured lawns rolling out into boxwood hedging and the severe bones of a winter garden. From his position in bed, he could see skeletal allium heads, the lacy remnants of hydrangea blooms, and a few curled leaves clinging to the rose bushes lining the brick path. Inside, the heavily panelled oak walls were relieved from dreariness only by the opulence of the chintz drapes hanging swagged at each window. The far end of the room was dominated by a massive stone fireplace, and Silas turned his head to examine the portrait hanging in the heavy gilt frame above the mantel. It was beautifully done, but even from this distance one could sense the coldness of the family grouping. The light playing over their faces revealed a tall, heavy-set man, seated, with a frail, grim woman standing behind him, hand resting on his shoulder. A young boy stood at the man's knee, small dimpled chin lifted above the profusion of lace on his collar. On the left, an awkward distance from the others, stood a young woman, tall and robust, a tiny smile quirking one corner of her mouth.

Silas looked at the portrait every morning, and every morning his stomach clenched to see the woman's face looking back at him, dark hair piled high on her head, eyes clear and frank. She looked so much like Ophelia, and the house was so like Wood Grange that he half expected it to be her looking out at him every morning. He turned his face away and took the last sip of his tea. His leg hurt, but he had already decided that today was the day he would make it to the end of the estate grounds, shattered bones be damned.

Pushing the tray back, Silas swung his legs over the side of the bed and reached for his trousers, draped over the nearby chair. Taking a deep breath, he pushed up from the bed, and pleasantly surprised that the pain didn't take his breath away, he slipped first one leg and then the other into his pants. Shirt loose, jacket and scarf on, he made his way to the thick double doors that shut out the activity in the rest of the house. Pushing one open, he saw Matron at her desk in the hallway, head down over patient charts, the grey roll of her hair visible beneath her starched nurse's cap.

"Out for air, are we, Mr. Larke?" she remarked, looking up briefly. "The wind is sharp today, mind you take your hat and gloves. And not too long on that ankle, yes?"

He nodded and turned to the left, making for the exit at the side of the house. Passing the door to the study, he was reminded of two years ago, before the carnage of France became his to carry, when he faced a man over a desk much like this one. When he considered what a wreckage his life had become since then, he felt small and angry all over again, the curdle of betrayal souring his gut. Pulling on his gloves and snugging the collar of his jacket up high around his ears, Silas stepped out into the garden, pushing away the memories. He would face those some other time. Right now, he needed to strengthen his ankle and be ready when his next assignment came from the War Office.

The morning was cold and clear, the bustle of the great house already fading behind him, replaced with the sharp tsk-ing of a thrush darting in and out of a hedge. He'd always loved this time of year, the keen nip of the cold, the clarity of the colours in the fields that faded to gauze at the farthest edges of the horizon. Before he could stop himself, he thought of the farm, so beautiful at the close of the year, everything quiet and still, all the rushing and grasping finished for the season. The barn filled to the rafters with hay, every shelf and nook of the farmhouse stacked with the spoils of summer. Even the animals seemed to know it was a time for tending the small dark seeds of the coming year, and set themselves quietly to their fodder. His stomach began to seethe at the memory, the threat against his family and their land still keen. Enlisting had been the right choice, he knew. The only choice, but God it still stung. And then returning from the front, leg a mangled mess, to recover within a day's ride from the man who had taken everything from him, well, he snorted bitterly, that was a cosmic joke of the first order.

Chest pumping from the long climb up the south side of the field, Silas found himself looking out over the downward slope. It twisted slightly to the right and ended at a magnificent willow fed by the winding creek running through the estate. It reminded him of a place that he and Ophelia had met a few times, talking and laughing beneath the green canopy of a similar willow on her father's estate. Exhausted by memories, good and ill, exhausted by the heaviness of regret, he turned around, tucked his head into the wind, and made his way back down the hill, ignoring the blackbirds that rose up, startled from their foraging at his approach.

Walking back toward Hartwood House from this direction

reminded him of the approach to Wood Grange, the ancient Somerset estate that contained the land his family had farmed as tenant labourers for as long as he could remember. His grandfather, and great-grandfather before that, had each carried on the hundred-year lease common among thousands of estates all over Britain. Slowing to give his ankle a rest, he thought of his family's farm; situated at the back of the main house, across the rolling flank of the pasture called Low Field, and on the rise of a slight hill, the house had had beautiful views over the valley and the less formal kitchen gardens of Wood Grange. A well-trod lane had led past its front door and the small front garden, fenced with ancient stones and a worn timber gate, on its way to the dairy, and from there to the nearest village. The traditional hundred-year lease between landowners and tenant farmers meant that it was the only place he, and his parents for that matter, had known as home. He remembered discovering a crooked set of initials carved into the lintel over the front door—JL, for his father, James Larke.

Reminding himself to pay attention while walking, Silas skirted the frozen puddles along the hedgerow, noting the expanse of barren field rolling away in rough, dark waves. Haven't even sown a winter cover crop; it's no wonder the country is mad with hunger and yields so poor, he thought. Everyone with any useful knowledge away dying in the mud or lying in some estate house hospital wishing they were dead. He stopped to loosen his scarf, his breath puffing out around him in silvery clouds, his ankle beginning to ache from the rough terrain.

He remembered walking the fields around the estate with his father, learning the names of the birds hopping in the hedgerow and dipping through the blue of the sky, the stages of the ripening wheat, and the signs of a heifer about to calve. His father's death in 1908, just months after his sixteenth birthday, had been a staggering blow, but he had felt held by the work of running the farm, prepared for the constant balance of sowing and reaping, breeding and butchering, producing and selling. He had felt sure of his place in the world, could see an outline of a future. His mother, sister, and brother had been an anchor in the grief. But it wasn't until the summer of 1916, when he had met Ophelia, their almost instantaneous friendship a surprise beyond any he could have dreamt, that the loneliness he had come to accept as his permanent state had lifted momentarily, and the light that seemed to surround her filled his whole world.

Climbing awkwardly over the last stile and into the lane, Silas forced himself to turn in the direction of the farmhouse. It reminded him so much of his childhood home that his chest felt tight. From the lower side of the property, he could see the line of apple and plum trees the owners had maintained and, folding in on itself in the far corner of the back garden, the rotting boards of the privy. The house stood, ancient and solid, the grey stone warmed by yellow lichens and the weather of countless years, but it had the air of neglect that always permeated empty houses. The skeleton arms of a massive rose clambered up the wall and over the doorframe, and a shutter hung lopsided on the front, and the bright red paint was peeling in strips from the front door. What had it all been for, he wondered. Was it ever real? This ancient, beautiful England for which he had slogged through mud and horror? It had all seemed so important, so vital, when he left.

God damn you, Merritt Blackwood, you dishonest arse. Swiping his hat off his head, he fisted it angrily. He had always known reaching for Ophelia was like reaching for the stars, hadn't he? The dumb luck of being befriended by a woman like her, out of his class in every meaning of the word, had always felt a bit like the last swig of beer before you're truly drunk or the high side of a swing, hanging weightless for a second before the inevitable plunge. Being sent to convalesce here at Hartwood House was like a knife in the gut, he thought for the hundredth time, assailed in turn by anger and anguish. Everything about the great house and the surrounding fields reminded him of what he had lost back at Wood Grange. The need to get away was becoming overpowering. He picked up his pace, though his ankle protested, and with a final glance at the farmhouse, turned back onto the lane toward the convalescent home.

CHAPTER 2

March 1918
Mrs. Darling's farm, Somerset, England

"Aargh!" Ice cold water streamed down Ophelia's leg, soaking her trousers and pooling in her boot. She dropped the water bucket and danced awkwardly around as the water seeped between her toes and squelched underfoot. "Bloody pump!" she grumbled, picking up the bucket and facing the ancient mechanism with a frown. It wasn't quite cold enough to freeze the horses' water buckets, but only by mere degrees. Ophelia's hands were stiff and clumsy with cold, and even before the pump had disgorged its contents down her leg, her feet had been freezing. She had discovered in the year since arriving at Mrs. Darling's farm that the only real cure for the cold mornings and evenings was to keep moving.

"I'll stoke the stove and you can hang those to dry," Mrs. Darling called as she passed by with an armload of firewood. "You've two pairs, haven't you?"

"I do," Ophelia said as she nodded. "I'll be in after I feed." Hefting a metal bucket in each hand, she made her way carefully toward the open door of the stable where the shadows of two large heads watched her progress eagerly. Placing her feet carefully on the damp cobbles, head high to help with balancing the slopping water, Ophelia remembered her short-lived deportment tutor, Madame Delacourte, clapping her hands in time to mincing steps and poking Ophelia under the chin to encourage a "regal" appearance. Her father had deemed it a waste of money when she failed to transform into an immediately marriageable woman, but she smiled to herself now, feeling entirely regal standing in the middle of a farmyard in trousers and boots, shoulder muscles aching with exertion. She manoeuvred each bucket onto the heavy hook in the wall of the horses' stalls, and checking their mangers to ensure they still had hay, headed toward the house to dry off. Hopefully Hannah has started the tea, she thought, shedding her boots and coat at the door.

"Get in here close to the stove," commanded Hannah when Ophelia came down the short hallway. "Catch your death and then we'll have your chores on top of our own."

Bess swatted her arm as she passed a bowl of porridge down the table, and Hannah winked broadly at Ophelia. She wasn't a chatty person, nor particularly soft in her ways, but Ophelia was coming to consider her a friend. One of her first, it had to be admitted, and she enjoyed the other woman's wry sense of humour. Their initial meeting at the WLA recruitment session had been frosty; Hannah making it clear that she thought Ophelia naïve, lacking in any useful understanding of how to become part of the war effort or the suffrage generally. Ophelia knew now that Hannah had been right, although at the time she had been irritated and offended by the accusation. She hadn't known the first thing about work, and even less about the situation faced by women of other classes. She saw now that she had been chafing against her own restrictions in the beginning, wanting out of a situation that she found unbearable, but with no idea that other women felt the same way she did, nor that so many were caught in situations far more impossible than her own. In the end, Hannah had been the one to open her eyes to the urgency of suffrage, the possibility of change for so many bound up in her own desire for freedom and agency. She couldn't quite put her gratitude into words yet, so she tried her best to demonstrate to Hannah that she was becoming less missish every day.

"It's alright, Bess," Ophelia said, smiling. "I'm developing a lizard's skin; Hannah's jibes don't even bother me anymore." She poked Hannah in the ribs when the other woman rolled her eyes in response.

"Push up closer so as you get warmed through," Mrs. Darling encouraged from her seat at the head of the table. "Chilblains are the very devil in this weather, and damp clothes are a quick way to bring 'em on."

Ophelia obediently scooted closer to the stove, heat rolling off its black, enamelled surface, some variety of stew bubbling away on the back burner. The scent of hot metal cut through the gentle wafting of softening onion and warming beef stock, wrapping her up in a blanket of homeliness. Tucking her toes closer to the leg of the stove, she sipped the tea Hannah had passed her.

"What's on your mind, gel?" Mrs. Darling asked. "Can see the wheels turning from 'cross the room."

Ophelia, still unused to those around her taking note of her emotional state, faltered. "Just feeling nervous to try the horses together with the plough. I know we need to start turning over the fields this week, and I feel a bit worried about actually doing it." She toed the edge of the cat basket, set near the stove to keep the mouser warm.

Hannah hummed from her place at the table, mouth full of toast and marmalade. Finishing her bite, she cleared her throat. "It will be a hard go, there's no denying it. Even with the practise you've had driving the team, the plough is a whole other beast."

Ophelia nodded, anxiety flaring in her belly. She had been working hard to prove herself on the farm, but self-doubt always seemed to be lurking in the dark corners. Perhaps she wasn't gaining as much strength as she had thought. She flexed her hands without thinking, feeling the twinge of stiffness in the muscles in her forearms.

"Not suggesting you're not up to it, Ophelia," Hannah said, noticing her fidgeting. "You're likely more ready than you think. Don't let the plough intimidate you and it'll not get the better of you. Just do as you did with the horses, you had their measure in no time."

"Aye," Bess murmured from the doorway. "You'll be fine, Ophelia. When you arrived, I didn't imagine a lady used to fine things could be as tough as you are, but already you're a farm girl through and through."

A feeling like giddy electricity snaked through Ophelia, the support of her friends lighting her up. They were right. She could do this. While Ophelia gathered the tendrils of happiness around her, Mrs. Darling began herding them into their outerwear and off to their assignments, pushing a dry sweater and tunic into Ophelia's hands.

Outside, the damp air bit into every exposed sliver of skin and wormed its way through each layer of cotton and wool. Ophelia gripped the wooden handles of the plough, the long metallic blade resting on the edge of the field behind Samson and Delilah. The horses stamped impatiently, Samson shaking his head and setting the harness to jingling in the cool morning air. Everything before her felt heavy and unwieldy—the long wooden arms, the high heavy rumps of the horses, the sharp club-shaped blade. Bess stood to one side, her voice low and quiet reminding her of the points they had reviewed in the instruction manual provided by the WLA. It hadn't been entirely clear to Ophelia how she might manage manoeuvring the plough through the soil, but standing here in the cold, her friends encouraging her, the horses waiting to be allowed to do the job they knew, she realized the only thing to do was to begin.

"Geeup," she called to Samson and Delilah, adjusting her grip on the plough, feeling the ridge of the cotton plough lines under her palms. Remembering to walk slightly to the side of the horses to ensure a straight cut, Ophelia stepped out into the field. It only took one step for the plough blade to catch the soft, damp earth, and then the horses were pulling harder, and Ophelia watched in disbelief as a slice of dark soil revealed itself. She danced farther to the side to avoid stepping into the divot and shouted, "I'm doing it!" over her shoulder. Bess and Hannah whooped loudly from behind her just as she tripped and fell directly into the turned earth. Samson and Delilah took a couple of tentative steps before stopping to wait for her to right herself. Ignoring the caking of dirt and the cackling of the women behind her, she stood and took hold of the plough once more. She clucked and the horses walked forward, and this time she made it all the way to the end of the row before the plough wobbled out of her control. Her arms ached, her back felt as stiff as a board, and sweat gathered between her shoulder blades, but she lifted her arms in triumph, crowing her success to the empty field. A handful of blackbirds lifted out of the oak at the field's edge, raucous and eager to scavenge in the upturned soil.

CHAPTER 3

The persistent press of sunrise against her eyelids forced Ophelia upward from a dream and into her narrow bed, the chintz eiderdown twisted and heavy around her legs. The room was as it had been when she first arrived at Mrs. Darling's, neat and spare, and the longer she woke here, the more beautiful she found it. The sun filtered through the lace curtain at the small window, picking out the simply carved handle of the wooden dresser, the belly of the floral pitcher beside the wash basin. When she had first arrived, fresh out of her training, she had wondered what it would feel like to wake up here, alone, in this room. No servant opening the curtains, tea tray waiting. No breakfast laid in the dining room below, no one's nimble fingers to help her dress for the day. It was exhilarating and, if she was honest, a little frightening. Her heart had raced and she had felt, for the first time since she had registered, the weight of what she had done. Was she equal to the task she had set herself? She remembered feeling unsure of everything that morning, except that at all costs, she must succeed.

Ophelia laid a moment longer, then hearing Mrs. Darling in the kitchen below, swung her legs over the side of the bed. She stretched, luxuriating in the pull of her muscles, the pang of discomfort from the week's work. She revelled in the capability of her body more than she had ever expected; at first, she was overwhelmed by fatigue, the weariness of muscles pushed far past anything she had known, but now when she woke with the faint twinge in her arms or a point of tension in her calves, she leaned into the sensation knowing it meant another day of productivity, of accomplishment.

Standing at the dresser, she splashed a little cool water on her face and pushed her hair back, gathering the thick, dark hanks into a loose braid. Catching sight of her reflection as she finished the plait, Ophelia catalogued the changes in her face. Her white skin was tanned from the sun and wind, colour always high on her cheeks now. The softness around her mouth had faded, leaving a tracery of fine lines around the sharpened outline of her lips. Her hair could hardly be tamed these days, always flying out from under her hat or the confines of her hair ties. *I've become the harridan Father always feared, not a hairpin in sight, breeches instead of a proper dress.* She almost laughed at the thought. But she'd never felt more herself, never imagined feeling this *right*. Ophelia slipped her corset over her combination, tugging the laces and adjusting it so she could move easily, donned her loose linen tunic, and reached for the breeches slung over a chair. Pulling the snug khaki fabric up her calves still felt illicit in the best possible way. It was new, this sensation of pleasure in one's body, and not in the socially proscriptive way of being judged fashionable or desirable. Ophelia had always felt just outside of what was considered attractive, being taller, more substantial than the sylph-like women in the fashion plates. Her features were not sufficiently soft to be strictly beautiful—her nose being a smidge too long, her lips a little too full, and her dark hair a little too unruly. In truth, none of this had bothered her a jot, was even a benefit in making her a slightly less marriageable prospect according to her father, but it had left her feeling lonely, an unknown future looming ahead, alone.

A sharp knock at the door drew Ophelia from her thoughts, and kicking out a leg to straighten the lacings on the outside of her calf, she hurried to finish dressing. Hannah, red hair tamed in a low bun, tunic straight and orderly, offered a quiet "morning" before ducking her head to avoid the old house's low Tudor beams.

"Morning. Sleep well?" Ophelia said.

"Hmm."

Emerging into the small sitting room at the bottom of the stairs, Ophelia heard the rumble of Mrs. Darling's laugh and Bess's infectious giggle.

"Morning, Bess," called Ophelia as she rounded the corner. "Ready for another day?"

"After this cuppa I'll be ready for anything," the other woman said with a smile, her pale, freckled skin creasing around the bright crescent of her smile. "I've a big day ahead. Mr. Bone is going to inspect the dairy today. *My dairy*," she added happily.

"That's marvelous," Ophelia said with feeling. Bess had trained in dairying with the WLA, and as Mrs. Darling had only the single cow, she was also working with the neighbour Casper Bone's larger herd. Mr. Bone, one of the larger landholders in the area, had worked for decades as a solicitor, and only returned to running his family's farm after his retirement from practise. A tall and craggy white man with tidy greying hair and a serious, observant air, he was lean in stature and even leaner in conversation. He conducted all his business with as little chatter as possible, but Bess had won him over with her practicality and skill. Improvements in efficiency and production had been so positive that he had proposed the idea of Bess running his dairy for him, even after the war concluded. He had no real love for the work, he said and could see the benefit of having a young person running the operation. No one was more surprised than Mrs. Darling, who had received the news with a quizzical smile.

When Bess had told everyone the news, months ago, they had all questioned her desire to work for such a taciturn man. Bess brooked no fools, but said she saw something lonely in the man and was determined to win him over. "He's not a bad sort, just out of practise with people," she had said amicably, a hint of her mother's Irish lilt in her voice.

"I'm impressed, Bess. I have to admit, I didn't think much of your chances when you first started talking about bringing Mr. Bone around, but I shouldn't have doubted you. You're a force of nature," Ophelia said, smiling at her friend. "I wish I was more like you, able to see the good in everyone."

"Well, not everyone is worth the time, but sometimes it only takes a bit of kindness to get past all that. Plus, I like to chat more than almost anyone I know, so it's easy for me to get to know folks. Even if they're not entirely willing," she said with a wink. "Honestly though, Mr. Bone is a business-minded man, and I think he sees that I can make his dairy profitable again if he's willing to take a chance on an unusual partner, and I've no intention on passing up the chance to run my own dairy."

Ophelia nodded, thinking how hard she found it hard not to dwell on the past, to nurture the hurts dealt by those closest to her, a litany of disappointments she couldn't quite let go of or forgive. Her father's total disinterest in her as a person, if she was being honest, sat like a stone in her chest. She hadn't truly hoped for more from him and wasn't surprised that he saw her only as a means of ensuring the future of the estate. That was, after all, what men of his generation thought of women, especially their wives and daughters.

"We're lucky to have you, Bess. The best kind of friend," said Hannah from her seat at the heavily scarred wooden table in the centre of the room. "Even Mr. Bone, though I'm sure he's loathe to admit it."

"Men usually are," said Mrs. Darling, deftly pouring tea and sliding plates of toast and bowls of oatmeal in front of each woman. "No one more than Casper Bone." She turned to pass Ophelia a cup of tea, indicating the plate waiting at her spot at the table. "Have a bite afore you have to go, it'll be a long one today."

"Thank you, Mrs. D.," she said, sliding into her place between Bess warming her hands on her teacup and Hannah methodically tucking into her breakfast.

"Enough about men," Bess said after a small slurp of tea. "Sleep well? How're your legs after harrowing yesterday? Lord, I'm sore today."

"Me, too," Ophelia said around a mouthful of porridge, "although it's my arms. I could barely lift them to braid my hair this morning."

"Makes no difference, always looks as though you've been dragged backward through a hedge anyway," Hannah deadpanned, giving Ophelia a crooked smile.

Mrs. Darling's laugh filled the room, eyes deeply crinkled, her wide smile revealing a chipped incisor. Ophelia smiled and rolled her eyes at Hannah. This easy camaraderie still felt like a gift to her, something she had encountered so little of. Relationships with women had always been competitive, elbows and teeth bared over whomever seemed like the best marriage material. There had been acquaintances at Wood Grange, girls and women invited to tea, garden parties, lavish dinners, but the business of social climbing, securing oneself above the others always took precedence over truly getting to know anyone. Despite all their differences, the women on the farm had taken her in, had welcomed her, not judging her inexperience. She found their acceptance thrilling, unexpected.

"Enough chatter, ye wee magpies. Get on with your breakfast, we've work to get to," said Mrs. Darling, wedging herself into a spot under the window and pulling a cup and saucer toward herself. She was almost immediately interrupted by a heavy knock at the door. Her chair scraped as she rose to answer it, and she was followed back into the kitchen by a tall, thin man wearing a battered trilby and a faded corduroy jacket with an arm band bearing the insignia of the County Agricultural Committee.

"Pardon the intrusion, ladies," he muttered quietly, swiping his hat off his head.

"No trouble, Mr.—"

"Garrett."

"Right. Have a seat then. Tea?" Mrs. Darling reached to refill the kettle on the stove.

"No, thank you, ma'am. Mustn't tarry. I've many stops to make today. I've been directed to give you notice that the War Agricultural Committee requires you to increase your wheat yield this year. Twofold, ideally, more if at all possible." He looked impassively at Mrs. Darling who stood, hand still on the kettle, mouth slack.

"Twofold?" she finally said.

"Aye, your yields have been low year on year and everyone is expected to do more to provide for the shortfalls. This winter may be our worst yet, they're saying." He shuffled restlessly, the defensive jut of his chin practised, mouth ready to press his point. Likely the result of many conversations like this over the course of the war, Ophelia thought. The women at the table watched him, Mrs. Darling making no reply.

"Of course, we at the county committee understand the strain you ladies have been under, pressed into doing men's work." He cleared his throat. "Ah—the good news is, the committee's been given government leave to enlist recovering soldiers to lend a hand wherever possible." He transferred his hat from one hand to the other. "Your farm is in the lucky situation of receiving that help sooner than most, and from a farmer, no less." Mr. Garrett smiled then, looking around at them, plainly expecting to be thanked for his officiousness.

Bess, Hannah, and Ophelia said nothing, only looked to Mrs. Darling whose face had clouded over as she listened.

"While I do appreciate the position of the committee and kindness of the offer, we've no need of help, Mr. Garrett," Mrs. Darling said. "Women we may be, feeble we're not. I've accounted for a larger planting, and Ophelia here is well-trained up with the heavy draft team for the sowing and harvest. There's no call to send us a man, we're more'n capable of getting the wheat in ourselves."

Mr. Garrett cleared his throat again and rolled the brim of his hat between his fingers.

"That's as may be, but the committee will have a soldier here or your land may come under consideration for repossession. As I'm sure you've attended committee meetings and read the pamphlets, you'll know that farms with unverified production levels become the concern of the local county committee, and if the situation calls for it, can be run under their supervision or reassigned. It would be in your best interest to be cooperative about the soldier."

When Mrs. Darling said nothing, he replaced his hat and dipping at the waist, bid them good day.

Hannah glared at the door. "Typical government interfering," she muttered, her cheeks flushed with anger. "You can always count on them to poke their noses in when women are taking charge of their own lives. Lord knows it ruffles men's feathers to see women succeeding at their work."

"And work we've to do," said Mrs. Darling after a moment. "Best get on with it. I don't plan on finding out whether his threats are idle."

The kettle whistled, high and keen on the stove. Mrs. Darling moved to lift it, automatically pouring it into the waiting teapot.

Her normally steady hands shook as she poured, the boiling water spitting as it hit the hot surface of the stove.

"Here, let me," began Ophelia.

"I've got it," snapped Mrs. Darling, rattling the teapot lid into place.

Ophelia sat down. If the County Agricultural Committee was assigning them help over and above the WLA, it must mean they thought the women unequal to the task. *Even I know being assigned a man to help out is a black mark*, she thought. She couldn't bear the thought of her work with the horses being the cause of Mrs. Darling losing her farm. *Stop it. You are doing your best and, as every bit helps, your work is useful, a contribution. Remember how far you've come since you arrived.* Hannah's sharp elbow in her ribs jostled Ophelia from her thoughts and sloshed tea across her plate.

"Thinking up anything useful, or just away with the fairies?" She smirked. "We'll need some kind of plan to deal with this Ag Committee nonsense on top of everything else."

"You're right about that," said Mrs. Darling, sitting down heavily in her chair. "This farm is the only thing I've ever had of my own, and I'll be damned if some bean counter from the village is going to take it from me." She spread her work-roughened hands out on the table and sighed. "I've always thought of it as a kind of reward for making it through my marriage, and I know the war demands something of each of us, some more than others, but the thought of losing this land just doesn't bear thinking on."

Mrs. Darling hardly ever spoke of her late husband, and though her face lit when she mentioned events in the past, she hardly ever spoke of the time before the women had arrived. Ophelia had pieced together that the late Mr. Darling had been a hard man to live with, not abusive but not kind, and she tried to imagine a younger Mrs. Darling being bent to another's will. It was hard to reconcile the woman that she knew with one who was afraid to speak her mind. When she had first arrived at the farm, Ophelia had been so intimidated by the older woman that she could hardly speak. Mrs. Darling was a tall white woman, big-boned, with sharp grey eyes and a lion's mane of silver-grey hair that she wore swept back into a loose bun at the nape of her neck. Her face, tanned from a life out of doors, was mapped by fine white lines creasing at the corners of her intelligent eyes and mobile mouth. Ophelia thought that she must laugh a great deal based on the lines at the corners of her lips, even though it took several weeks to see any evidence of that.

"We won't let them take anything," Ophelia said. "I'm faster with the horses now than last year . . . and I can keep them in a straight line," she finished with a comic cringe directed at Mrs. Darling.

"Ha!" Mrs. Darling gave a wry laugh. "Lord, remember at the beginning when all three of you got stuck down in the dell?" She cackled and shook her head. "Took us all afternoon to get the plough untangled and turned around."

Ophelia laughed, realizing she hadn't thought of the day in a long time, that driving the horses had become almost second nature, that living and working with these women had become an intuitive part of her. She thought of the first time she had heard Mrs. Darling laugh and had been caught totally off guard by the unselfconscious jangle of it filling the small sitting room. She had come to learn that Mrs. Darling loved a bawdy song, as well as the odd bit of village gossip, which she would tuck away in her memory for some future use. Now she kept her ears open for either, so that she might offer these bits up to Mrs. Darling over dinner. As a result, her repertoire of bawdy songs had increased tenfold, and her ability to read the subtext in a piece of harmless village news had improved by leaps and bounds.

And it wasn't just Mrs. Darling that she knew; over the months Ophelia had tucked away pieces about each of the other women. Hannah loved pudding more than the meal, was always in need of a hot water bottle for her cold feet, and was a bear until her first cup of tea. Bess was happiest in the garden, though better at baking than growing veg, loved novels of romance and piracy, and dreamed of travelling.

Ophelia reached out to rub her hand gently over Mrs. Darling's. "We will figure something out, I promise. I can push the horses a little harder, and we can take turns scaring the birds off the seedlings. Anything to improve our chances. We won't let them take your farm, will we?" she said, turning to Bess and Hannah who nodded in unison.

"We'll do what women do best," Hannah said firmly. "Succeed where no one thinks possible. Pass me the papers, and let's see what's expected of us."

Mrs. Darling slid the papers over to Hannah who began poring over them, Bess's dark head tucked close to hers, teeth holding her bottom lip. Ophelia stood and started to clear the breakfast dishes, filling the sink with hot water and a curl of soap from the dish at the edge of the porcelain drainboard. She sank her hands into the basin and looked out the window over the farmyard and out toward the pasture. The scrape of a chair on the flagstone floors drew Ophelia back into the room, her hands still in the now-cool dishwater. Hannah slid her cup and saucer gently into the sink, saying, "Well, it seems we're between a rock and a 'ard place with this new planting scheme. Under the War Act, the government says they've the right to take control of the land if we can't produce the required wheat." She pushed a hand through the wavy mass of ginger curls around her face and blew out a frustrated sigh. "Do you think you could push a little harder with the team, Ophelia? Even a half day more of ploughing over a week would mean we might seed another field in time."

"I—" Ophelia began, wiping her hands on the linen towel. "Samson and Delilah know their jobs, and I'm stronger than I was. Yes, I can do it. I *will* do it."

She raised her eyes to look at the other women in the kitchen, each here as part of their own story, with all their own cares and worries. It's not only the war effort, she thought, though that must come above everything. *I can't let Mrs. Darling or Bess and Hannah down now, not when they've been so kind to me. I came here thinking I had nothing to offer, but they showed me that I can contribute, and I'll not falter now when they need me most.* She shook out her shoulders and squared her chin, trying to physically embody the confidence she didn't quite feel.

"Aye, you'll be fine, Ophelia," said Mrs. Darling. "Ye've come a long way since you arrived." She patted Ophelia brusquely on the shoulder and turned to leave the room. "I've seed to sort out in the barn, you've all got your work for the day. No sense tarrying any longer. That wheat'll not plant itself."

The door off the kitchen scraped shut behind her, and the three women moved to begin their own days. Following Bess and Hannah out the kitchen door, Ophelia retrieved her wide-brimmed hat from the peg in the hallway, and emerging into the weak light of early spring, unceremoniously jammed it onto her head.

The horses were stabled in one end of the biggest barn on the property, their stalls opening out into a wide hallway opposite the empty calving stalls. Samson and Delilah were a matched pair of heavy draft horses. They stood sixteen-hands high with massive hindquarters, high, arching necks ropey with thick muscles, and glossy legs ending in dinner-plate hooves almost hidden by the great wispy feathers at their fetlocks. Their dark bay coats were rich despite their getting on in years, their manes and tails shot through with russet and white strands. Two chiselled heads, dark eyes curious, swivelled over the stall doors to take in her approach. The barn was quiet and dim, the smell of damp hay and animal mingling with the metallic tang of machinery and oil, the wet scent of earth and stone underneath it all.

"Hello, you two," Ophelia murmured, her hands going to her pockets for the bits of carrot she'd squirrelled away for treats.

Samson, the quieter of the two, snuffled delicately in her palm, the whiskers and velvet of his muzzle a wonderful scrape on her skin. "And for you, m'lady," she said, extending a hand for Delilah to burrow into. The mare's broad face was emblazoned with a bright slash of white from her right eye to her left nostril, and turning her head, she snorted eagerly into Ophelia's outstretched hand. Ophelia laughed and pushed her away when she'd ferreted out the last of the carrot bits, turning to lift their bridles from the rusty hooks on the wall.

Made of leather, worn soft and black with age, each bridle bore the horse's name on a small plate on the left cheek piece. A single brass medallion hung from each brow band: Samson's, a disc punched with a leaf motif, Delilah's, a bevelled crescent moon. Ophelia lifted the tack down and began her preparations for the day's work, the once foreign movements now familiar and comforting in their repetition. She clucked to Delilah and slid the bit between her teeth, letting the horse lick and chew as she settled the metal in her mouth.

Leading the team out of the barn, she stood, taking in the scent of animals and manure, the staccato of the hens pecking among the cobbles, the warm heft of Delilah and Samson stamping their impatience, massive hooves ringing metallic on the stone. She ran a hand down Delilah's silken muzzle, tugged gently at the reins and led them toward the sun, hanging apricot and gold at the far edge of the field. Sucking a deep breath, she filled her lungs with the scent of damp earth, clicked to the team, and braced as they scrambled to find purchase in the heavy soil. The brassy music of the harness blended with birdsong, and she lost herself in the rough rhythm of ploughing, each slice in the soil rolling back to reveal the dark underbelly of the field. Reaching the end of the row, Delilah tossed her head, flared her velvet nostrils, and swung out of Samson's way to turn.

CHAPTER 4

The same spring sun was almost hot on Silas's back, warmth blooming along his shoulders through his linen shirt. He looked over the patio, at the series of small tables set up on the ancient flagstones, each containing two or four men hunched over various projects, their shoulders bent as they placed puzzle pieces, extended arms to daub at a water-coloured cloud, paper clipped to a small easel. Some only sat silently, faces hidden by oversized fedoras or gauze wrappings, others paged one-handed through books, awkwardly making their way through whatever novel the nurse had been able to turn up for them. At least this grand library was being used for something other than smoking cigars, thought Silas, remembering Ophelia's disgust at her father's disinterest in his own estate's massive collection of books and manuscripts. These men'll be a sight more grateful for the distraction than Blackwood ever was, always more content to spend his days hunting and gambling than improving his mind.

"What d'ya think of this, then?" A man by the name of Scott interrupted Silas's thoughts, holding out a roughly whittled figure. The matron was of the firm belief that working with one's hands could lend the recovering men a measure of quiet solace while also giving them the chance to strengthen injured limbs. Silas took the figurine, turning it over in his hands. There was a head, a roughed-in face, and slouching legs that gave the figure a slightly comical feel.

"Not bad for a budding artist," Silas said with a grin, Scott laughing in reply.

"P'raps there's a spot for me at the Royal Institute yet," he said, affecting a plummy accent.

Returning the figure to Scott, Silas flexed his own fingers gratefully against his thighs, thinking that in the end a shattered leg wasn't so bad a thing to suffer. The nightmares were even beginning to improve, their regularity and intensity fading a little with each passing month. He still caught himself starting at certain noises, but life here in the hospital had begun to feel more solid to him, the muck and mayhem of the battlefield more like a terrible dream he was finally awakening from.

"So yer 'bout to light out, Larke?" Scott said, his brows gathered in concentration. His fingers worked slowly at the little figure, methodically scraping away at the wood.

"That's what the nurses tell me," said Silas noncommittally.

"Back to your family then?"

Silas hesitated, not sure what he wanted to share with the other man. He felt ashamed to have joined the army, leaving his mother and siblings, and angry that his injury made him unable to properly provide for them now. What the hell was the good of being the eldest son if he wasn't even able to keep them safe and secure?

"I'm not sure that I'll have the chance to see them," he said, settling on a half-truth. "Seems I'm to be seconded by the army for farm work. With so many men away at the front, farmers are having a hard time getting enough crops sown and harvested, and this last winter nearly did us all in, as you know."

"Oh, aye," said Scott agreeably. "'Tweren't one letter from home where my Margie didn't mention the trouble of getting flour and such. Felt as though she and the little 'uns might as well be in the trenches eatin' rations with me, such were the shortages." He sighed over the memory and patted his shirt pocket where Silas knew he kept his letters from Margie.

The memory of rations in the trenches made Silas's stomach clench. He felt guilty at his relief to be standing in the Somerset sun and not the muck of France. It made being put to work on some farm an appealing prospect; perhaps the physical labour would exhaust him enough to stop his mind from spinning endlessly every night, to quiet the guilt that crept in when he thought about his mother and siblings. "With so many convalescing soldiers well enough to work, but not return to the front, it makes sense for us to help with the farming. That's the gist of the letter I received, in any case," Silas said.

Scott nodded. Silas wondered whether he had received a letter of his own, or perhaps his injury prevented him from being recruited for the task.

"I'm headed back to the front m'self," he said quietly. "Got my papers earlier this week."

"Ah, I'm an arse, Scott. I'm sorry," he said, embarrassed.

"'Tis what it is, Larke. Could just as easily have been you than me, eh? That's the bloody mess of it all."

Silas nodded, wishing he had some pat reassurance for the man, but Scott had already been there, seen it all. Nothing Silas could say would make the return any less horrible. The situation on the ground beggared belief, and Silas fought the rising bile at the memory of standing knee-deep in the frigid mud, rats skittering over men's bodies in the maze of trenches, the haze of gun smoke and gas residue hanging like a pall over it all.

"Mr. Larke?"

Silas blinked and found himself back at Hartwood House, the matron watching him from inside the doorway. He stood slowly, giving the stiffness in his foot time to dissipate, and made his way toward the house.

"The cart is waiting out front. You'll find all the particulars regarding your farm billet in the envelope on the hall table."

He felt caught out, embarrassed. "Yes, Matron. I'll be on my way then."

She regarded him sharply for a moment then moved briskly past him and out into the sun. He saluted Scott with a casual hand, shouldered a small satchel, and strode toward the front hall, not wanting to linger lest this assignment slip from his grasp and he find himself in Scott's position. He still felt half a man, limping along with his shattered leg, returning to a country that seemed wholly unprepared to face the damage suffered by so many of its sons. At the doorsill, he straightened and tried to step into the future with a confident stride. Wincing as he stepped up into the cart, he tossed his bag into the back, and refusing to look back as they headed down the drive, he reminded himself that all the memories that now cut like glass had started out as wonderful. Let that be the lesson, he thought. Beautiful things can be turned to mud just like everything else.

The cart pulled gratingly along the narrow lanes, jolting and bumping past views alternately opening into wide vistas of undulating hills freshly fuzzed with the green of spring, sheep and the odd cow dotting the expanses between dry stone walls, or narrowed by head-high walls of hawthorn, blackberry, and crab apple. In those moments, the horse's bony hips shimmied along in a half-light shaded green by the wildly sprouting hedgerows, and Silas allowed himself to remember what life on a farm in spring felt like. It had only been a collection of months since his last spring at his parent's farm, but the intervening time had seen him first, in the most basic of military training, then the battlefields of France where spring anywhere felt like a wild, half-remembered dream, and then an entire spring missed while he lay abed, recovering.

The mud and madness of war had threatened to cover over anything he tried to hold dear, and so he had shut those earlier years, the ones he shared with his family as a young man, away. Not allowing himself to dwell on the memories felt like the only way he could protect them, keep them safe from the horrors he witnessed unfolding all around him. Sitting in trenches dug through what was once vibrant French countryside felt bizarre; a terrible echo of the life he had left at home, the life he had allowed himself to imagine unfolding peacefully, perhaps in the company of a loving partner. He hadn't allowed himself to think of Ophelia in that role. Her father had put paid to all that anyways.

Making his way slowly down the lane, the wooden cart seat under him so familiar he could have been back in his life before the war, he was struck by the feeling of being forcefully pulled away from the estate. Each hill and bend took him farther from Hartwood House, farther from his attempt to secure his family's future, and he felt the weight of the decision pushing at his back, a magnet working in reverse. He shrugged at the discomfort and fished in his pocket for the address of the farm where he was to be stationed. At the next village, he'd need to catch a small bus to take him all the way to the town of Banbury, but for now he could settle in and let the rhythm of the cart lull him, let himself watch the countryside scroll past like the pages of a children's picture book.

Soon enough, he found himself nodding off, head jerking awkwardly forward when he woke himself from a dream. The driver, silent as a tomb, almost entirely still but for the occasional click he gave to his ageing horse, chuckled as Silas jolted awake when they pulled up to the small station.

"Gods, man, have ye not slept lately?"

"It's been a while," Silas agreed. "Sorry that I made poor company on the trip."

The man waved this away with a grimace. "I've no love for prattle, get enough o' that at home. Some quiet does a body good."

He reached around to pass Silas his bag, and tipping his hat, slapped his reins on the horse's bony rump and passed out of the station onto the road. Silas waved at his retreating back and turned to join the queue for the bus. It lumbered into view, an awkward amalgam of a horse-drawn cart and a double-decker automobile. Only a few of the vehicles remained in England, all others having been commandeered for troop transport at the front. Silas was surprised by the sick taste rising in his throat, the unsteady tempo of his heart. *It's only a bus, get a hold of yourself. There's none here to harm you. Steady on.* He blew out a calming breath and stepped up into the vehicle.

"Tickets!" called a young woman in a loose navy-blue tunic, hat set at a jaunty angle on her dark hair. She brandished a hole punch and taking Silas's proffered ticket, clipped it with an efficient flourish. He smiled at her and took a seat toward the back, thinking his ankle might not handle the climb to the second floor. She wasn't much older than his sister, Delphine, he observed. *Wish she'd taken on a post at home as well. Better than her driving ambulances in France. Well, safer anyways.* But he knew Delphine would never settle for safer. She had always wanted to be at the center of everything, even as a child. He had only learned of her decision to join the nursing corps once she had already been accepted and travelled to France— a single cheerful letter urging him not to worry and to stay safe. Entirely worrisome and entirely Delphine. He knew from his mother that his sister sent her a postcard regularly with the same cheerful message. He imagined them standing in an ever-thickening stack on the kitchen shelf, always within reach and well-thumbed.

His mother had been suspicious when he announced that he would be enlisting; as a farmer, he was considered an essential worker and could be exempted from serving overseas, and that was what he had planned to do. He had seen too many farms fall into ruin when their farmers were called away, and he knew that his father would have wanted him to preserve what his family had built over the generations they had served as tenants at Wood Grange. He relied on the rush of other young men enlisting to cover his tracks, to convince his family that he, too, was caught up with patriotic fervour and the promise of adventure. In other circumstances, it would have been true; he loved the land he had grown up on, wanted to defend his country. Even the pageantry of the uniforms and the weapons stirred something masculine and protective in him, though that proved short-lived in the face of reality. Ironic then, that Blackwood refusing to grant him essential labour exemption and forcing him to enlist not only broke his link with the land but opened his eyes to the utter madness of war, the empty patriotic bellowing of the upper classes over the broken bodies and minds of men they considered expendable. When he returned, leg barely usable, the only thing he wanted from England was a quiet place to lick his wounds and make a plan to reclaim the scraps of what had been taken from him. It was his duty, he told himself, as the eldest son to protect the others, no matter the cost to himself, no matter what he might be called to give up. Being sent to help out on another family's farm made him all the more aware that what he wanted most—to be able to work the leasehold again, reassure himself of his mother's and brother's wellbeing—was again just out of reach.

CHAPTER 5

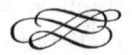

The sun was still high, warming the cobbles of the farmyard, the barn cats melted into a ginger and tabby puddle in the corner of the door jamb, when Ophelia pushed open the gate from the lower field a few days after the agricultural office's visit. She led the horses to the stone trough near the barn. They lowered their wide nostrils to the still water, long whiskers breaking the surface, their huffing breaths sending ripples across it. She dipped an old rag in the trough and squeezed it out over Samson's back, rivulets running down his withers, and snaking down his dusty legs. Methodically, as the horses drank, she ran as much water as she could over them, cooling them from the heat of the day and long hours of ploughing. They were on the skinny side of healthy, but forage was so scarce and money too tight to bring in much extra grain, so she tried to make up for it by taking care to make them comfortable. When she had first started with Mrs. Darling, she had worried she hadn't much feel for horsemanship and relied on the big animal basic training she had received from the WLA. A year out, she felt confident, in tune with her two charges. Directing them across the expanse of the field was satisfying; she felt powerful walking behind them, breaking the surface of the soil.

She had known, without having to be told, that the way her father had always managed the horses on the estate wasn't the proper way to treat them. He had loved big geldings, a stallion, if he could manage it, but he had treated them like an enemy to be conquered, a foe to be subdued, and the horses had responded in kind. They were wild-eyed creatures, angry and frightened, pawing and racing to get away from the spurs and whip of the creature they couldn't dislodge from their backs. Ophelia had felt sick watching him ride and avoided being out when he was in the stables, but consequently, she hadn't much hands-on experience with horses.

Samson and Delilah had intimidated her at first, the heft of their chests, the weight of their hooves in her hands when she checked them for rocks or signs of thrush, but slowly she had learned their moods, had learned to trust her instincts around them. "Horses need a master, Ophelia," Mrs. Darling had said the morning she had taken them out for the first time. "They want to know that someone is the leader, and that's to be you. Even when you feel worried, you mustn't show it." Well, I can do that, Ophelia had thought. I've spent most of my life hiding how I truly feel, surely, I can convince a couple of horses that I'm not afraid of them. And she had. Samson and Delilah trusted her, and she began to trust herself as well.

In the beginning it had been harder than she expected; doubt assailed her all the time, and the physical exhaustion made it even more difficult to feel like she was capable of what she had started. Her arms ached after only minutes of holding the reins or the plough, and her legs felt like leaden weights after two lengths of the smallest field on the farm. On the days when she could take a hot bath, Mrs. Darling passed Ophelia little cheesecloth pouches filled with lavender and peppermint to soothe her aching muscles, saying, "You'll get stronger soon enough, then we'll make a real farmer of you."

Wringing out the cloth and laying it over the edge of the horse trough to dry, she turned her hands over, examining their fronts and backs. They were tanned, with a line of dirt under each nail, palms covered with overlapping layers of fresh and healing blisters. Having read any number of requests for advice on keeping one's hands nice in *The Landswoman*, the magazine for WLA members, she knew she was not the only woman surprised, and sometimes dismayed, by the changes their war work had wrought in their bodies. Something about knowing that there were women all over the country slathering tallow and homemade concoctions on their hands or sharing recipes for sore muscle salves made her feel connected to a network of women in a way nothing else ever had. Hannah and Bess, having both worked from a very young age, considered her entertainingly spoiled, but were also generous with their own advice. Hannah swore by rosewater for keeping one's complexion clear and showed Ophelia how to gather the rose petals from the wild roses along the lane, boil them, and decant the liquid into tiny bottles she had saved. Using it each morning, Ophelia found it felt even more luxurious than any of the toiletries she had been able to easily afford while living on the estate.

Closing the door to Delilah's stall, she tidied the bridles on the wall before making her way to the house. She could murder a cup of tea and wondered hopefully if there might be leftover ham for a sandwich. Ducking to unlace her boots, she noticed a strange pair of boots by the door, suddenly noting the rumble of a man's voice under the familiar tones of Hannah and Bess. Something about it raised the hairs on her arms. Taking a breath to steady the skitter of her heart, she brushed the worst of the dirt from her coat and breeches before stepping into the cool half-light of the kitchen passage.

"There y'are, girl," called Mrs. Darling from beside the sink where she reached for a plate from the drying rack. "Sandwich and a cuppa for you?"

"Yes, please," Ophelia replied, emerging from the hallway to take in the scene before her.

Bess and Hannah sat in their usual places, but there was a strange stiffness to their posture, which Ophelia immediately understood when her she noticed the man sitting with his back to her. He was tall, his back and shoulders rising above the chair. Warm golden hair, a little long, curled almost to his shirt collar, and Ophelia could see that he sat with one hand on the table, one resting on a muscular thigh. His dark worsted work trousers were worn, but clean, and rode up slightly revealing not only the length of his legs, but angry red scars in the space between his trouser leg and his sock. She glanced across at Hannah and Bess who said nothing but watched her face intently. *This must be the soldier, the one sent by the War Ag.* Then he turned, the graceful movement of muscle under linen momentarily catching her attention so that she didn't immediately register his face. The strangled noise he made distracted her from Mrs. Darling, who handed her a plate of bread and cheese, which fell, unnoticed to the floor, smashing loudly. Ophelia's heart stuttered in her chest, her mouth open in a small, slack O.

How long had it been since she had seen him? It felt like yesterday. It felt like a decade. She tried to remember the disappointment of his leaving, but all she felt was a ridiculous surge of joy. She remembered every single detail of his face. The grey-green eyes, the sweep of dark lashes and brows, at this moment pulled tightly together above the line of his patrician nose. His mouth worked silently for a moment.

"Fee?"

Hannah's eyebrows shot up, eyes darting between Ophelia and Silas, cataloguing every flinch and pause. Bess stared at Silas, blinking slowly. Ophelia tried to marshal her reeling thoughts.

"It's . . . been a long time, Silas," she said, her hands moving restlessly against her jacket. She struggled to master her breathing, focusing on the clouds moving out the kitchen window, down from the hills, softening the bright summer sun that lay thick on the deep stone sill.

"Sit down, girl," Mrs. Darling said, tartly. "I'll make you another plate."

Ophelia sat woodenly across from Silas, her hands fidgeting in her lap. Her chest felt tight and the back of her neck hot. She pushed ineffectually at the strands of hair that had escaped her kerchief and wondered if it were possible that Silas could hear her heart racing from his seat.

Mrs. Darling turned from the table, picking up the broken crockery on her way, then lifted the kettle from the stove and poured a long stream into the waiting pot, saying, "Well, as you seem to know each other, I'll not bother with introductions. Tea then, Mr. Larke?" She plunked the cup and saucer down in front of him and reached around Ophelia to place the small creamer and sugar bowl within his reach. "And how *are* you two acquainted?" she asked as she arranged a thick slice of bread and a hunk of cheese on a new plate, placing it in front of Ophelia.

"We—"

"I, yes, w—"

They both began at once, tripping over each other's words. Silas dipped his chin slightly, indicating Ophelia should continue. Her eyes met his, and she felt the corner of her mouth lift in a smile. "Mr. Larke and I knew each other when we were younger, Mrs. Darling." His eyes flicked to hers at her use of his full name.

"It feels like years since we saw each other last," Silas said.

A lifetime, she thought.

"I suppose it has been," she said.

Hannah and Bess were practically vibrating in their seats, and Ophelia could tell it was taking every ounce of Bess's discipline not to blurt out a million questions about the situation unfolding before her. Hannah, on the other hand, had the pensive, withdrawn look that Ophelia had come to know meant she was examining something from all sides, assessing the information in front of her.

"Mr. Larke's family have been tenants on my family's estate for many years, long before either he or I were born," she said by way of explanation. "But it was really only by happenstance that we met the summer after the war began."

"What kind of happenstance?" Bess asked eagerly.

"Nothing so exciting as you might be hoping," Ophelia said with a laugh. She looked to Silas for confirmation and caught a flicker of emotion.

"A misdirected package . . . a book," he supplied, and Ophelia wondered if she detected a note of wistfulness in his voice.

Bess nodded, and Hannah's face took on a note of interest. "Hopefully some salacious pamphlet or a truly morbid gothic romance?" she said with a smirk.

Silas laughed, and Ophelia felt the sound spread through her like honey. She had forgotten how lovely and warm his laugh was. "Are you familiar with R. L. Hill's *Animal Husbandry*, volume eight?"

Hannah rolled her eyes and Bess cackled. Mrs. Darling, her mouth crooked in a half smile, nodded and said, "I've always found that one particularly useful . . . badgers and whatnot."

Despite the laughter around the table, Ophelia was suddenly conscious of how little she had thought of Silas or the estate since she had left. It was as though the train ride had deposited her in an entirely different realm, and she had been so busy learning and working that she didn't have the energy or the inclination to give her past much thought. She had been glad to push her father as far from her mind as possible, had been resolute in focusing on the reason she had joined the WLA—so that she might learn how to navigate a life on her own, out from under the influence of men.

While Silas explained the rest of the story to the other women,

Ophelia took a long sip of her tea, bumping the cup against the rim of the saucer as she put it down. She felt unaccountably nervous; the arrival of a piece of her past life highlighting how changed she felt. She wondered if she appeared immediately different to Silas. She stole a glance and found him regarding her, a puzzled expression in his eyes. Another thing she had forgotten—what it felt like to have the full weight of his gaze on her, the gentle intensity of his looking. He swallowed, and she watched the column of his throat working and was startled to find herself hungry for every detail of him. She found that he didn't look exactly the same, as she had first thought. There were subtle, but marked changes everywhere. His hair was the same honey gold that she remembered, a little longer, but his cheekbones cut a little sharper, his lips a little more stern, set in a firm, flat line.

It was his eyes that she noticed most, still the same mossy colour, but flattened somehow, the mischievous twinkle missing. New, fine lines emanated from the corners of his eyes giving his face a quiet, tired air. His hands on the table were calloused, the knuckles marked by healed scars, faded to silver, while a livid red line wound along the inside of his wrist up into his sleeve. She couldn't remember if he had been quite so broad and muscular, the hard balls of his shoulders snug against the fabric of his linen shirt, his heavy thighs clad in worn work trousers. An urge to reach out and touch him flooded Ophelia's fingers. It was a feeling she had experienced often during their summer of friendship; he was beautiful and kind and thoughtful, all things she hadn't ever expected in any man. The sudden awareness, that summer, of how lonely her life had been before Silas only made his friendship dearer, and she had mourned him keenly when he had enlisted. He had informed her of his enlistment in a short note, and she had felt no invitation to write to him in those few lines. She pushed down the squirming giddiness of once again being in Silas's company, and forced herself to focus on what she had come here to do: remake herself. Independent. Alone.

There was a lull in the conversation, and Mrs. Darling cleared her throat, saying, "So you're not only a reader, but a farmer then, Mr. Larke?"

"Yes, born and raised in the countryside, for my sins," Silas said with a smile.

"And now assigned to us by the War Ag, our soldier come to help, as it were."

Hannah snorted softly, fixing Silas with a challenging look. He acknowledged her disapproval with a nod of his chin, and Mrs. Darling continued. "So what kind of experience have you got then, young man? We're just lately under a great deal of pressure to increase our wheat yield."

"Almost anything, ma'am—"

"No need for the ma'am-ing, Mr. Larke, 'tisn't an audience wi' the queen. Just Mrs. Darling'll do," Mrs. Darling interjected tartly.

"Oh, right, sorry," Silas said, a little pink rising along his cheeks. "We sowed our fields in wheat and barley, kept milk cows and sheep at various times. There was almost always a horse for ploughing, sometimes a pig for the winter. I'm not bad with machinery, my father saw to that. We didn't have the most modern equipment, but it was kept in good nick. Oh, and we always had a flock of hens. My sisters mostly tended to those."

"The cows, here and over at Mr. Bone's, are my responsibility," said Bess, "and Ophelia's been a quick study with the draft horses."

"You always had a sense for animals, Fee. I remember that," said Silas, his eyes gentle on her face.

She felt herself blush at the nickname.

"A farmer is good news, indeed," said Mrs. Darling, pleased. "We've only time enough for one beginner, and that's our Ophelia, so I'm mighty glad you'll be a help and not a hindr'nce. The County Agricultural Committee have been by with warnings and seem to have a mind to order a temporary repossession of this land, so there's no time to waste. We'll need to sow a bigger crop than I've ever attempted on my own. The land's fertile enough, but it's the time constraint and amount required I'm worried about."

A beginner, thought Ophelia, her stomach turning sour around her lunch. Mrs. Darling might as well have said she was of no use at all, and in front of Silas, too. It had taken so much work for her to gain confidence; she didn't want to lose it because she felt inferior to Silas's experience. She was proud of the gains she had made since her arrival—the strength she could feel building in her body, the knowledge she was beginning to accrue, the contribution she was making to the farm and the war effort. The eager welcome Mrs. Darling had given Silas worried her; perhaps she had not been as helpful as she hoped. Even worse, would Silas's arrival change things with these women, these friends she had finally drawn close around her? She could feel him looking at her again, but she wouldn't let herself meet his eyes. Getting up from the table, she blurted, "I've work to do cleaning the tack and getting the harrow ready for tomorrow. I should really get started."

"I'll lend a hand," said Hannah, up from her seat before Ophelia could stop her.

From the corner of her eye, Ophelia saw Silas's shoulders drop as he raised a hand to rake it through his hair. He didn't turn to look at her, but she felt his awareness like a hand on her back. Damn, she thought, damn, damn, damn! *Why does everything have to be so bloody complicated?* She worried Silas's arrival was just going to dredge up everything she had turned her back on. Damn, she thought again, wishing for not the first time, that she knew some more satisfying curses. Ignoring her glare, Hannah linked her arm through Ophelia's and practically dragged her out of the kitchen. As they left, Ophelia could hear Mrs. Darling and Bess begin to pepper Silas with more questions.

CHAPTER 6

"So," said Hannah conspiratorially, once they had shoved on their boots and were crossing the farmyard, "what's the story with you and that fine young man?"

"There's no story, I knew him . . ." Ophelia began but faltered, not knowing how to explain what she and Silas were to each other. Or had been. Friends for such a short time, a single summer, but they had recognized something in each other, she knew it in her gut.

"Nothing, eh?" Hannah interrupted Ophelia's thoughts. "Doesn't seem like nothing to me, what with all the sighing and dark glances. I though he were about to come out of his skin when you marched int' the room."

"He wasn't, Hannah, what tosh," Ophelia blustered. "We met the summer before he enlisted and became friends, that's all. My father had no fond feelings for his family and discouraged our friendship at every turn." It was a gentle term for the war of derision her father had conducted against her friendship with a person he considered ill-bred, inferior, but Hannah already knew what a bully her father could be, how narrow his ideas, so Ophelia didn't give any further details.

"Ah, so he's handsome and forbidden, is he?" Hannah said, raising her voice in a sing-song teasing.

Ophelia batted her arm, trying to ignore the skittish happiness at seeing Silas again. "We're grownups, Hannah, not girls in plaits, and besides, what of your suffragette leanings? Surely a truly independent woman doesn't let the appearance of one handsome man turn her from the path?" She said it as a joke, but she wanted to hear Hannah's answer, realized she needed the answer to her own question.

"Ah, so you *do* think 'e's handsome!" Hannah crowed, pushing open the door to the equipment storage. The wide empty space was populated with all the farm implements Mrs. Darling could keep in running order with a very small amount of money and a great deal of ingenuity. The harrow, tiller, seed drill, and tedder waited in the low barn light, each needing almost daily tinkering to function and constant monitoring so that parts didn't wear through or jog loose out in the field. Hannah had shown a preternatural ability for repairing them, and Ophelia had come to rely on her to look them over regularly, so that her work with the horses could make the progress they so desperately needed. "I'm only cheeking," Hannah said with a smile. "But 'tis true, the tension in there was thick enough t' cut, and it weren't anything to do with the rest of us," Hannah said as she bent over to examine the trough on the seed drill. "And, Ophelia," Hannah said pointedly, "being independent doesn't necessarily mean being alone. One can be alone without having chosen independence, remember that."

"You say as much so often, but I don't know . . . It feels like a lifetime ago, Hannah. Things are different, *I'm* different." Ophelia took a breath to say more, but only let it out as a long sigh.

"It's no business of mine, I know," Hannah said. "It's only that I've been around enough gentlemen who were no such thing that I wanted you to know that I'll not say a thing to Mrs. Darling, nor anyone else, if you were wanting to talk about it. Only wanted you to know that you could talk to me, if you needed."

Her voice was gruff, but Ophelia heard the kindness in the words and wanted to hug her for it.

"There were times that summer when I wondered if we might be more than friends, but I'd no experience with anyone other than the suitors my father brought 'round. None of them were at all interested in anything I had to say, or who I was, so I suppose I felt special when Silas listened to me, showed interest in my thoughts." She paused, letting herself remember the summer days when they would happen to meet on the village road and ramble home together chatting. "We didn't know much about each other despite growing up on the same estate, my father having strong opinions on mixing with the staff or the tenants, so I didn't really consider it as anything other than curiosity on his part."

Hannah nodded. "Well, you may be different now, but I'd wager so is he. Perhaps you could both still use a friend."

Ophelia nodded, wondering if Silas had any interest in being her friend. Perhaps he lumped her in with bad memories of the estate and working for her father?

"Perhaps . . . I'm not sure," she said. "What if his arrival changes things here? Changes me?"

"I can see how you'd worry, but you're one of us, nothing'll change that, especially no man," Hannah said firmly. "No more fretting, we're losing time. We best get on with this," she said, gesturing to the machinery. They realigned the seed drill so that the holes were evenly spread along the trough, oiled the springs on the tedder and the blades of the harrow.

By the time they were done, Ophelia had managed to lose herself in the routine of the work and had almost forgotten about Silas's arrival. The coil of tension that simmered in her belly had relaxed, and she'd allowed herself to catch up on the latest WLA news from Hannah who often went through the village as part of her work with the forage corps. She knew she couldn't avoid the house forever, that she'd have to speak with Silas eventually, but she felt nervous somehow, wanted to put it off as long as possible. She wondered how he had actually fared in the war, aside from what seemed to be a nasty leg injury, and how his family was faring. The year after his enlistment had been long and, if she was honest, one of her loneliest. Her short friendship with Silas had cemented some unhappiness in Ophelia, a realization that her life might be something other than her father's to manipulate, and joining the WLA had felt like the answer to a question she hadn't known to ask.

"I've got to meet the forage girls to bring in some nettles from the banks near the bridge, so I'm off," Hannah said, turning to go. "And don't forget to ask Mrs. Darling to speak with the blacksmith about the tines on the tedder, a couple are loose enough to need a weld."

"I will. See you for supper."

Ophelia heard the door scrape and thinking it was Hannah back for something, called out, "What have you left, Hannah? Surely you're not back for your, what did you call it, supremely flattering, hat?"

Hannah didn't reply, and Ophelia turned to find Silas standing in the doorway, hands shoved into his trouser pockets. Her stomach fell, and she had the mad desire to run away, but she forced herself to face him, back straight, chin up. You've no reason to shrink just because his arrival is a surprise, she told herself. *You're not the same girl he knew back on the estate, you know yourself better, know more about the world and your place in it. You are doing something good here, something worthwhile.* She wiped her greasy hands on a rag. "Hello," she said, hoping her voice sounded confident.

"Ophelia," Silas said, ducking his head a little shyly. "I've just come to drop my bag. Mrs. Darling has made a room for me; she said it was the old groom's quarters."

"Oh, right. I can show you where that is. There's a door through here."

Making her way past the implements, she indicated a wooden door in the back wall. It opened into the same hallway as the horse stalls, and she moved down it to a small white-washed room furnished with an iron bedstead, a small desk, and a bentwood chair. An old chest, its leather straps worn through, sat at the foot of the bed. A ewer and washbasin were placed on a stand under the window, whose narrow view looked over the dairy yard. Silas placed his bag on the bed and looked around. He ran his hands through his hair, pushing the longish strands back from his face. He huffed a short sigh, his lips moving, about to speak. Ophelia suddenly felt that she shouldn't be standing in his bedroom and stammered, "Well, this is it, then," before turning to go. Silas's voice caught her at the door.

"I apologize if I seemed short in the house, Fee—I mean, Ophelia. I was just so surprised to see you. It had never occurred to me that we might be in one another's company again. What are the chances?"

His voice was low, urgent, rough in a way she didn't remember. It rumbled over her skin, wrapping her in him. He caught her eye and gave a cautious smile. She felt the need to shake her head to clear her thoughts.

"Oh, no need. You were lovely, I mean, just fine," she blurted, feeling her face flame. "I'm as surprised as you. I had no idea you were home from the front." The rush of words trailed off as she realized he might not want to be reminded of the war. She pushed her hands into the pockets of her tunic awkwardly. All the questions she had seemed to suddenly push up against her breastbone, threatening to escape the tight lid she was attempting to keep on them. Why he had enlisted so suddenly, and what had happened to his leg, and how were things for his family, still on the estate, and was he married as her father had implied . . . well, none of those things were appropriate to ask at the moment. She had chosen to make her focus this farm and the yield and these women who had helped her find her feet. She was done with the machinations of men, ready to take on a life in which she relied on herself. All the same . . . "*God*, it is good to see you though," she said suddenly and against her better judgement.

Silas smiled at her, warm and soft, his eyes crinkling at the corners in just the way she hadn't let herself remember. Seeming to read her thoughts, he said, "I've been away from the farm since I enlisted in 1915, but I've been back from the front and recovering in England almost a year." He gestured vaguely to his leg, and she knew the surprise must have shown on her face when he hurried to continue. "But it's a long story. Perhaps after I've settled in, we can catch up on each other's news? Most of all, I want to hear how you came to work on the farm, about joining the WLA."

"Of course. I should let you get settled," she said, feeling awkward and eager, and somehow irritated with herself. "I've lots to do today," she tossed over her shoulder before hurrying out.

CHAPTER 7

Watching her back disappear, Silas felt a rush of gladness, the happy comfort of seeing a familiar face. The whole day felt like a dream; long hours of travel dissolving in the shock of his arrival at the farm. He still couldn't believe Ophelia was here, couldn't stop drinking her in, reminding himself of her, revising the hundreds of mental images and remembered conversations he had stored away, and thumbed through in quiet moments. Alongside the familiarity, he saw all the ways she was different than before. The giddy coltishness he remembered was gone and her natural stillness felt heavier, despite the nervous energy emanating from her while they spoke. Her formerly pale skin glowed healthily, and he noted the contrast when she fidgeted with her sleeve, revealing a slice of milky skin at the inside of her wrist.

Having resigned himself to the impossibility of seeing Ophelia again after he enlisted, he hadn't let himself think about how he might explain his sudden departure for France or what she might have to say in return, but he saw that she was just as unsettled by the day's turn of events. He felt tongue-tied and awkward and longed for the easy conversations they had enjoyed in the past. Still amazed to find himself in the same room as her, he listened to her footsteps retreating down the cobbled passage and felt a heaviness lift in his chest. He had always liked the businesslike way Ophelia moved, and it made him happy to hear her boots tapping swiftly along again. Whatever the reason they had been thrown together again, he was glad of it.

But how had she come to join the WLA? And what had happened to her father's plans for her engagement? He had so many questions about how she had arrived here. The thrill of her proximity was tempered by worry, though. He had to keep their being together from getting back to Merritt; the man had threatened to evict the Larkes from the farm should Silas continue their friendship, and here they were together again. He remembered the early days of their friendship, the easy camaraderie that seemed to grow so quickly and naturally, and standing in the small room, her sharp footsteps fading away, felt the loss of that summer even more keenly.

Adjusting his braces, he moved to his satchel on the low bed, looking around to take in more of the room. No matter the surprises the day had brought, he needed to keep his focus on restoring some semblance of what he had lost, what had been upended by the war. He was still the eldest son, the head of the family; no one else could make up for the loss of his wholeness, the lack of strength in his leg, and the nightmares that hid in the darkest corners of his mind. Now that he was relatively healed, his focus had to be on making something with the land, gaining strength in his leg, providing for his mother and brother and sister. He had already lost so much time recuperating at the convalescent home.

Merritt's blackmail still galled him, and he had spent a good deal of time wondering if Ophelia could have known anything about it. But seeing her today, her cautious happiness at his arrival, he felt a relieved certainty that she knew nothing. He pushed his hair back, raking it through his fingers and told himself that he needed to get in touch with the War Office. Going AWOL wasn't an option, but perhaps Singer could put in a word to reassign him to a different farm. His commanding officer from the army had said he should send word if he ever needed anything, and Silas thought this qualified. He'd send a telegram from the village tomorrow asking about the possibility. Perhaps he could be on his way before he was forced to share anything about why he had enlisted. Perhaps he could still protect both Ophelia and his family.

He undid the latch on his worn bag and deposited his few belongings onto the floral eiderdown. A pair of trousers, a linen work shirt, knitted jumper, socks, thin cotton smalls, and a leather frame with a photo of his family, the frame edges worn smooth from handling, the photo already faded almost to white. He opened the trunk at the foot of the bed and placed the small bundle of items and the empty satchel inside, closing the lid carefully. Finished, he turned to the window, taking in the buildings in the dairy yard, noticing the warmth of the stone and the silvery, peeling planks of the doors, the weeds pushing up between the ancient cobblestones, the way the fields ran out, wide and rolling, to the feet of the sky. The stillness of the barn and the scent of the horses and hay all around him felt familiar and homey, and he was suddenly incredibly tired. Stretching out on the bed, its springs and iron fastenings creaking under his weight, Silas let his body be still, relaxing into rest, the dull ache of his ankle settling into a background hum. His mind returned to Ophelia hovering in the doorway, the way her eyes skittered over his face, not settling precisely, but stopping at his eyes, then his mouth. He remembered the way she had looked at him during the summer of their friendship; eager but shy, he had thought at the time. Now he knew it was longing he had seen in her eyes, to be seen, recognized, understood. Not alone anymore. Since the war, he had seen the same longing in his own eyes in the mirror every morning.

He mulled over everything, trying to parse out his feelings from the last few hours: relief to be away from Hartwood House, worry over how his leg would hold up to real work, shock and a punch of desire at seeing Ophelia again. Away from the hubbub of his arrival, he allowed himself to go over everything. Bess and Hannah had welcomed him with stiff politeness, obviously worried about his arrival, while Mrs. Darling had launched immediately into a list of reasons for why his help wasn't necessary, nor were they women who needed a man's assistance. He wasn't insulted or surprised by their resistance to his arrival; he could tell that they had an established rhythm and were not new to farm work. He had been in the middle of explaining that he had no intention or desire to disrupt their work, nor any hand in where he was sent, when Ophelia had strode into the kitchen and nearly stopped his heart.

It wasn't that he hadn't thought of her often since he had enlisted and left the farm, but he realized with sudden force that he hadn't nearly remembered her correctly. In his mind, she had been soft, almost girlish, but the woman who had entered the kitchen this morning was tall, close to lanky, and moved with the assurance of someone aware of their own capability. Her hair had been mostly hidden under her kerchief, but wild pieces escaped against her cheeks and dark waves of it hung past her shoulders. Silas had registered too late that he was staring, having realized he'd never seen her hair loose. Her face was lightly tanned, her lips a little rough with the sun, the wide fringes of her lashes dark against the grey-blue of her eyes. It had taken the crash of the crockery to break their stare, and by then a devastating blush had rushed up her neck and cheeks, and Silas wasn't sure he would ever recover from that sight. God, but she was beautiful, he thought and immediately pushed it away. He was here to gain back some strength and lend a hand for the war, not to make eyes at a girl he had known years ago.

Besides, Ophelia seemed settled in an entirely new life now, having broken away from her father's control and the unhappiness she had confided to Silas while they were friends. She clearly didn't need another friend, being surrounded by what he immediately recognized was a fierce posse of women. In any case, he thought, resigned, he had even less to offer her now than when they had known each other before. He was without land or work, damaged, body and mind, by the war; a man of little consequence who had failed to protect even his own family.

CHAPTER 8

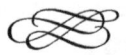

Bess's puckish face peeked out from the chicken coop as Ophelia hurried out of the barn, hands fisted into her pockets.

"Oi," said Bess cheerfully. "Looks like you could use some good news. Guess what I've got here," she said, gesturing behind her back.

Ophelia chuckled and stopped to look.

"Think it might be a double yolker!" Bess chortled, revealing a large creamy egg with a theatrical flourish. "Maybe we can talk Mrs. D. into a pudding for pudding."

"The luxury!" Ophelia laughed.

Bess slipped the egg basket onto her arm and fell into step with Ophelia toward the house. She was quiet, but Ophelia could feel her questions like an embodied presence.

"Go on, then," she said quietly, "I know you're dying to ask."

"Lord," said Bess. "That obvious?"

Ophelia huffed and said, "You're not obvious, Bess, but the last good gossip we had was Mr. Bone losing his temper at the county subcommittee chair and calling him a hog in armour."

"The look on the man's face was worth sitting through every minute of the meeting though, wasn't it?" Bess tilted forward, her lilting laugh shaking her shoulders and the mass of her jet-black hair. Subsiding, Bess said, "Go on, then."

"Well, there's not much to say. We became friends the summer after the war began, before I had any idea of joining the WLA or anything, really. His family hold the tenancy on my family's estate, have done for generations, and well. . ." She trailed off, feeling uncertain. She and Bess had shared many conversations about their backgrounds, and Ophelia was getting used to Bess's frankness when it came to the poverty she had grown up in, but she still felt gauche describing a life of ease to the other women who came from working class backgrounds. She couldn't truly understand what it meant to be poor, and that made her uncomfortable, suddenly aware of the sheer luck of her life, which she had always considered full of misfortune. She felt humbled by her lack of experience, by her realisation, so late, that other women her age were capable of caring for themselves, made decisions regarding their living and working arrangements that Ophelia had always been instructed were the concern of her father. She understood that Hannah and Bess had faced things that would have ruined her in the eyes of her father and polite society, and she had begun to understand that those things could make a woman as much as destroy her. She wanted to tell Bess about Silas, all the things she had enjoyed about him, all the futures she had imagined for them, but she couldn't find words that didn't feel girlish and silly.

So when Bess said, "Go on, Ophelia, I've been privy to a few heartbreaks," Ophelia tried to explain what the summer had meant to her.

"He enlisted. He left a note explaining where he had gone, but it was so sudden. I had never met anyone like him, Bess. He was so alive, so honest, somehow. The men my father wanted me to marry felt cold, calculating, which makes sense. I mean, marriage is a transaction to men of the class. But Silas was, I don't know, somehow so warm and alive. He made me feel that way, too."

Bess was watching her, listening.

"I was so naïve, still am, I know," she corrected when Bess huffed a laugh. "But I don't think I had ever realized that I could be *not* lonely . . . being friends with Silas opened a door to conversation and laughter and kind heartedness that I'd never experienced. He was from a family that loved him and the simple fact of our being friends meant that they loved me, as well. I have felt alone for most of my life and that was intoxicating."

"Aye, knowing you are loved makes all the difference, doesn't it?" Bess mused. "Must have made that summer special for you."

"It did," Ophelia said. "Perhaps it was that, even more than his looks, that I found myself falling for . . . I think I was half in love with him by the time September came. I was *such* a schoolgirl, I'm sure he didn't feel the same, for him it was friendship, but I felt like every moment together was precious." She smoothed her hands over her breeches, feeling the disappointment of what came next, even after all this time. "More so because I knew my father would forbid it, and sure enough when he caught wind of our spending time together, he was in a state. One night over dinner he threatened all sorts of punishments if I continued to visit the Larke house."

"Nothing like a little Romeo and Juliet to sweeten the longing, eh?" said Bess, ruefully. "I've seen it often enough amongst my friends, the forbidden fruit tastes sweetest and all that."

"I'm sure it was that, too, but also I'd never had the least interest in marrying anyone, and I'd always assumed it was because my only choices were men my father had chosen. I'd hoped not to be in a position like my mother, married to keep the family or the estate afloat, but I suppose I've always been too odd for people to offer for me out of genuine interest. But that summer with Silas made me wonder how else marriage could be. Made me wonder if there were men worth hoping after. But it wasn't like that in any case; we never even held hands." She glanced over at Bess wondering if the next part would sound melodramatic, a scene from a gothic novel. "It came to nothing, of course, because he enlisted. I swear something about it felt odd, and I did try to see his mother, but she only said that he had been caught up in all the patriotic fervour, and there wasn't anyone else to ask. My father had gotten his way again, just like always."

Bess was quiet for a moment then said, "So the way you felt about Silas made you wonder if you were truly opposed to marriage or just one version of it?"

Ophelia nodded, thinking. "I don't know if I had ever really thought about it at all, honestly. It was what was expected, and even though I didn't like my father's choices, I don't think I truly knew that there was an alternative. Aside from being a spinster, reliant on others for everything." She tried to think back to the summer with Silas, if there had been anything concrete in her thinking about marriage. She didn't think so, only upset with her father and relief for a few hours of freedom when it could be arranged.

"Is that what made you decide to join the WLA? Not wanting to marry?" Bess asked.

"I don't think so, or not entirely. I was at loose ends when I was given the flyer for the recruitment meeting, and attending felt a bit like throwing a cat among my father's pigeons. But when I listened to Hannah speak that night, it suddenly seemed possible that I might have another bigger choice for myself. Irritating my father seemed like such a small thing to do compared to war work and choosing an entirely new life. So I joined up. You know the rest," she finished.

"Hannah can be quite the firebrand, can't she? I was already desperate to sign up when the parade came through Bristol, but seeing her standing up on the back seat of that motor car, her voice ringing out over all our heads. Well, it was thrilling, is what it was." Bess shook her head. "Couldn't get my name down fast enough."

They both smiled, taking a seat on the bench outside the house. "Thank you for letting me ramble about all this business with Silas. I've never really had any friends to talk about things like this." She grimaced and hurried to change the subject. "How have things been with you the last few days?"

Bess had been the subject of some amount of gossip when she had arrived at Mrs. Darling's farm, and one or two of the more ignorant villagers continued to question her work ethic. Weeks back, she had mentioned to Ophelia that one farmer in particular had taken issue with her assignment, but whether he opposed it on the basis of her being Irish or a woman, Bess couldn't say.

"He hasn't bothered to show his face at the farm this week. And he never has the nerve to say anything in front of Mr. Bone." Bess blew out a breath and turned to Ophelia. "I've thought about your offer to speak to Mrs. Darling about it and while I appreciate you asking, I don't need you or her to speak up for me. I can stand up for myself, I've plenty of experience dealing with bullies, been doing it for most of my life. Most don't 'ave the stomach for going toe-to-toe."

"Right, of course," said Ophelia quietly, thinking that she had experienced few bullies, outside of her father, and certainly no one thought less of her because of her ethnicity or skin tone, though she had always been treated as inferior by virtue of being a woman. "I'm sorry, that was presumptuous of me, Bess. I know you're capable of dealing with these things. I hate that you have to, though."

"Well, it'll take more than one fancy lady like you standing up for me for things to change, but I do appreciate the offer," Bess said, leaning into Ophelia's shoulder with a friendly bump. "It's what I deserve, but oftentimes not worth the effort of asking, if you see what I mean?"

"I think so," Ophelia said.

Bess had popped to her feet and reached to pull Ophelia up by the hand, saying, "Let's see about tea now, I'm famished."

"Be right in." Ophelia smiled.

Alone, she rolled her shoulders, trying to ease the tension that had settled in between them, partly the result of the strain of working the horses, and partly the result of Silas's arrival. *Speak of the devil.* Ophelia caught sight of him leaning on the rails of the main gate looking out over Bottom Field. Hidden from view by the back wall of the house, she took the opportunity to look her fill.

He was still unreasonably good looking, she thought petulantly. The late afternoon sun lingered in his golden hair, catching the longer bits in its warm rays. His braces stretched to accommodate the broadness of his shoulders, pulling his trousers tight against his firm backside and long, muscled legs. He shifted to look down the long drive to the lane, and Ophelia caught a glimpse of the cording of muscles in his forearms where his shirt sleeves were rolled to the elbow. Tilting her head back to rest against the wall of the house, she allowed herself to remember how capable he had seemed three summers ago, how she had surreptitiously admired his strong arms, his long, nimble fingers, and how the intensity of their friendship that summer had allowed her attraction to him to feel somehow safe. A rough sound caught her by surprise, and Ophelia found herself looking up into Silas's face. She blushed and shot to her feet.

"Sorry, didn't mean to startle you, thought you heard me approaching," Silas said.

"No, lost in my thoughts," Ophelia blurted, brushing the dirt of the day from her work jacket. "I, um, shall we go in?"

Silas watched her with disarming frankness. Eyes intent, he seemed to be taking in the sight of her in breeches, and finding it a pleasing revelation judging by the flush of colour in his cheeks. *Well, that's unexpected.* Her hands stilled mid-brush. It had been a long time since she had felt Silas's approving glance, and the reminder filled her with pleasant warmth, quickly doused by the knowledge that these feelings would make working together awkward. She reminded herself that she was dedicated to this farm and the work that needed doing here, and nothing, not even Silas, could come in the way of that.

He cleared his throat again, and meeting her eyes, said, "Right, yes, of course. I s'pose it'll be dinner shortly."

"Mhmm," she agreed, going into the house.

She thought she heard an intake of breath, as though Silas was about to speak, but he said nothing, only stooped to undo his boots before following her into the kitchen.

CHAPTER 9

After only a few days on the farm gathering around the kitchen table felt almost cozy, familial. Silas was reminded of family dinners and the waves of conversations happening simultaneously, how the sharing of small things gradually wove people ever closer together. Mrs. Darling and Bess were discussing a newly broody hen and the possibility of chicks, and Hannah had fresh gossip from the village. Ophelia seemed quiet, though she laughed about Delilah shying at a rabbit and described how dry the soil had been under the plough. He watched her as unobtrusively as he could, catching the flick of her wrist when she buttered a slice of bread, the press of her lips, top to plush bottom, when she savoured the tang of salt and potato, the smooth movement of her throat when she drank. Seeing her, taking her in, was like the first sip of strong cider, fizzing through his veins, followed by a punch to the gut when he remembered he couldn't afford to be around her, indulge in the old hunger for her.

Silas reached for the pitcher of water in the centre of the table, inadvertently brushing Ophelia's hand. He froze, the sizzle of heat singing through his hand and down his arm, shocking in its intensity. It seemed absence had only intensified his unspoken attraction to her; his want flared like flame in dry tinder. Her eyes darted to his face as she quickly withdrew her hand, shoving it into her lap. He wanted to laugh at himself, undone by a touch of her hand like some untried lad. Hannah cleared her throat, breaking into his thoughts, bringing him back to the table where three sets of assessing eyes watched him carefully.

"Still not much for mixed company, I'm afraid," he said. "Been a long time..."

"Course it has, my dear," said Mrs. Darling. "Don't worry yourself about it, we don't stand on ceremony here, do we, girls?"

"So long as there's butter and tea enough to go 'round, we're a forgiving lot when it comes to manners," said Hannah with a smile.

"That's a relief," said Silas. "Even at their best, my manners aren't what you'd call ideal. Being a farm lad, and all." He ducked his head, hoping he'd added a little levity and drawn the attention away from Ophelia.

"They're just fine, young man," said Mrs. Darling, patting his hand. "We're glad to have you and your strong back here in time for the season. I've an inkling that we're going to need every square inch of the land this year, and there are those who'd be happy to see us fail. It's good to have an extra pair of hands."

Silas felt his stomach sink at her words. He didn't think it wise to stay on the farm with Ophelia, but could he leave when he had been assigned by the War Office to help them? Leaving anyone in a situation when they needed help set his teeth on edge, and when he received this post, the letter from his commanding officer had made it clear that the farms receiving soldiers were expected to make significant improvements in production. So much of farming depended on timing, and if Mrs. Darling lost his labour now it meant losing time, which could mean losing her farm. Christ, he hadn't thought things could get any more complicated. He pushed his hands into his thighs, breathing through his frustration and trying to quiet his mind enough to make a plan.

"Have you family nearby, Silas?" Hannah asked.

"Oh, uh, yes, they're just outside Wells."

"You're practically local, then." She laughed.

"Aye, I suppose I am. Though I didn't travel a great deal, mostly at home on the farm. Basic training was the farthest away I'd been 'til France." He paused, not wanting memories of that time to sink their claws into him. "My father passed away some years ago, and my mother and younger sister and brother and I stayed on at the Wood Grange estate. As you likely know, a tenant farmer can't afford any disruption in crops or earnings, so my mother relied on me in my father's stead. It was a hard time."

"I'm sorry for your loss," said Hannah. "It's never easy to lose a parent."

"No, though it has begun to fade a little as the years pass," Silas said, thinking about how often he still thought of his father and wished he could speak with him one more time.

"Both my parents had passed by the time I were finished in service," said Hannah. "I'd not lived with them for many years though, so p'raps not quite the same as your situation."

Silas nodded, wondering how it would have felt to grow up alone in another family's house. He thought of him and his siblings, like a litter of puppies, always tangled up, playing and fighting together. "I was fortunate to have been born into my family, even with my father's death. We all love each other a great deal. I'm sorry you didn't have the chance to grow up with yours."

Hannah waved him away with a casual hand. "And have you a sweetheart or a wife back at the estate? With your mother perhaps?" she asked.

Ophelia's fork hovered at her mouth.

"No, 'fraid not. I'm on my own," said Silas. "My mother and younger brother have stayed on the farm, working it as best they can." He swallowed the thickness that gathered in his throat every time he thought of them being forced from the house and home they had always known. Knowing that he had caused this danger for them, in befriending Ophelia, and angering Merritt, made it all the harder to live with.

There was silence around the table for a moment and Silas couldn't bring himself to look up from his plate. Then Mrs. Darling said, "We're not more than a day's travel from Wells," her voice kind and low. "And I see no reason why you shouldn't have the same free days as the girls. Perhaps you can take the train up to see them soon. I'm sure it always does a mother's heart good to see her children no matter how long it's been."

Ophelia caught his eye, and he knew she was thinking of how sweetly his mother had spoken to her, how they had sometimes sat in her garden for tea, how Ophelia had treasured her care that summer. It was not only Silas who had been cleaved from his mother, but Ophelia, as well. When Merritt had confronted him with accusations about their friendship, Silas had been woefully unprepared. Despite how often Ophelia had warned him about her father's selfish and erratic behaviour, he hadn't understood the lengths to which Blackwood would go to try to marry Ophelia off for his own benefit. Ophelia had known her father far better than he had. She had been right that he would use anything at his disposal to get his way. He tried to smile reassuringly at her, but she had already ducked her head back to her dinner.

"Have you settled into your room, then?" Hannah asked.

"Yes," said Silas. "The room suits me just fine. Being quiet and clean, it's more than a sight better than where I've had to bed down."

"Were you at a convalescent hospital nearby?"

"I was." He paused, then said, "It was just south of my home, an estate in the Mendip Hills called Hartwood House."

Ophelia dropped her knife, her eyes flying to his face. Hartwood

House was only a day's travel from the farm and even closer to Wood Grange. He knew she was thinking of him recuperating so close to the estate. He wondered if she ever spoke with her father or anyone on the estate and felt sick at the thought that she might casually mention Silas's arrival.

"Excuse me," she murmured, regaining her composure and placing her knife carefully on her plate. "I had no idea you were so close to home all this time."

Her chest rose and fell rapidly under the loose fabric of her tunic, and he could see her trying to make sense of what he had revealed. Bess glanced at Ophelia, and seeing she was unsettled, asked about the nurses at the estate hospital, how long he had stayed, and what the other soldiers had thought of the estate.

Silas felt awkward speaking about his time at Hartwood House, not having truly worked through how he felt about it, nor having yet spoken about it with anyone. He had, of course, been absurdly grateful to be there, away from the front, and despite the pain of recovery, he had woken each day with a sense of purpose. It was his duty, he told himself, to recover and be of service in whatever way was possible. Regaining his strength and fighting to master his body became his all-consuming task. He didn't know how else to account for his returning home while so many others, far more deserving than he, languished in hospitals at the front or under the horrible sucking mud of the trenches. It mattered less that his sense of that duty was fuzzy on the best days, cynical on the worst days; he just knew he had to keep moving forward. Staying still too long left him open to contemplation, and that led to considering what he had done and for duty to whom.

Before France he had held patriotic feeling lightly, considering it more in terms of his love of his community, the place he had been born, and a boyish, far-away sense of doing right for a benevolent sovereign. The reality of basic training and war had been a jarringly ugly awakening. Jeering classism among officers and pat jingoism as a bandage for terrorised men pushed beyond all limit dimmed Silas's youthful belief. He had acted to protect his family, to keep Blackwood from punishing Ophelia, to defend the home that he feared would disappear in the fog of mortar blasts and gas. In the hospital, he had plenty of time to pick at the memories, to dissect each decision, to wonder whether he might have been better to stand up to Blackwood, take the chance that his threats were all bluster. In the end, no matter which way he turned it, he couldn't imagine there had been a way to solve the puzzle of protecting the people he loved any differently.

"The nurses were true marvels," he said, returning to the conversation. "Caring and knowledgeable. I'm one of the lucky ones, really. I roomed with men who were injured beyond anything I could imagine." He paused, his mind filling with the men still living at Hartwood House, some who might never recover enough to leave. "It was difficult to be there . . . at the estate . . . it, uh, reminded me a great deal of a place where I was once very happy." He finished abruptly, self-consciousness overtaking him.

Ophelia was watching him, her eyes unreadable, spots of colour high on each cheek. She tucked a strand of hair behind her ear, and Silas wished to be her fingers, caressing the satiny lock.

"I intended to volunteer as a nurse," Bess said. "But I heard Hannah speak and knew the WLA was for me, and as it turns out, I've found me feet with dairying."

She laughed easily, her dark eyes merry, a small dimple appearing in her chin. Silas liked her and was glad of the good company Ophelia had around her.

"It's no mean feat to be good with animals," he said by way of a compliment. "They'll nose out a false person faster than most humans."

"True enough, the dairy herd over at Mr. Bone's are suspicious of anyone who approaches in a rush. A calm mind is the only way to get anything done with them. In a funny way, I'm glad I've been working under Mr. Bone; he seems unfriendly, but 'tis really just a very quiet man. He's gentle as a lamb with the herd."

"Have you been with him long?" asked Silas.

"About six months, now. He's agreed to take me on as manager when the war is finished. It's a chance I never imagined before all this," Bess said seriously.

"He's lucky to have you," Hannah said before scooping another serving of potatoes onto Mrs. Darling's plate. They finished their dinner slowly, picking away until there was nothing left of the ham and potatoes, and only the smallest crust of bread still on the cutting board. Silas couldn't remember the last time he had felt so satisfied or sleepy. It reminded him of home, which made him think of the telegram he still needed to send.

"If you'll excuse me, I have an errand to do in the village first thing tomorrow, so I think I'll turn in," Silas said.

"Right you are," said Mrs. Darling. "Best get things cleaned up here and into bed, everyone."

Ophelia watched Silas rise from the table, carrying his plate to the sink, speaking quietly to Mrs. Darling and offering to wash the dinner dishes.

"Ah, away with you, now, Silas! A man offering to wash dishes, pssh! That's a sight more charming than good table manners." She laughed.

"Just want to lend a hand," Silas replied quietly. "Only where it's wanted, of course."

She had the strangest feeling that she was dreaming this moment; Silas standing in the kitchen, plate in hand, the softness of his stockinged feet on the flagstones suddenly unbearably domestic, intimate. Something was amiss though; she had seen it on his face during dinner when, for a second, his eyes had filled with anguish. It was there and gone, his green eyes clear, forehead smooth, but a sad, tight line had bracketed his mouth for the rest of the meal. She felt cross and out of sorts at how his change in mood made her feel;

his arrival had already thrown her confidence into disarray. She considered the possibility that what she had said to Bess was untrue; perhaps they would not get used to working together. If Silas's strength and experience was more than enough to help Mrs. Darling meet the production quota, would she still be of any use on the farm? The thought felt like ice in her chest, but she couldn't deny that things had suddenly gotten more complicated with his arrival. Working here was the only thing of her own she had ever had, and Silas's arrival made her want to clutch it harder to prevent it from slipping away, keep it for herself. But the most important thing was securing the harvest; her feelings about the farm, her friends, Silas . . . they couldn't come into it.

CHAPTER 10

*D*ays on the Darling farm began in a flurry of activity, but for the first few seconds of every morning, Ophelia let her mind sink back into her body, reinhabiting the self she was still getting used to. On the mornings since Silas's arrival the knowledge that he was waking up somewhere nearby unsettled her. She imagined the room she had shown him to, how his lanky frame might be sprawled across the iron bedstead, quilt rumpled around him. Or perhaps he slept curled in on himself. She didn't know. They had seen each other often after meeting over the mistaken book, but almost always outside, on their way to or from somewhere, only rarely seated in the cool cavern of the Wood Grange kitchen while Mrs. Greene worked her culinary magic around them. Ophelia remembered feeling a little drunk on the intensity of their friendship and the conversations they had had about what it meant for them to continue meeting. Silas had argued that it was dangerous for her, that his company could only be a negative for her, which she had rebuffed with immediate and, she later realized, naïve exclamations. She didn't know much about the world, how people talked, he had said. His concern had only made Ophelia dig her heels in harder.

Her father sought her out very rarely, usually only when he required her to be on display for dinners and parties, so prior to meeting Silas, this had meant spending time with Mrs. Greene in the kitchens and the garden, visiting some of the more elderly villagers with goods from the estate, and long hours reading in the library or wandering the grounds. She knew that this made her odd, a young woman always on the fringes of everything, but she hadn't had any real desire to change it. Silas and his friendship, then, were like a treasure to her, something of her own, not tainted by her father or the needs of the estate. It had seemed worth it to flout her father's rules at the time, but Ophelia wasn't sure she felt the same way now that it was Mrs. Darling's farm on the line. She worried that somehow the news of a soldier of Silas's age arrived to help might wind its way along the lines of village communication and that her father would get wind of it. She hadn't left a forwarding address for her father, didn't expect to hear from him, and hadn't exchanged letters with anyone but Mrs. Greene, but she knew better than to put it past him to act in his own best interest, no matter the consequences to others. Something had happened between Silas and her father; she was sure of it now. It occurred to her that she had always suspected this, but something about Silas's arrival had cemented it in her mind.

She slid out of bed, rubbing her eyes and pushing off her nightgown to dress. The bite of cool morning air on her skin made Ophelia think of Silas again, dressing for the day in his own small room in the barn. She conjured an image of him, as best she could, naked to the waist, pulling on his linen shirtsleeves. She imagined the shift and slide of the muscles down his back as he slipped the shirt over his head, the way his shoulders would bunch and release under the worn fabric, how his hair would fall forward into his eyes as he did up the buttons. Her mouth was strangely dry, and a thready beat began to throb between her legs. She realised she was avoiding thinking of his hands moving to the buttons of his trousers or the way the leather of his braces would slide across the palms of his wide hands as he settled them on his shoulders.

Downstairs, there was a loud knock at the door, and Ophelia heard Mrs. Darling hustling through the house to answer it. Her voice, rich and commanding, filtered up the stairs.

"Morning to you, sir. What it is I can help you with?"

"Morning, ma'am. Apologies for the early hour, but I come on urgent business from the War Agricultural Committee."

Ophelia hurriedly dressed, pulling her work jacket closed as she descended the stairs, Bess close at her heels, Hannah emerging from the sitting room. Ophelia wondered at the tension in Mrs. Darling's shoulders, whether it arose from the nature of the visit or her host's familiarity with being treated as incapable by men in positions of authority. For the moment it was hard to tell. The man at the door, tall and whip thin, produced a sheaf of paperwork, and leaned down to place his leather briefcase at his feet. Ophelia caught sight of Mr. Bone holding the reins of his dogcart out in the farmyard. He feigned nonchalance, but it struck her as odd that the neighbour would appear in tandem with the War Ag. It appeared that Mrs. Darling thought so as well because her back stiffened and she called out to him.

"To what do we owe the pleasure of a visit from you, Casper Bone? 'Tisn't often you are over on our side of t'hill."

Mr. Bone shook his head and said, "'Tisn't a visit, Arabella, only dropping the government man where he asked." Clearly wanting to end the conversation, he turned to fuss with something on the piebald horse's bridle. Ophelia could feel Hannah tense behind her while Bess poked her gently in the rib to mouth "What do they want with Mrs. D.?" Ophelia shook her head, wondering the same thing.

"If we could just get back to these papers, ma'am," said the official. "It's important that these instructions are communicated to you as soon as possible." He cleared his throat. "In order that you might take action with all due speed."

"I don't even know who ye are, let alone what I'm to do with all due speed, sir. P'raps you'd best explain yourself."

She motioned him into the kitchen, toward the table. Hannah quickly sat opposite him, eyes darting between him and Mrs. Darling. Bess pulled out a chair for Mrs. Darling before sitting beside her. Ophelia slid in next to Bess and waited to hear what the man had to say.

"In the course of our meetings, it's come to the attention of the County Agricultural Committee that there are potentially two acres or more of under-utilised land on this farm." He consulted a map on his clipboard. "At the north end of your property, there is a plot that seems to have been let go wild for some years. A wheat crop might be had there, were it cleared and cultivated. As I'm sure you understand, the government cannot allow the country to go hungry when there is arable land left fallow." He paused to take a breath, his sandy moustache quivering a little as he prepared to continue, eyes flicking up to Mrs. Darling's stony face. "The chair of your subcommittee has granted you until the twenty-first of May to have the indicated land prepared for cultivation, which with the help of the soldier seconded to your farm, should be feasible. In the unfortunate event that it is not, the land may be forfeited to the government or potentially reassigned to another landholder who is able to get it sown and harvested."

Mrs. Darling rose from the table and stood silent in the doorway for a moment, then lifting her chin gracefully, she fixed her eyes on the figure of Mr. Bone, who stood toeing the dirt of the farmyard. Refusing to meet her eyes, he cleared his throat and frowned at something on the footrest of the dogcart.

"So, Casper, 'tis to be this way, is it?" called Mrs. Darling, her voice strong and carrying. "Well, you know I've no stomach for games, so I'll tell you what I've always told them. I'll not be bullied into submission by any man, no matter what committee he serves."

"Now, Arabella—Mrs. Darling, that's not the case at all. I've naught—"

She turned her back without letting him finish and snapped at the official, who stood awkwardly in the kitchen, "Leave the papers with me. We'll have the land ready. Good day." Taking the papers he thrust toward her, she closed the door. She let out a long breath, and reaching out to pat Bess's shoulder, she said, "Let's have a cuppa and puzzle this out. Someone on the Agriculture Committee is certainly doing their homework, but I'll be damned if some snake from that trumped-up band of busybodies gets a single centimetre of land from me. If there's someone desperate enough to be stirring trouble for us with the Agricultural Committee, they'll be desperate enough to try anything. Come now, Ophelia, get that kettle on the stove."

Ophelia crossed the room to fill the kettle, and looking out the window above the sink, saw Silas enter the farmyard from the lane. He must have come from the village, she thought, as he was already dressed in a thick cotton work coat, the shoulders and back faded by the sun. Running his hands through his mussed, golden hair, he looked toward the house and then toward the two men about to depart. Mr. Bone, his shoulders broad from work and without a hint of roundness due to age, despite the grey of his hair, shook Silas's hand and spoke a few words. Ophelia started as the kettle overflowed, splashing cold water over her hand. Did Silas and Mr. Bone know each other? Was it possible she and Silas's past wasn't the only coincidence about his arrival? She couldn't imagine Silas being involved in anything nefarious, but it was also possible he wasn't the same person she had known at Wood Grange. She couldn't ignore that he hadn't chosen to share much about his current situation. *Be fair, Ophelia, there hasn't been much time for him to explain anything to you, assuming he intends to.* But she couldn't help feeling that something was wrong as she watched Mr. Bone clap Silas on the back before settling himself back into his cart with the irritable-looking official at his side.

Turning from the sink to place the kettle on the stove, she heard the scrape of the door as Silas entered. He looked more rested than the previous day, but Ophelia noted the brevity of his smiles when he greeted the other women and the way he pushed his hands into his pockets, then removed them to run his hands through his hair, the burnished golden strands waving back behind his ears and curling slightly at his temples. He looked worried, Ophelia thought, and that worried her.

CHAPTER 11

Silas could feel the change in Ophelia as soon as he entered the kitchen. Her eyes darted to his face, then away, and she fussed with the cutlery and plates on the sideboard. Mrs. Darling was fuming, head pressed together with Hannah, discussing the papers the khaki-clad man had dropped off. He wondered who the man was and why he had arrived on the farm with Mr. Bone. Perhaps Mrs. Darling was thinking of selling her property? Would be a hell of a thing to run this all by herself under normal circumstances, never mind wartime. Maybe she had run out of steam and thought to find a little cottage somewhere by the sea? But there was something about the tone of her conversation with Hannah that Silas thought seemed unhappy, almost angry. He looked around at Bess forming dough for scones, her nimble fingers flying over the floury surface, one of her front teeth catching her lip in concentration, then again at Hannah, whose face was serious and set in concentration while she carefully looked through the documents Mrs. Darling pushed toward her on the table. Finally, his eyes found Ophelia, a stack of plates held to her chest, one hand full of cutlery. His brain stuttered a moment at her beauty, his body coming instantly to life as he took in her trim breeches and the swell of her breasts under the workaday tunic. The green WLA armband stitched with a crimson crown circled her bicep. He wanted to run his hands over the band, feel the new strength evident in the muscles of her arms. He was stunned, and irritated, if he was honest, by her effect on him. Just seeing her again set him aflame with longing. His body had been a stranger to him since the war, a physical thing that seemed only to feel pain and fear, but being thrust together with Ophelia for only a few days made it thrum with desire, made him aware of himself as a man again. It was inconvenient, but he had found himself noticing the morning air against his face, the brush of shirt against skin, the weight of his braces on his shoulders. He felt alive to his senses as an instrument of pleasure again, after so long.

He realised too late that they stood in awkward silence, that Ophelia's eyes were on him, as if she had been watching him observe herself and the others. He wondered what she saw. He gave her a tentative smile and gestured toward the plates.

"Like some help with those?" he asked.

"Thank you, no," Ophelia replied, her eyes narrowing ever so slightly as he made to move toward her.

"Uh . . . right."

"How do you know Mr. Bone?" she asked suddenly, two spots of colour high on her cheeks.

Bloody hell. So she had seen him shake hands with the other man and had drawn her own conclusions. No wonder she was watching him like a hawk; God only knew what she thought he was up to. Silas pushed back his hair and met her eyes, trying his best to project open honesty.

"Don't know him from Adam, actually. But you know how it is with farmers—all the families tangled up in each other's business. I suppose it didn't take long for the news to go round that a soldier had arrived to lend a hand."

"Hmm. A surprise from your past," she said quietly.

"Indeed," Silas agreed. "I suppose he wanted to get a look at me for himself. In spite of the war, idle chatter still brings people together. P'raps we need it more now, small things to prattle about and all that."

"It just seems strange," Ophelia persisted. "You're assigned here, to help Mrs. Darling, but the War Ag wants to check up on us more, not less."

"Well, I certainly didn't orchestrate the visit, if that's what you mean," Silas said, feeling defensive. "I don't even know what the committee man wanted, let alone why he arrived with Mr. Bone." He pushed his hands into his pockets as they stared at each other. Why would she think he had anything to do with any of this?

"I don't know what I meant," Ophelia said with a sigh, putting the stack of plates on the corner of the table. "There's no shortage of people in the village who have wanted to see Mrs. Darling fail for years . . . I guess I'm beginning to wonder whether all these War Ag visits have something to do with that. And then you arrive in the middle of it all." She twisted the hem of her tunic around her finger. "It's just unsettling and made me wonder what your connection to all of it was."

"None at all, honestly, Ophelia," Silas said, voice low and urgent. "I was assigned straight from the convalescent home, didn't even know where I was headed until I arrived. I promise I have nothing to do with any of this."

She nodded. One up and down of her chin that loosened two silky strands of dark hair at her neck. They slid against the pale skin of her throat and Silas wanted so badly to touch them that his fingers felt aflame. Ophelia watched him, the grey depths of her eyes as cloudy as the seabed on a stormy day.

"Do you know what the inspector wanted of Mrs. Darling?" He cleared his throat, trying in vain to distract himself from his wayward thoughts.

Ophelia sighed. "More wheat. It's always more wheat."

He nodded, knowing what it felt like to be under constant pressure to produce more. He had been lucky that his family's land had been productive and well-managed by his father, but nevertheless, the relentless demand for more wheat, more milk, more food had been ever present.

"I know I'm not a farmer in the traditional sense of the word," she said, voice a little breathless, as though she were rushing the words, "but I have been working here with these women, my friends, for a year, and I'm starting to feel like one of them. I can't bear the thought of someone working against us, wanting us to fail." She continued before he could speak. "It's not just the war effort, though I know that's what's most important. It's that this is Mrs. Darling's place, land she has tended to for decades, land that's seen her through all sorts of things, married and alone. And she's ... she's welcomed me here, made me part of the farm. I will not," she said, her voice hard on the word, "just stand by while she is pushed around by people who see a chance to benefit themselves."

She turned away to look at Mrs. Darling and Hannah for a moment, and he could see the tense set of her back, shoulder bones high and sharp against the khaki linen of her WLA tunic. He took a chance and reached out to gently touch her shoulder. When she turned back to him, he said, "I'm no saint, Ophelia, but I promise I've nothing to do with any of the War Ag business in the village. I don't know anyone in these parts, and I've no interest in disturbing Mrs. Darling's farm." He paused to watch her reaction, silently begging her to feel the truth of his words. "I can see how much you and these women mean to each other, how well you all work together. I would never do anything to endanger that, you have my word."

She nodded. Her shoulders dropped the tiniest bit, but it was the relief in her eyes that eased Silas's worry.

"But," he said, voicing his thoughts as they occurred to him, "something does seem odd about the sudden increase in pressure, doesn't it? Would they give an assignment that they know is impossible, do you think?"

"I don't honestly know," she said wearily. "We've followed all the instructions sent out, and at least one of us attends every meeting. I thought we were doing a good job."

"I'm sure you are, all of you. Perhaps it really is a case of the demand for grains increasing suddenly, as the man said." She looked grateful for his encouragement, and before he could think better of it, he lifted a hand to her shoulder and squeezed gently. The heat from her body and the feel of the firm muscle of her shoulders under his fingers went to his head like a stiff drink. He thought of the telegram he had sent from the village that morning and hoped that a reply from Singer with reassignment details might come quickly. The week he had been on the farm had left him feeling tossed about the open ocean; the rising tide of lust watching Ophelia's face, animated and happy, followed by the nauseating fall when he recalled that if her father found out they were together, he would evict his mother from her farm. He was almost entirely sure that Ophelia would never have been silent had she known what her father had done, but a small, sibilant voice in the recesses of his mind, hurt and afraid, whispered that he could afford the risk of being together much less than she could.

"You're fortunate to have landed among a group that suits you so well. Does the WLA give you any choice where you are assigned?"

She shook her head. "I can't imagine a better farm to have been sent to. I don't think I really considered where I might be billeted when I filled out the form, but thank heavens I ended up with Mrs. Darling." She turned to look out the window above the sink. "Sometimes there are letters in *The Landswoman* that make veiled references to struggles with their billets or the farmers, you know, hours of work, questionable accommodations and so on . . . but I feel like I've found . . . I don't know . . . a family. I've been ridiculously fortunate."

"I'm happy for you, Fee. You deserve it, not having had much of a family for so long."

She shrugged casually, but her face clouded.

"How did your father take it? Your leaving, I mean?"

"I don't know," she said frankly. "He made his disapproval about the WLA abundantly clear, but when I actually left it was under cover of darkness to meet Hannah waiting in a wagon by the side of the road."

Silas whistled lowly. "Like a highway woman slipping along the moonlit roads, eh?"

"Well, it didn't feel that glamorous. I thought my nerves would devour me from the inside out. I still can't believe I actually went through with it, but honestly, leaving Mrs. Greene was the only part that gave me pause."

He could understand that, knowing both Ophelia and Mrs. Greene. The housekeeper had been as much a mother to Ophelia as she had ever had. Silas remembered hearing bits and pieces of the story from his own mother; Ophelia's mother, Iris, had died young, only a few years after giving birth to Ophelia. When he was young, he had wondered what it might be like to be an only child growing up in a house bigger than anything he could imagine, thinking as he squeezed round the kitchen table next to a sister and brother that it might be quite nice to grow up alone. No one pushing past you on the stairs or squabbling over who had more covers in the bed, no elbows jostling for the last sausage at breakfast. Sometimes it had seemed bliss to Silas, but when he had finally met Ophelia there was a loneliness to her that never dissipated, despite hints of wildness, rebellion. It was as though she existed entirely unto herself, unlike Silas who existed as son, brother, villager, tenant—cemented firmly into his world by a multitude of roots, generations deep. Ophelia, despite being literally to the manner born, stood alone, untethered to her father, unrooted by siblings or even a mother. Looking at her now, he could see that the loneliness had lifted a little, that she was valued here, that the place was forming itself around her.

As far as Silas could tell, the one and only person who looked out for her in childhood was Mrs. Greene, the Blackwood's portly, middle-aged cook and housekeeper. Stout, with a fuzz of honeyed grey hair, and kind, sleepy eyes, Mrs. Greene was Ophelia's champion in all things, clucking and cooing over the "poor wee girly, alone in every way that counts, rattlin' 'round that big 'ouse on 'er own."

At his mother's table, a wedge of cake and a cup of hot black tea in front of her, Silas had often overheard Mrs. Greene and his mother sharing the village gossip. He could still recall their voices and much of what they shared. "She's a good gel, really, so sweet and thoughtful. Though her father's left her too much on her own all these years, poor dove," the cook would murmur to Mrs. Larke before setting her teacup down forcefully, leaning forward and resting her elbows on the table in a gesture that indicated she was about to share a particularly important opinion. "Iris was always a means to an end for Merritt Blackwood. Poor woman hadn't a chance, really. 'Twas nothing but sadness in that house after they married. Mrs. Lyons and I used to mourn somethin' fierce for the mistress, kept under his thumb with all the shouting and strong armin'. No good'll ever come o' this, Mrs. Lyons and I used t' say, and no good ever did. 'Cept Ophelia, o' course."

Careful not to attract attention, he stepped closer to Ophelia and ran a hand down her arm to her hand.

"I'm sorry. You must miss her a great deal. I know how much she means to you."

Ophelia smiled a watery smile and nodded.

"Are you able to write to her at all?" Silas asked.

"I am wary of attracting my father's notice," Ophelia replied, "so

I don't write often. She writes me when she can, and thankfully, I've heard nothing from him."

Before he could ask anything more, Mrs. Darling cleared her throat and pushed back from the table, her plate still loaded with most of her breakfast. Deep worry lines creased her forehead and her mouth was an unhappy slant.

"Well, everyone, it's a mighty good thing that Silas arrived when he did, as the committee has well and truly forced my hand. According to these papers, as Hannah reads them, we've to get two and a half acres into cultivation by May, which gives us roughly three weeks. And that's on top of the current fields Ophelia's prepared." She rubbed her hands together on her lap and continued. "We'll need everyone pulling together to get this done, and even then, it'll not be a sure thing, the areas the agriculture man has indicated haven't been ploughed under for years, more hedgerow than field. I've no earthly idea how we'll do it . . . I really couldn't bear to lose the farm," she added, almost to herself.

Everyone was silent around the table, the weight of the task and the cost of failure as heavy as lead. Then Hannah spoke.

"We'll do it as we've done everything so far, strong backs, chippin' away at the task," she said, resolutely. "As Mrs. Darling says, 'tis a good thing we've Silas's back now. We'll put it to good use breaking through the blackberries and crabgrass." She looked over at Ophelia, then said with an encouraging smile, "Between that and your work with Samson and Delilah, we'll have the fields cultivated in time."

Silas didn't miss the grateful smile Ophelia sent Hannah and wondered about it. She seemed relieved by the other woman's encouragement; did she worry he had come to replace her?

Still pondering this, he nodded, saying, "Ophelia and the team will be invaluable, as I'm not yet sure how my leg will fare on rough ground. But for what it's worth, you can count on my back to help in any way I can. I'll have no part in you losing your land, Mrs. Darling."

"Thank you, Silas," said Mrs. Darling seriously. "I'm feeling awfully grateful for the lot of you, I must say."

Ophelia beamed at him, her eyes warm and happy. Hannah and Bess nodded in agreement.

"Alright, then," Mrs. Darling said, looking around the table. "We'll take this on together, yes?"

Bess, Hannah, Ophelia, and Silas all nodded. Despite the agreement, the rest of the breakfast was sombre and quiet. Just as Ophelia rose to clear the plates, another knock sounded at the door.

"And who's that now?" said Mrs. Darling, getting up to answer it. She returned momentarily with a small yellow paper, folded in half. "For you," she said, passing it to Silas. "From the army, judging by the telegram boy."

He rose from the table and, standing with his back to the women, read the abbreviated message from his former commanding officer.

Good news re: your recovery. STOP. Regrettably, reassignment not possible. STOP. I, and the army, thank you for continued service. Cpt. L. Singer.

Silas stood stock-still, disappointment warring with relief. The decision had been made; he had to stay, could not abandon this post, nor his duty to these women and his country. He would have to find a way to keep his assignment to this farm, and his rising attraction to Ophelia from bringing everything down around his head.

"Everything alright?" Hannah asked.

"Oh, uh, yes, just an update from the regiment I was attached to. Nothing to concern us, really," Silas said. He shoved the telegram into his pocket and turned to help clear the table.

CHAPTER 12

The sun was cresting the tops of the oak trees when Hannah and Ophelia emerged from the house into the farmyard after breakfast. The ginger barn cat leapt down from the fence rail and slouched over to weave itself around Ophelia's legs. She stooped to scratch its back, fingertips moving over the knobby ridges of the cat's spine. It purred and flopped down to expose a long white strip of belly. Hannah laughed. "Yer like a fae, Ophelia, charming all the animals around you."

Ophelia snorted in response. "'Tis because I was never allowed a pet as a child. My father only believed in animals for work, even the dogs he kept were only for hunting. I tried to bring a treat to the dogs once and he caned my hand. Said it made them soft and they needed to be sharp." She stopped petting the cat and looked over at Hannah. "I suppose I always felt the animals might be my friends where people had failed to be."

Hannah nodded. "I had no pets of me own, neither. No place for that in service, and once I were on me own, I'd no money to spare for that sort o' thing. 'Tis horrible lonely on your own, isn't it? The first time I ever felt cared for was after joining the WSPU. The other women looked out for me, looked after each other. I felt as content as that cat there." She gestured to the cat, indolent under Ophelia's fingers. "A funny thing isn't it, that loneliness can come to anyone, monied or poor, educated or not."

Ophelia nodded, thinking about the difference in their lives, how easily she might never have met Hannah, nor gotten to know how strong and intelligent she was, how fiercely she fought to survive in a world that told her women were worth little. In a strange way, having her hand forced by her father was the catalyst for some of the best things in Ophelia's life; joining the WLA, meeting Hannah, Bess, and Mrs. Darling, understanding that she could direct the course of her life, that she was capable of so much more than she had ever known.

She nodded, thinking as she spoke. "I didn't know that women could have such different lives, come from different classes, and still have so many of the same experiences. Even though I hated the way my father spoke about people who were from lower classes than ourselves, I suppose I still thought of them that way ... as *other* than us. I truly thought you and I had nothing in common. I'm embarrassed, really, at how callow I was, how unquestioning ... I know I'll be learning a new way of seeing the world for a long time."

"Ah, come now, Ophelia. You couldn't have known what you weren't taught. And you're practically a card-carrying suffragette now," Hannah said with a smile. "In any case, that's why Mrs. Pankhurst was always saying we've to spread the word ... though we wear no mark, we are everywhere," Hannah intoned. "So she says, in every class from high to low." Hannah's face always lit when she spoke of the cause and Ophelia felt grateful for the other woman's willingness to overlook her flat-footed understanding of how the world worked outside the bounds of the gentry.

"Speaking of animals"—Hannah shot a sly look at Ophelia—"that was quite the breakfast after Mr. Bone arrived with the War

Ag man, wasn't it? Thought Mrs. Darling might toss him in the dung heap for a minute there."

Ophelia laughed. "I was surprised to see him, too. I've never been certain what the story is about their past, but there must be something . . . I don't think I've ever seen her so cross. And he looked as though he would rather be anywhere else on Earth."

"And well he might, Mrs. Darling isn't to be trifled with. The timing is strange though, isn't it? I hope Mr. Bone has'na gotten himself mixed up with those toads on the county committee, stirring trouble more than doing any good, I'm sure of it."

"I'll ask Bess at dinner. She'll surely have picked up some idea of the situation, working around Mr. Bone at the dairy every day. Bess says he can be quite friendly now that she's gotten to know him."

Hannah's eyes flicked up over Ophelia's shoulder as someone emerged from the house, scraping the door closed over the stone lintel. Ophelia turned from Hannah to find Silas standing in the lee of the doorway. He wore a dark grey waistcoat open over his shirt and the soft wool of his brown work trousers clung to his muscular thighs, hems brushing the top of his work boots. The sun in her eyes gave Silas a halo; warm copper and golden light illuminated his hair, throwing his face in shadow. She could feel his eyes though, their mossy green dark and intense as he stood quietly under her scrutiny. She couldn't tell whether the tightness in her chest was because of the situation on the farm or his undeniable beauty.

"Mrs. Darling has errands for me in the village and says I'm to find out if there are any repairs you need from the smith before ploughing . . ." Silas said when neither woman spoke. "I, uh, if there's anything you need, I can bring it to him today."

Mrs. Darling clearly recognised him as someone meant for places such as the farm. Ophelia was surprised how insecure that made her. Here he was, immediately at ease, whilst she sometimes still felt out of place, the odd man out on the farm. It was frustrating how easily she reverted to her old insecurities in his presence; she knew that he had more experience, of course he did, but she didn't like her own assumption that his skills rendered hers useless. It was an old pattern, thinking that she as a woman was less than, learned early and hard from her father. She thought she had rid herself of the habit during the last year, but it had raised its head again with Silas's arrival. She wished the newer, bolder part of herself would put it back in its place. Hannah shifted beside her, pushing Ophelia gently toward Silas. "Ophelia's the one with her eyes on the machinery most often, she can tell you if there's anything needed. I'll be off now," she said, waving as she turned to leave the farmyard.

They stood for a moment longer, Silas watching Hannah's back. Ophelia tried not to stare at him, but stole quick glances, memorizing him for later—broad shoulders bulky beneath his linen shirt, worn but clean, under the leather braces she remembered. They had been a gift from his mother one Christmas, she recalled. Clearly treasured, soft and flexible with wear.

"Right, then. I've not had an in-depth tour of what you're working with. We could do that now, I suppose?"

"Over here," Ophelia said, distracted by his nearness and her own musings, unable to manage anything more conversational.

She walked toward the large opening in the barn, Samson and Delilah stamping in their stalls, eager to move on hearing her approach. She stepped into the dim half-light, dust motes floating in the sunlight that pierced the cracks and knotholes of the barn walls. It was hushed other than the odd clomp of a large hoof and the intermittent *tsk*ing of the swallows shunting in and out of the high ceilinged space. She heard Silas follow her and felt her heart thudding madly in her chest. Was it wise for her to be alone with him? She couldn't quite parse her feelings about Silas this morning —irritation? attraction?—and that frightened her a little.

Walking ahead of him, she approached the collection of

machines housed in the barn. Harrow, seed drill, plough, all of various ages and states of repair, and in the back corner the dull metallic barrel of the roller. She returned to her earlier worries about her abilities and felt a hum of satisfaction when she began describing the situation with each of the machines. Of course, Silas knew what each was and how to use them, but she knew these specific ones and how they performed in these fields. She knew the cant of their wheels, the finicky ways they needed to be attached, and the yawing turns they made at the end of each row. She had been learning all these things all year long, and now she could share her knowledge with him. Silas followed her, listening as she pointed out each piece, outlining their status and what repairs might be needed. She didn't pause once, and Silas seemed to understand that he wasn't to interrupt. He simply nodded and moved quietly along beside her.

"The seed drill needs to be realigned after each use, as the pins holding it in place get jogged out of position in the fields, but it's not too much of a bother," Ophelia said as she reached the final machine. "And that's about everything we have here, aside from Samson and Delilah, who you've already met." She nodded toward the doorway leading to the horse stalls. "We're lucky that Mr. Bone sees fit to do some small repairs for us, otherwise things would be even more makeshift than they are. He can be a hard man, so we are grateful for his help with that."

"It's good you have a handle on things. If we can't rely on our equipment, it will be nigh on impossible to have the extra land cleared and sown in time."

He paused, and she thought again of the task that lay ahead of them, of the miracle, and inconvenience, of his arrival.

"It adds to our work to be sure, but the main fields have already been harrowed, seeded, and rolled. That's fifty acres of wheat and then there are the two small fields by the house. We've sown those in sugar beets, for the horses and cows."

"You've gotten so much done with so little, Ophelia. It would be impressive, even for a seasoned crew," Silas said, running his hand over the chipped paint of the drill.

"Mrs. Darling is an excellent teacher, and we all had at least some training from the WLA. We've managed to pull together so far." She realized she hadn't quite kept the defensiveness from her voice when Silas ducked his head to make eye contact.

"I was in earnest, Fee," he said, the nickname between them before he caught it. "What you are doing, not just with the farm . . . it's impressive. All of it. Something's changed in you, not just your clothes or that you've left the estate . . ." He trailed off a little.

"I feel it, too," she said quietly. "I think it's my mind that's changed, even more than my body." She wondered briefly if she should have spoken of her body aloud, but decided not to examine that thought too closely. "It's like all of this"—she gestured between herself and the room full of machines—"was in me, but not even I knew it. I had to come here and do this to truly realize it." She wanted to explain to Silas what it meant to work on the farm, to be useful in a concrete way; she wanted him to understand what she was trying to build for herself. "When I told my father my plans with the WLA, he was so angry and I was so afraid." Silas nodded when she paused. "But I did it anyways and maybe that's the most important part, the *doing*, even more than whether it was farm work or nursing or something else."

He was quiet beside her, his face thoughtful, his body still. She appreciated that he hadn't tried to minimize her leaving the estate, but also hadn't made it the most important part of what had changed. She wondered if he also felt relief at leaving the farm and before she could help herself, she was asking him.

"Why did you leave, Silas? I mean, I know you enlisted, which surprised me, honestly. I suppose I imagined that you would always be there, as your family was, hadn't realized you were patriotic in that way."

He met her gaze, his green eyes dark as a forest glade, and if Ophelia hadn't been watching so closely, she would have missed the moment his face shuttered and rearranged itself into something resembling neutrality.

"I hadn't considered it originally," he admitted slowly. "Had planned on applying for exemption to keep the farm going, grain and milk off to market, all that . . . but I suppose I worried that wasn't enough, wouldn't protect anyone if it came right down to it." He pushed his hands through his hair, the strands immediately falling back into place across his brow. "It felt important to defend something, what I think of as my country, my family and friends, of course." His long fingers gestured in the space between them as he said friends, and Ophelia couldn't help remembering how lovely their short summer had been. A reprieve she hadn't known to hope for.

"Your mother must have been beside herself with worry," she said, thinking of how close Mrs. Larke and Silas had been.

"Aye, surprised and grieved. I know she'd been counting on me to keep things going for all three of them. Samuel hadn't really taken on much of the farming then, and Delphine, well, she was just as she always was, driving my mother to distraction."

The fondness in his voice was like an ache Ophelia could feel in her own chest. She wanted to take his hand or draw him close. She reminded herself that she didn't need to soothe him, that she didn't have to take on his past or responsibility for his feelings. She looked up at Silas, still standing with his back toward the door, his face lost in shadow and memories of his family.

"Have you been to see them since you were sent home to recover?" He shook his head, and she saw that she had hit on the real point of pain. "Why not, Silas?" She couldn't understand why a man so devoted to his mother and siblings would stay away, but when she looked up to continue her questions, she saw his face twist with anger and sadness.

"I've nothing to offer, have I? My leg is only just shy of a wreck and I feel of no more help to them than when I was across the Channel. I'm"—he swiped a hand across the back of his neck—"I'm ... there's reasons I can't visit them, in any case," he gritted out, his jaw sharp with tension.

Ophelia didn't know what to say, hadn't realized that Silas, strong, capable Silas, might feel himself less for his injury, and immediately understood what a silly assumption it was. There were expectations of manhood, not as inflexible as those for women, but expectations just the same. The rigid set of his shoulders and hands fisting at his sides told her everything she needed to know.

"That isn't true, Silas, it could never be true of you. It isn't your duty to protect everyone, even if it were possible," she said gently. She wanted to say more but he was already shaking his head, so instead of pushing him further, she motioned while moving across the passage. She lifted the horses' bridles down from their hooks and swiped the jar of leather cleaner from its place on the shelf. Her hands felt unsteady as she worked the buckles on the horses' bridles, her fingers tripping over the familiar movements. Silas lingered behind her in the doorway, his broad shoulder resting against the rough boards. He said nothing, but she could feel the weight of his eyes on her, and it made her neck hot and her hands clumsy. She whirled around, desire and sadness hot in her chest, and said, as breezily as she could, "Well, you may as well make yourself useful if you're going to stand there."

Silas dipped his head and stepped across the hallway in one easy stride. Next to her at the waist-high shelf, he pulled one of the bridles toward himself, and taking a piece of rag, began gently wiping down the leather, removing the dust and grime of the previous day. Almost immediately, Ophelia realised her mistake; sharing the jar of cleaner meant that he stood close enough to brush her elbow with his. She couldn't help but watch his long fingers moving against the leather reins, every stroke of his hand sending ripples of movement along his muscled forearm, the pale skin sprinkled with golden hairs, revealed by his rolled-up shirtsleeves. He made no attempts at conversation, nor came any closer, but worked steadily at the task, his body seeming to fall easily into the rhythm of the work. Ophelia found herself listening to the steady metronome of his breath, instinctively matching her own movements to the timing of his. They worked in silence, surrounded by the soft snuffing of the horses eating and the clucking of the hens.

It felt so easy to work next to each other like this, Ophelia thought. She tried not to let herself imagine a future version of her life where there was nothing that they couldn't face together, no burden they could not shoulder side by side. But even as she felt her body sway ever so slightly toward Silas, their shoulders companionably close, she had an inkling that he hadn't shared everything with her.

"And what of you?" His voice was soft and worn like the leather they worked on.

"What of me?" she said, irritated by her unsteady voice.

He snorted softly, and she could feel the warmth of his smile against her cheek. "I've spilled my guts and still know no more than that you arrived here without your father's blessing." He paused. "Which I have to say is no mean feat given the sway he held over your life last I saw you." He turned toward her at the bench, his hands stilling in their work. "I can't imagine how much has changed in your life and I find myself eager to know. If you're willing to share, of course."

Ophelia huffed a small laugh into the warm air and tried to ignore the sizzle of nerves in her belly. She wasn't sure why she felt nervous to tell Silas about her move to the farm. They were both here now, so surely it made no difference how they had arrived. He had enlisted, and as much as that had thrown his life into disarray, the decisions she had made in his absence had changed the course of hers. She cleared her throat.

"Things were much the same after you enlisted, with my father, I mean. There was another potential proposal, and when I told him I didn't intend to marry his choice, he threatened the usual retributions." She paused, and Silas nodded to show he understood her shorthand. "I wasn't supposed to visit your family, though I did stop by a few times. I saw that the visits made your mother melancholy, so I didn't continue." She kept her hands moving to keep her mind from dwelling on the loneliness of that time; the empty manor house seeming colder than she could ever remember, the bleak, sere fields echoes of her own isolation, pushing her to seek change, connection, some new version of her life.

"When I met Hannah at the recruitment meeting, she was doubtful of my intention. But by the time I got home that night and got over the embarrassment of being called a lightweight, I knew I would join. The WLA makes sense to me, did then, and still does now."

"How do you mean?" Silas asked.

"Well, women have had to put aside suffrage arguments for the duration of the war, but this work"—she gestured with her hands toward the horses and the machinery—"proving that women are equal to the tasks that have been men's domain, well that's still suffrage. It's showing that women are as valuable a part of this country as its men and deserve the right to vote for its government." Silas made a noise of agreement in the back of his throat and Ophelia continued. "Really though, the women here rescued me, tolerated my flat-footed attempts at both farming and feminism, pushed me to strengthen my mind as much as my body. I might have left my father's estate of my own volition, but I could never have imagined what billeting with Mrs. Darling, Hannah, and Bess would change."

Silas was quiet, his brow furrowed as he listened, thumb

rubbing absently along the length of the cheek strap he held. Ophelia chanced a look at him and he turned immediately, eyes intent on hers.

"Everything is different for you here," he observed. "I almost can't imagine you as you were before. You're more . . . vibrant, maybe? But also, mmm . . . sharper?" He pursed his lips trying out the words in his head, deciding if they were apt. "Not sharper, like harsh, but somehow more keen, like a new blade."

"Oh," she said, taking this in.

He laughed and shook his head, pushing a hand through his hair. "I expressed that clumsily, I'm not sure I can describe it properly. More you, somehow. Like you've changed from a watercolour to an oil painting. Your self is so clear here."

"Perhaps, but things are also muddier. So many things I held as facts have turned out to be incorrect. I have lived in a pond my entire life, Silas, and mistaken it for the ocean. I could scarcely argue for my own enfranchisement, let alone anyone else's. Before I started reading the books and pamphlets Hannah recommended, I assumed all women thought as I did. I didn't realize that Hannah, who grew up poor, and Bess, who is Irish, or even Mrs. Darling who does both men and women's work on the farm, would all have entirely different views on almost everything. That a woman might choose to pursue work or love another woman or love no one at all, and that having those choices benefits everyone. It is all related and I never knew that, never understood." She felt her heart pounding as she spoke, wondering if he would be discomfited by her thoughts, if she was expressing them well. Speaking her mind was still new to her, even after a year, and she felt slightly wary of sharing her thoughts with a man. But Silas needed to know that she was working to change. Ophelia didn't want him to mistake her for the person she had been on the estate. "My father thought me little more than a child, and his protection of me was concerned only with preserving what he considered his investment. My only thought was to marry someone not chosen for me by my father, but the more I learn, the more I wonder if the question is whether to marry at all." She took a deep breath. "I've come to see that so much of the protection we women gain from marriage is really just ceding control to our husbands. If we were actually treated as adults, capable of rational thought and decision making, there might be an argument for a marriage of equals. As it stands, those cases are few and far between, I'm afraid."

Silas was quiet, and Ophelia wondered if he was thinking of his own parents' marriage or if she had simply said too much, too quickly. She cleared her throat, prepared to defend herself, when Silas spoke.

"I also find myself questioning many of the ideals I held before France." He gestured vaguely toward his leg. "Being back is uncomfortable and not only because of my injury. I don't know quite where I stand these days . . . though I am certain that enfranchisement is the right of all, and that loving another person is no one's business but one's own. I certainly didn't slog through hell only to tell other people what to believe or who to care for."

Ophelia nodded and waited for him to continue.

"Not sure what I did slog through hell for in all honestly," he said almost to himself, then shook his head. His overlong hair slid forward across his brow, and Ophelia had the urge to brush it back for him. She imagined the slide of it between her fingers, the way it might feel to tuck the strands behind the fine ridge of his ear, and squeezed her hands into fists to make them behave.

"You've given me a great deal to consider, Ophelia," Silas remarked, turning a crooked smile on her.

"I'm still considering much of it myself," she said, then noticing the changed angle of the sun through the barn door sighed. "God, I've a deal of work to get done today, so we'll have to continue another time." She wiped her hands on the rag hooked on the nail above the workbench and ducked outside before her desire to keep standing next to Silas, talking and listening, got the better of her.

"Course. I'll put these on their hooks," he said, replacing the lid on the tin of saddle soap and gesturing to the bridles.

* * *

Silas stood beside the pump in the farmyard, silvery drops plinking into the tin bucket beneath the spout. He wiped the remnants of saddle soap from his fingers, running the rag around the edge of each nail, and took a deep breath. He couldn't settle his thoughts; they raced like grasshoppers around his head, leaping and beating their wings while he tried to cage and order them. Ophelia's questions unnerved him, not being able to tell her the whole truth gutted him. He tried to assess the situation, his options; reassignment wasn't a possibility, the potential repossession of the farm worried him, *and* he had nowhere else to go. He would have to stay, and he would have to find a way to ignore the hungry desire for Ophelia he could feel taking root in him.

Hands dry, he walked toward the long field that bordered both the house and the lane. He thought of his mother and the way that his father had cared for her before his death. Silas thought of the moments between them—the quick kiss at the door before the day began, his father's hand at the small of her back, the way his mother passed her hand over her husband's shoulders as he sat at the kitchen table. Was his father not protective of his mother? Of his sister? He tried to imagine whether his mother had felt childish for the care his father bestowed and found he couldn't form an answer.

Wasn't a man meant to protect those he loved or who were under his care? Silas had always equated protection and care of one's family with the state of a man's character. It was how he had understood his father as a loving presence. He tried to understand how Ophelia could say it wasn't his duty to protect those he loved.

If he wasn't able to do that, what else had he to offer? Silas felt heat rising up his neck and the now-familiar ache beginning to pound in his ankle. He had been stomping across the uneven ground without realizing it, his confusion and irritation gathering force in his body. "Bloody leg," he muttered, leaning down the massage his calf and ankle. Even through the fabric of his trousers, he could feel the hard lines of scar tissue, the pitting in the muscles of his leg. It made him feel weak to have to stop and rest, to tend to his body, which he now understood he had always taken for granted. He rubbed gently at his calf and down the hard line of his ankle, trying to soothe the ache that persisted months after the injury. He felt the disappointing, salty burn of tears at the back of his throat and tried to swallow them away. What kind of man was he now anyways, he thought bitterly. Worrying about whether he should protect someone he loved when he couldn't even walk halfway across a field without stopping to rest. Half a man at best, broken at worst. He pushed his fingers more firmly into his leg, trying to loosen the knots of his scars.

CHAPTER 13

The day after the committee official's visit, Ophelia made her way along the edge of the top field, Samson and Delilah on either side of her, their heavy hooves denting the softening soil as they plodded along, heads low, harnesses jingling. The afternoon of his visit, Ophelia had taken a quick walk over to the new field to acquaint herself with its terrain. She was nervous to plough an uncultivated area; so far, all her practise had been on ground that had been turned over for decades, but this new plot resembled nothing so much as a patch of wildness, covered with crabgrass and dotted with the odd primrose, edged by waist-high blackberry, wild rose bushes, and the remnants of a laid hedge, now gnarled with age. Having been sown with a cover crop for a number of years, the land had eventually been let to go wild when Mrs. Darling's workload on the rest of the farm became too much. It was neither the worst nor the best piece of land, forming a kind of crooked dog leg between Mr. Bone and Mrs. Darling's farms. It was a little hard to get to, and Ophelia wasn't entirely sure that she could command the team well enough to get the ground broken with sufficient speed and to the correct tilth, and it preyed on her worry that she wasn't pulling her weight on the farm. She didn't want to let Mrs. Darling down, but she also didn't want to make more work by doing her job poorly because she was afraid to ask for help.

Cresting the rise, she saw Silas at the far end of the track. He was stacking the unearthed stones at the base of a hedge in his shirtsleeves, back already dotted with sweat, waistcoat hanging from a thick pleach.

"Woah, Samson." The gelding stopped obediently, the traces jingling gently between he and Delilah. "There's a good boy, eh?" she murmured, scratching behind his ear and down his neck.

Hearing the horses, Silas straightened and put a hand to his eyes. "What do you think? Can we make something of it?"

Ophelia surveyed the land, noting how much he had already cleared that morning, and nodded. "Not sure we'll be ready to plough this afternoon, but I brought the horses with me in case. Let me secure them, and I'll help you finish up this end."

Silas stepped forward. "I noticed a stout beech a little farther down, we could tie them there until we're ready."

"I've kept them in their halters so we can graze them for now." Ophelia tugged Samson forward and she and the horses fell into step behind Silas. She took a deep breath and tried not to watch the way his trousers hugged his backside or the way the muscles in the broad expanse of his shoulders moved, smooth and sinuous, under his shirt. As though he sensed her thoughts, Silas turned, a sly smile on his face.

"Alright back there? You're awfully quiet."

"Uh, yes, f-fine," she stammered, sure her blush could be seen from the other end of the field.

She was tongue-tied and awkward, and what would she say anyways? *I suddenly find myself thinking of kissing you, but I am terrified that wanting you means I must give up the independence I am imag-*

ining for myself for the first time? The curse of a broad chest and a fine arse, she thought irritably.

"I suppose I've been thinking about how strange it is to be here, together. After all this time."

Up ahead he nodded, then stopped and waited.

"It was lovely to talk with you yesterday . . . made me think of that summer, I suppose," she finished, her voice lifting with uncertainty. "How different it feels not to hide, to just have a conversation."

"God, yes," Silas huffed, his mouth hitching up at one corner. "There are some who find subterfuge enticing, but I've no stomach for it, myself. I'm a simple man when it comes down to it and prefer my conversations out in the open."

Ophelia's mind stuttered to a halt as Silas approached, reaching out to take Samson's lead rope. His fingers brushed hers, but when she made to pull away, he slid his hand up to her wrist, circling it with his long fingers. She could feel her pulse hammering against his fingertips and looked up just as he turned her hand over, running the fingers of his other hand across her palm. She almost clamped her hand shut, surprised at the tickle of his thick fingers moving across the creases of her skin. Her breath rushed out, delight and shock filling her when Silas lifted his head, eyes heavy lidded. He still held her hand, his blunt forefinger circling the flesh of her palm hypnotically. She pulled away, closed her hand, and rubbed it self-consciously against her thigh.

"I shouldn't have—" he began, stepping back.

"No, I didn't mind," she blurted. "I mean . . ." But she didn't know what she meant. She more than *didn't* mind, but they needed to work together, needed to secure the harvest and the farm. She worried this strange flame flickering between them could derail it all.

"I'm sorry, Ophelia. I overstepped. I know we need to work together," Silas said. His voice was soft and low; from a distance they might be discussing the best place to tie the horses, and Ophelia was grateful for his consideration. She felt giddy and disappointed. She wanted him to take her hand again, wanted to feel his lips on her skin, instead she only nodded and said, "No need to apologize. Let's get to work, shall we?"

Silas smiled, his mossy eyes warm and bright, and she felt her stomach roll unsteadily. He looked so reassured; she couldn't tell whether she was glad or disappointed. She looped the horses' lead ropes over two thick branches, hurrying through the task so she could move away from Silas's warm bulk. The V of skin visible at his throat was distracting, and she was horrified with herself for noticing the sunlight on the dusting of hair that disappeared into his open collar. She made sure the horses had plenty of room to graze without becoming tangled, and finished, strode after Silas. He stopped to reach into a wooden trug and handed a sickle to Ophelia, then turned to pick up a scythe. Spreading out across the new field, they bent to the task of pushing back the brush and thorns.

Ophelia was glad of the mostly silent work, forcing herself to focus on the necessity of working well together. Surely this fluttering in her belly, the shivery anticipation she felt around him was mere attraction; it was only natural. He was beautiful, thoughtful, and gentle in his speech. He had occupied her thoughts since his arrival, if she were being honest. But she had deliberately chosen this path for herself, away from a conventional life, the conventional ties of partnership. She didn't see how the two could coexist, and she knew she was not willing to give up on her own liberation.

It wasn't just that he had appeared in the middle of her new life, like some particularly handsome spectre from her past, his presence threatening to upset the carefully balanced bridge she was building between her old life and a still-unknown new one. It was, Ophelia discovered to her horror, that she wanted him; his friendship, but also his smile, his kisses, his regard, and she wanted them with a hot, uncomfortable urgency. She didn't know how to reconcile this desire for Silas with her desire for a life not circumscribed by marriage to a man chosen by her father, or perhaps marriage at all. She was upset by the strength of her feelings for him and discomfited by their resistance to her attempts to ignore them.

They worked through the morning and until the sun rose high in the clear sky. Sweat trickled down Ophelia's neck and along the dip of her back, slid into the valley of her breasts. She stood and wiped her brow with the scrap of calico she had learned to carry in her pocket and looked to see where Silas was. Toward the farther end of the patch of weedy land, he stood and swiped a hand across the back of his neck. He gestured toward the trug where he had stowed a jug of water and a few apples. Ophelia nodded and headed toward it. Slumping onto the ground, she tipped backward and let her feet splay out in front of her. The bright blue dome of the sky extended past her field of vision, filling her with its enormity. A flight of birds darted and swooped across the blue and then Silas's shaggy blond head came into view beside her.

"Drink?" he asked.

She sat up, laughing, and nodded. He passed her the heavy earthenware jug and she drank gratefully, the water cool and sharp in her mouth. Taking the jug back and replacing its stopper, Silas handed her an apple and bit into his own.

"God, I missed this," he said, almost absently.

Ophelia looked at his profile. Aquiline nose a sharp outline against the shrubbery in the background and those obscene lips—almost a pout, in direct contradiction to the masculine planes of his face. She turned away before it became staring.

"When I was in France, it seemed possible I might never see another English summer."

"God, Silas," she breathed. Her chest felt tight at the thought of him at the front, the thought of him injured, alone. Dead, even. She couldn't imagine a more alive person; even injured, he radiated a kind of generous vitality. "It must have been horrible." The words felt useless and trivial even as she said them.

"I'm just so fucking glad I was wrong," he said. Then, "Pardon my language."

Impulsively, she grabbed for his hand and squeezed. He froze, and she swore she could see his pulse at his throat when she looked up from their clasped hands.

"I'm glad you were, too."

She was holding it too long, she thought, and it was becoming awkward, but she couldn't bear to lift her hand from the warm skin of Silas's. Didn't want to lose the contact that confirmed he was very much alive next to her, his handsome face tilted inquisitively toward her. Any words she could find to describe the unsteady gladness at his continued existence skittered around her mind unhelpfully. Embarrassed, she pulled her hand back into her lap. Then both of them were clearing their throats and making to stand awkwardly. They stowed the water and remaining apples, and before either of them could acknowledge the conversation, they turned to their tools and the seemingly Sisyphean task of the brambles.

* * *

Silas dropped into the rhythm of scything, the easy lift and swing of the blade, the satisfying *shik* of the brambles and grass as he sliced through them. His arms and back ached pleasantly, but he was aware of a deeper ache in his ankle and hoped he wouldn't pay too dearly for the exertion. For the most part, his leg had slowly strengthened, but sometimes at night the scars ached painfully, and until now he hadn't pushed himself much past the walks encouraged by the nurses at the convalescent hospital. Standing up to stretch his shoulders, he took a moment to watch Ophelia working to his left along the hedge. She seemed to be humming as she worked the sickle through the thick growth of cleavers, grass, and buttercup. She wore a kind of khaki bloomer overalls that should have been unflattering, but tucked into her boots and cinched in at her waist, emphasised the generous swell of her hips and the tempting curve of her backside. She had rolled up the sleeves of her collared work shirt, and her hair was pushed up under the same wide-brimmed hat that all the WLA women seemed to wear.

He watched as she bent, reaching forward to slide the sickle through the plant stems. He felt his throat tighten as her shirt pulled snug, and he caught the silhouette of her breasts swinging forward against the worn cotton. He wondered what it might feel like to cup their silken weight, wondered if she might make a sound if he released them from her corset. Distracted by the movement of the muscles in her shoulders and arms, he could have stood there all day, chest tight with desire, his head full of all the things he imagined people might do in a field they had all to themselves. He shook his head. *Get yourself under control, you're to work together, not be messing about.* She'd thrown off her father's expectations, but Ophelia was still a proper lady, not to be ogled by a farmhand. Almost certainly still a virgin. *Well, at least we'll have that in common.* He wondered what Ophelia might make of the fact. Perhaps nothing, she was after all, a straightforward person at heart, someone who valued honesty and simplicity in most things. Perhaps, should anything ever come of this, she would feel happy that they were equals in intimacy, that he had not shared this part of himself with anyone else.

In truth, he'd never shared anything of substance with anyone, save his short and treasured friendship with Ophelia. Even the men in his regiment had been ghostly figures to him. He had felt disinclined to reveal much of himself lest he or they not live through the night. He had held the memories of he and Ophelia's meandering talks and long walks tightly to himself, a life buoy in a sea of chaos and fear. Although there had been plenty of opportunities during his time in the army to rid himself of his virginity, he would only have been one among many soldiers finding solace with willing local women. He had felt disloyal in his heart, though he had known there was no one waiting for him at home. He felt no disrespect for the women, working or otherwise, but he hadn't been able to imagine pressing his body to a stranger when he couldn't even admit to himself which woman he really wanted. Lost in his regrets of the past and his improbable hopes for the future, he didn't hear Ophelia approach.

"I suppose I oughtn't have brought the horses today seeing as we didn't make it to ploughing," she said.

"No, but we've cleared enough that we'll be able to crack on tomorrow," said Silas. "Help you bring them back to the farm?"

She nodded and moved toward the horses, clucking and calling their names. Samson lifted his chestnut head at her voice but quickly returned to his grazing.

"Greedy beggar," she said fondly. "'Twould eat himself sick, this one."

She reached the horses' tethered ropes and handed Delilah's to Silas before taking Samson in hand. She moved them along the edge of the field and toward home. Silas's stomach growled, and he thought eagerly of the warm meal likely waiting for them when evening chores were finished. He lengthened his stride to catch up with Ophelia and, switching Delilah's lead to his opposite hand, was able to walk beside her, both of them caged on either side by the swaying barrels of the horses. Their shoulders bumped companionably every few steps, and he breathed in the warm, soft air of the spring evening. He watched their feet moving alongside each other, evenly matched despite his limp. It felt perfect.

*　*　*

OPHELIA HAD HEARD Silas's stomach growl on their walk to the farm, and though she was likely as hungry as he, she was dreading dinner. In the last week, mealtimes had become a game with herself, wondering whether Silas would be present or occupied elsewhere. Despite her determination to remain unaffected by his presence, a not-so-secret part of her always hoped he would occupy the seat opposite her, so that she might enjoy the elegant planes of his face as he ate and conversed, the pleasure of his rough-hewn hands on the cutlery. Or failing that, that he might sit next to her, their shoulders and thighs close enough to enjoy the heat and substance of his body, to surreptitiously inhale his singular scent of linen, sun-warmed grass, leather. She felt possessed by him, her body strung tight as a bow with longing and unfulfilled desires, yet the more she wanted him, the more disappointed she felt in herself. A woman of suffragist leanings, Ophelia thought, a woman intent on a life of her own should be able to withstand the proximity of a man with whom she has some history, even if that man is Silas Larke. Did the way he affected her mean she hadn't truly left her old life behind? She wasn't sure that desiring equality as a woman was compatible with the kind of lust Silas inspired in her. She wanted to ask Hannah what she thought but was worried that her friend would find her ridiculous. She valued Hannah's opinion too much to make a fool of herself, but she longed to have her trusted insight. For the time being, she kept it to herself, worrying away at the thought while she worked and ate and lived in Silas's presence.

She felt moody and short lately, even with Bess, who was unfailingly friendly. Unable to fall asleep at night, though her body was leaden with fatigue, she found herself turning every mundane interaction she and Silas shared over in her mind, embellishing it wildly. She tried to imagine Silas's lips on hers, the scrape of his hands at her waist, his chest and thighs solid against her. Awake and aroused, she rucked up her shift while her hand stole between her legs. Letting herself imagine Silas moving against her, she stroked into her wet heat, fingers slippery and eager. Inexperience clouded the exact details of his movements, but she knew how to draw pleasure from her own body, making tighter and tighter circles until her orgasm washed over her, and she curled, sated, into sleep.

Waking in the morning, the longing and questioning began all over again. She knew something had to give, but what? Ophelia couldn't deny that Silas's physical closeness drove her to near distraction, but she didn't think that was all. She longed for something else, too. Something like the closeness that she imagined might emerge from friends who became lovers, who knew each other's bodies, as well as each other's minds. The unfettered access she now had to Silas was revealing a person she was eager to spend her days with; he was already diligent with the tasks Mrs. Darling set him, he was winning Bess and Hannah over right in front of her eyes, and Ophelia could see that he genuinely enjoyed their company in return. He was respectful of her boundaries, and while he never pushed her in any way, she felt certain that he was always keeping a part of himself under tight control. Something pulled between them, filled the air with unspoken weight when they were together. Ophelia supposed the real question was: Did she have courage enough to find out what Silas wanted? And how to do that while they all laboured under the deadline for the increased yield? One couldn't simply stride up to a man in a field and casually proposition him, could they?

CHAPTER 14

A few mornings later, Hannah popped her head round the doorjamb as Ophelia reached the bottom of the stairs, then a moment later, pressed a cup and saucer into her hands. The steam from the cup warmed Ophelia's face, and she smiled at the first sip. Hannah had made it just the way she liked it—too sweet and milky for anyone else's taste. She grinned at her friend and hummed her appreciation through another sip.

"Sleep alright?" Hannah asked, sliding into her seat at the table.

"Mhmm," mumbled Ophelia, joining her. "My back and arms ache from cutting back the field, but I slept like the dead." She pulled the plate of thick sliced bread toward her and buttered a piece before topping it with a slice of cheddar and slumping into her chair. She fidgeted with her teacup while she chewed, squirming in her seat like a child at church.

"What is it, Ophelia? You're jumpy as a cat this week," said Hannah, around a mouthful of toast.

Ophelia looked up, wondering if she could truly say what was on her mind. She took a bite of her breakfast to buy herself some time.

Hannah didn't usually wear the heavy WLA tunic; instead she wore a man's linen shirt tucked into her breeches with elasticated braces and a kerchief at her neck. This morning, she was still in her shirtsleeves, the indigo kerchief around her neck, but unknotted. She had pulled her braces on, bunching the worn fabric of her shirt at the shoulder, and she sat sprawled in her chair, one socked foot propped up on the chair next to her. She looked like a gentleman pirate, Ophelia thought, or perhaps a robber queen. Her hair was wild and thick, pulled into a loose roll at her nape, and she still had the dregs of sleep about her eyes and mouth. Somehow in their months of friendship, Ophelia had never really noticed how beautiful Hannah was. Sitting across from her now, Ophelia saw a wild, wary beauty. An uninhibited honesty in the way she moved, worked, was still. She inhabited her body in a way Ophelia found confounding and attractive; she didn't seem to feel the need to make her physical presence small or tidy, and yet there was something welcoming about her. She seemed at home in herself and Ophelia couldn't quite understand how she achieved that.

Growing up, Ophelia had always understood that women were to fit themselves around every situation like particularly useful furniture. Helpful, but unobtrusive. So she didn't quite understand how Hannah could be both radical and generous. It had been her experience that women were either desirable or denigrated, and it had gone without saying at Wood Grange that women who were not quiet and malleable were denigrated. As her friendship with Hannah deepened, Ophelia was coming to see that the aspects of Hannah that made her an excellent companion in fleeing one's father were also things that made Ophelia uneasy, wondering whether she would ever feel brave enough to truly step into a new life, expect equality as her due.

"So?" Hannah asked again, her long fingers playing with the handle of her teacup while she waited for Ophelia to answer.

"I—" Ophelia hesitated, then plunged in. "I find myself thinking far too often of Silas, wondering what he's thinking . . . and, well, I'm distracted . . . not doing a good job, I think. I'm already slower than you and Bess and"—she could feel her cheeks heating with embarrassment—"and I wish I knew what to do about it. Him, I mean."

There. She had said it aloud. The secret shame she had been fretting about since Silas's arrival. She almost couldn't look at Hannah, worried her friend would be staring at her in horror.

Hannah's laugh rang out in the kitchen. "Is that all?" she cried, her wide grin echoed in her laughing eyes.

"Yes, but—"

"But nothing, Ophelia! You're a woman who's come face-to-face with a man with whom she shared . . . well, something," Hannah said plainly. "Of course, you're distracted, you're wondering where he's been, why he left, what're you to do now you're here together." She reached across the table and patted Ophelia's hand. "Thinking of someone or even wishing for something with someone doesn't mean you aren't doing a good job. Lord, half the world would shut down if people couldn't work while having feelings for someone else!" She laughed at the thought.

"I do *not* have feelings for him," Ophelia protested, hotly.

"To be sure," replied Hannah with a wry twist of her lips. "But his being here is stirring something up, yes?"

Ophelia nodded.

"You think his being here means you can't start afresh, as you planned?" She watched Ophelia carefully as she asked her next question. "Or perhaps you aren't quite as immune to him as you thought you were?"

Ophelia picked at the rough skin around her thumbnail, thinking she needed to remember hand salve tonight. She didn't know what to say to Hannah's questions, wasn't sure what she felt. She had thought it was because Silas left so abruptly, but now she wondered what she had expected him to do differently. So she *was* angry, but maybe more at herself than at Silas. For being hurt when he left and for feeling caught out when he arrived on the farm and for doubting herself when her past showed up in her present. Ophelia didn't want to feel anything for Silas, certainly not an inconvenient amount of desire.

"I, oh, I don't know . . . I had thought when I left the estate and joined you here that I would be free of those things that were part of my old life. I thought I would feel certain, not being in my father's house any longer . . ." She trailed off, not sure how to express the surprise and hurt that Silas's assignment had caused. "I thought I had left behind childish things, and him being here nettles me somehow. Everything feels so upended, *I* feel upended . . . not at all like an adult who might make their own decisions."

"Ophelia, the past isn't a coat you can just cast off and walk away from," said Hannah. "You have to carry it around with you, until you decide how you'd like to deal with it. It's what you do with the things you've learned that determine if you go forward on solid ground." She poured more tea into her and Ophelia's cups. "Believing in suffragism and equality doesn't make one more or less brave, it is only a lens through which we might see the world and make our decisions."

"But do you think it's compatible? Attraction and suffrage, I mean? I suppose part of what I thought I was leaving behind was concern with those things, someone else having power over me because of them . . . and now that he's here, I'm not sure what to think anymore." She floundered around for the words. "Can someone who believes in the cause also believe in love? Want it for themselves? I mean, if you're attracted to someone, are you letting down the cause?"

It was the mostly clearly she had ever articulated what plagued her about Silas's arrival, what had been tangled up in memories of the past, and his arrival. She felt both nauseous and relieved to have spoken it aloud. Hannah was silent for a long moment, her head nodding almost imperceptibly. Then she spoke.

"Well, I've come to see there are as many different experiences of suffrage as there are womanhood. In any consideration of the problem of equality, we must always keep that in mind. Bess, for instance, has lived a life different than you or I or Mrs. Darling, even considering the shared factor of being female. But your question was about love and equality, wasn't it, and to my mind there is only one answer."

Ophelia waited.

"Love is at the heart of equality, I think, for why else do we undertake risks to our person, our livelihoods, our reputation, but out of love for others, for ourselves? We believe that all women are equal, that all people are equal, worthy of respect and dignity. That is love, is it not? And what of Silas and the other soldiers? Going to war to protect those they love, but protecting so many more they will never know." She began tying the knot in her kerchief, her fingers moving through the motions while her eyes held Ophelia's. "I don't think love is frivolous, nor is it only relegated to romantic love, mind . . . I felt more loved among my friends in the WSPU than any time I can remember." She finished her tying and stood up. "Love can make us brave, Ophelia. Don't forget that in your fretting about your situation."

"I-I've never thought of it that way," Ophelia said slowly. "Love was really more guilt or power in my family, not something noble. I've wondered if it was a weakness, something I must push away if I care about suffrage."

"Anything can be a weakness, but I don't think the cause demands that we be alone. 'Twas only through people coming together that Mrs. Pankhurst was able to effect any change at all. What is it all about if not for giving women the freedom to choose our own paths, meaning marriage or not, careers or motherhood, voting or abstaining, as we see fit."

"But sometimes ownership might seem like love, mightn't it? Someone wanting to protect you, that isn't love, is it? It's assuming you aren't capable, that you're a child who must be cosseted away from the reality of the world." She took a breath, realizing her voice had risen, her words coming out high and breathless. "I mean—"

"I have a feeling we've left the abstract and entered the personal," Hannah said, dry as sand.

Ophelia felt herself colour. "I-I don't know how to tell, I suppose, what is kindness and what is control," she said lamely.

"Well," said Hannah, "I suppose that would depend very much on the man."

She watched Ophelia, her intelligent eyes missing little. When Ophelia remained quiet, mulling over her words, Hannah pushed back from the table.

"On with the day, then? Now we've set the world to rights."

Getting her hat from the hall, Ophelia turned over her conversation with Hannah, lost in her thoughts. Her friend's points seeming to chip away her stagnant thinking, letting her see the situation in new light. It had seemed prudent when she left Wood Grange to exchange her old beliefs for different ones, ones she had thought were more aligned with what she was hoping for. Ophelia saw now that she had only replaced one set of rules with another; if she was truly going to be the mistress of her own life, she would have to get comfortable with nuance and truly thinking for herself. It was more daunting than ploughing this new field. She would have to develop her own sense of direction, not relying on her father's rules any more than she could rely on another woman's rules for her own decisions.

CHAPTER 15

*D*inner was a hurried affair that evening; Mrs. Darling rushing to place the dishes on the table as the sinking sun, spreading its last rays of the day across the farmyard, sent long, coral fingers of light through the open kitchen door. Ophelia had just hung her coat on the peg in the hall and was following the sound of cutlery and conversation toward the kitchen when Silas appeared at her shoulder. From behind his back, he produced a bouquet and reached around her to hold it before her. Clutched in his large, tanned hand were lilacs, their scent already swirling around Ophelia, and gauzy white umbels of cow parsley surrounded by a phalanx of dark, glossy leaves. A late-April lane in the form of a bouquet. Ophelia leaned forward to push her nose into the flowers, delirious with surprise and delight.

"Is that garlic?" she cried, snorting back a laugh.

"Needs must," said Silas with a gentle huff. "I had only the length of the field to gather them, and even less time before I lost the nerve to give you them."

She took the bouquet from his hand and turned to face him, raising the flowers to her nose again.

"They're beautiful, Silas. Thank you."

"My pleasure," he rumbled, and she had the distinct impression he was not referring only to the flowers. "Wondered if you'd like to take a walk with me after dinner? It's a lovely evening."

She dipped her head, suddenly shy and mightily aware of something warm and alive between them, but nodded jerkily. "I'll find a jug for these," she said, backing into the kitchen, her eyes locked on Silas's, their mossy green darkening to charcoal as he watched her retreat.

She hurriedly placed the flowers in a jug on the Welsh cupboard, shaking her head when Hannah made to ask her about them. Hannah grinned and pulled out the chair next to her at the table, and having washed her hands, Ophelia sank gratefully into it.

"Long day?" Hannah asked.

"Indeed. Lots of progress though, perhaps even enough to have the ploughing finished tomorrow."

"Ah! Many hands make light work is right, then!" Hannah sang. "We'll have that land under cultivation, and the committee'll be eating crow, won't they?"

"The day those men eat crow'll be a cold day in hell, mark my word," said Mrs. Darling darkly. "Don't trust them not to have summat else up their sleeve."

Bess placed her hands on Mrs. Darling's shoulders, squeezing gently. "Now then, we're well on our way, so there'll be no need to worry 'bout that," she said confidently.

"Aye, perhaps you're right, Bess. Let us hope so," said Mrs. Darling, her face drawn and worn. "Now dig in, all of you, before the food is cold."

Hannah patted Ophelia's knee and said, "Pass the potatoes and tell us about those horses of yours, Ophelia. According to Silas, if we're to have this done by first of May, we'll be counting heavily on you."

"I was able to get a first pass done today; it was tougher going in the new field as the ground is harder and longer since it was cultivated." She paused, wondering if she really were equal to the task, trying not to dwell on everything that rode on her succeeding. "But I'm getting better at holding the rows straight and the horses are strong. I think we can do it. We must," she said, as much to herself as everyone else.

Hannah patted her shoulder, smiling encouragingly, and at the head of the table, Silas lifted his glass to her, saluting her with a quiet smile of confidence and pride that made her blood warm. I can do this, she thought, looking around the table and taking in the belief she saw in each of her friends' faces. *I might not have been born into farm work, but I have worked hard to learn what I need to know to help Mrs. Darling and my country, and I belong here.* The thought surprised her, having never felt like she truly belonged anywhere, but the longer she let it linger, the truer it felt. The women had accepted her, naïve and unworldly as she was when she arrived, and had supported her as she gained confidence and understanding of what it meant to work on a farm. They had shared their pasts with her, had been generous, if a little stern, in educating her on suffrage and equality. She no longer felt on the outside but held by a web of interdependence defined not by family, but instead by friendship, shared work, and mutual respect. Then she thought of walking out with Silas after the meal, and her stomach tipped nervously. Eagerness warred with apprehension. She fiddled with her napkin in her lap and pushed her food around on her plate until, at last, Mrs. Darling suggested she put the kettle on and put an end to her "infernal fiddlin'."

* * *

SILAS WATCHED Ophelia pushing her dinner about her plate and wondered if she felt the hollow ache of nerves in her stomach like he did. His own plate was nearly empty; out of long habit he made his way through the last of the hearty colcannon and chops Mrs. Darling had prepared, grateful for the food after a long day of work in the field. He felt a visceral delight in a puddle of butter in mashed potatoes or the sharp tang of fresh greens dressed with a bit of vinegar, pushing away memories of dry rations in trenches and the soldiers who were still surviving on them.

Hannah's hearty laugh cut through his thoughts and he glanced round at the women, deep in talk of preparations for the May Day celebrations in the village. Bess was gathering suggestions for games for the children, as well as soliciting Mrs. Darling's reportedly excellent Victoria sponge for the dessert table at the fete. But it was Ophelia's face that caught his attention, as usual. She laughed while telling a story about a May Day fete at Wood Grange, and Silas was struck by her ease with Bess, Hannah, and Mrs. Darling; her high cheekbones were merrily pink, her white teeth flashing as a broad smile broke over her face, sunrise lighting the morning sky. He'd never seen her so in her element; he'd always known her in relation to her father, the estate. Here she was free in a way that suited her, on the cusp of becoming fully herself. He could see the vitality in her, in the way she spoke and held herself. The kernel of the girl he had known at Wood Grange was there, always, but a woman, intelligent and independent, was blooming around it.

He saw that she had given up everything he had mistakenly thought made her who she was; she was no more the estate than he was the tenanted land. He didn't have to continue on with things as they always had been—Ophelia had chosen something entirely different for herself, perhaps he could choose something different for himself, as well. Silas worried that if Blackwood knew he were home from the front, and even worse, assigned to a farm with Ophelia, he would follow through on his threat to evict his mother and brother. But, he thought, what if he could find a way around Blackwood's blackmail? If the secret of Silas's enlistment were no longer a threat, surely that would leave Blackwood no bargaining chip? *Yes. Yes? If I had some legal advice and could ensure their safety, then I'd have nothing to hide, nothing to keep from Ophelia.* The thought was like nitrogen bubbles in his blood, fizzing and popping, making him lightheaded. He wanted so much to tell her everything, to have nothing between them, least of all her father. As soon as he had a way to protect his mother and Samuel from Merritt's blackmail, he could visit them. Tell them how sorry he was to have left, that he was safe, and that he would find a way to provide for them properly. And then he could finally come clean to Ophelia.

* * *

AFTER DINNER, Ophelia and Hannah stood at the sink in the kitchen, Hannah wiping the film of suds from a plate while Ophelia tucked the last teacup into its spot in the Welsh cupboard. Returning to the sink, Ophelia watched Hannah's profile as she worked. Hannah's eyes were on her hands in the soapy water, but her mind clearly elsewhere. She hummed to herself, and Ophelia joined in while turning to tuck the last plate away on the shelf, surprised to see Silas standing in the entrance to the kitchen, a navy-blue knitted jumper pulled on over his work shirt, hands in his pockets.

"Care to join me for that walk, Ophelia?"

Nerves skittered along her spine making her want to fidget or laugh, but she schooled herself, attempting to modulate her voice into a calm, reasonable reply. She could see the nerves in Silas, too, the way he held his shoulders stiffly, eyes searching and eager. She realized in a rush that he thought she might rebuff him, and her insides melted disobediently, pooling warm in her belly.

She nodded and turned to Hannah. "See you in the morning?"

Hannah swivelled from her spot at the basin and smiled. "Aye, you will. Enjoy your stroll."

CHAPTER 16

Ophelia followed Silas down the hallway, slid her feet into her boots, and closed the door quietly behind them. The night air was warm, and looking out across the farmyard, Ophelia could see just a hint of the sunset, coral and mauve, left in the arms of the trees, hear the bright chirrup of robins settling to their nests all around them. Standing next to Silas, she listened to the whir of night insects and the thuds of animals subsiding into rest.

"Shall we?" He began to extend his arm toward her, then the movement stuttered and he tucked his hand back into his pocket.

They moved, as if by agreement, toward the lane. At the end of the drive, Silas opened the gate into the long field and they made their way along the grassy verge. Heading up the long slope to the top of the hill, Ophelia felt a shimmer of heat where their hands swung between them, felt the warmth of his body so close to hers travelling in waves along her skin. She tried not to bump into him as they walked, but the uneven ground and Silas's injured leg caused her to stumble against him.

"Sorry."

"No, 'tis this leg. Makes me unsteady when I'm not paying attention." His voice was quiet, and Ophelia detected a note of sadness, of resignation in it.

"Does it bother you much? The injuries, I mean?"

"I've not had to test it on much beyond the therapy the doctors gave me while convalescing. Some days my leg and ankle aches, but I imagine some work will do them good, make them stronger. Make me stronger."

"I'm sorry, Silas. I can't imagine what it must have been like . . ." She was unsure how to ask him what had happened to call him to war.

A flood of emotions flew across his face: sadness, surprise, embarrassment, and then settled into a wary defensiveness. He stopped and toed the loose dirt with his boot.

"There's no need for pity, Ophelia," he said quietly. "I'm far better off than so many others. Able to return to my life mostly the way I left it—" He broke off midsentence, an odd look in his eyes.

"I didn't mean that I was sorry *for* you like that, Silas. Only sorry you had to go," Ophelia said into the silence. "I didn't mean to pry."

"No, you're alright," Silas said through clenched teeth. "You're not prying, only making conversation."

Ophelia felt irritation rise in her chest. "Not making conversation, Silas. Wanting to know about your life since the estate, wanting to know how you really are."

"I . . . ah, Christ, I don't know what's wrong with me." He ran his hands roughly through his hair, blowing out a long breath. "I feel so prickly 'bout it still." Gesturing vaguely to his leg, he shook his head and motioned for them to continue on.

Ophelia fell in beside him once again. Silas extended his arm, and flustered by their conversation, Ophelia forgot to maintain her distance and took it. Too late, she realized her mistake. Heat and awareness bloomed where her hand rested over his arm. She felt the press of his bicep against hers and couldn't keep the image of Silas in his shirtsleeves from her mind. He made to lead them along the outside edge of the field, and she let herself be carried along, matching her steps to his. She liked the feel of his warm, solid body next to hers entirely too much.

"How did—"

"I meant—"

They both spoke at once, then Silas, gruff, said, "You first."

"You left a letter saying you'd enlisted, and I know earlier you said you felt your work wasn't enough . . . but it did seem so sudden. I guess I thought perhaps there was something else to it," Ophelia finished softly.

It felt important to her, suddenly, to know the reasons. The vague worry that her father had influenced him somehow took on more substance in her mind. His leaving and her leaving had always felt intertwined somehow, not cause and effect, but something more tenuously tangled. He was quiet for so long that they had made their way up over the rise and down the other side toward the setting sun before he spoke. Finding a wide stile built into the fence, he stopped, turning to look at her. His face was lit on one side by the fading light of sunset, all angles and planes, the sweep of his eyebrows and eyelashes dark against skin turned golden.

"I suppose I caught the same patriotic fever that all the foolish young men did . . . a plough handle felt useless in my hands, and I thought a rifle would feel more . . ." He paused, his eyes travelling slowly over her face. "Something," he finished on a breath.

They stood almost chest to chest, Ophelia's hand still resting on his crooked arm. She could see the glint of the dying light in his eyes, the green-shot golden and moss. She felt rooted to the spot, pinned like a moth under his gaze.

"It was horrible," he said, voice so low she had to pitch the tiniest bit closer to hear him. "Well, basic training was boring, endless drilling and posturing by boys so young all I could think of was Samuel. And then France." He dropped his arm and turned away from her, looking out across the field. "I still hear it in my head, this roar of weapons and commands and men, like animals, screaming. Sometimes I wonder if it will ever fade."

She watched his back, his shoulders a tense, dark outline in the sunset. She didn't know what to say to him, didn't have any idea how to offer comfort in the face of such utter devastation. He didn't move or say anything more, so she closed the distance between them, not examining her motives too closely, and took his hand. It was warm and firm in hers, larger, so that she had to flatten her palm against his to be able to wrap her fingers all the way around and squeeze gently.

"I can't imagine what it was like for you there." She waited to see if he would ask her to stop or tell her she needn't try to comfort him. When he didn't, she went on. "However you feel about all or any of it, you can talk to me. Without fear of judgement." She tried to emphasize the last words, tried to tell him that he needn't be alone in this. He squeezed her hand in reply, and she felt the calluses on their palms rough against each other. Two sets of working hands, she thought.

"I don't know if I can talk about it," Silas said, his voice rough. "I don't know if I want to."

"That's okay," Ophelia replied, hazarding a sideways glance at him. "I just wanted you to know that you could talk to me . . . that you oughtn't be alone in what you saw."

She saw him nod out of the corner of her eye and then he was pulling her to him, his long arms wrapping around her back. She stiffened, then felt Silas lower his head and press his cheek to her hair, and she let herself relax into his embrace. He said nothing, just held her, chest to chest, thigh to thigh, the warmth of his body seeping into hers through their clothes. She shuddered out a breath and raised her arms to circle his waist. She wasn't sure how long they stood like that, silent, while the light faded from the sky and the air began to cool. Moments, probably, but she felt her heart, tight almost to pain, somersault in her chest. Then, with a final press of his body to hers, Silas whispered, "Thank you," and stepped away. Ophelia's arms fell to her sides, something inside her irrevocably rearranged.

"Shall we go back?" he asked, arm crooked out toward her.

Ophelia didn't trust herself, so she fell into step with him without taking his arm.

* * *

THE BIRDS WERE quiet in the edges of the field, only the odd rustle and the early evening *hoo* of an owl let one know they were there. This far from the main buildings of the farm, there were none of the daily noises, and Silas suddenly felt very alone with Ophelia. The quiet of the countryside at dusk was a balm to his soul; it had taken him months in the hospital to stop expecting the peace to be broken with shouting and explosions. At first it had been eerie, an absence like a vacuum that only reminded him of innumerable deaths, but gradually it was becoming soothing again, a quiet stillness that he remembered from his childhood. Tonight though, the stillness was infused with a thread of tension, a filament of awareness flickering between he and Ophelia that seemed to glow brighter every day. He couldn't decide whether holding his tongue would break the tension or thicken it. He heard himself say, without any real thought, "Do you remember the cake you made me for my birthday that summer?" It had seemed an innocuous memory when safely in his head, but out loud it reminded him of a thousand other things better left alone. Ophelia's step stuttered the tiniest bit and she chuckled, her laugh low and throaty.

"Calling it a cake was generous then and still is now, Silas," she said, a smile in her voice, and squinted at him doubtfully. "It was an utter ruination," she said decisively. "Batter held together with jam more than a cake."

That wasn't untrue, Silas had to admit, but the cake wasn't what he remembered about that day anyways. "Oh, aye, but it's the thought that counts, isn't that what they say?"

"It is," she agreed, her long hair slipping over her shoulders with the movement.

He let the sound of her laugh ripple around him in the open field, let it take him back to that day on the estate.

"Didn't you blindfold me?" he asked, knowing perfectly well that she had. Remembering exactly the way her hand had felt in his, firm and warm, as he, eyes covered by his own kerchief, followed the sound of her breathless laughter. She had pulled him along through her father's house, one of his arms outstretched, stumbling over the lintel and getting caught in the curtains at the French doors. Her whispered "Come on!" had washed over him, excitement and desire skating over his skin.

"I did, didn't I?" she said, slightly aghast. "How terribly forward of me."

He watched her for a moment, the very last of the day's light slanting through the loose waves of her hair, and tried to think of a response that didn't reveal too much of himself. Nothing came.

"Hmm," she said slowly, her chin puckering in remembrance.

"Regardless, it was a cake for the ages." He tried to make his voice light, casual. Tried not to reveal that he remembered everything about that day. How, that afternoon, inside the estate house, still holding his hand tightly, she had stopped suddenly, and blindfolded, he had tumbled against her. The warm solidity of her back against his chest a pleasant shock that drew him up sharply. That close, he had felt the hard ridge of her corset pushing against his ribs with every breath she took, the muslin of her shirtwaist thin and filmy. Her bottom, full and rounded even under her heavy walking skirt, had fit snuggly against his groin. He had wanted to wrap his arms around her, pull her even more tightly against him, drop his head to inhale the fresh air scent of her hair. Instead, they had both stepped away from each other at the same time, and the loss of her warm curves against him had been like a gust of winter air. Ophelia had made a startled noise in her throat and made to drop his hand, but he had laced his fingers with hers and asked, his voice strangely loud to his own ears, for the promised cake.

Her shoulder bumped his and dislodged him from his memories. A silvery heat radiated across his skin at the contact and he hardly heard what she was saying. "For the ages indeed . . . it was a disaster. I was so excited to give it to you, and by the time we got there, it had almost slid to the floor. Good thing you were likely hungry from the day's work and none too picky," she said, and her mouth curved in a secret smile, his favourite, where one corner of her plush top lip lifted against an uneven incisor.

"I remember it looking a little unstable," Silas said, trying to recover his equanimity by forcing himself to remember the most lopsided, ill-conceived cake he had ever seen. It had careened wildly on the cake stand, looking for all the world as though it wanted to throw itself off the plate onto the floor. The layers had been uneven, and thick rivulets of raspberry jam were leaking through the patchy whipped cream spread over its surface. He recalled the single taper listing on top, its small flame wavering in the breeze from the open door. "I loved that you had thought to make it, though," he said. "I used to think of food from home when I was at the front, and that cake was one of the things that always came to mind."

She blushed and ducked her head, a pleased smile on her lips. "What else?"

"Oh, um, let's see . . . tea, hot and black, my mother's bread slathered with cold butter, snap peas from the vine, oh, Christmas cake stuffed with candied fruit." He looked down at her, face tilted up, taking in his list. He felt embarrassed suddenly, perhaps he was gluttonous to admit he had thought so often of food. But it had felt like home to think of those things, mostly because when he thought of them, he thought of the people he had shared them with, the places they had sat, the conversations they had had. The scarred oak dining table in his family's kitchen, squashed onto a settee with his brother on Christmas morning, the garden behind his childhood home.

"I don't suppose it was only the food that you were missing," Ophelia said quietly, and his heart somersaulted with relief. She understood. She had heard what he had fumblingly expressed.

"No, indeed . . . I missed home so God damn much," Silas said fervently, the words scraping his throat.

Ophelia nodded and reached to open the gate. Without his noticing, they had made their way back to the farm lane. He didn't want to go in and didn't know how to prolong their parting. Before he could think of anything intelligent to say, Ophelia slipped through the gate, and his hand shot out to catch hers. They stood frozen like that for a second, then Ophelia glanced down at their hands and slid hers from his. His heart plummeted before he realized she was turning and moving toward him. She paused for an instant, took a shaky breath, and then lifting her chin slightly, she brushed her lips gently over his. It was more breath than kiss, but he felt the warm, dry press of her mouth to his, and his mind reeled. She stilled as if to draw back, so he slid his hands gently down her arms and ducked his head. He waited, hardly breathing, for her decision. When she leaned into his hands and found his mouth again, he thought he might die of relief. Her lips were more firm this time and Ophelia pressed them first to the bow of his top lip, then to the corner of his mouth, opening hers to sip at his bottom lip, gentle and persistent. He felt the warmth of her breath feather across his lips, then her voice, hushed and breathless, in the space between their mouths.

"Is this okay?"

He nodded and felt his hands flex on her biceps. He didn't dare allow more of his body to touch hers, didn't know if he could withstand the hunger that rose up in him. Her lips were wreaking havoc on his again, and something embarrassingly like a growl escaped him when he felt the firm tip of her tongue dart out against the seam of his lips. Ophelia smiled against his mouth and he pulled back.

"Christ," he breathed.

Ophelia laughed shakily. "I'm sorry to be so bold. I've wondered about kissing you for ever so long," she said.

"And?" He wanted to feel nonchalant about her answer, but his chest was tight and he could hear the blood rushing in his ears.

Ophelia touched her lips gently as if testing for difference. Silas felt his cock twitch with interest at the sight of her long fingers pressing the kiss-damp flesh. She hummed with pleasure or happiness or some combination, and the sound went straight to his groin. He felt ridiculous and giddy, electricity skating over his skin, pulling his mouth into a wild grin.

"We should—" they both began.

"Go in," he said, reluctantly.

"Do this again," Ophelia said at the same moment, her eyes crinkling with an impish smile.

"Oh, I . . . uh, yes please," said Silas, scrambling for words.

"Yes to both then," she said, nodding her head as she pushed through the gate toward the farmhouse. Silas followed behind, dazed, wondering how he'd ever fall asleep that night.

CHAPTER 17

Ophelia practically floated through the kitchen door and into the hallway. She could feel the quiet warmth of the house embrace her and was glad of it. Her heart still thudded against her ribs and she didn't let herself think overmuch about kissing Silas yet. She took a seat in the empty kitchen, turning the chair to rest her feet against the stove's still-warm front. All the adrenaline seemed to leak out of her; she felt shaky, as though she wanted to laugh. It had been so much lovelier than she'd imagined, his lips warm and firm, the scrape of his stubble a perfect rasp against her palms. She could still feel the press of his hands on the skin and muscles of her arms, the taste of him on her lips. God, did she ever want to do it again, and soon.

She sat, lost in reverie until her backside began to go to sleep. She needed to check the horses quickly before she made her way to bed. The increased workload had made them hungry, and she had taken to bringing them extra hay each night. She slipped across the barn yard and moved through the now twilit barn. Ophelia's stomach fell when she saw Samson's stall door ajar. In her own stall, Delilah paced irritably, her tail swishing as she moved.

Rushing forward, Ophelia threw the door open, but the stall was empty, Samson nowhere to be seen.

Ophelia's heart beat wildly against her ribs, fear sizzling through her like heat lightning as she hurried back out the barn door. Samson was a clever horse and prone to fiddling with latches and chains, but she had always been careful to latch his stall properly. Could it have slipped her mind this afternoon? *God, if anything's happened to him, I'll never forgive myself.* Then it occurred to her that Samson might have escaped the farm entirely, and she felt the tears begin to trickle down her cheeks. She swiped them away angrily and burst out into the courtyard. There was no sign of the big gelding there, so she continued around the house toward the top field, calling his name softly, not ready to alert the others to her mistake. To her right, Ophelia heard a sound, perhaps a rustle? She skirted Mrs. Darling's kitchen and hurried along a path leading down a hill to Mr. Bone's lower pasture where he had sowed an early crop of alfalfa. There, almost to his knees in lush green, stood Samson. Relief slammed into Ophelia, and she bent double to catch her breath, tears now running down her face in earnest.

"Easy, boy, easy," she said, straightening and approaching the big bay. "How did you find yourself all the way here, then, hey?"

She waded through the thick, green plants, their tiny leaves like clover all around her. Ophelia hoped they might bring her some luck; Samson could be funny about being caught, and she realised too late she had run out of the barn with only his lead rope. For the love of God, she thought, can anything else go wrong tonight? Moving slowly toward Samson, she crooned and murmured to him, "Good, beautiful boy. Come now." Slipping the rope around his neck, she secured it in a loop with a loose knot and prepared to lead him home. She ran a hand down his dark neck and was surprised to find her hand damp, the coat under it cool and wet with sweat. In her panic, she hadn't registered the odd cant of the gelding's hips; he stood awkwardly, his belly distended, his rump tucked in discomfort. Ophelia moved toward his head and noted his glassy stare, the short, panting breaths coming from his wide nostrils.

"Oh my God, oh my God," she chattered, her thoughts scattering like leaves before a wind. "What's the matter, Sam? What's happened?"

The horse gave no answer, but swung his head toward his belly, butting against it repeatedly. Ophelia felt like she ought to remember something from her training, anything at all, but her mind was a terrible blank. Samson kicked forward with a hind leg, pulling the rope out of her hand when he swung toward his belly again. Ophelia remembered a horse of her father's who had acted in a similar manner, and her stomach slithered with fear. The groom had been inexperienced and left a mare too long in the new spring grass where she had eaten herself sick. Ophelia had come running when she heard her father bellowing, just in time to see the writhing mare sink to her knees. She remembered the rolling eyes and the long legs flailing at her belly.

"Oh God," she moaned. "Please don't let it be colic . . . please, please, please," she begged aloud.

She focused on Samson and tried to remember anything at all about colic and how to respond to it. The gelding kicked a leg up at his belly again, his neck and withers dark with sweat. She remembered the groom tugging on the mare's halter to keep her standing, and her father's shout when she went down. Don't let the horse lay down, she thought. That's important and . . . keep it moving, her brain provided. *Right! Movement helped horses digest. I definitely remember that from training. I'll get him out of the field and up to the barn, then I can walk him along the lane. I can get Samson back in his stall before anyone knows what's happened.* She knew she had followed all her usual routines, but she couldn't shake the feeling that she was responsible, had endangered the animals who relied on her care. She thought of how relieved Mrs. Darling had been at Silas's arrival. A real farmer, she had said. Real farmers didn't make these kinds of errors. She pulled at the rope around Samson's neck, urging him forward. They needed to get back to the barn.

Samson had no intention of moving from his spot. His splayed hind legs stayed rooted and he regarded Ophelia with blank, shuttered eyes. She imagined he had a fatalistic air. Absolutely not, she told herself. *Get this horse moving, or everything will come down around your ears. All the things you've learned mean nothing if you are stupid enough to leave a gate unchecked and have a horse die on your watch.* God! How could she face Mrs. Darling and admit her utter failure? The tears began again, and she pulled desperately at Samson's rope, not managing to budge him an inch.

Be gentle, she reminded herself, Samson doesn't like a lot of commotion. She let the lead fall from her hands and turned away to have a really good sob before pushing the heels of her hands into her swollen eyes and sniffing loudly. *Okay, Ophelia. You've had your cry, now figure out how to get him moving.* Blowing out a long breath to calm herself, she faced the gelding once more and forced her shoulders to relax, trying for a soft smile as she approached.

"There's a good lad, Samson. We'll get home all in good time, won't we? Delilah will be waiting for you, and Mrs. Darling for me, no doubt. Let's try a small circle, shall we?"

Her voice was as low and calm as she could make it, and she made sure to move quietly and slowly to his side. Taking up the lead once again, she began to move the horse's head from side to side in an effort to get him to turn a little. Finally, his weight began to shift to one side, and Ophelia was able to get him to move one foot a little to the left. She crooned and petted his neck, scratching gently at his favourite spot behind his ears. Eventually, he grudgingly stepped forward, his hind end obviously still uncomfortable. His ears were plastered against his head, and every so often he swung his head around toward her, teeth bared. Dodging his mouth, Ophelia kept up the pressure, knowing he was lashing out in pain. They made their way toward the edge of the field, the progress agonisingly slow. It was now fully dark, and Ophelia could see nothing but the faintest line of the sunset fading along the horizon. The cool of the night was seeping through her tunic, and she felt still colder as the initial burst of adrenaline left her body. Her teeth began to chatter, and she felt the drag of her breeches against her legs as they gathered dew. Pulling Samson forward felt impossible, but she feared stopping, even to change direction.

"Come on, love," she quavered to the horse. "Let's try to get up to the barn, shall we?"

She chivvied and pulled until she could tell by the lack of alfalfa that they were near the opening of the path. Samson's breath was laboured and he resisted every step, but Ophelia's desperation made her strong and determined, and she pulled them forward. Just as she thought they might make it to the path, Samson decided he had gone as far as he was willing and planted his feet firmly, pulling back against her paltry weight. She didn't know how long she had been walking him, but her arms shook with fatigue, and her mind spun in frantic loops. *I need to keep going. The only thing that matters is keeping Samson safe until the colic passes. God, please let it pass.*

And then the doubts began to assail her. Ophelia heard all the criticisms her father had levelled at her: weak, useless, unintelligent, good only for bearing children. His voice taunted her and morphed into the more specific nastiness she had experienced during her service: unnatural, divisive, forward, immoral. You only had one job here, Ophelia, she told herself. *No wonder everyone was so happy for Silas to arrive, they likely knew it was only a matter of time before you bollocksed something up.* Shame curdled in her belly, winding itself, vise-like, around her insides. She wanted to sink into the ground before anyone found out. The humiliation would be unbearable; she would lose her friends, her place on the farm, whatever was unfolding with Silas. She hadn't the work experience, nor the life experience, to get work in a town or city like Hannah or Bess. Perhaps she was as useless as her father had said, after all. *No!*

She made herself listen, stern. *It's true you've made a total hash, but you're not useless. Look, you remembered to keep him moving, and you're close to the path now. Keep your head. Keep going. You can fix this. You will fix this.*

Her arm jerked suddenly backward and Ophelia cried out at the pain in her shoulder. She turned and felt, rather than saw, Samson's knees beginning to buckle and pulled hard at the rope, his mane, anywhere she could get a grip.

"No, Samson, no! Stay on your feet, you must!" she cried, moving to push at his large rump, then dashing forward to pull him ahead by the rope.

His footsteps were muddled and slow, and he kept stopping to kick at his stomach, but she pulled him along until her entire body ached and she felt the old blisters on her palms reopening. Samson struggled along behind her, slowing and then finally, in a horrible slow-motion sway, began to crumple to the ground. Ophelia shouted and cried to him to get up, to keep going, but he was too heavy for her to move once he began to kneel. His great head tipped forward as his front knees met the soft earth, and even though Ophelia could barely see in the dark, she felt the gravity shift as he sank down. Oh God! Why hadn't she gone for help sooner? She was such an idiot, trying to fix this on her own when she had no business calling herself a horsewoman, no business playing farmhand. She begged Samson to get up, pulled at his forelock and mane, but she could feel the tremor of his back legs getting ready to sink fully to the ground and knew she had lost the battle to keep him standing. She had no idea what to do. Her mind was a riot of panic and fear, and she heard herself babbling.

"I'm sorry, Samson, I'm so sorry. This never should have happened. I'm sorry, I'm sorry."

She knelt and ran her hands through his thick mane and cried, great heaving breaths shaking her shoulders.

"Ophelia! For God's sake, girl, where are you?"

Mrs. Darling's voice came loud and close in the night air. Ophelia stood so suddenly black spots danced before her eyes.

"Here," she croaked.

A bright slice of lantern light cut through the dark, illuminating the bottom of the path and the edge of the field, then swung forward until it shone across Samson and Ophelia.

"God in heav'n! What's happened?" said Mrs. Darling, hurrying over.

"I'm so sorry . . . the latch . . . he's gotten into the field . . . I tried . . . tried to keep . . ." Ophelia stumbled and stuttered, the words like stones in her mouth.

"Christ almighty," swore Mrs. Darling. "Bess! Go straight to Mr. Bone's and tell 'im we've need of him in his top field. Don't leave until 'e comes back with you."

Ophelia registered the sound of Bess hurrying away, but little else as she tried to push Samson to his feet again. She said nothing to Mrs. Darling, afraid that the woman might release her immediately. But Mrs. Darling only lowered her voice and moved closer to Ophelia, taking her hands and chaffing them, saying, "Come now, Ophelia, ye must be sore from keeping him upright for so long. We've been looking for you since I heard noises down here and found his stall empty."

"I'm sorry," Ophelia cried, drawing her hands back from Mrs. Darling.

"That's enough of that, now, girl. We've a job to do to get this one back on 'is feet an' it'll take all our focus to do that. We'll discuss the rest later."

"But, I've ruined everything," Ophelia said, brokenly. "And poor Samson, I've harmed him . . . perhaps even k-k-kil—" But she couldn't even make herself say the words. "I'm no use to you here, have only caused trouble and made us behind. I know you'll need to send me away."

"Do you know that, now?" said Mrs. Darling.

Ophelia was silent, waiting for her to say the words.

"You think you've made such a grave mistake that I'll not forgive you, is that it?"

Ophelia nodded, not sure the other woman could see her.

"You've looked about and decided you're responsible for everything going wrong, have you? That if I toss you out, things'll pick up and be done better without you? That I'm better off on me own?"

Ophelia felt the older woman nod and run her hands over Samson's neck and withers.

"Well, I see you've not learned the most important thing about farming yet, Ophelia." She paused so long Ophelia thought she wasn't going to continue, but then her voice came out of the night, soft and low. "The most important thing about farming is leaning into each other, asking for help, and knowing when you need it. The tricky part is finding folks ye can count on, but once you do, mark my words, you hold on tight and keep 'em close."

She reached out, covering Ophelia's shaking hands with her warm, rough one.

"You might not know much about farming yet, but I can see that you know something of bein' alone, and it makes you skittish around others, thinking you can't rely on them. But I'm telling you now, you can rely on me, on these people. We'll come through this if we help each other, and so will Samson, greedy gelding that he is." Mrs. Darling said this last bit with a gruff laugh, and Ophelia felt the tears begin again.

She wanted to thank Mrs. Darling and to be sick all at once, to tell her that she had no idea how to rely on anyone, no idea how to feel safe without making herself useful to others. Helpful and pleasant were the only ideals to which she had ever been told to aspire. It felt awkward and frightening to admit that even though she had learned so much, there would be times like this when she was in over her head with the farm, and the people on it. But before she could figure out how to say any of this to her host, the sound of deep voices penetrated the dark, coming closer and closer. Ophelia heard the gravelly tones of Mr. Bone and the deeper rumble of Silas, Bess's lighter voice rising and falling over them. They all seemed to emerge into the field at the same time, and Mrs. Darling lifted her lantern to their faces. Silas's chiselled cheekbones and ruffled hair gave him the appearance of Michelangelo's *David* while Mr. Bone looked like a storybook villain, the lantern light carving his fierce mouth like a trench across his angular face. Bess came to a stop, one hand at her mouth when she saw Ophelia and Mrs. Darling crouched next to Samson.

Mr. Bone swept his eye over the scene, then passing one of the two ropes he held to Silas, said, "Stand up, ladies, and lend a hand with these ropes."

They stood, and Mrs. Darling said, quietly, "I do thank you for coming, Casper."

He looked at her sharply, but only nodded his head and set to work.

CHAPTER 18

The blue-black of night was falling all around them, and the calls of crickets and frogs echoed at the edge of the field. Lanterns set at the edge of their tableau sent their shadows off across the field, horrific silhouettes stretching long, petering out into the dark. Silas and Mr. Bone had worked the ropes under Samson's legs and were organising to help him stand and, hopefully, walk home. They quietly directed Bess and Ophelia, needing their extra hands everywhere. Hannah had gone straight away to the village to see if the vet might come in time. Ophelia worked without thought, pushing away the nausea that threatened in her throat, concentrating only on the sound of Samson's breathing and the next instructions. Mrs. Darling soothed Samson, stroking his aquiline nose and murmuring softly. She moved quickly to Mr. Bone's side when he seemed ready to begin moving the horse.

"Lucky 'e's not rolled, Arabella. Just might be the thing what saves 'im," Mr. Bone said, his breath coming sharper as he prepared to move the gelding. Looking across the horse's sweaty flank to Silas, he continued, "One of you needs to take his head and work to get 'im standing . . . the rest of us are going t' 'elp 'im up."

Silas nodded and got a firm grip on the thick rope. Ophelia watched his fingers grasping, the cording of muscles in his forearms, and wished with all her might that she had come to him for help earlier. This whole night, the injured horse, eyes rolling, nostrils flaring with fear and pain, was her fault. She would never forgive herself. Of all the irresponsible—

"Ophelia?" Silas's voice cut into her thoughts.

She realised by his tone that it wasn't the first time he had said it. Her eyes snapped to his, and she nodded.

"Take the rope at Samson's head. He knows and trusts you. Speak to him softly, but firmly . . . anything to get him up and standing. Stay close, but watch that he doesn't knock into you when he rises, he might be clumsy or lash out. Understand?"

She nodded, feeling unshed tears hot behind her eyes. She had wanted to prove to Silas that she was capable, not a lightweight, but she had done the exact opposite. Even though the fear that she had done harm, perhaps irreparable, to Mrs. Darling and the farm felt suffocating, she tried to hold on to Mrs. Darling's words, to remember that she was part of this team. She could lean into their help now. She felt the tears begin to push past her lashes and blinked miserably.

"Fee," said Silas, soft, but firm. Catching her blurry eyes he made a tiny nod in her direction, his chin sharp, but his mouth soft. *Focus*, his face said, *you can do this*. She dipped her chin in response, acknowledging his reassurance.

Then it was a blur of coaxing and pulling, moaning and heaving, every muscle straining to make headway. At last, Samson was standing, supported on all sides, and the exhausted group stumbled and lumbered the short distance to the barn. Mrs. Darling disappeared into the house to return with a dusty bottle of brandy, which she passed round, each one of them taking a swig. Mr. Bone wiped his mouth with his sleeve appreciatively, and Ophelia coughed when the sweet liquor burned its way down her throat.

The fire in her belly reminded her of the sweet burn of desire. Silas accepted the bottle from Bess, who had taken a sailor-like gulp, and taking a deep breath, took a drink. Ophelia watched him hold the brandy in his mouth for a moment before he swallowed, the column of his throat lean and smooth against his rumpled collar. While the others took their sips, Mr. Bone had taken Samson's lead and was slowly walking him around the farmyard, his rough voice persuading when the gelding's footsteps faltered, praising when he walked on. Ophelia watched the man as he moved in and out of the lantern light. He was not as old as she had first estimated. His hair was mostly silver, standing out in spikes from under his cap, but his face in the lamp light wasn't goblin-like any longer. More craggy, as though he had been formed from the local stone, his cheeks a little lean, but the cheekbones high and strong, lips wide and set firmly. She wondered at the change in him, or perhaps the change in her own seeing. He had seemed so miserly when she first met him, but tonight had changed something. There was an air of confidence, of willingness to help she had never noticed before. Before she could think on it any longer, it was her turn to walk Samson.

The night passed more slowly than Ophelia thought possible, and she couldn't ever remember feeling so tired. When the first rays of the morning began to prick through the velvet cloak of the night, she thought it was her imagination. Passing her hand over her eyes, she clucked softly to Samson, pulling him forward for yet another circle past the barn door. Inside, Delilah pawed and stamped in her stall, calling to Samson every once in a while. For the entire night, he had made no reply, and Ophelia could not even be sure he heard the mare's whinny, but this time, he raised his head a little, one ear pricking forward, and nickered softly.

"Good boy, Sam, good boy," Ophelia murmured against his warm, flat cheek. She continued on her circle, passing a sleeping Bess crumpled against Mrs. Darling on the stack of hay bales next to the door. Silas emerged from the barn with a bucket of water, motioning Ophelia to let Samson drink if he was interested.

"I think you've got him through the worst of it, Fee," he said quietly. "Thank God you found him when you did, it all could've been much worse."

He set down the bucket and reached to run a hand down her free arm. Even exhausted and anguished over the night, she felt the hairs on her arm lift, the blood in her veins stir toward his hand. She wanted to drift toward him, to take shelter in his arms, against his broad chest. Samson only sniffed the water, not ready to drink, so Ophelia began moving forward, worried to let him stop too long. Silas managed to brush a hand against her shoulder as she moved. His fingers squeezed gently before dropping.

"Proud of you, your instincts were spot on."

She didn't feel proud of herself, she felt anxious and embarrassed. Despite Mrs. Darling's reassurances, she still worried that she had let everyone down.

CHAPTER 19

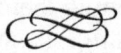

Ophelia's body was leaden with fatigue, all the anxious fire from the night having leached out with the watery light of dawn. She concentrated on the movement of her feet on the cobbles.

"Hallo? Where are you all? I've brought the vet!" Hannah's voice rang from down the lane.

Passing Samson to Mrs. Darling, Ophelia turned toward the edge of the farmyard, between the house and the machine shed, and there framed by the hedgerows along the lane, was Hannah. The early morning light was fiery in her hair, the sides of her coat sailing out behind her like wings, and at her side, a tall, lean man with very dark hair. He carried a small leather doctor's bag in one hand, and manoeuvred a walking stick with the other. Hannah gestured as they approached, her long fingers flying, and the man nodded as he listened. Arriving in front of Ophelia, Hannah said, "Here's the vet, though I see you got Samson up an' going."

"Only an assistant, ma'am," the man insisted, his voice low and rough with the hint of a Scottish burr. "Dr. Mill is delivering a particularly difficult foal, so I'm here in 'is stead. Edward Crane, at your service."

"We're very glad of your arrival, I'm sure," said Ophelia warmly. "We've been walking him all night, but I'm not sure he's any better than bef—"

"Hallelujah! By God, ye've done it, that's my boy!" Mrs. Darling hollered and laughed from behind them.

Ophelia and the vet turned to watch Mrs. Darling cackling and running her hands up and down Samson's neck. Behind him was a steaming pile of manure.

"Ah, good lad, good lad," said Mr. Bone, emerging from the house with a teacup in his hands. "I'm sure the vet will confirm, but a movement is the best sign in a colic-ing horse." He moved toward Mrs. Darling, still at Samson's head and proffered the cup of tea. "'Ere, Arabella, I'm sure you could use a cuppa after the night."

Mrs. Darling looked sharply at him for a long moment, and then her face relaxed, a small smile playing across her mouth. She took a sip and sighed deeply. Dr. Crane stepped quickly in their direction and deposited his bag, taking a stethoscope and thermometer from it. He tucked the thermometer in his coat pocket with a deft movement, and speaking softly to Samson, ran his hand down the gelding's flank. Ophelia noticed he didn't use his cane while examining the animal, but left it standing against the barn wall. Leaning forward, he pressed his ear to the horse's side and listened carefully, then placed the stethoscope to the same spot and listened again. Moving slowly around Samson, Dr. Crane examined him from every angle, missing nothing, his thick, blunt fingers moving efficiently over the horse.

"Well, he's most likely over the worst of things, and as Mr. Bone said, having manured is an excellent sign," said Dr. Crane. "Offer him as much water as he'll take and only a handful of dry hay at a time. If he continues to improve and behave as normal, he may have half a flake of hay in four hours, and another four hours after that, then a full flake by this evening. Keep him moving, and no matter how sorry he makes you feel for him, don't offer him too much hay. In fact, you want him a bit angry at his lack of food."

"Thank you so much, Dr. Crane," said Ophelia. "I'm so relieved he'll be okay. It was my error that he got into the field, and I feel sick about it."

"You all seemed to have it under control when I arrived, and had done all the right things early on. You'll need to be extremely vigilant about him for the next little while though; he mustn't overeat nor get into anything too rich. Horses' stomachs are finicky at the best of times, and now that he's had an episode, he's a little more likely to be set off again. It's an easy mistake to make."

Ophelia felt herself blanch, thinking again of how close she had come to truly endangering the farm. She blinked back tears and nodded quickly.

"Ah, I've upset you, miss. I apologise, it's a hazard of dealing with animals all the time. You've done fine. He'll mend and be on with life 'afore you know it. Horses are the most delicate, but stubbornly resilient creatures I've ever worked with, and a horse that knows it's valued seems a hundred-fold more likely to perk up than one who's not. Seen it time and time again."

She felt a soft hand squeeze hers and she looked up to find Hannah standing beside her, a small smile on her face. Ophelia squeezed Hannah's hand back and let out a sigh, trying not to let the tears come again.

"'S okay, Ophelia," Hannah said quietly. "What's done is done, and there's no sense in dwellin' on't. I feel sure Dr. Crane is right about Samson recovering. Speaking of recovering, you've not had a bite all night, so let's take care of that." She nodded her thanks to the vet's assistant and guided Ophelia toward the house.

Ophelia pulled back, protesting that she needed to settle Samson in his stall with water, slipping past her friend and into the dark cool of the barn. She just needed a moment to sit, calm herself.

Her head felt both empty and full of persistent thoughts blaming herself, berating her irresponsibility and carelessness, pointing out every failing. If she could just sit for a minute, gather herself, she could assess things properly. She found herself in Silas's bedroom and made her way to the iron bedstead, sinking onto the eiderdown. The tears were coming in earnest now, as much from spent fear as from sadness, and she let them fall. Living with her father, she had been careful not to let any emotions show while in his presence lest it invite a lecture on the weakness of the feminine person, but here on the farm she had discovered the catharsis of a good cry. She let the feelings wash over her, trying her best not to let her mind hook on the bad ones. Yes, she had made a mistake, a serious one, but with the help of the others, Samson was likely to recover, no real harm done. She noted this, and also her mind's insistence that her mistake was the more pertinent piece of information. "Ophelia Mae," she said aloud, trying to think of what she most wanted to hear, what she imagined someone might say to make her feel better. She immediately thought of Mrs. Darling's kindness in the night. "Things go wrong, they always will. *And* you still have a place here."

It didn't entirely dissolve the remonstration that sat in the pit of her stomach, but it felt less overwhelming. A thing that might be dealt with, not the end of the world. She snuffled a little, her nose wet from the tears, and rummaged around on Silas's bedside table for a handkerchief. She found one tucked next to the small portrait of his family. Pulling at it loosened a small stack of papers which fluttered to the floor. Blowing her nose, Ophelia leaned forward to gather them. A letter or two, much folded, covered with small, spidery hand, and underneath those, the distinct yellow of a telegram from the War Office. Ophelia had seen the type when the committee man came to inform Mrs. Darling of the required increase. Not thinking before doing so, she smoothed the papers on her lap, her eyes skimming the text.

The telegram was brief, a reply to what was obviously Silas's request to be reassigned. The superior officer wished him well but assured him no other assignment was possible. Ophelia held the telegram to her lap, not sure what to think. It was dated two weeks ago, when he arrived, and she recalled her own thought that perhaps she ought to leave rather stay to work together. It made sense even if it hurt a little to contemplate his desire to leave. She wondered if he still felt the same way. Placing the telegram on the bed next to her, she smoothed the small pages of the letters in her lap. She didn't know his mother's hand well enough to know if the letters were from her, but she guessed they were. The heavy footfalls in the hall startled her and she stood up just as Silas came through the doorway. The letters fell from her lap to the floor, and she darted to pick them up.

"I wasn't reading them, Silas, honestly, though I know that's what it must look like." She knew she was gabbling but couldn't seem to stop. "I came to sit down for a moment, and when I pulled your handkerchief from the table they fell out. I wasn't snooping, honestly." She paused when Silas stepped forward.

"It's okay, Ophelia." He raised a hand, motioning her to be calm. "You're okay."

"Still, it was rude of me to handle them. And I *did* actually read the telegram." She could feel the embarrassment flame up her neck and across her face.

Silas said nothing for a breath. "I should have told you right away," he said. "Don't know why I didn't honestly. When I first arrived, I thought I had better find another posting."

"Because of me?" Ophelia asked.

"Not you, but because we knew each other, and I guess I worried that we had parted on strange terms." He pushed his hands into his pockets and rocked back on his heels trying to find the words. Ophelia waited. "I could see you were uncomfortable with my arrival, and I didn't want to disrupt anything here."

She wondered why he hadn't spoken to her about it at the time. But then, they hadn't really known what to say to each other about anything at that point, had they?

"Oh."

"I was just trying to make things as smooth as possible for everyone," Silas said, a bit edgy. "Didn't really even know what this assignment was going to require of me, and then here you were..."

Ophelia set the letters aside and pushed her hands against her thighs. She knew she was exhausted and emotional from the night, but instead of admitting to it, she gave in to her irritation. "I think not speaking about things generally makes them more awkward, not less. And you don't give either of us much credit, assuming we couldn't have come to a solution." She took a breath to steady herself. She had, after all, worried about the same thing when he arrived. "I've been trying to face things head on these days, not keep it all in the shadows as I used to. I want to see the shape of the challenge before I decide I'm not up for it . . . I feel . . . well, I actually feel a little angry that you made the decision for me. For us." She hadn't known exactly what she wanted to say until the words were out, but now that they were, she felt their honesty. She was tired of having decisions made for her, tired of not being consulted on the matter of her own life. In hindsight, it was a large part of why she had left the estate, joined the WLA. It rankled that Silas had acted without speaking to her, as if she didn't even signify.

*　*　*

"Well, I hadn't any idea what your thoughts might be, not having seen you in years, had I?" Silas heard the tension in his own voice, his mouth tense at the corners. "You're not the only one who's trying to figure out what to do with their life, Ophelia," he said. "Damn it, that came out wrong."

Silas felt an ugly slither of fear in his chest. It mingled with the coil of self-preservation urging him to push back. He heard the hurt in Ophelia's voice, saw the irritation playing across her face, felt the fear of losing the connection they were building. He was coming to love seeing her every day, sharing their work, looked forward to more walks in the evenings. He didn't know how to explain his desire to leave the farm without revealing how her father had used blackmail to force him into enlisting. Didn't know if he could properly explain the fear he had felt when faced with the choice. Didn't know anymore if he had made the right choice.

"I can see you don't want to discuss it, Silas. I apologize again for looking at your things. I had no right to do so." Ophelia's voice was somehow frosty and disappointed. She stood looking at him, her hands fiddling with the hem of her tunic.

"No, 'tisn't that, Fee. I promise. I do want to discuss it, I really do." He petered off, then sucked in a breath, decision made. "When I arrived, I was so taken aback to see you, I hadn't a clue what to do. I was so glad and then worried—"

"About what?"

"There are things about my enlisting that I wasn't able to explain at the time, things about it I thought I would never have to tell you. I didn't have any idea that we would see each other again, not like this."

She frowned, a tiny wrinkle gathering between her brows, her lips settling into a firm line.

"I don't think I understand, Silas. What has any of this to do with me? Or the telegram?"

He wanted to walk away, wanted more than anything to not have to tell her this piece of his past. He forced the words out, ignoring the taste of bile that rose in his throat. He hated thinking of those days, the threat in Blackwood's voice, the derision in his eyes. The utter horror of what he faced in France.

"I, uh . . . I wasn't planning to enlist, as you know, but your father approached me that fall." She made a noise like a growl, and he paused, looking up.

"My father," she ground out. "This has to do with my father?" Her voice was quiet, laced with an anger he'd never heard before.

He nodded. "He was, as you already know, unhappy with our friendship, and when I brought my essential services exemption papers to him for his signature, he refused. Not many people know that essential labourers require the signature of their employer to be eligible for the designation, but he did and was prepared to use it to his advantage. I tried to argue with him, but he said it was either enlist, or he would end my mother's tenancy on the farm."

"But you did enlist," Ophelia said slowly.

Silas nodded again. "I'm not sure . . . I don't know what he will do if he finds out that we are stationed here together. I can't risk my family being turned off the land . . . my mother . . . it would destroy her." The bile continued to rise, the acid heat of it stealing his breath. He swallowed hard, wanting to finish what he'd started.

"God damn him!" Ophelia swore, pacing to the window. "That vile snake of a man, what an utter shite!"

Silas had never heard her swear and was simultaneously impressed and, if he cared to think on it, turned on. Hardly the time, he told himself.

"And you didn't want to say anything to me because . . ." She paused, looking at him carefully. Then realization lit her face. "Because you thought I might have known what my father did?"

Silas felt the anger fizzle in the pit of his stomach, cold ash. "Well, I had no idea. I suppose I didn't think it was out of the realm of possibility . . . we'd not spoken after I enlisted. Perhaps you were angry with me for going, or perhaps your father had already told you. I just didn't know."

Ophelia turned, hands on hips, colour high on her cheeks. Her hair, mussed from the night's trial, was a soft cloud, wild tendrils backlit by the light of the window. The terrible truth was Silas thought she was the most beautiful creature he'd ever beheld. He wanted so much to make her understand, to turn the contents of his mind inside out so that she might see the agony he felt in making the decision. Might see how he had tried to protect everyone he loved and ended up failing all of them.

Ophelia's arms dropped to her sides and she moved quickly toward him. "My God, Silas, didn't you think you might speak to me?" she said, coming to a stop in front of him. "How could you think I would have played any part in my father's games? Forcing you to enlist? Threatening your family? Are those things you think me capable of?" Her eyes were cloudy with tears, and she reached out for his hand. Grasping his larger one in her smaller one, she squeezed. "Knowing my father as I do, I can't say I'm surprised by this, but it is despicable, even for him. Of all the horrifying things." She made a tiny movement toward him so they were standing toe-to-toe, hands still clasped.

Silas brought his free hand to her cheek, cupping it carefully, slowly running a thumb back and forth along her cheekbone. Her cheeks were still flushed and her skin satin-soft under his thumb. He watched her, thoughts flitting like birds across her face. She stilled, and giving a gentle tug on his arm, she said again, "Why didn't you just speak to me, Silas? I know being billeted here was a shock, but we've managed to talk of other things that required some trust in me. We might have worked out a way to protect your mother's rights to the farm. God help me, if you don't think that's what I would have wanted."

"I didn't want to worry you, and I didn't know the details of your leaving the estate. I wasn't sure on what terms you had parted from your father."

"Both of which could have been solved with a conversation," she said, frowning a little. "Did you not think it concerned me as well? Your arrival, I mean."

"I, um, well, I didn't think of it that way, to be honest. It seemed best for me to remove myself from the situation and barring that, that I work as quickly as I could to find a new situation for my mother and family. I didn't know what you might think about any of it."

"No, indeed," she said tartly, sliding her hand from his. "And you didn't bother to find out, did you?"

"I was trying to protect you from all the mess, trying to fix it before it all came apart," Silas said, feeling caught out, defensive. He had been trying to do right, to fix the mess he had made. His hand clenched around the empty place hers had been so recently.

"I don't need to be protected from everything, Silas. I am capable of making decisions and facing hard things. I didn't want to be manoeuvred about by my father, and I certainly don't want to be managed by you. If there is something concerning me, I expect to be included in the conversation. If you have a question, you need only ask. I am not a child to be placated."

"I understand that, but try to see it from my perspective, Fee. I had no way of knowing you had changed, had these new ideas, demands of your own. Damn it, I didn't even know how you got here. I just knew what your father had threatened to do."

He wasn't sure she had heard him because she continued, "But that's almost how you think of me, isn't it? A little woman to be coddled and kept from the mess of her own affairs." She was breathing hard now, her upset writ in every angle of her body. "Can't you understand this is what makes my choice to be here so important, independence so vital? I don't want to be told who I might marry, nor do I want to be told what I am allowed to be involved in. Control under the guise of protection is still control. I don't want to be controlled any longer."

Silas felt hot and angry. Or hurt. He couldn't quite tell. "For God's sake, Fee. I've been pushed into nothing but failure year after year. I'm only trying to keep my head above water and you're yelling at me about rights and protection. I tried to do right by my family, *and* to do right by you, Fee. I don't know what I've to offer if it's not some kind of protection, some action to smooth your way in the world."

"But don't you see? You haven't smoothed anything," she said, frustrated. "Keeping the secret made everything more complicated."

He opened his mouth to speak, her words swirling around in his head, and closed it again. But no, he couldn't let it stand. "How could it be more complicated?" he snapped. "My family's in danger of being evicted, you blame me for keeping secrets, and I've no way to fix any of it." He was so tired he wanted to cry—tired of pain and worry and expectations and failure. He looked at Ophelia, no longer sure what to say, and saw the moment she understood the stakes for him, that as high as they were for her, the ground he stood on was equally unsteady. The dark slashes of her eyebrows relaxed, the hard set of her chin softened, and instead of irritation, there was resignation.

"I'm too tired to talk about this anymore," she said quietly.

"Damn it, I'm sorry. I shouldn't have spoken that way, Fee."

"No, it's alright. I just . . . just can't right now." And then she was gone, out the door before he could call her back.

CHAPTER 20

Ophelia moved quickly through the barn, slowing when she passed Samson in his temporary paddock, a comically tiny pile of hay at his giant hooves. He ducked his head and blew a breath out over the hay, sending it fluttering. Then his mobile mouth was moving over the ground capturing each stray piece. His ears were floppy and relaxed, his tail swishing absently. Ophelia's heart squeezed with relief; he was going to be okay. Everything was going to be okay. Everything except Silas. She ducked her head into the house to let Mrs. Darling know that she was taking a walk and would be back directly. "Just need a minute to get my head together," she replied when Hannah called out to ask if everything was alright.

"Absolutely not," Mrs. Darling commanded, emerging from the kitchen hands on hips. "Upstairs and into bed. You've been walking all night, what you need is a rest."

Suddenly unable to even form an argument, Ophelia registered the aching weariness of her body for the first time since sitting down on Silas's bed and gave in without protest, her leaden legs carrying her up the stairs. When Mrs. Darling came up to bring her a cup of tea, Ophelia was already asleep on her bed, still fully clothed.

Waking with the next morning with a pounding headache and a stiff neck, Ophelia hobbled through changing into a fresh shirt and breeches before making her way down to the kitchen for tea and anything still left from breakfast. The house was quiet and empty, so she had obviously slept through everyone leaving for the day. Pocketing a scone from the larder, she headed around the kitchen garden and across the long field. It wasn't quite warm yet, but there was the promise of it in the late April air. Her tunic and breeches felt tight against her stiff body, and the faint smell of stale sweat still clung to her. She wanted to wash away the lingering fug of fear.

Heading to the bottom of the field, she made her way along the edge of the creek that made its wrinkled way between Mrs. Darling's property and Mr. Bone's. A higgledy-piggledy hedgerow demarcated the property line in front of which the green bank sloped down to the creek. On Mrs. Darling's side a grove of willow trees formed a shady spot in the crook of the creek before it dashed off into the distance. It was deeper here, a calm, shaded pool that Ophelia had discovered on a ramble one day in the depths of winter. Seeing the still water steadied her, and she felt the breath she had been mentally holding since the night before leave her lungs in a rush. Crouching to remove her boots, gaiters, and socks, she made a pile on the bank and stepped into the water. It was cold enough to make her toes curl, but it felt so good. Crisp and clear and real. It emptied her mind, drawing all her attention to the sensation of the gritty gravel under her soles and the cold water lapping at her ankle bones. The longer she stood in the water, the more urgent it seemed to take a dip. Stepping back onto the shore, she shucked her tunic and shimmied out of her breeches. Fingers already unhooking the busk of her corset, she was toeing the clothes into a pile beside her boots before she thought better of the idea.

Wading in up to her thighs, Ophelia almost regretted her eagerness. In for a penny, in for a pound she thought and let her body sink into the water up to her chin. She gave a little shriek of surprise when every fibre of her being contracted at being submerged in the creek. The hairs on her arms and legs rose in a vain attempt to generate body heat, and her nipples tightened to dagger points in protest. On the other hand, the cold had chased every thought of the previous night and day from her mind, scouring away the dread and worry. Afraid she might not last much longer, she forced herself to lay back in the water, letting her feet drift off up the bottom, and felt the cloud of her chemise float out from her body. Closing her eyes against the sky, she let the silence fill her ears and her mind focus on the gentle shush of her own breathing.

The clinking of pebbles under the water alerted her to movement before his voice did. Ophelia opened her eyes and blinked a tall figure into focus. His familiar face was upside down, shaggy hanks of golden-brown hair framing his high cheekbones. His careful smile was a lopsided question mark. She thrust her feet down, pitching awkwardly to stand. Water streamed down her body, her wet hair pulling at the back of her head, and she clutched her arms across her transparent chemise.

"How long have you been here?" She gulped, adding as she came to her senses, "Pass me my tunic, please."

Silas moved to step backward and lifted the tunic from the pile. Passing it to her with averted eyes, he said, "Only a moment. You heard me as soon as I stepped into the water."

She fisted the fabric in front of her before clutching it around herself. "I rose late and thought I might clear my head," she said, gesturing to the creek behind her.

Silas nodded. "I came across this spot a while ago myself. Mind if I stay and dip my feet, too?"

She shook her head and watched as he toed off his boots and

slid his socks from his feet. He stepped gingerly over the pebbly bank and hissed when he stepped into the water. "Jaysus!" he yelped. "How'd you get your whole body in this? It's bloody freezing!"

Ophelia laughed aloud, the sound loosening her body. Silas took a tiny step forward, and Ophelia watched his feet, long and palest white, in the green water. He wriggled his toes, and the flex of tendon and bone under vulnerable flesh sent a wild flash of tenderness through her.

"I want to say again how sorry I am for reading your telegram, Silas." She wasn't sorry to have discovered the truth behind his enlisting, but she was sorry about how it had come out. He was silent for so long that she raised her head to look at him. His eyes were dark and serious, roaming over her face. She felt her shift clinging and cold. Her hair stuck to the back of her neck, beginning to curl slightly at her shoulders. Unaccountably, she felt shy. He pushed his hands into his trouser pockets, and his shoulders lifted and bunched under his linen shirt.

"It's alright, Ophelia, honestly it is. I do wish I'd told you sooner. Having it all inside has been killing me." He took a deep breath. "I've been an arse, I know. I feel like I've no bearings anymore, like all the things I thought about being a man, a person, no longer apply. I believe in suffrage, I truly do, and I'm also a bit lost about where it leaves me. I truly thought I was doing right to shield you, to not bring the problem to you, only a solution, once I had one. But you're angry about it, I can see you feel betrayed and I'm not totally certain how I should have done it differently. Honestly, I feel a bit angry about it all, too." His face was stern, a furrow of unhappiness carved between his dark brows, his mouth drawn down at the sides. "I don't mean for you to solve it or pat me on the head, of course, only I wanted to tell you, well, tell you that I want to do better. That I'm trying so hard to figure out if being here with you will harm my family and how I might change that."

Ophelia wasn't sure what to say for the space of a breath; her heart and mind couldn't seem to agree, to say nothing of her body. She was covered in gooseflesh, somehow freezing and burning at the same time. She clenched her fists in the tunic. "It wasn't until I left the estate that I realized I had been existing on the periphery of my own life, and I promised myself I'd never feel that way again. I know it's entirely presumptuous of me, as I've no idea what we are to each other, but I wish you'd spoken to me. At least let me know my father's part in it. Asked if I might have been involved, rather than wondered."

He was quiet for so long that Ophelia thought the discussion was finished. Looking up, she found him watching her. "What we are to each other?" he echoed quietly.

Her rabbiting heart leapt wildly in her chest and she looked down, focused on his pale watery feet, the hems of his pants clinging, sodden, to his ankles.

"I only meant, here in this situation, this time." She was babbling now and she hated how unsure she felt. "I think that what we felt for each other that summer is still here, but we are different people, want different things . . . and some days I don't even know what those things could look like." *Drat.* This had gone off course quickly, and Ophelia wasn't sure how to get back onto safer footing.

"I suppose they could look however you'd like them to," Silas said. "I hadn't imagined a farm run entirely by women before the war, but now I can't see any reason why it shouldn't be the norm. Perhaps all the things that feel impossible to us are only that way because we've not seen it done yet? I think if people let themselves experience an unfamiliar thing before judging it, we would all be better off."

She nodded, looking over at him, still standing in the creek. His arms hung loosely at his sides, hands gentle, face open. His green eyes were dark today, like moss in the rain, and they skated over her face, the weight of their gaze like the brush of fingertips. She stepped toward him, the water moving against her ankles. A stilt-legged plover dashed along the bank behind Silas's shoulder, and for a second its movement distracted her from his hands coming to rest gently on her biceps. The touch moved like a current over her damp skin. Her lips parted, and his pupils flared darkly. Almost without thinking, she pitched forward and his arms slid around her. The tunic slipped from her hands into the water between them. Her breasts, cool and pebbled, pressed against the broad expanse of his chest. He straightened, made to step back at the contact.

"Might I hold you? I should have asked," he said quickly, moving to release her.

"You might," she said, leaning back into the contact, letting the warm scent of him fill her senses.

The linen of his shirt was rough, and a button pressed into her cheekbone, but the thud of her heart in her chest drowned out everything else, and she let her arms rise to circle his broad back. He made a contented hum in the back of his throat, pulling her closer, and Ophelia thought she had never felt so secure in all her life. Closing her eyes, she breathed in the green, wet scent of the creek, the hint of nearby farms, and over it all, Silas. The only other man she had ever been this close to was her father, and he always smelled of stale tobacco and too-strong cologne, but Silas smelt of sun and fresh air, of tea and fire, leather and new earth. Freedom and future, she suddenly thought. She pressed her nose into him, breathing deeply. His large, warm hand came to the back of her head, stroking her hair and down her back. The familiarity of it shocked her, the rightness of it, even more so.

"Fee," he rumbled under her ear.

"Mmm?"

"Could what is between us be one of the things that we haven't imagined yet?"

"Oh, I've already imagined it," she blurted before her brain could stop her mouth. Heat flushed her body and she groaned with embarrassment into Silas's shirt.

"So have I, if we're being honest," he said, huffing a laugh.

Raising her head gently between his hands, Silas stroked his thumbs across her cheekbones, his warm, rough fingers sending a cascade of heat through her. She felt it pool, golden and warm, in her belly, and turned her face to press her lips to his palm. Everything in her moved toward him. Leaving all the complications of the situation behind, she could only think of deepening his caress, that he might even kiss her again. Her breath stuttered at the thought, seesawing in her chest, filling the space between them.

Seeming to read her thoughts, Silas lowered his head, whispering against her lips, "May I kiss you, Ophelia?" She felt the question as a rush of air against her mouth and nodded uncoordinatedly. She realized in the seconds before his lips met hers that everything had been leading up to this. All the pent-up feelings, the surprise that it hadn't been so odd to see him again, that they did work well together, that really in this moment, she was just *not* kissing him. She tilted ever so slightly toward him. He took a steadying breath, and she saw that his chest rose and fell almost as rapidly as her own. How incredible, she thought, to be stumbling in a haze of desire, together. Was it always like this when one was to be kissed? She thought not. And then she didn't think anything at all as the first brush of Silas's lips against hers obliterated everything.

Tenderly, he pressed a soft kiss to her upper lip, so lightly she found herself chasing the touch as he drew back. His hand rose to smooth down her cheek and along her neck as he leaned back in, taking her lips with his, exploring their plush warmth. Ophelia's blood sang through her, hot and heavy, coiling languorous and bright along her limbs. Her hands fisted in Silas's shirt, giving her pleasing leverage to draw him closer. He grinned against her mouth, and she was overcome by the feel of his firm, soft lips. He nipped gently at her bottom lip, then drew a fiery line with his tongue to the corner of her mouth. She felt explosive, full to the brim, sensation pouring over her skin. Opening her mouth as Silas ran his tongue along the seam of her lips, she obeyed an instinct she didn't recognize and caught his tongue with her own. He made a heavy noise in the back of his throat and deepened the kiss, his tongue tangling with hers in the wet heat of their mouths. Power and hunger surged through Ophelia. She sighed and pressed herself to him, incandescent, voracious. She could feel Silas's desire, tightly leashed, emanating from him, and she revelled, head spinning, in their mutual abandon. Releasing Silas to draw breath, Ophelia pressed her fingertips to her lips, exploring their stinging, tingling surface. She felt reborn somehow, new to the world, new to herself. Silas shook his head and laughed, resting his head lightly against her shoulder. A low "Hmm" was all he managed before pressing a gentle kiss to the curve of her neck.

"I," she began, "I . . . wanted that so much." She was as surprised as she was sure.

"God, so have I," Silas muttered, the words slurred when his lips caught against the damp skin of her neck. "And you feel even better than the first time, Fee, which is impossible."

She felt herself blush and pushed closer to him. She hesitated then lifted her hands to run them through his sandy hair. Had she always wanted to do this? To feel the cool silk of his hair in her fingers? It suddenly occurred to her that she had no idea how she had lived before being able to touch Silas. How had she never reached out to run her hand down his sharp cheekbone or press her fingertip to the perfect bow of his top lip as she did now? He sucked that fingertip into his mouth and every nerve ending in her body exploded into life. He drew the sensitive pad of her finger deeper into his mouth, and she felt her breasts grow heavy, nipples tightening against her shift. His eyes had gone dark with desire, and she felt her mouth slacken as every flicker of his tongue coursed through her like molten honey. Ophelia felt the drugging pull on her finger deep inside and, lost to sensation, only dimly registered the evidence of Silas's erection pressing firmly against her belly.

This was not at all what she expected when the ladies' manuals had warned against "loose behaviour." Nothing about Silas's hands and mouth on her felt loose; she was drawn tight as a bow, but more importantly, Ophelia realized, she was directing the action as much as he. This did not feel like being taken advantage of—it felt like being set free. No, that wasn't right. It felt like setting herself free. Releasing her finger, Silas pulled back, stroking a hand along her jaw. Their chests moved like bellows, harsh breath mingling in the space between them, eyes glassy with lust and surprise. Ophelia loosened her hold on Silas's shirt front, smoothing the fabric over his chest, and laughed unsteadily. She felt wobbly, like all her joints were filled with warm liquid.

"You're getting cold," Silas said sternly, taking in her pebbled skin. "Here." He guided her out of the water and reached for his discarded coat. Wrapping it around her, he chafed her arms and back, heat blooming through the heavy linen. It smelt of him, a now almost-familiar scent, and Ophelia sucked in a lungful, already greedy for more of him.

"I should get back. I've not done a thing yet today," she said, apologetic, and felt her cheeks heat at the breathiness of her voice.

"Right . . . o' course."

He drew her, clumsy in the oversized coat, back into his arms. She sagged against him, wrung out from everything that happened in the last two days.

"I don't want to let you go," Silas said into her hair. "I wish we could stay here forever."

She didn't reply, only nodded against his chest.

"I know it's uncomfortable, but please, let's talk when things are hard," she said. "We should have done that before, and I regret it."

"Yes. I promise."

She wanted to be able to talk about what was between them, as soon as she figured out how she felt about it. But before she lost her nerve, she said what was weighing on her. "Silas, do you think it possible to want a relationship with someone and also to want independence? Could a person have both?"

She pushed back from his embrace to look at him. Reluctantly, he let her slide from his arms.

"I don't know," he said carefully. "Could one not have independence within a couple? Surely there are marriages that are happy and equal?"

"I suppose I was more wondering whether marriage is a requisite for every relationship."

"I don't know how else people could truly have each other, Fee, out in the open," he said. "For all its failings, marriage is the only way I know of for a man to provide for a woman he loves or a family."

She felt disappointed. Unaccountably. "You had parents who were good to one another, but for those of us with no such model, marriage can seem like a risk. Even more so now that I've realized the possibilities of suffrage. Can you not see that there must be some other way for two people to love one another? A way that doesn't involve subjugation of one party to the other?" He was silent while she felt her irritation grow. She crossed her arms, hugging the soft warmth of his coat to her one more time, then shrugged out of it. She didn't bother with her corset, but pulled her breeches on over her chemise and shrugged into her still-wet tunic.

"I would never see you that way, Ophelia, in case we are even discussing the two of us in a marriage."

"I know you wouldn't, but others would. Women are expected to exist as foils to their husbands, the homely little wife tending to her husband while he is free to go and tackle the outside world. People expect women to stop being interested in their own lives, to be satisfied with cookery and birthing babies. Society expects it, and then men wonder why it shouldn't be that way after all."

"I think you'll find that I'm the last person who's interested in what other people expect. I've had enough of other peoples' expectations and ideas to last me a lifetime and more." He stood, still ankle-deep in the water holding his jacket loosely. "You don't want me to make assumptions about you, so I'd ask you for the same courtesy."

He was right. She had assumed she knew what he wanted, had let everything become about her own worries.

"Do you want those things?" he asked, his eyes clear and calm. There was no pressure in his question, only curiosity. "The cookery and the babies?"

She felt caught between honesty and the fear of what it might cost her. "I . . . things were not easy growing up. I don't see myself wanting children in the future," Ophelia said, her voice growing quiet. "I *am* sure I want a life, one of my own choosing, my own direction."

He watched her quietly and she was forced to admit that it hadn't occurred to her that a man could feel constrained by expectations, too.

"Do you want those things, Silas? Not cookery, but babies?"

"Babies," he said quietly. "I don't think so. I had always thought so, before, but I don't know that I want to bring a child into the world that I have seen. There is so much to repair for the people already here, I suppose I've been thinking that might be work I could do. Cookery though . . . perhaps I might try my hand." He said it with a smile and his voice was light, but Ophelia felt the weight behind his words, the choices he had already begun to consider. She was embarrassed she hadn't asked him sooner.

* * *

SILAS STILL FELT punch-drunk from their kiss, the taste of Ophelia heady and cool on his tongue, but he forced himself to think about what she had asked. Was marriage the only way to live as a couple? Of course, it wasn't *literally* the only way. He knew that, knew there were men and women who lived outside the bounds of what society gave its assent to, knew there were spinster friends who cared for each other their whole lives, bachelors who shared rooms with their lifelong friends. But he didn't "know" any of those couples, wasn't sure they would be welcomed at respectable tables or in the circles of people he had encountered. *Don't be an arse. Your circle of experience is laughably small, and just because you don't know them doesn't mean they don't exist.* Still, the thought was a barb in his chest; he feared an arrangement without marriage would push Ophelia to the very margins of society, and he couldn't imagine her there. She belonged in the very centre of things, not society per se, neither of them had any use for that, but amongst friends, able to move freely, without worrying about judgement. He wanted her to have everything she wanted, but he wasn't sure he could give her this.

"I don't know, Fee," he said at last, slipping unthinkingly into the nickname. "Suppose you've come across a great deal of new thinking since you left Wood Grange, but I'm not sure I'm such a modern man, as it were."

"I think at heart you are, Silas. Perhaps your habits of mind need time to catch up with your instincts." She gathered her gaiters, stockings, and boots into her arms and straightened once more. "I'm sorry I sprang all this on you. It's a lot, I know . . . I think I'm more than a little wrung out from last night. Everything feels a little intense at the moment."

Silas nodded, thinking that that wasn't all that had inspired the conversation, the brand of her lips on his still as present as the conflict between them. It cut him to the core to say it, but he wanted her to know that he held her under no obligation or assumption. She was free to kiss him and have nothing come of it, reputation or relationship be damned. He didn't want that, of course. He realized as the words hung between them that he wanted to kiss her again and again, to run his hands over her body, to have hers hot on his own skin. To explore what was so tenuously growing between them, to hold on to this new thing with both hands. Instead, he schooled his face into neutrality and tried his best to believe the words he said aloud. "If this conversation has made you feel uncomfortable about our kiss, you need think no more of it, Ophelia. It will stay between us and need change nothing. You have my word."

"I'm not uncomfortable," she said, hugging her corset to her chest, a streak of colour rising up her neck. "I liked . . . *really liked*, kissing you, I want to do it again. But . . . but I don't want you to think I aim for marriage," she said, her chin lifted, eyes steady.

"I see," Silas said. He wasn't sure if Ophelia was testing him or herself, so he paused before saying, "I feel like a fussy old woman." He chuckled. "Worrying about marriage and protection when you are ready to cast it all aside. I need to figure out what I think, but God, I want this, whatever this might be, so badly I'm sorely tempted to throw my assumptions about all of it out."

"Me, too," Ophelia said quietly, shifting her bundle of clothes to take his hand.

They crested the hill hand in hand. For the first time since he had met Ophelia, he didn't worry whether anyone would see them together. He squeezed her cool hand, and she squeezed back.

CHAPTER 21

The terror of Samson's colic lessened each day as the gelding continued to perk up, back to his old self: friendly and a bit bossy. Ophelia still felt her heart drop each time she went into the barn and didn't see both horses eyeing her from their stalls, but she knew it was irrational; the loose screw that had let the latch give under Samson's fiddling had been fixed and remained so every time she checked. The other arrhythmia had nothing to do with horses and everything to do with kissing Silas. She couldn't help but run her fingers over her lips from time to time, trying to understand the alchemy wrought by two people pressing their mouths together. It wasn't as though she hadn't thought of it during that summer and even afterward, she most definitely had, but it had always been within the context of there being no possibility of she and Silas marrying.

Under her father's roof, and in her own stilted understanding of class, Silas was considered beneath her socially, and now here on the farm, Ophelia had thought she was certain that marriage, any marriage, was off the table for her. But just as she had realized that living independently meant taking responsibility for your own beliefs and actions, any relationship was going to have to be something she and Silas would craft from the pieces of their respective lives that spoke to them. And she was finding herself wondering what a true marriage of equals might look like, never having seen one. She would need to imagine it with what she was learning about herself and the world. Leaving the estate had been the first step in not letting other people think for her, but she had discovered that the entire world was this way, that she needed to think for herself all the time. *Drat! Things were significantly easier when you let someone else do your thinking. Easier, but less satisfying.*

The days after their conversation at the creek had been so busy with preparations for more sowing, Bess's work at the dairy, and Hannah's long days with the forage corps, that Ophelia hadn't found herself with a moment to spare, to say nothing of a moment alone with Silas. He continued to work at every task Mrs. Darling set him—mostly construction and repairs on the ancient outbuildings with the occasional day of work at Mr. Bone's. One sunny morning, Ophelia ducked out of the house and into the machine shed to prepare the seed drill for the day's sowing. Over breakfast, they had discussed the possibility of having the seed in the ground in time for everyone to have a break for May Day. If they could sow both fields today, they would be in good stead with the wheat crop, and provided they didn't lose too much to birds or dry weather, Mrs. Darling and Silas both thought they just might make the quota. The pressure made her jittery, but Ophelia schooled her thoughts and focused her mind on the machine in front of her. Its long metal tray was dented and the paint chipped, the words Barrow Seed Drills barely visible any longer. Ophelia ran her fingers lightly along the tray checking the holes and the tiny funnels underneath, moving to check the hinges for the lid and then the mechanism for attaching it to the harness. Everything looked in order, so she bent her knees and grasped the front end of the machine, preparing to pull it out of the shed and into the yard, ready to be hitched to Delilah and Samson.

"Give ya a hand?" Hannah called from the doorway, Bess beside her in her dairy tunic.

"Ta," huffed Ophelia gratefully.

They hauled the seed drill out into the sunny yard, and Hannah and Bess held it while Ophelia went to harness the horses.

"No good'll come of it," Hannah was saying when Ophelia emerged with Samson and Delilah in tow.

"What's that?" she asked.

"Marriage," said Bess gloomily. "Hannah's on her high horse again about women's rights and the institution of marriage," she said, her voice a nasally impression of a lecturer.

Hannah swatted at Bess, who laughed and danced out of her way. "I only said that there was little to justify the romantic veneer that's often applied to it. For the pleasure of caring for a husband," she said in a tone that suggested it was no such thing, "we relinquish our names, our ability to work or own property, even achieve higher education. We've no recourse should he do a runner or worse, nor even the custody of our children before the law."

Bess's laughing face clouded over. "Course you're right, Han. There's not a lick of sense in any of it. I love my da, but he'd be lost without my ma, like a ruddy child himself. Least he has the sense to admit as much and treats her with respect. Does make me think hard on the prospect though, especially now that I know I can run a proper dairy on my own." She paused and her brow furrowed. "I've a real chance at good work, and I'd not really considered what it might feel like to have to let that go before I joined up with you lot. Doesn't feel like many men would be happy to countenance a wife who works, and doesn't that just beggar belief."

"A wife who works," Hannah scoffed. "Are there any that don't? Just don't want us out from under their thumb, is the real truth."

Hannah looked at Ophelia. "What of you, now that your Silas is here?"

"What of me? And he's not *my* Silas any more than... than, well I don't know what," she finished, irritated at Hannah and Bess's knowing smiles.

"If I had to bet, I'd say you're thinking a great deal about marriage, eh?" Hannah said, nudging Samson forward so Ophelia could attach the traces to the drill. "Am I right?"

Ophelia wanted to cross her arms and pout, but her hands were full of machinery and Hannah was both right and unlikely to let it go. Bess watched her over Delilah's rump, a smile tucked into the corner of her cheek.

"Suppose I have been," Ophelia said, not ready to relinquish her mood. "Not marriage exactly, but a relationship or, you know, relations." She dipped her chin to gesture vaguely at her own body.

"Oh, sex," said Hannah. "Well, course you are. Marriage is the snare that we end up in when all that's really wanted is sex."

"That's a little harsh—"

"Isn't there something—"

Bess and Ophelia both began at once.

"Romantic notions the both of you have, 'tis preposterous," crowed Hannah. "Marriage serves men because women must be faithful no matter their treatment, bearing children with no thought to their health or welfare, with no recourse for ill treatment or the sheer indignity of existing as chattel. We've no say in a government that makes decisions regarding our lives." She straightened from her position behind Samson, and Ophelia could tell she was getting ready to dig into her arsenal of suffragette talking points.

"You're right, of course, Hannah... but what if there were a way for a couple to be partners that didn't involve subjugation, or perhaps they could simply enjoy each other's company," she said this last word with emphasis indicating she didn't mean tea parties or morning visits.

"Course there is," Bess said. "Been all kinds of arrangements since the beginning of time, and not just the business kind. Surely, we can all acknowledge that not all the spinsters and bachelors sharing rooms are just good friends," she said simply. "I know you've said Silas is worried about what people will think or the legality of marriage, but it's silly to think there aren't all kinds of ways to be married or support one another." She paused, a thoughtful look on her face. "Hannah's right; if you and Silas can come to an agreement on a partnership that satisfies you both, you should make it so."

"Or not," interjected Hannah. "There's nothing wrong with sex, so long as you're cautious and protect yourself. It needn't be complicated."

Ophelia wasn't sure she agreed with this last bit; everything seemed impossibly complicated. But they had reached the field now, and Bess and Hannah headed off to their work while she straightened the horses and took a sight line down the field. It was the section of land the War Ag had insisted be made productive, and she wanted to be sure she had done everything just as instructed; the harvest could well depend on her having sown to the correct spacing and depth. Blowing out a long breath, Ophelia clicked to the horses and felt them lean into the traces, the metal of the seed drill juddering as they took their first steps.

Hours later, the sun had slunk behind the clouds, and the first drops of rain were soaking her shoulders. She looked across at the three long rows she had managed. The rooks were already congregating in the hedgerow and the oaks, shiny, covetous eyes on her freshly scattered seed. She readied herself for another turn up the long slope and felt the popping sound before she heard it. The right side of the seed drill tilted and sank to the ground with a metallic grinding. Letting the reins drop, Ophelia watched as the large metal-rimmed wheel doddered awkwardly off to one side.

"Bloody machine!" She bent to look at the spot where the wheel used to be. The axle had completely shorn through leaving nowhere for her to reattach to the wheel. She'd need to find some way to fix it, or they'd be seriously delayed. The familiar whirl of nerves began in her stomach; she hated making mistakes, hated the way shame crept in at the corners, insinuating itself until it was the only voice she heard. She made herself think about the night with Samson, made herself remember Silas's face in the lantern light, his steady encouragement, Mrs. Darling's words—forgiving, kind—which she remembered so often, Hannah and Bess's helpful hands. Even Mr. Bone, present and neighbourly. She didn't need to do this alone. Wasn't in fact, alone. Had only ask for help, and it would be given. Nodding her head, as if in agreement, she unhitched both horses, leaving the seed drill listing in the middle of the field, and headed for the farm, Samson and Delilah in tow.

Hannah appeared from the barn doorway when she clattered into the yard and agreed that mostly likely the axle had worn through, the metal exhausted to the point of collapse.

"S'no good for today, I'm afraid. We'll need the blacksmith to weld a new piece or replace the axle all together. Either way, we've lost today," she said.

"Damn," Ophelia said and tried not to worry that she hadn't cared for the machinery as well as she should have.

"Don't go blaming yourself, Ophelia. 'Tis not something that's happened in the time since you were here, likely it's been working against itself for a few seasons now."

"I just wish I'd . . . I should have noticed earlier, and then we'd not be caught out like this."

"I've not been farming much longer than you have," said Hannah, coming over to sling an arm around Ophelia's shoulders, "but I've come to see there's no end of things to go wrong, and only so many hours in every day. Don't be hard on yourself. We'll get it to town and hope to have it back in a day or two. Let's go tell Mrs. Darling."

They found the farmer in the kitchen garden tying up the floppy pea shoots. She stood, dirt-caked hands on hips, and listened as Ophelia described the wheel-less seed drill. Her mouth thinned, and Ophelia's heart kicked wildly in her chest. Having to give Mrs. Darling bad news that affected the future of the farm reminded Ophelia of the stakes of her work here, made her think of having to tell her father something that would displease him, and her stomach clenched with nerves.

"Well, that's a bloody shame, isn't it?" Mrs. Darling said after a long pause.

Ophelia opened her mouth to begin apologising and offering to make it right however she could.

"Ah, my girl, don't get to babbling about your mistake, eh? 'Twas nothing you could have done differently that would have made that wheel stay on a minute longer." She swept the straw hat from her head and swiped the back of her hand across her forehead. "Farming's a son of a bitch, if you'll pardon my language. Everything would just as soon go wrong as right, and there's not a thing you can do about it. Remember what I said to ye the other night, eh?"

Hannah squeezed Ophelia to her side, and Ophelia felt herself sag into her friend, relief flooding her body. She smiled weakly at Mrs. Darling, grateful for the woman's sanguine approach to things.

"There now, you look as ruffled as a wet hen... there's no need to tie yourself in knots. Get the wheel to Stevens at the smithy and see what he says. We'll get the wheat in the ground one way or another." She paused in the act of putting her hat back on her head. "P'raps we might all attend the May Day celebrations the day after next, as we'll be waiting on the drill anyways. What do you say, girls?"

Hannah whooped. "Let's tell Bess!"

Ophelia let herself be pulled away to find Bess over in the Bone dairy. She turned back to smile at Mrs. Darling who waved her off with a fond smile before turning back to her legumes. The rest of the day was spent in a whirlwind of activity getting every other chore completed so that the holiday might be spent entirely in leisure. Ophelia helped Mrs. Darling weed and tidy up in the kitchen garden, currycombed the horses, picked their stalls, and prepared their grain for the next morning. Hannah, finished with her forage duties, hung out the washing on the line and set the bread to rise for the evening meal; Bess headed back over to Mr. Bone's to finish the dairying tasks for the day. Silas, on his way to the village to see about having the wheel repaired, had called to Ophelia in the garden to see if she might ride in the wagon with him.

"Happened to overhear some of your conversation with your friends today," he said with a grin once they had left the farm and were some ways down the road.

Ophelia felt herself colour and she batted his arm. "Silas Larke! Were you eavesdropping on me?"

"No, ma'am." He shook his head. "Just took an opportunity to listen to what women say when they're amongst themselves."

Ophelia waited for him to continue. Delilah's rump moved steadily between the traces of the cart, the long swish of her tail scattering flies.

"Do you agree with Hannah? That marriage is only a trap for women? I wasn't sure if that's what you were trying to say at the creek, but hearing you all discussing it, I suppose I understand why you feel that way."

"I suppose I do . . . only it's not only about marriage. I know there are plenty of women who are part of the cause and are married." She sucked in a breath, trying to speak through her nerves. "I am afraid of losing myself, of being lost in someone else when I've only just started to find out who I am."

"Perhaps it needn't be complicated, Fee?"

"For you, perhaps," she said. "For me, it feels like potentially giving up everything I've accomplished since leaving the estate. Being tied to a man's decisions just as my mother was, just as Mrs. Darling was. I am free for the first time in my life, Silas. Free to earn money, to use my time as I choose, to work with my hands and body. I don't want to lose that . . . I'm . . . I'm afraid of losing it." She picked at the seam of her tunic, focusing on a loose thread, trying to find the words to explain what she wanted, what she could only now dream of for her future. "I wish that people could be what they wished to each other, not posessions or subjects, but equals."

"I'm not opposed to it on principle, but I'm not sure how it would work, Fee," Silas said. His eyebrows pulled together in a furrow, his green eyes searched hers, troubled and cloudy, before turning back to the reins.

Ophelia nodded. Despite how much she wanted Silas, she was also having trouble figuring out the particulars. Perhaps Hannah was wrong, and love and independence were mutually exclusive, as she had feared. She sighed, and Silas moved one hand from the reins to take her hand in his. They travelled the rest of the way to town in silence, save for the steady clop of Delilah's hooves and the creak of the cart.

By the end of the day, they all slumped around the dinner table, exhausted and quiet. They moved through the ritual of cleaning up after the meal and each taking a cup of tea, made to trundle off to bed. Ophelia turned to hand Silas his cup and saucer and found that they were alone in the kitchen. Was it just her imagination or were the others always making themselves scarce around she and Silas? She was too tired to give it much thought at the moment, so she just kept stirring in the milk and honey.

"You remember how I take my tea," he said softly, surprise and delight in his voice.

"Oh," said Ophelia, not sure whether she had always remembered or just since they had been together on the farm. "It's nothing, I know how Hannah takes her tea, too."

She tried to make it into a joke, but he took a sip from the cup, then placed it on the table. He lifted her hand and held it gently between his two larger ones, his fingers hypnotically stroking the underside of her wrist.

"It's not nothing to me, Fee," he said, seriously. He looked up from their hands, his mossy eyes darkening. "Everything you do is something to me."

He stroked once more over the pulse at her wrist, then letting her hands go gently, he raised a one of his own and skated it along her jaw, cupping her head with a large, warm palm. She felt herself sink into the pressure of his fingertips against her skull, her breath ghosting over her lips. He leaned closer, his eyes on hers, lips parted. Then he pulled her gently to him, letting his hand stroke down her spine to settle on her hip. She pressed into him and fitted her mouth to his just as he leaned into her. She felt his fingers flex on her hip, his mouth sliding open to admit her seeking tongue. The suction of his mouth on her tongue drew a whimper from her even as she widened her stance, notching herself closer to Silas. He sucked harder on her tongue and smoothed his hand down over her behind, hitching her tight to his thigh. The darkness of his mouth tasted of warm tea, a surprising tang when his tongue slid against hers. She felt herself getting wet, the heat pooling between her legs, and she moved against his thigh to ease the ache. Silas returned the movement and then pulling back, his teeth scraping her lips as he withdrew, he whispered, "I forget myself when I'm with you," against her mouth.

Ophelia nodded, belatedly releasing the grip she had taken on his biceps. She murmured a hasty apology and brushed the wrinkled linen of his shirt down smooth, stepping back from the warmth of his body. "So do I."

Good God, but she didn't want to stop, wanted to push herself closer into his arms, wanted his mouth on her neck, her breasts, anywhere she could think of. Instead, she smoothed her own tunic and picked up her abandoned teacup. It shook very slightly as she lifted it to her lips, the tinny music of china on china loud in the small kitchen. He leaned back against the edge of the Welsh cupboard and crossed his feet at the ankles. The movement gave the impression of relaxation, but Ophelia could tell he felt nothing like casual; his body vibrated with their kiss, just as hers did. He looked at her with a strange, dreamy quirk on his lips.

"I should say good night, Silas," she said sheepishly.

"Sleep well, Fee," he said, nodding and straightening from his place against the cupboard. "Sweet dreams."

He chuckled as he made his way down the hall. Sweet dreams indeed.

CHAPTER 22

May Day dawned bright and warm, the slightest breeze stirring the still, soft leaves on the trees and setting the heads of cow parsley dancing at the edges of the lane. Having fed the animals and laid the table for dinner when they got home, Hannah, Bess, Ophelia, and Mrs. Darling dressed for the day. Ophelia was glad she had impulsively packed her favourite dress when she had left the estate. She had chosen it, a lifetime ago, for its delicate handwork; the botanical imagery in the lace detailing had always made her feel ethereal. The ankle-length skirt fell in tiny gathers from her waist to three bands of lace and embroidery at the hem. The puffed-sleeve top had a slightly outmoded silhouette, but she loved the pin tucks and the insertion lace that decorated the bodice. She extended her arm to admire the delicate balloon of batiste fastened at her wrist with tiny mother-of-pearl buttons. The whole thing was a frothy confection entirely different from the khaki uniform she now wore daily, and a reminder of the things she used to enjoy as a lady of leisure.

Getting dressed had been unexpectedly enjoyable, donning her prettiest shift and drawers, lacing herself into her good corset, remembering the delight of ribbons and silk against her skin. Surveying her reflection in the looking glass, she faced a woman with a tanned face, unbound hair, a straighter set to her shoulders. The fit of her dress was not quite right due to the leaner and broader figure her new muscles had given her, but Ophelia was enjoying the feel of her changing body too much to fuss about snugger shoulders or a looser waist. She felt the changes in her spirit, too, an easy anticipation of a simple day with her friends, not to mention spending all day with Silas. At Wood Grange, there had been so much leisure, so much time doing nothing that the teas and dinner parties had blended together into a blur of disinterest. Looking forward to the fete today was a real change from her working days. She fished a small reticule out of her top drawer, placed a few coins and a handkerchief inside, and headed downstairs to meet the others.

Hannah stood in the kitchen, the wing-like sleeves of her blue gingham dress swinging. Her hair was looped up into a graceful knot on top of her head and her narrow ankles were sharp in polished black boots. She leaned over the sink to scrub at her hands with the small brush and muttered, "I'll never get all the stains from my fingers, but that'll have to do for today."

"Oh, Hannah, you look lovely! It's going to be so much fun."

"Indeed, 'twill be lovely to have a day with no thought of forage," she said, smiling. "It's been ages since I've been to a May Day celebration. When I was in service, the cook used to sometimes take us parlour maids to the fetes, and I always loved those days. Just to wander and look about..."

She let the rest of the sentence fade away, then moving quickly, she took up her shawl and held out her arm for Ophelia.

"Best get going then."

Ophelia slid her arm through Hannah's and they made their way down the hall to the kitchen door. Ophelia felt a thrill of nerves, excited by the prospect of the day out and the thought of spending more time with Silas. Her face heated when she let herself sink back into the memory of their kisses. She was slightly surprised to realise that the heat had nothing to do with shame or regret, but with a slow-burning desire to explore more, everything, with Silas. But she still couldn't tease apart being together and being someone's wife, someone's property, and she had sworn to herself when she left the estate that she would never allow that to happen, never allow herself to be in a relationship like that of her father and mother's.

All around her, she had seen evidence of the way women were expected to disappear into their marriages, abandon themselves for their husbands, and she knew that she could no longer ignore that prospect in her own life. So independence meant being alone; it *had* to, didn't it? No matter how much she wanted Hannah's words to be true, Ophelia feared they were not. Look at Mrs. Darling, Ophelia thought, she has run this farm on her own since her husband passed, and Hannah lives as she chooses exactly because she is unmarried. Even Bess, who longed for love, was considering how to balance her burgeoning career with marriage. It seemed obvious to Ophelia that if she and Silas continued to circle around each other, they would be forced to make some kind of decision. She didn't want to become a mistress any more than a wife, but she wasn't certain of any other options. Silas wasn't conservative and could be considered a suffragist by any measure, but she knew that he held his parents' marriage close to his heart, having grown up in the shelter of their love. He worried about the implications of an unconventional relationship, and she found herself wondering if there was any way to bridge this divide.

Hannah tugged at her arm, pulling her into the bright sunlit day. At the edge of the yard, next to the clump of volunteer hollyhocks, Bess swayed happily, the embroidered hem of her walking skirt swinging around her ankles.

"I never thought I'd miss wearing a dress and all the bits, but I have to say it's lovely to be out of that uniform. Drab does nothing for my complexion," she said, smile bright.

Ophelia laughed. "Lord, you're so right, Bess. I feel stones lighter without my tunic and jacket. What a day we'll have, dressed up with somewhere to go."

"Somewhere, indeed," said Hannah with a wry smile. "Funny that Banbury should feel like a destination all of a sudden when we see it all the time."

"Oh, but being on our own time makes it all feel more celebratory, doesn't it?" Bess said.

"It does indeed," Mrs. Darling said, closing the door behind her and poking a hat pin through a wide-brimmed hat trimmed with velour and satin flowers and a faded ribbon. She swung a small basket onto her arm. "I want you all to have a lovely day and enjoy the break. We'll be back in harness as soon as that wheel is repaired, so throw yourselves into the day with abandon."

"Thanks, Mrs. D.," said Bess. "And what a day we have, bluebird skies and everything!"

Her loose curls waving, Bess headed down the lane, Hannah in tow. Their voices floated above their heads as they disappeared down the dip in the lane.

Mrs. Darling called into the barn, "Mr. Larke! You joining us today?"

Nothing for a moment, and then Silas poked his head out, pulling on a light linen jacket, his hair, still damp, tucked behind his ears. He had shaved and wore a clean shirt in slightly better repair than his usual work shirt, and Ophelia caught her breath at the sharp, smooth line of his jaw and neck against the crisp white collar. Letting her eyes travel down, she noticed he was wearing trousers in a fine herringbone wool, grey on dark grey, and that he had polished the toes of his boots. Looking back up to his face, she saw him noticing her perusal. His mouth softened, and his eyes grew so dark Ophelia feared she would drown in their depths, but instead of speaking to her, he turned to Mrs. Darling.

"Pass inspection, ma'am?" he asked, clacking his heels together playfully and tugging at the lapels of his jacket.

Mrs. Darling laughed, a long, loud cackle ringing out on the cobblestones, and saluted him under the floppy brim of her hat.

"With flying colours, sir," she said, smiling. "Now let's be off. Mrs. Perkins's sponge won't last long with the vicar milling about, and then we'll be left with those awful bricks Mrs. Oliver tries to pass off as biscuits."

Ophelia laughed despite herself, and Silas gave her a broad wink behind Mrs. Darling's back. He was so handsome she felt a bit fluttery in her stomach. Like some agrarian Apollo come to earth to celebrate a hedonistic day among the country folk. Self-conscious in the clothing she had not worn in so long, she smoothed down the pleats at her waist, straightening the embroidered lawn and fidgeting with the ribbon belt she had added at the last minute. Silas was suddenly in front of her and took her hand in his, his thumb rubbing in a gentle circle.

"You look so lovely, Fee . . . quite takes my breath away, you in that dress. Though, in truth I like your trousers a great deal," he said, his voice rough as stone, dark as midnight.

"Thank you," she rasped. "It's strange to be back in these clothes. I've not worn a dress in so long now, it almost feels unnatural." They both laughed at her word choice, and Ophelia thought of all the times she had heard and read men complaining about the "unnatural" suffragettes and WLA workers. It still rankled to be judged so weak-minded as to be corrupted by two columns of fabric.

"Looks perfectly natural," Silas said. "I quite like the contrast, if I'm honest—knowing how you look in trousers makes it a little exciting to see you in skirts again."

"Silas." She actually giggled, impossibly charmed by his

comment. "I was a little nervous to dress today . . . I thought that, well, you might prefer me like this, or maybe that I would prefer myself like this." She felt nervous to admit this to him, to say aloud how much his opinion mattered, but she didn't let herself look away.

He nodded, thoughtful for a moment. "I prefer you however you feel most yourself, Fee. You take my breath away in trousers . . . all that strength and capability." She watched as two patches of pink rose on his cheeks. He swiped a hand through his hair, sending the strands into disarray. "Honestly, I feel the same about you in a dress. It's not your clothing I care about, it's you."

She could feel her smile, giddy and wild, before she snapped her mouth shut, heat creeping up her neck and across her cheeks. She felt herself tilting toward him, a sunflower toward the sun, pulled ever closer by the charge between them, by his earnest desire to learn more and do better along with her. She wanted to pull him into her chest, to feel his arms around her, to press her mouth to his again, and it all made her feel wildly out of control, insufficiently serious about her desire for independence. Tension roiled in her stomach and she could feel Silas's eyes upon her, the warm scrape of his calluses over the back of her hand, and all she wanted to think about was a whole day in his company, away from work and the worries of the farm. She didn't know how to answer the sweetness of his words, so instead, she looked up at him and noticed how similar in height they were now that she wore her higher heeled boots. She could almost meet his eyes straight on, and she liked the sense of equality it gave her.

"It feels surprisingly luxurious to wear a dress again, though as Bess said, I didn't really expect to miss it." She fingered a sleeve and said, "The fabric feels lighter and softer than our uniform, but it feels strange to have my legs bare again."

There was a noticeable pause as they both processed the image of her bare legs under the frothy lawn skirts of her dress. Silas made a choked sound in his throat and muttered, "Christ, Fee," under his breath, rubbing a hand across the back of his neck.

"Sorry, I didn't—I only meant—"

"No, no, 'tisn't you. I find myself drunk with you these days, hardly able to focus on anything else. You only spoke aloud what I was already contemplating in some detail."

"Oh," she said. Lord, was this to be her only reply to anything he said? She frowned, then said, "I see."

"I'm not sure you do, Ophelia," Silas countered. "Have you any idea how beautiful you are? Truly? How entirely distracting that cloud of embroidery and filmy fabric is on you? I pride myself on being a man capable of restraint, but now I know what it feels like to hold you in my arms, kiss you . . . and, well, my restraint is in what might generously be called tatters."

She opened her mouth, felt at a complete loss for words as Silas's admission swept through her, and closed it again. Her chest felt hollow and too tight at the same time, each breath dragged from deep within her. Silas extended his hand to her, a soft smile on his lips.

"Let's go before Mrs. Darling comes back for us, or I find I can no longer resist you."

Ophelia laughed and swatted at him, but slid her hand into his. They made their way down the lane toward the road in companionable silence, each lost in their own thoughts, their palms pressed warmly together. The verge was lush, alive with nodding bluebells and delicate clusters of lady's smock, and Ophelia felt sure she had never felt more alive, wandering along next to Silas. It felt completely right. Did she dare to dream of this for her future? She pushed away the worry and squeezed Silas's hand. He squeezed gently back. They reached the bottom of the lane and turning out into the road, saw Mrs. Darling's tall silhouette ahead of them in the distance.

* * *

EMERGING from the dark of the barn into the bright sunlight of the May morning, all Silas had seen ahead of him was a halo of pale light, Ophelia at its centre. Now moving down the pebbled drive to the winding lane that led into town, Silas couldn't totally remember what he had said to Ophelia once he had blinked her into focus. He glanced down at her now, her dark hair swept up into loose rolls looping away from her face, gathering in a soft cloud at the base of her neck, and found his throat tight with longing. She strode along beside him in a dress so fine it might have been made of cobwebs, the shiny toes of her good boots swinging into view with each step. She was slightly taller than usual, her shoulders only an inch or so below his own, so when she turned and caught his gaze he found himself close enough to see the marine blue of her eyes shot through with gold and grey. She blinked and the fan of her inky lashes gave a momentary reprieve. He tried to gather his thoughts to make conversation, but his mind refused to provide him with anything but images of Ophelia in this disastrous confection of a dress. The tissue-thin fabric clung to her curves emphasising the swell of her breasts, the easy glide of her waist into ample hips. He noticed that it was a little snug around her biceps and recalled with pleasure the muscles he had felt flexing under her skin when they kissed. Her shoulders were broader, and she held them more confidently, straight and powerful, even as she looked shyly at him, so many questions in her eyes.

He couldn't remember ever noticing so many things about a woman's dress before; the way the tiny mother-of-pearl buttons caged Ophelia's slender wrists, or the way the blue satin ribbon she had tied at her waist had him thinking of positively bone-melting things he could do with it, or the way the high collar ran all the way up her graceful neck highlighting the freckles that ran across her cheeks and disappeared into the prim, lacy fabric at her throat. He felt entirely unmanned by the vision of Ophelia in a dress now that he had seen the outline of her legs in breeches every day and could imagine their naked contours under the thin layers of linen and lace. He wondered if it had been wise to let Mrs. Darling start off ahead of them, leaving him stranded like a sailor before his own personal siren. He focused on the feel of her hand in his, grasping for a foothold, like a drowning man at sea. *Don't maul her like an animal, Larke. She deserves better than a mangled wreck like you, still haunted by the war, casting about for a purpose.* But he couldn't make himself listen. He wanted to be certain she was real and not his most fevered fantasy come to life. Her skin was warm under his thumb, and he felt the pulse at her wrist fluttering unsteadily against his fingertips. And when he told her that she was beautiful, a vision in both dress and trousers it was because he could not yet say the words that were in his heart, the truth. That he was already half in love with her, that he could think of nothing but her lips on his, that he felt at the end of every rope he used to keep himself bound to his better nature, that every moment away from her felt like a lifetime.

Before he could blurt out any of his ill-advised thoughts, he tugged her along the lane, following the others as they made their way to the fair. He couldn't be sure, but he thought he caught a ghost of disappointment flit across Ophelia's face, but then it was gone and she fell into step beside him. The warm glide of her palm against his was wonderful, and though their hands were both a little rough from the farm work, he loved that Ophelia's smaller, fine-boned hand fit perfectly into his larger one.

CHAPTER 23

Hours later, Silas watched Ophelia's head fall back against Bess's shoulder. She and Bess had the look of childhood about them, and he imagined Ophelia's stomach sore from laughing, fingers sticky from iced buns and jam tarts, feet aching from dancing and wandering along the high street and around the village green. Late afternoon light filtered through the trees turning everything golden and mellow. *She* made everything golden. He still wasn't entirely comfortable out in the village with everyone; he still had a feeling of restless worry that Ophelia's father might appear, like a storybook villain, to ruin the beauty of it all.

"What a day," Ophelia was saying. "I can't remember the last time I ate so much or had such fun."

"It's true. My cheeks hurt," sighed Bess.

"I never imagined one day could feel like such a holiday," said Ophelia. "I thought it not enough time to truly rest or recuperate, but I feel I've packed a week's worth of merry-making into a few hours."

Silas watched them making a dent in Mrs. Darling's fruit tarts, Ophelia's eyes half-closed with pleasure, her lips slippery with jelly. He wanted to look away, could feel his cock stirring at the little noises of enjoyment she made. Finally, rigid with desire, he thrust himself away from the tree where he leaned and gulped down the last of the lemonade from the tin cup Mrs. Darling had produced from her basket. It was sweet and slightly warm and slid down his throat with a lazy, pleasant feeling.

He paced around the bench where Ophelia and Bess lounged to look out at the green, where earlier they had cheered as the village children wove haphazardly around the Maypole, coloured ribbons fluttering gaily as the tiny heads bobbed and wove. Proud mothers had stood in clutches around the edge along with elderly women and a few older men, whom Silas assumed were grandparents. The missing men, away fighting in the trenches, were a conspicuous absence, and Silas had pushed away the nausea that threatened to join the crowd rallying to enjoy the day and celebrate a fruitful sowing season. The village green was hung with bunting, and small tables in front of the vicarage held plates of biscuits and tarts, cakes, and sandwiches. A group of Morris dancers, diminished in numbers by missing members, had made their way around the green, jolly and loud, followed by a group of screeching children who scattered at the appearance of the tall figure of the Green Man.

Ophelia and Silas had stood to one side watching the children laughing and pushing each other as the tall figure moved in their direction. Its face had been covered with leaves and bracken, its body draped in a long forest-green cloak. Despite the shrieking giggles of the children, it moved slowly along the green and out of sight with no one the wiser as to its identity. People had fallen out of their clusters and begun chatting or sampling the wares. Ophelia and Silas had joined Hannah and Bess in wandering among the children's games, the few boys playing a game of cricket just off the green, and the village ladies gathered, heads together, catching up on news. Mrs. Darling had found a seat among friends, the easy rhythm of the conversation proof of long acquaintance.

"You okay?" Ophelia had asked quietly, the edge of her little finger brushing his momentarily.

"Hmm?"

"Wondered if the children reminded you of your family, of Sam when he was little," she said.

"Oh, aye, I suppose. It's hard for me to think of them. I'm afraid I've let them down."

"I'm sorry, Silas. Have you spoken with your mother lately?" Her face was concerned. "Surely she didn't tell you that?"

They had wandered, rounding the corner of the green, a little distance from the crowd, and he rubbed a hand across the back of his neck. "Not about this, only letters with some news, how I was recovering, where I'd been sent after the hospital. I don't . . . I don't know what to say, how to ask her forgiveness for how I've involved all of them in this. I don't know how I can see them without alerting your father, and that will only make things worse."

He could feel anxiety and shame tightening his chest, the memories of the war gathering like a cloud at the back of his head. He began to wish he hadn't come to the fete. Was this going to be his life forever? Every event haunted by ghosts of men who no longer drew breath while he did, the shame of his failure malingering over it all? The dreams and starting at noises were becoming less intense, but the guilt still appeared, sudden and vicious. He took a long slow breath to center himself.

Ophelia stopped and turned sharply to him, brows drawn together in a frown. "Do you mean to say that you haven't spoken to her about any of this?" She waved vaguely, indicating, Silas thought, that her father had betrayed the Larkes and their tenancy.

He shook his head. "I did write that I was healing well, would be better eventually, and that I would visit when I could, but nothing more."

"Silas! Don't be so daft!"

He blinked.

"Men so often seem to think they know how other people feel or what is good for them. My father thought he understood me without ever having to actually speak to me and find out. And though I'm sure you think you have better reasons, you are doing the same thing." He watched her fists ball at her sides, ruffling the fine lawn of her dress. "Don't assume you know how your mother feels. Do her the courtesy of letting her tell you, for heaven's sake. Let the women in your life tell you how they feel, and stop making choices about what you think they are capable of knowing."

He felt her irritation like a slap; it brought him up short. *Had* he assumed he knew? He stood looking at her silently for a moment, her cheeks bright with anger, shoulders stiff while she waited for him to speak. He felt muddled again; protection had gotten tangled up with assumption, and he hadn't even noticed it happening. The truth was, his guilt about Blackwood's betrayal had made him feel small, and he hadn't wanted to admit that to himself or his mother. Or Ophelia, if he was honest. It felt more difficult to rebuild his ways of thinking than to rebuild his leg.

"I did assume, Fee, and I didn't even notice I was doing so."

"Don't you think she would want to know everything about your circumstance? She loves you a great deal and surely wouldn't hold the choice you made against you . . . it was impossible and forced upon you. But she'll not get to tell you that if you don't give her the chance."

She reached out to take his hand, threading her fingers in his. "I know it's hard to change the way you've always thought. I don't mean to be harsh . . . I'm still reminding myself of so many things every day."

He looked down at their hands, then instinctively glanced

around to make sure no one was watching them. He hated having to do it, but he didn't want to be naïve about Blackwood, and he was the one who had been banging on about reputations, after all. Satisfied that the fete carried on without them, Silas caught their clasped hands to his chest and pulled Ophelia in for a kiss. He slid his free hand around her waist and nipped at her lips. He drank in her noise of surprise and met her open mouth with his own, tasting lemonade and sugar on her tongue. As quickly as it had begun, he ended it, afraid to let his body run away with him.

"My word, Silas Larke, you do go to a girl's head." Ophelia laughed unsteadily. She tucked a loose strand of hair behind her ear and stepped back from him.

"And, you to mine, Miss Blackwood." He grinned.

They wound their way around the green and back to the stalls and chatter, but Silas kept thinking about his mother and whether he had been missing something all this time. Perhaps she was no more in need of protection than Ophelia, perhaps what she needed was to know she could count on her son to help her make a plan, to be honest about his situation. He wondered if he had lost too much time wading through his own guilt. But he thought of what Ophelia had said about his mother's love and knew that she was right—Lettie Larke would want to help, but not rescue. His heart lifted like a bird taking flight in his chest; maybe he could trust himself to find a new way of being. Maybe he could do more than just react to situations.

The afternoon had crawled by, and everyone had eaten their weight in treats, visited, and spent a good deal of time lolling around on benches or under trees, lazy with sunshine and sugar. Silas and Ophelia stood in the shade of the tree, and Hannah, stretched out on the picnic quilt, grinned sleepily up at Silas.

"How're you finding the day, Silas?"

"Ah, lovely, thanks, Hannah. I've eaten well and had my ear

talked off by Mr. Graves who's thinking of ordering an Albion binder this year. How about you?"

"Just the same. Have even gotten in a nap," Hannah mumbled.

"Thought I might begin the walk home, actually," Silas said, looking at Ophelia. "Care to join me?"

Ophelia nodded and Hannah waved them off, saying that she would join the others when they were ready to return to the farm.

CHAPTER 24

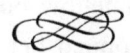

"Ready to go?" Silas smiled at Ophelia and offered her his arm. Her stomach pitched like she stood on the deck of a ship and warm waves of desire licked up her insides. Silas had slung his jacket over his arm and undone the top two buttons of his shirt, exposing a V of tanned skin. His linen shirt and trousers were slightly wilted from the heat, and his hair curled deliciously forward over his forehead. She took his arm, and he swung her gently onto the road back to the farm. They were quiet as they walked, their footsteps on the tarmac the only sound aside from the zigzagging song of a skylark high over the fields and the pipping of chiffchaffs in the hedgerow. Arm in arm, they wove along the road, stepping onto the verge when the odd cart passed by. Ophelia felt heavy and warm next to Silas, her breathing slow and easy, the steadiness of his step and the heft of his body next to hers a lovely anchor that she allowed to pull her steadily home to the farm.

Within the hour they were standing in the doorway of the barn, having made their way there by some silent agreement. Ophelia turned to look at Silas, their shoulders barely brushing together.

She had to feed the horses their evening grain and water them, but she wanted to linger just a bit longer in this moment with Silas. The delight of being alone with him made her a little giddy, her stomach fluttering like when she'd had too much wine or the moment just before one jumped into the sea. It was hard to concentrate when he looked at her so keenly, his green eyes gone smoky and intense, his mouth drawn into a line somehow both firm and sensuous. Her bravery faltered, and she dropped her eyes to their hands, Silas's long fingers firm and warm around hers. He lifted her hand, bringing it to his lips, and pressed an open-mouthed kiss to each knuckle. Ophelia sucked in a breath and her stomach lurched, a delightful drop followed by a sizzling awareness of the wet warmth of his mouth on her skin. She watched him watching her over the back of her hand, his lips moving incrementally toward her wrist, placing soft kisses as he went. Reaching the fine knobs of her wrist bones, his tongue flickered around each, sending an arc of electricity flying up her arm to explode in her chest. She felt a shiver raise the fine hairs on her arms, tightening her nipples to hard points. He held her hand in his, her arm extended, his tongue worrying at the tender skin on the inside of her wrist. She felt herself sagging, her body turned liquid heat, pools of it settling in her belly and between her legs. Silas drew her gently toward him, a slow smile etching tempting curves in the corners of his mouth. Ophelia let herself move toward him, feel the heat of him slowly surround her, his scent of grass and leather and linen flooding her senses.

"I'd not even hoped to have you alone, Fee," he breathed, their lips almost touching, his breath skimming across her cheek to ruffle her hair. He pulled back, eyes bright. "But I do, I mean we are, and . . ." Two bright spots rose along his cheekbones. "Would you come to my room?" he blurted. "I so badly want to kiss you again."

"Oh," she breathed.

Concern etched a tiny divot between his eyebrows. "Have I misread the situation? Oh Christ, Fee, I'm sorry," he groaned.

God, no. "No!" she blurted, trying to forestall his embarrassment. "Not at all, I just need to tend to the horses, their evening grain. Would you... would you wait for me?"

Relief flooded Silas's face. "Until the stars dimmed," he said. "May I give you a hand?"

She nodded. "You could fill their water buckets while I do their grain."

She watched as Silas strode out into the yard, a bucket in each hand. The sun had turned from the high, bright yellow of midday to the hazy, honeyed light of late afternoon, and it lay heavy and hot on Ophelia's face, a corollary to the heat she felt watching Silas's shoulders ripple as he worked the ancient water pump. Back in the barn, he hung the horses' buckets on their hooks and laughed at Delilah's pinned ears when Ophelia placed the low pan of grain on the floor of the mare's stall. Latching the stall door, Ophelia went to wipe her hands down her the fronts of her pants, remembering just in time that she wore a dress.

"Damn, just need to find a rag," she muttered aloud.

"I've one in my room, and a pitcher of water," came Silas's voice from down the hall.

"Oh," Ophelia said under her breath.

Drawing herself up to her full height, and careful to keep her hands away from her clean dress, she followed him to his room and stood, as calmly as she could, in the doorway. He bent over the washstand, pouring water from the pitcher into the low bowl. In his hand was a worn washcloth. Ophelia wondered if he had used it to wash that morning, imagined the fabric moving across his sharp cheekbones, catching in the morning's stubble that would have shadowed his jaw. Had he wiped down his neck, over his chest, even under his arms? Like a bomb, the idea of the same cloth skating over Silas's body and then hers obliterated all thought, replacing it with hot need. It was all she could do to remain on her feet when Silas reached for her hands. He wiped each of her palms clean, lingering on the webbed spot between each finger, the touch so sensual Ophelia felt as though his hand was between her legs. Her breathing came short and harsh until he put them both out of their misery and crushed her to him, his mouth covering hers.

His lips were firm, nipping and sucking at her own hungrily, and she responded in kind, eager and greedy. Silas ran his tongue along the seam of her lips, kissing her and whispering her name as he went. She welcomed his explorations, the warm swipe of his tongue against hers, the smooth nip of his teeth at her bottom lip. Opening for him, she licked at his tongue, exploring, the soft slide of it against her own sending a spiral of liquid heat to her core. She could taste him, minty and warm with a hint of ale from the picnic, and the familiarity of it, the intimacy of tasting each other made her tremble. Silas pulled back, searching her face.

"Is this okay, Fee?"

She nodded her head firmly and looped her arms around his neck, bringing him down to her once more. She pressed her lips to his, his mouth a still point in the storm of desire that was ricocheting around her body. Silas stroked her cheek with the backs of his fingers, then ran a finger under her chin to lift her eyes to his. The rasp of his fingers against the smooth skin made her shiver, which broke the spell long enough for her to speak.

"I . . . I haven't changed my mind about marriage, Silas," she said quickly and as firmly as she could. "I want you to know that before we continue. I want this, want *you*, but I don't want marriage to be the price of it."

He was still save for the fingers that stroked the back of her neck and tangled in the loose hair there. His eyes were steady on hers when he assented.

"Okay, then we continue," Ophelia said, her voice a little

thready. "And we must be careful, Silas, I do not wish to be with child. Will you help with that?"

"Yes, you have my word. Uh . . . we were given condoms while in France, and I did save one, but it needs time to prepare. Would you like to wait until I can do that?"

"I'd . . . I'd prefer not to wait," she said, colouring. "Could you not . . . not spill inside me?" Ophelia asked, refusing to give in to the embarrassment of the moment. "Hannah says that's a reasonably reliable way to avoid pregnancy. She's my best source of information at the moment," she added, a little shyly.

"I imagine we're both grateful for the knowledge if it means not waiting." The corner of his lips lifted in a smile, but his eyes were intent on her, hungry.

Her blood was rushing in her ears, loud and chaotic, and Ophelia wanted so much to be kissing Silas again that his words took a moment to sink in. She stilled. He had heard her. Their feelings about marriage weren't totally aligned, but he respected her autonomy, her choice. She felt a flush of heat that had nothing to do with his hands on her, his parted lips so close to hers.

He leaned forward. "We can change our minds at any point, Fee. Either of us, for any reason," he said gently, his eyes serious on hers. "We'll figure this out together. Agreed?"

"Yes," she said, dreamily, rubbing her chin against his fingers. "I know we can. I want you, Silas . . . I want to do this with you."

CHAPTER 25

I want you. The words rang like a bell, echoing through every part of him. Ophelia wanted him. Even after his clumsy attempts to offer something she didn't need, she still wanted him. She believed in the man he could become, just as he believed in the woman she was becoming. He tried not to think about his maimed leg, about how she deserved someone perfect and whole, untouched by war. But his heart and body were greedy, and so instead of putting distance between them, he ran his fingers down her spine, feeling the ridges of her corset laces through the thin fabric, each tiny button holding the dress tight around her body, smooth under his fingertips.

"We'll take care of each other, love, won't we? We'll listen to each other."

"Promise," Ophelia murmured. Her arms were still around his neck, and she had thrust her face into the crook of his neck, kissing and licking the sensitive skin above his collar, nipping at his earlobe. Her keen mouth was slipping against his skin, her fingers sliding through his hair. Being more eager than experienced himself, he recognised the fumbling fervency in Ophelia's touch, like she couldn't get close enough to him, like every barrier was a monumental frustration. Taking her hands in his, he pressed a kiss to her damp, swollen lips and spun her in his arms. Drawing her back against his body, he held her hands, palms open, to her breasts. Covering them with his own, he spoke into the halo of hair at her ear.

"Fee, my own sweet Ophelia. My God, you're so bloody beautiful. I've waited so long to touch you."

She arched back, one hand flying to his neck, her arse, free of trousers and tunics, grinding into him. He hissed a curse and gently placed her hand back on her breast.

"God, Fee, when you move like that, it's . . . I mean, your arse against me is—"

"It is, isn't it?" Ophelia said half laughing, half awed. "I can feel you, Silas. Everywhere, especially here." She wriggled farther back against him, fabric and flesh rubbing against his aching cock. "Oh . . . please hurry, I want to turn around again."

"Fee," he ground out, "you must stay still if I'm to get these cursed buttons undone."

His fingers felt enormous, the buttons lilliputian and endless, as he worked each one through its embroidered eyelet. The pieces of the high collar of the dress fell apart revealing the long column of Ophelia's neck, pale and delicate where it disappeared into the thicket of her wild, dark hair. His throat felt tight, and his hands froze in their work. He wanted to brush his lips against the skin he was revealing and for a moment, he forgot that he could. Forcing himself to move slowly, he placed a kiss at the base of her neck, just where the dress opened and her shoulder blades began to fan out. Silas heard her breath leave her lungs in a gust and felt goose bumps rise along her skin, under his lips. He kissed upward until he reached her hairline, and sweeping her hair aside, stroked the tender spot behind her ear with his tongue.

"Oh," she said and tilted her head to give him better access to her neck.

He let himself taste her in long, lingering strokes. Sweet like honey, a bright explosion of fruit, and the tang of summer heat. It all went straight to his head. His senses were filled with Ophelia, her scent wrapping itself around him, the glorious curves of her body soft against his, the small sound of surprise and delight she made when he kissed the lobe of her ear. He felt flustered by the magnitude of his desire, like his mouth couldn't cover enough of her skin, his hands not able to fist enough of her clothing, his body never close enough to hers. She squirmed against him, pulling one of his hands back to her breast. He ran his fingertips over her, feeling the heavy softness of her breast against the stiff ridge of her corset. He imagined her nipples, just out of reach, and groaned, his body a riot of lust and anticipation.

"Buttons," he growled.

"Buttons?" echoed Ophelia, dimly.

"Buttons."

Silas straightened her in front of him and set to work on the back of her dress again, each slice of creamy skin further incentive, urging him on. Finally, the dress and petticoat could be slid down her hips, and Ophelia stepped out of them, turning to stand in front of him in her corset, chemise, and drawers. Her legs were bare to the embroidered hem of her chemise, and it was all he could do not to drop to his knees before her. She was so beautiful it took his breath away. What a hackneyed phrase, he thought, for the punch-drunk feelings Ophelia inspired in him.

All the time he had spent remembering their summer, their friendship, thinking he had embellished her in his mind. Surely, he had told himself, surely no woman is so perfect. But she was. Her hair curled down around her shoulders now, loosed of its pins, and one shoulder of her shift slid down, revealing the smooth ridge of her collarbone and the expanse of her breasts, lifted by the cut of her corset. The fabric was something with a slight sheen, and the light from the small window lit upon it, gilding Ophelia, making her shimmer. Silas was familiar with corsets in principle, but unsure of their workings in reality, and so for a few moments he only stared, taking in the contour of her waist and hips, the tempting line across the tops of her thighs where the corset ended. He knelt before her and pressed his forehead to her stomach, hands holding her hips. He could feel her intake of breath, then her hands in his hair, fingernails carefully scraping his scalp. She whispered his name above him, and when he pressed a kiss to her belly through the satin and boning, he felt her quiver, rubbing her legs together.

"I want to touch you, Fee, may I?" he asked against her stomach.

"Yes," she said, solemnly, her fingers tightening in his hair.

His forehead still against her middle, he ran a hand up either leg, clasping her slender ankles then moving slowly up to the taut muscles of her calves. She wove a little the higher he went, so he slowed and traced gentle circles at the back of each knee. The skin there was unbearably soft, a secret revealed only to him. Ophelia moaned and pressed her knees against him.

"Your skin, Fee . . . I've never felt anything so smooth." Still circling with his fingers, his cock harder than he could ever remember, he muttered, "God, I want you so badly."

She groaned and pressed herself against him, lost in the moment. He pushed up her chemise to reveal her drawers, the split between the legs drawing his eye to the shadows there. Looking up and catching her eyes, he traced a fingertip up the inside of one leg, up under the thin fabric, moving slowly as much to give her time to adjust to his touch as to give himself time to think of how and where to touch her. He was aware of his inexperience, nervous that he might not do this right, but then her hands clutched at his hair and she whimpered when his fingers brushed the damp curls of her mound, and he let himself follow her lead.

"Bloody hell, Ophelia, you're perfect," he said, his fingers stroking the wet seam of her sex.

His body was screaming at him to move more quickly, but he wanted to take his time to learn her, couldn't bear to rush through these first glimpses. Ophelia sighed and writhed against his hand, her fingers tight in his hair, her legs quivering when he stroked a finger between her lips. She was incredibly wet and warm, her flesh smooth and muscular against his finger. He had never felt anything like it. His cock strained against his trousers, and he couldn't seem to fill his lungs properly. *Fuck* was the only word that came to mind, and so he chanted it quietly as he pressed kisses to the insides of Ophelia's thighs, his damp lips catching on the thin linen of her drawers. He pressed his nose to her centre and inhaled the sweet, earthy scent of her arousal, and gathered his courage to ask for what he had been wanting to do for so long.

"I want to put my mouth on you, Fee . . . would you let me taste you?"

"I . . . is that what people do . . . lovers, I mean, I don't know all the—" She fumbled through the words, her voice thick and slow.

"I'm not sure if other lovers do it, but kneeling here in front of you it's all I can think of," he said, nuzzling against her thigh, his body afire with the feel of her.

"Yes," she said, running her hands along his shoulders. "I want that, too. Show me . . . please?"

He leaned back, his hands on his thighs and took a deep breath. Ophelia laughed and reached for him.

"Shall I hold my chemise for you?" she asked, lifting the sheer lawn and holding it saucily above her waist.

He smiled and nodded, reaching around to undo the knot holding her drawers up. The beribboned and embroidered fabric fell to the floor, and Silas reeled at the revelation of Ophelia completely bared to him.

CHAPTER 26

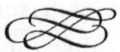

The look in Silas's eyes was so intense, Ophelia could hardly keep her legs from buckling under her. She held the edge of her chemise up like a cabaret dancer, her legs and pussy bare to Silas who sat back on his heels before her, palms spread wide on his thick thighs. His long fingers flexed against the muscles of his legs, and she could see the bulk of his erection hard against the fabric of his trousers. His eyes darted up to hers, seeking permission, and taking a deep breath, she nodded quickly before her nerve deserted her. Silas's golden head ducked toward her and she felt his breath fanning out over the inside of her thighs. He slid one hand up the side of her leg, his long fingers spread over her backside, his thumb anchored in the crease of her hip, under the edge of her corset. The other, he began moving up the inside of her thigh with strokes so light she barely felt them. A heavy aching pulse beat between her legs, and she rubbed them together trying to ease it.

"Please," she said, "please."

Instead of replying, Silas pressed his mouth to her, then used one finger to part her lips, his tongue hot against her wet centre. The pleasure of it sang through her and she bowed up against his mouth. He gripped her behind harder to keep a hold of her and swept his tongue through her lips, surprising a cry from her when he flicked over her clitoris. He paused for a moment and she felt him smile against her, humming a sound of understanding, then he pressed the flat of his tongue experimentally to the tiny nub and she writhed against him, breathing out his name. The sensation was so intense she felt her mind go black, every molecule in her body focused on that tiny patch of friction between the knot of nerves and his tongue. She held him to her, legs shaking with the effort of staying standing, nipples drawn exquisitely tight. She could feel the release building, threading like quicksilver along her limbs, gathering like a storm cloud. It burst upon her, fast and furious, his tongue still licking and pressing as she came.

"Oh," he said after a moment, drawing back, lips slick with her. "It isn't as I thought at all . . . it's so much better." He smiled lazily at her; pupils blown wide with desire. "Incredible . . . you're. . ." He trailed off, stroking the curve of her hip.

She didn't know what to say, felt turned inside out by all of it. Silas on his knees before her felt entirely too good to be true, his eager attention to her pleasure felt like a gift she hadn't known to want. But her body didn't care, wasn't interested in parsing the finer points. It only wanted Silas with a single-minded ferocity.

"*You're* incredible, Silas, God, how did you know how to do that?"

"Not sure, really," he said a bit sheepishly. "I just tried to listen to the sounds you made . . . and your body let me know when it was good, I think."

"It was *so* good," she said and knelt down to him, kissing him deeply, their tongues finding each other quickly now, tangling in the dark heat of their mouths.

He pulled her into his lap and then breaking apart for air, said, "I don't think I'm ready for you kneeling on the floor, Fee. Up on the bed with you."

She nodded and let him lift her, his arms tight under her shoulders and the backs of her legs. He stood and swung her gently down onto his narrow bed. She scurried back to make room for him, but he only stood watching. His hair was wild around his head, tousled by her fingers, his clothes rumpled, the front of his trousers snug against the thick ridge of his erection. Ophelia swallowed and sat up, coming to kneel at the edge of the bed. She ran her hands down the front of his shirt, over the placket of his trousers, feeling the hot pulse of him beneath the linen. Silas hissed a breath, his stomach muscles tightening under the fabric when she slowed, pressing a hand to his length and squeezing gently. She wanted to follow his lead, to pay attention and learn how he liked to be touched, to know the feel of him, how to take him apart as completely as he had her.

Before she could ask him, Silas motioned to her corset, saying, "Shall we take this off, love?"

The endearment settled like sunlight in her chest, warm and golden. She nodded and came off the bed, reaching behind her to unknot the laces.

"Give you a hand, if you like," said Silas.

"I've taught myself to do it, but I'd like your help anyway," Ophelia said, turning to smile at him.

Silas slid the laces loose until Ophelia could unhook the metal busk at the front. Laying the corset on the trunk at the foot of the bed, he reached for the hem of her chemise, slowly sliding it over her head, and adding it to the corset and her discarded stockings. Entirely naked now, Ophelia thought she might feel nervous or ashamed, but the dark heat in Silas's eyes pushed everything else away, and she let herself sink into the warmth of his desire. He stroked down her back and over her bottom, his hands coming back up to linger on the fleshy curve of her hip. He kissed her neck, sucking gently at her skin. Trying not to be distracted, Ophelia began to unbutton his shirt, pushing it off his shoulders to reveal a muscled chest, firm from work. She ran her fingers down his sternum, moving across his pectorals to the coppery discs of his nipples. He shivered when she brushed a fingertip across one. She smiled, enjoying his tight groan and the way the flesh puckered at her touch. Without thinking, she leaned forward, flicking her tongue across it. The reaction was electric; his hands came to her jaw and he pulled her to him, his mouth taking hers in great greedy kisses. Still kissing her, he manoeuvred Ophelia back onto the bed. Unbuttoning his trousers, he pushed them to the floor and followed her down, his light cotton smalls doing nothing to hide his erection or the long, tight muscles of his thighs. Ophelia caught a glimpse of the scar rising up the side of his left calf to his knee, but before she could see it clearly, Silas was looming over her and she was lost in the beauty of him.

He brushed her hair back off her forehead, pressing kisses to each of her eyelids, then cheeks, and finally, her lips. She opened for him and he swept his tongue into her mouth, his lips almost bruising in their ferocity. Ophelia felt excitement thrum through her, and she arched up against Silas, kissing him for all she was worth. Desperate for more of him, she reached down to push at the band of his smalls and he wriggled out of them, laying bare between her spread legs.

"Silas, I want, may I touch you?"

Her words felt clumsy compared with the incandescent light that was filling her body, the easy conversation she and Silas seemed to have through touch, but she persevered, determined to make this moment fully hers, theirs.

"Will you show me how?"

He had been gently rubbing himself against her thigh as he brushed seeking fingers over her clitoris and through her lips to her entrance, but he stilled now, raising his head to look at her. His grey-green eyes were nearly black, pupils flared wide and dark.

"Uh, oh, aye, I'll show you. Pretty simple, really," he said, a cheeky grin lifting one side of his smile.

She laughed and thought that he was still, always, the most beautiful man she had ever seen. A giddy thrill shivered through her at the thought of what she was about to do, what she had decided to do with Silas. She was taking ownership, taking it by the horns, as Hannah always said, and making this about pleasure and not ownership. There would be no "before" and "after," no change in her value. Silas thought it was simple to pleasure him, to know what he liked, and Ophelia desperately wanted that knowledge, to feel his body respond to her the way she could feel hers responding to him. She leaned up to catch his mouth with hers, sucking his bottom lip into her mouth so she might nip at its fullness. He let her pull at him, then kissed her back, licking into her mouth when she opened for him. He took her hand in his, wrapped it gently around his cock, then began squeezing and stroking so that she could feel the slip of his foreskin against her palm and the warm rasp of his callouses against the back of her hand. He murmured into the skin of her neck, curses and praise that made the tips of her ears burn and a flood of heat pool between her legs. She never wanted him to stop. His length was heavy and satiny in her fist, and she found she couldn't look away from her hand on him. "Okay?" she heard herself whisper. He didn't answer with words, and she didn't ask again, just took in the bellows of his chest above her, his shuddering movement when his foreskin pulled back to reveal the ruddy, swollen head of his cock.

"Jesus God, Fee," he breathed raggedly into the space between their bodies, hips thrusting into her hand in earnest.

Looking up at him, Ophelia felt awed by their intimacy, suddenly aware that her bare-bones knowledge of sex had prepared her for something entirely different, something mechanical, transactional, not the raw beauty and terrifying purity of Silas in the throes of desire. She wasn't afraid, but overwhelmed by her reaction to him, to the frenzy she felt holding him in her hand, feeling his mouth on her thighs. She wanted him like this, naked, spirit and body bared to her always, but she feared that Silas would continue to want to protect her with marriage, shield her from judgement by giving her his name. She hoped she wasn't being unrealistic in thinking they could find a way to share a bed, but perhaps not a name. Pushing the sharp sadness away, she concentrated on Silas moving more frantically against her, one elbow supporting his weight, his hand fisted in the tousled mass of her hair.

"You're so beautiful like this, Si," she whispered.

His face, sheened with perspiration, softened instantly, and he brushed his lips gently across hers.

"Please . . . don't stop," he mumbled, pressing soft kisses to the centre of her mouth, one at each corner, finally nipping at her bottom lip until she opened for him.

Sinking against her searching lips, he shuddered, and she felt the warm spatter of his orgasm coat her hand and belly. They moaned into each other's mouths, their kisses becoming softer, slower, more tender. Pulling back from her, Silas reached for his discarded shirt, and sitting up to kneel between her legs, began cleaning her, carefully wiping her stomach, then her hand. He pressed a long kiss to the centre of her palm and Ophelia felt an invisible string tighten between her legs, desire sliding warmly around her belly. She smiled up at him, heady with lust and triumph. His eyes were unfocused and hazy, his mouth a languorous curl up into his cheek. She pulled his hand and he tipped toward her, coming to rest his head on her breast, his legs long against hers, one hand resting warm and solid across her middle. He sighed contentedly and turned his head to kiss her breast. Ophelia felt every single point of contact between their bodies, the roughness of his chest hair against her ribs, the press of his kneecaps against her calves, the cool satin of his hair against her shoulder and chest. It was perfect. He was perfect. She hadn't expected that they would fit together so well, his body against hers like the last piece of a puzzle. And he hadn't even been inside her yet, which, if she was honest, she was now looking forward to with a great deal of anticipation. She ran a hand through Silas's hair and snuggled farther into him.

CHAPTER 27

Minutes passed, perhaps even half an hour, while Silas listened to the sounds of the room, the steady thrum of Ophelia's heartbeat under his ear, the whoosh of her breathing, and watched his hand rising and falling on the round curve of her belly, his tanned fingers skating over the tiny silvery lines that spread toward her hips. He was trying so hard to lay still, to enjoy the velvet of her skin against his, the soft, dusky cloud of hair between her legs, the way she absently rubbed one of her feet against his shin while she sifted her fingers through his hair, but the eiderdown was bunched up under him, pressing his cock against the long muscles of her thigh and he could feel himself getting hard again. He shouldn't be surprised, he thought, though he had barely recovered from the sight of Ophelia's hand around him, the surprised moan she made when he came, her nipples tight as she arched against him. Thinking about it brought his cock fully to life and he felt Ophelia's surprised huff against his hair. He was about to tell her they needn't rush into anything right away, when she wriggled, pressing one leg to rub gently against him. *Oh*, his brain registered dimly.

She turned toward him, eyes crinkled with a smile, and sliding her free arm around his back, pulled herself up snug against him. Pressing a kiss to his forehead, she said, "Perhaps it's too soon to want you again, only it felt so good."

"Not too soon," he murmured, running a finger from her belly down into the crease of her hip. "I might not come again right away, but perhaps you can?"

"I can sometimes," she said, colouring slightly and stretching her hand over his, "when I do it myself."

Sweet Jesus. The thought of Ophelia, coming, her own fingers stroking herself, was something he thought he might die to see. Still contemplating the image, he let out a strangled noise when she slid down and hooked a leg over his, her warm, wet centre suddenly pressed against his lengthening cock. Ophelia made to hitch backward in surprise, but he grabbed her, pleased to find that his hand was big enough to cover one cheek of her arse, and snugged her hard against him. He couldn't quite believe that he was holding her, naked, against himself, that she was as eager for his touch as he was for hers, that they had by ridiculous, dumb luck found themselves with a chance to be together. *I never want this to end.* His hold on her tightened instinctively.

He wondered if she felt the axis of her world tipping as much as he did, if she could also feel herself changing, shedding her old skin like a summer-sleek garter snake. A horrible thought struck him—perhaps she thought of this only as a dalliance, a casual one-time event. She was after all, leaning more and more into her suffrage beliefs. Perhaps there was no room in her life for a man like Silas? Or she thought him conventional in an unappealing way? He was scarred now, not whole as he had been when she knew him at the estate, weakened and broken in ways that had nothing to do with his leg. He could see that her friendships with Hannah and Bess buoyed and enriched her, and he wondered how he might fit into the world of a woman building her own future. The thought constricted his chest like a vise, small and sad. Ophelia twisted in his arms, pushing against his hand on her backside, and he forced the worries down, boxing them away for later examination, focusing on the warm woman rising up on one elbow in front of him.

She looked at him solemnly, her blue eyes missing nothing. Her cheek rested on her hand, head cocked, and she searched his face for a long minute then said, "Is everything alright, Silas? Are you . . . do you regre—"

He didn't let her even finish the word, but slanted his mouth over hers and licked between her lips, tasting the sweet tang of her mouth. "Not for a second," he said against her warm lips. "Only wondering . . ." He paused, trying to find the words for his feelings. "I suppose I wondered if not wanting to be married might change how you feel about me now, after this?" It was coming out wrong, he could tell by the crease of tension that had appeared at the corners of Ophelia's eyes. Stupidly, he kept talking. "Perhaps this is only a dalliance for you? Only it would be good for me to know, as I feel I've lost my footing here, Fee. You've upended my whole world and well . . . I find I'm not sure I want it righted."

"Nothing with you is a dalliance," she said firmly, and he saw the truth in her face, the tension at her eyes gone. "I've no idea what things look like after this, I only know I don't want marriage, for convenience or otherwise, to be the only thing we consider. I've only just tasted a life outside of what I imagined, and I'm not ready for that to be over. Sex"—her cheeks pinked slightly—"between us is a commitment from me. There are so many things I am fearful of —becoming with child, being discovered, shamed—but I am more afraid of not making my own choice about it." She was pensive, a finger tracing back and forth along the ridge of his shoulder. "Can we still be together like this, knowing that?" she asked softly.

"I'll have you any way you see fit, Fee. We'll make it up as we go along."

She surged up against him then, mouth and lips everywhere, hands clumsy, skimming up his back, clutching at his arse, electric and wild and beautiful, and more tempting than he could ever have imagined. He kissed her harder and held her against himself, fingers firm on her hips, the rub of her belly against the head of his cock an unmitigated disaster for his self-control. The need to be inside her was overwhelming, pressing like weight behind his eyes, gathering at the base of his spine, tightening his balls against his body.

Pulling back from their kiss, he put a hand to Ophelia's cheek so she met his eyes. He stroked a thumb across her pouting bottom lip, its round, pink flesh reminded him of her nipples, and he knew he had to get out the words before he lost his focus.

"I want to be inside you . . . may I, Fee?" he asked, lust making his vowels slip together.

Her eyes widened a fraction of an inch, and he saw her cheeks hollow with a sharp intake of breath. The pink point of her tongue darted out, tracing the bow of her top lip, and Silas thought her might never have seen anything so beautiful. But then she nodded and her blue eyes turned dark with longing, and he knew he had been wrong.

"Are you sure?"

"I want you inside me, Silas. I want it to be you . . ."

He was perfectly still for long moments. The words hardly felt real, sounded like every dream he had ever had. But he could feel her heart beating frantically against his chest, and there were her hands at his shoulders and her lips at his ear.

"I want it so much, Silas."

And so they were sailing together, out past the bounds of any map he knew, in uncharted waters. Here be monsters, he thought. Love, jealousy, heartbreak. He would risk it all for this moment with Ophelia, this shared adventure. *Sod off*, he told his worries, and flexing his hand in her hair, he kissed her with everything in his heart.

* * *

S ILAS'S MOUTH was a rogue waving lashing her lips, pushing past the boundaries of her teeth and tongue with a hypnotic rhythm. Licking warm and wet into her, then sucking gently to pull her tongue into him. She liked being inside his mouth, feeling the muscular slide of his tongue against hers, the momentary clack of their teeth when they took the kiss deep and clumsy. She liked the darkness of his mouth against hers, the unmissable echo of his tongue in her mouth thrumming between her legs like a heartbeat. He had asked her so tenderly if she wanted him inside her, waiting for her reaction, holding himself still against her. She should have known that Silas would be as self-possessed in this moment as he was in all the others, when she felt like a Valkyrie driving an out-of-control chariot of desire, everything in her screaming for satisfaction. She wanted to demand he immediately make good on his question, but then she was distracted by the slip of his cock against her wet sex and, she groaned and tried to spread her legs so she might make tighter contact with the rigid length of him. An unmistakable ache was building in her, the heavy liquid slide of anticipation already slippery between her legs.

"P-please," she whispered against his neck, running her tongue around the hollow at the base of his throat. He was salty and musky, entirely male, she somehow knew.

Silas slid her onto her back, and kneeling between her spread legs, blew out a whistle of admiration. She didn't feel embarrassed to be so exposed to him, but her body felt open in an unexpectedly vulnerable way. As if sensing her thoughts, Silas smiled softly at her. She felt herself blush as his fingers brushed the springy hair between her legs, then, so gently, traced the seam of her vulva. She watched his face, awed and slack with desire, and felt her insides liquify. She hadn't known that another could care about the sheen of her skin, the flush of desire along the line of her lips, didn't know someone might sweep a finger so gently along the slippery edge of her sex, watching her reaction or the movement of his finger so intently. She hadn't known. And yet, there was no other person she could ever imagine doing this with, being seen and touched like this. She felt herself combust under his gentle ministrations, the heat of his curiosity and intent.

Silas muttered, "God damn, Fee," then pressed a little more firmly to spread her labia and circle her entrance. Desire, sharp as the bite of a whip, hit her, and she bowed up off the bed.

"That's a good spot, then," said Silas half to himself, half to her, and a smile hitched up one corner of his mouth.

"Uh-huh," Ophelia said, dazedly, settling back into the eiderdown, wriggling her bottom closer to Silas's knees.

She felt his thick finger circle her entrance more firmly, then sink into her. The feeling was indescribable. Lovely, invasive, thrilling. Everything whittled away until nothing remained but his finger moving inside her, his thumb sliding upward against her clitoris. Her breath rattled through her, passing her lips in sharp huffs. Silas was growling low in his chest, possessive and possessed. He took himself in his free hand, and Ophelia watched spellbound as his hand shuttled up and down his thick length, wondering at the mechanics of what they were about to do. She could see the shimmer of moisture at the tip of his cock, feel the unsteady rock of his hips against his hand, and suddenly could wait no longer. She reached for him, fingers skating over his hips, bending her legs to make room for him.

"Fee," he ground out. "I'm so ready, will you have me?"

She nodded, her blood hazy with desire and nerves. He slid his hands under her bottom and scooted her toward him. Still kneeling, he notched himself at her entrance, muttering, "So fucking beautiful, Fee. I wish you could see yourself, see us." And then he was pushing forward, gently rocking the head of his cock, smooth and hard, into her. She froze suddenly, waves of sensation lapping at every atom of her being.

"Please don't hurt me," she whispered. He stilled instantly, one hand at her hip, one still gripping himself.

"Have I been too rough? I'm sorry. God . . . I feel appallingly clumsy," Silas said, his eyes cataloguing her face, concerned. He brought one hand up to stroke her cheek, feathering over her skin. "We can stop, Fee. Everything's moving so fast, maybe we should slow down."

"No," Ophelia said, more sharply than she meant to. "I mean, no, you haven't hurt me or pushed me. I want to do this Silas. With you." She took in a shaky breath. "I meant my heart. Please don't hurt my heart."

Her eyes flicked to his, and she didn't know what she hoped he would say. I'm already in too deep, she thought; this is going to hurt no matter what happens.

She cupped Silas's hand, still resting against her cheek. "Please, let's not stop now."

Silas nodded and slipped a hand between them. After a moment of searching, he found her clit, his blunt finger stroking and circling, clumsy and not quite right at first, but he was as good as his word, listening to her body and the sounds she made, and suddenly it was right, the thread of desire in her belly winding more and more tightly. A low animal sound of satisfaction grew in her throat, humming and growling out of her before she could stop it. Silas smiled and kissed her and she thought she might die of the pleasure of his hands on her, the pleasure of being wanted, of being seen.

"So soft," he muttered against her neck, kissing and nipping at the skin behind her ear, then the smooth curve of her collarbone. "I want to run my mouth over every inch of your skin. Fuck, Ophelia, you taste so good, like sunshine and honey and I don't know . . . happiness."

His lips moved over her chest, down into the smooth valley between her breasts, frantic, reverent. He stroked a hand up her ribs, testing the silk of skin over bone, then cupped the heaviness of her breast in one large hand. He ran a knuckle, then a palm over her nipple, drawing a pleased gasp from her when it tightened to a hard knot. Everything felt like pure sensation; there seemed to be no difference between she and Silas's bodies, his touch and her flesh melded together in one symphony of call and response. She moaned and pushed her breast up into his hand, wanting to feel the rough skin of his palm against her nipple again, wanting to feel possessed, desired. She could feel his erection, hard and silky against her centre and an echoing hollowness, a wanting so deep it felt like a cave in her chest.

"Now, Silas, please . . . now."

He pushed forward, his hand on her hip trembling, his sharp white teeth biting into his bottom lip. Fire circled her entrance, hot and keen, then sweet and liquid, every infinitesimal thrust from Silas making more room for himself until he was fully seated in her. And then the magic began. The drag and slide of his cock inside her stunned Ophelia, rearranged her molecules, every nerve in her body rising to the surface until she was alight with sensation. Silas worked himself against her, experimenting with depth and speed, hissing when she wrapped a leg around his hips to pull him deeper. Ophelia tried to concentrate on how everything felt, but Silas was kissing her neck and palming her breast, picking up speed with his thrusts, and she spun away on a river of pleasure. She could feel her orgasm coiling low in her belly, gathering strength when Silas rubbed against her in just the right way, but he was growing uncoordinated, and just as the sensation began to unfurl, he pulled out of her.

"Finish together?" he panted.

She nodded, so relieved that Silas had kept his head when she had been so swamped by sensation and lost to reason that she didn't immediately register his suggestion. But when he raised an eyebrow suggestively at her and stroked himself long and slow, she quickly caught up. Sliding a hand between them, she worked herself, the rhythm of her circles almost matching Silas's strokes. And then they were coming, her fingers slipping against her swollen clitoris, Silas's hips jerking, his eyes hawk-like on her hand. He moaned softly and sank against her, their chests heaving, bellies sticky with Silas's orgasm, Ophelia's hand still pressed between her legs. Silas stroked down her waist and hip in long, gentle caresses, his fingers lingering in the hollow of her hip.

"Thank you," he whispered against her skin.

CHAPTER 28

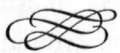

*I*t was almost dark when the distant clatter of shoes on the dry lane and happy voices sing-songing along the hedgerows penetrated the cosy nest of Silas's room. Ophelia's back went stiff against him and she straightened up, her hair a wild nest, tendrils and curls escaping in every direction. Silas couldn't help but notice the way her breasts moved when she leaned forward, their satiny curves tipped by now-soft, pink-tinged nipples. He loved this glimpse of her, sated and rumpled, as though they were waking for the day, as though she were his. *His.* The word made him feel both possessive and infantile. Ophelia was a person, not something to be owned, but he had to admit he liked the feeling of it, of being the one the who could stoke her pleasure and hold her in the night, of being the one she turned to and in whose arms she woke. The noises of the others returning grew closer.

"Sounds like they're almost at the bottom of the lane," Silas said, running a finger down Ophelia's spine, coming to rest in the soft crease of her back and hip. It was warm, and he let his fingers push toward the front of her pelvis and the pliant skin of her stomach.

"Hmm," he growled appreciatively and sat up behind her, his chest curving around her back.

"I should go," she said, distractedly turning to kiss his cheek, then hurriedly rummaging around the bed for her clothes.

Silas pushed thoughts of possession and waking together aside and handed Ophelia her corset and chemise, reaching under the bed to retrieve her drawers. She blushed prettily and stepped into them. Bringing her corset up around her waist, she hooked the busk closed and turned her back to Silas.

"Will you help me with the laces? They don't have to be tight, just tidy," she said, already reaching for her dress, which hung on the foot of the bed.

Silas grasped the laces and wound them once around each hand, tugging the corset closed. The cotton cording pulled tight across his palms and he found he liked the bite of it. He wished he and Ophelia had more time . . . no, that wasn't it. He hoped they had more time, hoped there might be more days like this. Wishing felt passive, while the hope he felt was muscular, active, willing him to make what he hoped for real. Ophelia reached around, her fingers tangling with his.

"Si? Is the knot tied? I need to get my dress back on before they are all here."

"Right, sorry, distracted for moment. Yes, knotted for you," he said, patting down the laces so they lay flat on Ophelia's back.

Her shoulder blades rose above the line of her corset, sharp and delicate, working like the most beautiful hinges he had ever seen when she leant forward to step into her dress.

"God, Fee," he whispered, his hand hovering over the skin and bone of her. "How am I to go on as usual now that I've seen you like this?" He stroked a hand across one shoulder blade, her skin instantly pebbling under his touch. "You've ruined me, love."

He could see her breathing was short and sharp, her shoulders and ribs moving jerkily, but she didn't turn, only stood, her back to him, the unbuttoned top of her dress gathered in her hands at her waist.

"Say it again... please, Silas?"

"Which part? That you've ruined me?"

"No, the last part."

"Love?"

"Yes, that part," she said, swaying backward into him.

His arms were around her in an instant, his mouth on her neck, behind her ear. She sighed, turning in his arms, her mouth finding his, already open and soft. He let Ophelia lick into him, the scent of sex and her warm skin blending with the lavender water from his sheets to fill his senses. She pulled back, her eyes blue and stormy, lips kiss-swollen.

"How will I see you again? Like this, I mean..."

"As soon as possible," he huffed. "Could you find a moment to slip away tonight, perhaps? Later?"

She nodded, humming a dreamy assent and indicated her dress. "Buttons?"

He turned her away from him, and kneeling, began the task.

* * *

SILAS WAS on his knees behind her, and Ophelia could practically feel his breath on her backside as he worked the buttons into place along the opening of her dress. Her mind and body were careening around in opposite directions, the one urging her to get dressed and out as quickly as possible, the other demanding she linger, perhaps find another reason for Silas's nimble fingers to touch her, and most definitely find a way to recreate today. At the moment, her body was winning, and it took all of her willpower not to politely request he begin working the buttons in the opposite direction and take her immediately back to bed. Bed. What a revelation that had been. She couldn't stop thinking about how Silas had looked, looming over her, his face tense with pleasure, neck corded with exertion. Nor could she forget how he had *looked*, taking note of every part of her body he uncovered, noticing each sigh and shiver and responding to it with more pressure, a softer touch, a faster rhythm. The sensation of him inside her lingered; she felt tender everywhere, each ache a reminder of his body inside hers. She wished they could stall the world a little longer, that she could curl back into Silas's warm bulk and rest, but the noises of the returning group were getting closer, and she wanted to keep this private, their own, for a while longer.

Silas was at her neck now, his breath ghosting past her ear and ruffling her hair. His hands stilled, and then she felt his lips at the nape of her neck. It was a soft and gentle kiss, not seeking, but leaving a scorching sense of possession. She imagined his lips making a mark and found she liked the idea more than she was comfortable with. Possession was a slippery thing, she thought. Too much in one direction and a woman was chattel, but with the right man, in just the right amount, perhaps it was an entirely different proposition? Perhaps a woman could possess a man in turn? The imprint of Silas's lips on her neck felt like the latter, but perhaps that was only her body talking? She didn't yet know if she could trust her reaction to his touch, it all felt so incendiary and volatile. Their lust for each other was combustible, but was it enough to find their way to an agreement about what they could be to each other? She wasn't even sure if what she longed for was possible.

Ophelia straightened, putting more distance between her skin and Silas's fingers on the last of her buttons. But she couldn't stop thinking about his lips and all the marvellous things she had discovered he was willing to do with them. She stepped away from him, reaching for the boots she had hastily unlaced and tossed next to the trunk.

"I wish I didn't have to go," she said, pulling the boots on and wrapping the laces untidily around the ankles.

"Will I see you later? Perhaps this evening?"

His eyes were serious and hopeful and Ophelia felt her resolve falter a little.

"I just need to figure out what this . . . I mean how to—" She stumbled over the words. Her body still sang from Silas's touch. She imagined the blood in her veins, sweet and heavy with sated lust, and knew she needed to collect herself before she lost sight of everything she had set out to do.

"I'll try to come," she said to Silas, almost avoiding the disappointment in his eyes by turning quickly for the door.

She heard him say her name quietly as she left, but didn't let herself turn around.

* * *

It had been long past dinner when the others had arrived home, so there was no need for food, but Mrs. Darling had made a pot of tea. Their conversation flowed around the kitchen table now—the identity of the Green Man, the state of the other farms according to their owners, and the relative merits of everyone's contributions to the picnic. There came a lull and then Silas spoke.

"I'm thinking of visiting my mother. I've actually been speaking with Mr. Bone about her tenancy, and he's agreed to look over some papers for us. I'm hopeful he might be able to help us. And, I have to admit that a very wise woman recently told me that I should let the women in my life tell me how they are feeling, instead of assuming I know."

Ophelia felt herself colour.

Hannah rapped her knuckles on the table, grinning. "Here, here."

Silas smiled across the table at Ophelia. "So . . . that is what I'm going to do. See my mother and find out what she would like to do about her future. Find out if she would like my help with these tenancy issues. I hope she will ask me about my future as well, so that I may share some hopes I am harbouring." Quiet sincerity filled his face now, all golden shadows in the light of the candles at the table's center.

Ophelia couldn't stop herself from smiling, could feel the upward movement of her mouth loosening her shoulders and the tension in her neck. He was putting things to right, doing the work they had talked about. The thought of it made her want to kiss him again, but she just smiled again and said, "I can't imagine how glad your mother will be to see you, Silas."

"Grand news, Silas," said Bess. "Your mother'll be so happy to see you well and recovered."

"Thank you, Bess. I hope so," said Silas. "I was thinking of catching the train next week, if that suits, Mrs. D.?"

Mrs. Darling agreed, and the conversation moved on to the rest of the week's work, the weather, and the fast approaching first cut of hay. Ophelia let herself be held in the eddy of everyone's conversations and basked in the warmth of Silas's heated glances, her mind drifting back to their afternoon in his bed.

CHAPTER 29

The following week passed with frustratingly few stolen moments with Silas, and Ophelia found herself craving the times she could slide into the chair next to him at meals or stand beside him at the stove sipping a tea before heading out for the day. It wasn't that they weren't sharing space, most days they were together from sunup to sundown, but they were in constant motion. Checking the progress of each field, weeding the cereal and root crops with the horses, spreading manure on the newly cleared field, an endless wheel of work under the warming dome of the summer sky. Confident with the horses, Ophelia kept an eye on Samson, but pushed them as hard as she dared to keep the weeds under control. Bess was busy each day with her dairying work at Mr. Bone's, and Hannah arrived home from the forage corps each day red-faced and weary. Word had also arrived from the War Ag that they would be sending a committee member to inspect their progress. They retired from the dinner table soberly one night, taking their tea to the sitting room and sinking onto the sofas. Much later, work assignments organised, tasks allotted, tea drunk, only Silas and Ophelia remained. The flames had died to almost nothing and the moon hung in the inky sky out the window. They sat in companionable silence, thighs and shoulders snugged tight together. Silas was due to leave for his mother's the next day, and Ophelia didn't want to lose a minute with him.

"I could do this with you every night, Fee."

"What, ruminate on the arrival of an unfriendly War Ag inspector?" Ophelia said, half sigh, half laugh.

"Nah." He ran a hand down her thigh, stopping at her knee. "Sit with you in front of a fire, tea in our mugs, a long day done."

She hummed in response.

"It's nice to end the day together, no?"

"It is. Though we're really only able to sit here because there's five of us doing the housework and dishes and chores. Were it only you and me, I'd likely be still cleaning up after dinner, and you'd be in here enjoying the fire on your own."

"It needn't be like for us," Silas protested. "I'd take on all the tasks with you. Fair is fair."

"Do you think it could be, outside of this time and place? There'd be so many reasons for you to go back to the way things were before—you in the field and me in the house. Everyone will expect it, there's already so much talk of returning to life as it was. I fear people have little interest in equality when it affects them personally."

"Men, you mean."

She nodded, thinking that there were also women who worked to maintain the status quo. That she might have continued to be one, but for meeting Hannah, joining the WLA.

"To hell with what everyone else expects," Silas swore quietly, his body going tense against hers. "I'll burn it all to the ground if it means being with you, building something that matters together."

It was giddy and electric, the possibility of being together on their own terms. Of taking a step into the future on *her* terms. She nudged his shoulder with hers. "Let's burn it to the ground, together."

He stared at her for a moment and then she took his mouth with hers, opening to bite at his soft lips. Ophelia felt him go pliant, and she wrapped her arms around his neck to pull him onto her. The upper half of his body over hers was a heady weight, and she let herself enjoy the feeling of being held down while their mouths roved hungrily over each other. Silas pulled back and stroked a hand down the side of her face, lingering on the angle of her jaw, running a rough thumb along the crease of her mouth. Ophelia opened her eyes.

"Walk me to my room," he rumbled.

Yes. She scooted up from under him and they stumbled, clumsy with desire, through the kitchen and into the farmyard. The moon had risen higher, its watery light leaking into the corners of the buildings, gilding everything silver. They hurried across the cobblestones, shadows distorted like fairies or thieves in the night. The dark arch of the barn door enveloped them, and then Ophelia was pulling Silas across the small room toward his bed. He caught her about the waist and spun her, laughing, toward him.

CHAPTER 30

Silas's head thrummed with the electricity of a thousand lightning strikes, stars sparking behind his eyelids. The heady joy of Ophelia in his arms again, her broad smile turned up toward him, madcap with excitement and desire. Lust streaked through him, hot and dangerous, but he forced himself to concentrate; he wanted to remember everything. Stroking her hair tenderly, he catalogued the exact second Ophelia's lips met his, the particular weight of them against his own, the distinct taste of tea and honey on her tongue when she swiped it against his, eager and questing. He singed the memory of her fingers curled at the nape of his neck into his mind, pulling at the roots of his hair just enough to bring his cock to full attention, his entire body adrift on sensation, anchored only at the places where their bodies met. Breasts and chest, hips and thighs. He tried to steady himself, pressed kiss after kiss to her lips, but when she drew her warm tongue across his mouth, begging entry, he had felt himself go under, sinking into the honeyed warmth.

A low growl rumbled between them, captured almost instantly by Ophelia's sipping kisses, her languorous explorations of his mouth. Silas wondered if one might go mad from desire, thinking that at least he and Ophelia would do so together. When she pressed herself more firmly against him, he could feel her body trembling, her shuddering breaths rubbing the edge of her corset against his nipples distractingly. He couldn't remember ever wanting to do anything more than he wanted to unbutton her shirt and lay her bare to him. His mind reeled at the memory of Ophelia's breasts overflowing her corset, he want to figure out more ways to pleasure her with his hands and tongue. He opened his mouth wider, trying to taste more of her, bumping their noses when he tilted her head to better meet his tongue. She pulled back, rubbing the bridge of his nose, a rueful smile on her still-damp lips.

"Sorry." Ophelia giggled breathlessly, before running her hands along his jaw and up into his hair.

"S'okay," Silas replied, leaning in to press open-mouthed kisses along the line of her jaw and down her throat.

He lingered behind her ear and licked into the dip between her shoulder and neck, sucking the tender spot gently when he paused. Running his hands up Ophelia's arms and cradling her face in his hands, he pressed a soft kiss to her lips. She smiled against his mouth, and before he knew it, he was giving in to the firestorm of desire burning through him. He didn't wait or lap gently this time, but plunged into the dark warmth of her mouth, tongue tangling wildly with hers, teeth nipping at her kiss-swollen lips. Silas felt his cock swell, his trousers uncomfortably tight, just as Ophelia arched against him, then drew back, her chest heaving.

He raised his hands to the top button of her shirt, pushing the tiny mother-of-pearl button through its stitched hole, looking up to see whether he had her permission to continue. She nodded, her breath catching when his fingers brushed against the rise of her breast. Pushing the straps of her overalls off her shoulders and carefully peeling back the fabric, Silas ran a finger along the embroidered edge of Ophelia's corset, considering the creamy expanse that rose and fell quickly under his gaze. The skin of her chest was smooth and pale, dotted by the tiniest freckles, a constellation only he could see. Watching her face carefully, he ran the backs of his fingers gently down her sternum, dragging a finger into the cleft of her breasts. Her skin was so soft and warm, her reaction to his touch so electric, Silas thought he might come right there. Ophelia let her head fall back, sighing as she did so. Silas kissed the base of her throat and dipped a long finger beneath the edge of her corset, finding the hardening point of her nipple. His breath left him in a rush, and Ophelia arched against him with a tiny whine of pleasure. He could feel her pushing her breast up into his palm, trying to increase the contact, and his mind blanked, utterly blackened by a haze of desire. It hummed between them like a gossamer thread, electric and impossible, and he was struck anew by the miracle that Ophelia mirrored his desire so exactly, so hungrily. Hunger. It clawed and howled in his chest, like something wild and too long denied. Dipping his head to where his hand cradled the satiny weight of her breast, he opened his mouth and let it out.

The swipe of his tongue around Ophelia's nipple threatened to bring him to his knees and he tightened his grip on her hip to keep his balance. Desperate to be inside Ophelia again, to be that close, he let his tongue linger over the pebbled skin of her nipple, exploring the texture even as he felt it tighten almost to a point. Unable to resist Ophelia's broken sighs and the thrill of pleasuring her, he took her nipple into his mouth, sucking gently, then with more force when she threaded her hands in his hair and held him to her. She arched against him, and the press of her softness against his cock was more than he could bear, so he pressed his thigh between her legs. Hitching her up against him, and begging his body to withstand the exquisite torture, Silas ground Ophelia against the muscle of his thigh, his free hand skating over her hip, clutching at the extra fabric of her overalls, trying to make contact with her body. She made hot, needy noises, so pressed his leg harder against her centre, felt her arch into it, legs tensing to find purchase against him.

"I'm . . . Silas . . . God," she intoned, rubbing harder, uncoordinated, against him.

Painfully hard, he tried to ignore the friction of her leg as her orgasm overtook her. Head thrown back, pale neck exposed, she shuddered and cried out, clutching his shoulders for support. He ran his hands up and down her back, feeling an aching tenderness pushing from behind his ribs. She looked up at him. Her blue eyes were fathoms deep, pupils muzzy and blown wide with desire. Like a goddess, hair wild, colour high on her cheeks, she looked both surprised and completely at ease. Her desire was plain on her face and Silas loved the frankness of it, wanted to kneel before her, give her everything she desired. He didn't know what that looked like, but he found he didn't really care. He would find his way to something new. Could already feel how tight and stiff his old thinking felt. They would build something beautiful. Together.

* * *

NOT HAVING any words at all, Ophelia sagged into him, letting her cheek press into his chest. She listened to his heart pound beneath her ear and felt the echo of it in her own chest. *Here, here, here* each beat seemed to say. She had half expected the cold rush of self-recrimination, but it didn't come. Satiety lifted her on a tide of pleasure and she pushed away her worries. Later on, when she was alone again, she would have this to remember, when they were for each other and the world was quiet for a moment. Silas pressed a long, soft kiss to the top of her head, his hand smoothing down the coils of her hair, and she ran her hands up his back to pull him closer to her. Right now, Ophelia told herself, she had Silas, willing and impressively eager, and she intended to take every advantage of the moment. She nuzzled his chest and raised her head to kiss him, which he returned, then murmured, "Let's get these off," and pushed her overalls down over her hips, pulling her to step out of them.

Indicating her corset with a wave of his hand, he said, "You might be quicker with that," and proceeded to unbutton his waistcoat and the buttons at the neck of his shirt. Shucking the vest, he slid his thumbs under the worn leather of his braces, and Ophelia stopped unhooking her corset to watch. He grinned, vulpine, and made a show of teasing the leather over his broad shoulders. Shirt off, braces hanging down his legs, he began to unbutton his trousers. Ophelia's throat dried instantly.

"Leave those just like that," she said, her voice rough.

A dark eyebrow flew up, but he didn't protest. Only nodded and waited for her to finish with her corset.

Bare and settled against the pillows on Silas's bed, Ophelia felt like a woman in a painting: admired, sated, doted upon. Silas bent, then crawled up the bed toward her, and she reflexively pulled the sheet up to her chest. He shook his head and pulling the sheet gently away, settled his wide shoulders between her spread legs. "I want to taste you again," he whispered, looking up to meet her eyes, before lowering his head and pressing his mouth to the damp curls at the apex of her thighs. She hummed a ragged agreement as she let her head fall back against the wall. Silas's tongue was moving delicately along the seam of her vulva, dipping into the sensitive folds with tiny licks, then sucking kisses that dragged her swollen lips into the heat of his mouth. Ophelia felt lost to the world, floating on a sea of sensation so wide she could no longer see the horizon, anchored only by Silas's tongue lapping into her, his spread hands firm under her backside. She squirmed to get closer to him, a low keening in the back of her throat.

"Silas," she managed, "don't stop."

She felt his smile against her wet flesh and, sliding a thick finger inside her entrance, he pressed the flat of his tongue to her clitoris, catching the rhythm quickly this time, working in perfect, teasing circles. Ophelia's stomach tightened, strands of lightning running along her arms and legs, nipples and clitoris gathering tight as she raced toward her orgasm. It shattered over her like fireworks in a night sky, her body clenching around Silas's finger while he continued to work her gently with his tongue. When the last ripples faded and her body was perfectly limp, he slid his hand out from under her, skating it up the outside of her thigh to find her hand and thread his fingers through hers. He laid his cheek on her thigh with a low, happy sigh. His eyes were glazed, pupils blown wide with desire, his lips and chin slick from Ophelia's orgasm.

"Come here," she murmured, pulling him up, reaching to run her hands over the taut muscles of his back, the broad sweep of his shoulder blades like wings under her palms.

Then she reached between them, running her hand down the front of Silas's body, over his ribs and the smooth hinge of his hip. Remembering how firmly he liked to be held, she reached into the opening of his trousers and smalls to run her fingers lightly over Silas's jutting cock. He sucked in a breath, the air whistling through his pursed lips, and Ophelia felt him bob against her hand. Wrapping her fingers around his length, she stroked slowly up and down, loving the trembling praise Silas mumbled in her ear.

"Ah, God . . . so bloody good, Fee. You're so beautiful, have I told you that already? So God bloody beaut—Jesus!"

He came suddenly, surprise and satisfaction flaring in his green eyes, and Ophelia felt power surge through her. It was a heady feeling, new and freeing, and it burbled out of her in a laugh. Silas looked at her and then began to laugh as well, a low chuckle that built until his shoulders shook. They collapsed back on his tiny bed, snorting and giggling, their legs twined together, arms around each other. Silas kissed her between chuckles and murmured, "Fee, my own sweet, salty, Fee."

He rose to clean himself, shed his trousers and crawled into the tiny bed next to her. He wiped her hand gently, sliding the cloth along each finger, then they curled around each other, Ophelia on her side with Silas's leg slung over her hip. She ran her hand over the long muscles of his thigh and the hard globe of his arse, tracing the knob of his knee and sliding a finger into the tender skin behind it. Reaching farther down his leg, she felt the top edge of his scars. He hadn't done anything obvious to hide it when they had fallen into bed, but she suspected from the way he had moved his leg out of her sight that he felt self-conscious. He flinched now, and her finger froze over the tracery of scars and rough skin.

"Do you want me to stop?"

"No, it's okay. It's just a part of me, now," he said, but his voice was as tight as his breathing.

She let her fingertip rest gently on his calf, waiting for him to become accustomed to the feeling. The skin had been puckered in some places, drawn tight in others, and it looked painful even though the skin had entirely healed. Sitting up, she took his long, elegant foot in her hand and ran her palms along his instep and up the inside of his ankle, slowly making her way to the outside where the shrapnel had shattered his skin and bone. She turned and found Silas watching her closely, his face shuttered. She caressed the skin and then without thinking, brought her lips to the scars and pressed soft kisses to his calf, running her tongue softly over the sculpted knob of his ankle bone. Silas shuddered, and when she looked up his face was broken open, the sheen of unshed tears fogging his green eyes. He rose up and crushed her in his arms then, his mouth rough and hungry on hers. She didn't know what he had seen on her face, but something tight and sad unravelled in him, dissipating in the heated space between their mouths.

"You're whole to me, Silas," Ophelia whispered against his lips. "I know you feel broken, but you aren't, only different than before."

He pressed his forehead to hers, a long breath rushing out

against her face. He stroked her hair back from her face, tucking it behind her ear. "I . . . oh, Fee," he said. "For so long after I came home, I just wanted to be who I was before, to erase everything. But I couldn't, nor could I seem to go forward, and so I was stuck in this no man's land." He rolled to lay on his back, looking up at the ceiling. She watched his profile, lashes sweeping his cheeks, sharp, soft lips moving as he spoke.

"The last few weeks though, I've begun to see things ahead of me, ways I might be. My leg hasn't occupied my thoughts the way it did before." He paused, and she slid her hand across his middle to hold herself close to him. "I'm glad we're here, together, Fee. No matter what comes of it."

She nodded against his chest. "Me, too."

CHAPTER 31

The station platform was still shaded and cool when Silas arrived, his satchel in hand. Standing on the platform, he watched the sky beginning to colour, warm and soft. Caught up in the movement of light, he didn't notice the man appear at his side.

"Morning, Larke," Mr. Bone murmured, tipping his hat briefly.

"Morning, sir," Silas replied, his eyes still on the sky. "Appreciate you making the trip with me today."

"Ah, well, it's been years since there's been a need for my lawyering, and I'm only in Bess's way at the farm now that she's got it all set up. I was glad you came to speak to me about all this. It's good to be of use."

They stood silent while the screech of the engine faded to a mechanical wheezing and then boarded. Silas hadn't splurged for first-class seats, but the cars were mostly empty, and they took seats next to each other facing the front of the train.

"So," began Mr. Bone, "I thought we might begin by looking over whatever papers your mother has at the house to see whether there's anything to suggest Blackwood might have cause. Seems more than likely to me that it's nastiness."

Silas blew a long breath out, steadying his nerves. He knew what kind of nastiness Blackwood was capable of and didn't feel much like chancing it while his family hung in the balance. "So what do I, we, do, then?"

"Well, if it is as you think, a hundred-year lease, I would guess your mother has more than a decade before she'd need to renegotiate. So my suggestion is that we call a spade a spade, as it were." The older man's hands settled on the leather letter case on his lap. "There's usually a provision in the case of a death to assume the tenancy, provided the remaining family is able to keep the land worked or the animals profitable, so I propose we call his bluff."

"Do you think that's wise? I don't want to complicate things for my mother—"

"Silas, that man owes you a good deal more than just fulfilling his legal obligations to your family. By God, he's lucky we haven't brought the constabulary with us."

Silas nodded, grateful for the fatherly vigor. He actually felt a bit sick at the idea of setting foot on the estate properties again, but there seemed to be only one way of making the things that had been weighing him down right. He wanted to know his mother was safe in her home, Samuel given the option to continue running the farm. He and his brother had never spoken in detail about Samuel's plans, but he did know that Sam loved farming and the land he had grown up on. It wasn't only settling the score with Blackwood that Silas looked forward to though; he was eager to sweep away the final obstacles to his committing to Ophelia. She deserved a partner that could come to her without shadows hanging over him, and for himself, he wanted to be able to consider their future clearly, not under threat or secrecy. Being able to understand his own needs and work out what he truly felt about marriage could only happen if he wasn't looking over his shoulder or worrying about who might know what. He was done letting Merritt Blackwood run his life, and for the first time since he had been sent away by the man, exemption papers unsigned, he felt close to relief.

It hadn't been easy to approach Mr. Bone for help, and it had really only come about when Bone's career as a lawyer came up in conversation one night during dinner. When he had realized the man's former profession might be an answer to his conundrum, Silas pressed Bess and Mrs. Darling for more information. Bess hadn't known much about his work, but Mrs. Darling had said the former lawyer had worked for many years as the village solicitor and was likely quite familiar with wills and tenancy issues. Silas had noticed an unusual tightness around her mouth when she spoke about Mr. Bone, but she had praised his diligence and work ethic.

Hopeful, Silas made time to visit him and soon enough, the older man's sharp tongue and quick mind had drawn out the salient facts, and the former lawyer was on the case.

After writing to his mother, he had spoken with Ophelia about confronting her father and when she had agreed to the idea, he had asked Mr. Bone to look over the papers in person. Before Silas could think better of his plan, they were on their way to settle things.

"I do appreciate all you've done for me about this, Mr. Bone," Silas said before passing the man a packet of sandwiches that he had wrapped up in the dark kitchen that morning. "I wasn't entirely sure how to approach all this, as I said when we first met."

"'Tis naught." Bone took the bread and cheese with a nod. "I've never had a stomach for bullies, though it's been years since I 'ad the chance to go up against one." He chewed thoughtfully. "I think it were partly the reason I went into law in the first place . . . I faced my own bully when I was not much younger than you. Though I weren't strong enough to best that one, I've had good results in my career since."

"Oh?"

"Funnily enough, it was even in regards to a young woman." Mr.

Bone glanced over at Silas, his eyes crinkling slightly at the corners. "If I'm not entirely mistaken, I think a young woman might be at least partly the impetus for this trip?"

Silas nodded. "She's the best part of the reason, but I've let this all hang over me for long enough. I want it cleared up so that I can focus on my future. Despite Blackwood's best efforts, I'm still alive and I need to remember that."

Mr. Bone lifted his sandwich to cheers Silas. "A good woman can bring out the best in us," he said a little wistfully.

"Yes, sir, I believe that as well. Did you ever consider marrying yourself?" he asked after a pause.

"Ah, well," said Mr. Bone thoughtfully. "I could never quite put my feelings into words when it came to the moment of truth. The law, now I can talk about that damn near all day, but a woman is a different matter. I 'spose I was a prickly young man, in addition to everything else."

Silas nodded. "Feelings are a tricky business, indeed."

Mr. Bone huffed a gruff agreement and subsided into quiet. Silas let himself relax into the movement of the train, shunting more quickly now through the countryside. It was quiet in the car, the machinery of the engine muffled by the upholstery, and Silas found his head getting heavy. He closed his eyes and tried to marshal his thoughts before they arrived.

At the Wells station, he and Bone alighted and made their way to the pony carts, managing to secure a ride on a ramshackle vehicle pulled by a shaggy chestnut. They started off, and the closer the trap drew to his childhood home, the tighter Silas's chest felt. He started when Mr. Bone lifted an arm to clap him gently on the shoulder.

"Whatever happens today, you'll have me at your back. This isn't something to face alone."

"I'm grateful, sir. It does give me a good deal of comfort."

The farmhouse seemed almost exactly the same as when he had

left it almost two years ago—the low-slung, honeyed stone building with its small windows and dark wooden door waiting for him as though preserved in amber. The front garden circled by the low stone wall still protected his mother's veg garden from the worst of the rabbits, the rose bushes still scrambled up the corner of the house. Bone indicated that the trap should stop there, and after paying, Silas hefted their bags down. He took a deep breath before pushing the gate open and indicated that Bone should proceed first. Before they could reach the door to knock, a collie waddled around the side of the house and gave a half-hearted bark.

"Puff!" Silas exclaimed. "There's a good girl." He ruffled the collie's dark ears and patted her rump. "Looking a bit plump there, eh? Is Mother feeding you from the table again?"

"Silas Larke, don't you be spreading rumours about how I care for my dogs," came his mother's laughing voice. She stood at the side of the house, face concealed by the wide brim of her straw hat.

Silas's heart leaped. "Ma!" he cried and moved to scoop her up in a firm hug. "God, it's good to see you."

She felt smaller in his arms than he remembered, but she smelled just the same. For a second, it felt as though his entire childhood came rushing back, staggering in its clarity. He hugged her hard, then let her stand again. She clutched his hand and wiping her watery eyes, said, "Lord, I've waited so long to have you back. You can't imagine how good it is to see you with my own eyes."

Silas could only nod. Remembering that Mr. Bone stood behind him, still waiting to be introduced, he said, "Mr. Bone, this is my mother, Lettie Larke. Mother, this is Mr. Casper Bone. He's come to help us with the matter I wrote you about."

Lettie's face instantly clouded, her mouth going hard. "That man," she hissed. "May the devil take him."

"Well, I've no affiliation with the devil, ma'am, but I do know my way 'round a legal document, so I hope I may be of some use to you. Silas has apprised me of the bare bones of the thing, and if I might look through the papers you have, I'm sure we can find some resolution. Whether the devil is interested in him is another matter, I suppose."

His mother laughed and shook Mr. Bone's hand, ushering them into the house.

They sat around the kitchen table, and his mother served tea from the same teapot he had used all his life. His mother seemed at ease with Mr. Bone, and they spoke of Mr. Bone's dairy and the increases he was having with Bess's leadership. Silas let the conversation fade into the background as he looked around the house, letting himself really see it. He had been half afraid to come back here, to see it again after being at the front; he didn't know if he could hold the innocence of life before together with what he had seen overseas. But the sun was streaming in the small windows, laying down its warmth on the old flagstone floor, pushing into the corners of the room, just as Ophelia's light was pushing into the corners of Silas's fears. He could do this, he needed to do this. Facing Blackwood was part of moving forward.

"I found the documents that you asked about, Silas," his mother said, patting his hand. "Your father always kept those types of things in the desk in the sitting room. Shall I get them now?"

"Let's take a look."

The paper was old and folded so often the creases were almost translucent. His mother spread it out in front of Mr. Bone, who unfolded a pair of wire-rimmed spectacles, and putting them on, leaned forward. He read through the document, humming and nodding to himself. Silas's mother hadn't sat down again, but fussed with dishes at the sink and refilling the kettle.

"It's going to be okay, Mother," Silas said, coming to stand next to her at the sink.

"I still can't understand why you didn't tell me immediately, Silas. How could you have kept that secret when you were going to war?" Her face was small and sad when she looked up at him. "What if, God forbid, something happened? I'd have never known about any of it."

"But nothing happened, Ma, look at me, strong as an ox," he said.

"Don't make light, Silas Larke," she scolded. "You might be a grown man, but I'm still your mother, and you know I would have moved heaven and earth to prevent you from going to war, especially because of blackmail."

"I didn't want you to worry, Ma. And it was my fault that Blackwood was angry in the first place, he hated that Ophelia and I were becoming close. He didn't care a bit about patriotism, only took an opportunity when he saw it. I couldn't let you and Samuel suffer because of me."

His mother's hands stilled on the dishes she held. "Nothing about this is your fault, Silas. I will always be grateful for your choice, but I would never have wanted you to sacrifice yourself in order to keep us housed here. It grieves me greatly to think what might have happened." She took his hands with her soapy ones and squeezed. "My God, I'm so grateful you are home safe."

He only nodded because the words were stuck in his throat.

His mother turned back to the sink and continued, "Now, tell me about our Ophelia. How is she? I must say, I was more than a little surprised that you were both stationed at the same farm. What are the chances?"

Silas smiled. "Slim to none, I imagine, but there you have it. I couldn't believe it myself when we first saw each other. But she is doing well, Mother, happier than I've ever seen her, and making great friends among the WLA women. She asked after you before I left."

"She is a lovely girl, always was," his mother said thoughtfully. "I'm glad she's found her way. She always deserved better than her father. Funny how things turn out though . . . her being from the big house and now turning to farming."

Mr. Bone cleared his throat then, announcing that he had gone through the tenancy agreement. There was nothing, he said, to indicate that it could be nullified without cause. "Having been signed by your husband's father, it seems likely you still have more than a decade left before renegotiation would begin. Now to the matter of the refusal to sign the war exemption papers, that is a matter of public record, and I should think it wouldn't be too difficult to show that Blackwood was acting out of malice."

Relief surged in Silas, tempered only a little by his worry that he should have thought to challenge Blackwood on this at the time. *You didn't know any better. There was no shame in trying to protect your family.* He forced himself to remember why he was here, what dismantling Blackwood's threat would do for all the plans he had for his future.

Lettie poured more tea into her cup and gave Mr. Bone a funny little salute before drinking it down. "Well, I am more grateful than I can say, Mr. Bone. For passing your eyes over our papers and for coming here with Silas. We'll think no more on this then, Silas. Samuel and I'll stay put, and when you are released from your duties by the War Office, we'll decide what to do next."

Silas laughed at her no-nonsense ways, grateful for the visit, for her stalwart love. Finishing his tea, he agreed with Mr. Bone that they might walk down to the estate grounds for a conversation with Blackwood. Silas's mother bade them be careful and promised a hot dinner when they returned. Samuel would be home, she reminded Silas, eager for her boys to be at the same table once more.

CHAPTER 32

⚜

They reached the circle of the drive, boots crunching on the gravel. Climbing the wide stone steps, Silas faced a brass lion's head knocker glowering from the center of the glossy black door. His stomach was heavy with dread and nerves. They stood silent, shoulder to shoulder, for a moment before Mr. Bone reached out to press the bell. It rang inside the house, hollow and loud, then the shuffling of feet and the door opened to reveal a stout woman with dark eyes in a merry face. Her greying hair, still strawberry blonde in places, was loosely held in place with a lacy mobcap.

"Help you, gentlemen?" she asked without opening the door farther.

"We're here to see Blackwood," said Silas with as much confidence as he could muster.

She looked at him then, as if seeing him suddenly. "Silas Larke? Oh my stars, boy! I'd no notion you were back." She clutched at her cap and then at the shawl tucked round her shoulders. "Mrs. Greene, d'you remember? I used to make biscuits for you and

Ophelia. Oh, lord, don't get me started!" The housekeeper dabbed at her eyes and shook her head.

"Of course I do," Silas said. "I'm so glad to see you again. As to Ophelia—I've a letter here from her. She wanted me to bring directly to you." He pulled a small envelope from his chest pocket and handed it to Mrs. Greene.

She dimpled at him, tears still leaking from the corners of her eyes. "Oh my stars! How lovely of her. Do come in, then."

Mrs. Greene motioned for them to come into the foyer, and they both stepped forward into the house. It was quiet inside with a palpable feeling of emptiness about the place. Nothing much had changed that Silas could see, but he had only been inside perhaps three or four times, and never through the front door. Mr. Bone held his leather case to his chest and nodding to Mrs. Greene said, "Mr. Casper Bone, at your service, ma'am." The housekeeper tittered and took his hat.

"Is he in the study?" Silas asked, knowing it was rude, but not feeling able to make his way through all the niceties without losing his nerve. He needed to get this done. "I know it's not the done thing, and I would enjoy longer to catch up, but there is a matter of some urgency, Mrs. Greene."

"Oh, yes, I see, o' course." She motioned them toward the largest of the doors off the foyer. "In there."

The room was heavy with age and dark wood, anchored by the plush Aubusson carpet and the massive desk in the centre of the room. Bookshelves towered along the far wall, still stuffed with volumes, but the mantel was missing the large landscape that had hung above it, and Silas noted that the trinkets, silver snuffboxes and jeweled cigarette cases, that had been displayed on the sideboard were gone. Blackwood was bent over paperwork when they entered, and Silas took him in, in the moment before he looked up; greying black hair, shoulders hunched over his scrawling hands, the fabric of his expensive suit greasy with wear even from this distance. He continued writing for a fraction of a second longer before he raised his head, an expression of disoriented shock on his face. Silas pounced, not waiting for Blackwood to gain a moment's equilibrium.

"I've come to settle my mother's tenancy, Blackwood. I was a fool to agree to your threats before, and I'll not leave here until she's properly titled on the leasehold."

"So you managed to make it back, did you, Larke?" Blackwood's face had settled back into its regular territory, a derisive sneer. "Well, I have to admit, I didn't think much of your chances overseas, but here you are."

"Here I am." Silas took the papers that Mr. Bone had ready for him. "She's years left on the lease, and according to my lawyer, there's no way for you to break the lease without proof of dereliction."

"Oh ho, your lawyer, is it? And who might you be, my good man?" Blackwood turned his beady eyes on Bone, fingers steepled over his paunch. "And has Larke let you know what his part of the bargain was? That's he's already broken it, settin' foot in here." Then to Silas, "Give it up, Larke, you were outmanouvered before you even got to France . . . unsurprising considering your father. A man unsuited to anything but standing behind a plough, not a clever bone in his body. Much like yourself," he snarled, a superior tilt to his lips.

"Ah, well, sir," said Mr. Bone. "You may not be aware, but the courts don't look too kindly on blackmail, so you've not much of an argument as to Silas's breaking it. However"—he stepped forward and took a seat in the chair in front of the desk—"there is the matter of the lease signed by your late wife's father in . . . oh"—he scanned down the document with a long finger—"1835, it looks like. That was the traditional renewal of a hundred-year lease with Silas's grandfather, so by my reckoning, that gives Mrs. Larke until 1935 before she need worry too much about moving on. So unless there's any proof of dereliction, your tenants are well within their rights. I suspect the courts are run off their feet at the moment, what with all the war work, so might not look favourably on such a nuisance case."

Silas wanted to laugh at the pinched look on Blackwood's face, but he schooled his features into neutrality. Bone slung one long leg over the other, waiting for Blackwood to speak. It was interesting to see him in his element here in the grand house, shoulders straight and firm, hands relaxed on the arms of the chair. Silas had only seen him on the land prior, and through the implacable eyes of Mrs. Darling. He had seemed harder there, more ossified in his position, but today he had been inquisitive and kind, and now commanded the room with confidence and ease.

"It's nothing to me who stays in that hovel, but I'll not hesitate to evict her if the land shows the slightest dip in productivity. I'm not running a charity," Blackwood spat.

"There'll be no question of that, Blackwood," Silas said. "My family has been working that land for generations, and so it will continue. My mother is more than capable."

Mr. Bone rose, calmly gathering up his papers and closing the latch on his briefcase. "Good day, sir. These papers will be stored securely, along with the notes outlining our business today, should you have any notion of trying to destroy or alter them. It was not a pleasure doing business, but I trust I fulfilled my duties as a voice of reason."

"Get out!" Blackwood growled.

They made their way out into the foyer and through the front door, a rectangle of light with a dazzle of green in the distance. Silas sucked in a breath on the threshold and stepped onto the porch, as if into a new life. He wanted to laugh or sing, something to release the bubble of relief that filled his chest. Instead, he turned and shook Mr. Bone's hand.

"I can't thank you enough, Mr. Bone. You've no idea."

"Casper, please. And it is sincerely my pleasure. I've no stomach for aristocrats run amok, faced my own version of that man decades ago, and it still needles me." The older man patted Silas's shoulder. "It was good to work the legal chops again, it's been a long while."

Silas laughed, and they began the walk back to the Larke farmhouse. He was looking forward to dinner with Samuel and his mother, but in truth, he was desperate to get back to the farm to see Ophelia. He felt the distance from her like an ache in his chest.

CHAPTER 33

Silas had been gone three days, but as Ophelia contemplated his empty chair at the table all she could think of was how late they had lain in each other's arms the night before he left, how little sleep he must have had. She had crept back into the house close to two o'clock, sliding as stealthily as she could into her bed, the sheets cool and tight. Laying there in the dark, she had thought of the disarray of Silas's bed; the sheets wrinkled and loose around him when she rose, eiderdown crumpled at the foot of the bed, pillows piled under his golden head. The lines of his body had a sleepy languor, but his eyes were sharp, watching her dress. Leaning over to kiss him good night, he had slid a hand up the back of her leg, caressing her behind through her overalls. The electricity of his touch had kept her awake the rest of the night.

"Sleeping ill lately, Ophelia?" Mrs. Darling said. "You've the look of too much work and too little rest this week."

Ophelia shook her head, trying to hide what she was sure was a guilty blush. "It's nothing, just had strange dreams last night, is all," she mumbled. "Just need another cup of tea this morning."

Mrs. Darling hummed vaguely while pouring more tea into

both their cups. "We'll need to keep going on the field work today. I've no intention of giving the War Ag a leg to stand on when they come for the inspection, and with Silas away this week, more of the work will fall to you, I'm afraid."

"It's no bother. I'll check on the new field and make sure the scarecrows have been keeping the birds off. I had planned to weed in the long field today as well. Samson and Delilah can be turned out in the small pasture for a few hours, I think."

Mrs. Darling nodded. "Best get on then."

It was hours later when Ophelia returned from weeding the wheat and checking in on the progress in the newer field. She called to Samson and Delilah as she emerged from the shelter of the barn and outbuildings. They grazed behind the farmhouse, in the small paddock next to the kitchen garden, heads down, thick tails swishing at flies. A small black bird landed on Delilah's rump, stretching out a wing gracefully before lifting into flight again. Ophelia watched the hot, lazy dance of the late May day before her, the ever-present hum and tick of insects like the breath of the land around her, interrupted only by the odd call of an animal or rumble of a farm vehicle. Suddenly both horses raised their heads, ears pricked, bodies erect and watchful. A high whistle came from behind the house and Ophelia thought of the lips that were pursed together at that exact moment, throwing a jaunty tune out into the air.

"You're back!" She flung herself at him as he crossed into the farmyard.

He dropped his satchel and caught her up in a hug, grunting at her impact. He was warm from the walk, smelt a little of sweat and warm linen, and she was so bloody glad to see him. He glanced quickly around, then pressed his lips to hers in a soft greeting. She wrapped her arms more tightly around his neck and opened her mouth to deepen the kiss.

Pulling back enough to grin at her, Silas said, "What a welcome.

I might leave every couple of days now that I know what awaits me."

She boxed his shoulder and stuck out her tongue, laughing. Silas silenced her with a kiss.

Once they made it back to Silas's room, she sank onto his bed while he emptied his bag and placed his items back in their spots. She was dying to ask what had happened with her father, but didn't want to push.

"I saw your father," he said, closing the lid on the chest at the foot of his bed.

Ophelia nodded, her breath caught in her suddenly too-small chest.

"I think it helped to have Mr. Bone, but I did it, Fee . . . I stood up to him. I stood up for my family."

"I'm so glad, Silas. I'm so happy for you and proud of you. How does it feel?"

"Strange . . . like there is something gone that I can't quite put my finger on. Lighter, I think. Like I can finally be here without looking over my shoulder. Like something is finished." He came and sat next to her on the bed, lifted her hand to thread his fingers with hers. "I'm so bloody glad to see you."

"So am I."

"Tell me everything I've missed. How's the field? The horses? Any word from the War Ag?"

They stood and Ophelia told him all the news, little as it was, while they walked out toward the fields.

Hours later, only the bread crust and a few radishes, their shiny, red skins bright against the blue and white of Mrs. Darling's china, were left of dinner. Silas watched Ophelia toy with her teacup, fingers fidgeting with a tiny chip in the curve of the handle. Over dinner, they had all discussed his visit with Blackwood, the women listening with smiles at Mr. Bone's swashbuckling return to lawyering, and his joy at knowing that his family was safe in the house they had always known, working the land they loved. She seemed to be taking it all in, but now she sat silent, far away.

"Penny for your thoughts, Fee?"

She looked up, owlish eyes blinking slowly at him. "Hmm?"

"Thinking about your father?"

"No," she said slowly. "Well, yes, but only in that I've used up enough time thinking about him, worrying about him, talking about him. I realized today that I'm finished. I think I'd not properly understood that he's had no bearing on me since I left the estate; I thought I was walking away from something, but it turned out I was travelling toward the beginning of my life. *This* life. *Here*." Her words were slow, he could almost see the thoughts forming as she spoke. "I've been free since I got into the wagon with Hannah, but I didn't truly realize that until just now."

Silas reached a hand across the table, letting the tips of his fingers rest against the tips of hers. She blinked again and slid her fingers in between his, squeezing gently. Looking up from their hands, she smiled and said, "It doesn't matter anymore what he does or doesn't do. I'm free of him. And now you are, too."

Silas took a slow breath and looked up. She was watching him, taking everything in, her grey eyes cloudy, but certain. For the first time in many, many months, he felt certain, too.

CHAPTER 34

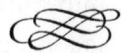

Silas had been back from the estate a week when Ophelia was out in the front field checking the wheat for signs of predation when she heard a clattering of hooves on the cobblestones of the farmyard. She pushed up from her knees and brushed her hands down her tunic, making her way around the farmhouse. She was tucking a stray strand of hair behind her ear when she came into the farmyard. Two large bay horses, dark with sweat, one foaming at the mouth, stood facing her from across the yard. She put a hand up to shield her eyes and took in the arrivals. A younger man accompanied an older and held his horse slightly behind the elder man.

"Get down and find the beasts some water, man," the older man directed, irritably. "Bloody useless fool," he muttered as the younger man swung down from his horse.

"Water, miss?"

"This way." Ophelia turned in the direction of the pump behind her, indicating the large stone trough that was also full. She turned back the second man and watched as he slid awkwardly down from his mount. He moved to lift the reins over his horse's head and the animal shied away from him. She saw spittle fly from his mouth as he cursed the horse's behaviour. Catching the man's face fully for the first time, her stomach twisted with fear; her father threw the reins to his groom and turned to face her.

"Well," he snarled. "Here you are, then."

His face was hard, pulled into a habitual glower, and Ophelia was momentarily surprised she hadn't immediately recognized him. The familiar feeling of a hare snared by his gaze raced through her body. She needed to say something, she could feel his eyes on her, like he was gaining strength with every second she remained quiet.

Ophelia felt sick. "How did you find me?" She felt herself choking on the words. The next came as out as a croak. "What do you want?"

"Larke delivered your location straight to the house, had it right on the front of your letter to the housekeeper. Really, Ophelia, writing to the staff? How simple you are." His voice was acid.

"What do you want?" she repeated. "I've work to do."

"Ah, work is it? Left your own family to hare off here and play farmer," he said, speaking before she could get any more words out. "I'll get right to it then, I've no more time to waste with you." The horses were fussing at the water trough and Blackwood turned to shout back at his groom about settling them. "Blasted idjit," he swore.

"Father," she began.

"Hold your tongue, Ophelia."

She felt her head begin to heat, flames beginning to crackle over the sound of his voice.

"I find I have need of you. A number of the staff had to be let go recently. Despite you being a disgrace to respectable women"—he gestured angrily in the direction of her boots and breeches—"you know the house and what is required." Ophelia wanted to laugh, felt a hysterical bubble rising in her throat. Had her father really just told her she was to return to the estate, run his household for him? "You may start by finding their replacements as soon as you return," he finished.

If the idea of being stuck on the estate with her father, his unwilling helpmeet, weren't so repugnant, she might have let herself laugh at his audacity. *I can't be here, having this conversation again.* Her father took her silence for acquiescence and began speaking again. Ophelia pressed the heels of her hands against her eyes and realized there wasn't even a question in her mind, no doubt that she would ever return nor ever run his household. Taking a breath, she noticed that her heart had stopped racing, her chest no longer strained against that familiar tightness. She felt the firm weight of her feet on the ground, the strength of her legs running up into her waist and chest. She wasn't afraid. Angry, yes, and upset, but not afraid. The knowledge dawned on her like light in a darkened room. She no longer feared him. She saw his anger for what it was; the tantrum of a privileged, ridiculous man grasping at straws to maintain his hold on what little power he had. Ophelia looked at him. He looked like a schoolboy playing at being a man. The shadow he had cast over her shrank the longer she watched him. He had been a giant when she was a girl, had thrown his weight around, and demanded loyalty, but her time away had changed her and instead of a giant, she saw a sad man, alone in a huge house, unloved and uncared for.

"I won't do it, Father," she said over his ramblings about the incompetence of the house staff. He continued as though he hadn't heard her and for a moment she wondered if she had said it aloud at all. "I won't do it, Father," she said again, more firmly.

His fever-bright eyes found hers. "Won't do what, Ophelia?" His voice was quieter now, but still weighted with the same assumed authority.

"Return to the estate to live. Keep house for your benefit," she said as plainly as she could. "You can't bully me into line any longer, I know that I am capable of more. I deserve more than what you have always allowed me. I can, and will, make the decisions about my own life. Your opinions are not welcome."

He laughed then, a menacing chuckle that ran uncomfortably up her spine. He turned his long fingers toward himself, seeming to examine his fingernails. "You'll do as I tell you, daughter. The war will be over soon, along with all this farm nonsense. Traipsing all over the country doing God knows what, you've been avoiding your duty and letting the estate fall into disrepair." He finished with a smug look, as though he had thoroughly trounced her. "Go and change into something appropriate. I intend to return you home today."

Rage and disbelief flooded Ophelia's head for a moment. *The absolute nerve of him, acting as though I'm a child to be ordered about.* She turned away from him, recalling the ribbon of steel threading Mrs. Darling's voice when the War Ag officer had become pushy, how she stood her ground when he attempted intimidation. Then, when she felt in control of her voice, she turned back. "I've learned a lot of things in the time I've been away and the most important ones aren't even to do with farming. I am not afraid of you, Father, nor your threats regarding the estate. If anyone has abandoned their duty, it is you, turning out staff who have served our family for decades, lining your own pockets instead of investing in the land, threatening loyal tenants. It beggars belief."

Merritt's mouth moved soundlessly, his hands working in the air at his sides like claws. "Well, I never—" he spluttered.

"Being here, on this farm with these people, I finally see that the land is a promise to the people it supports, to the country itself, and you have broken that promise just as you broke your promise to Mother—"

"How dare you!" he thundered, anger clouding his face.

"Don't interrupt me when I am speaking," Ophelia said before continuing. "For a long time, I believed that you knew best, that you had the measure of me, but I know now that you have no idea what I'm capable of and I find I no longer care about your opinion of me, good or bad. I am finally free of you. I choose to live my life as I see fit, not according to your rules."

He was silent for a moment. Ophelia felt the blood fizzing in her veins, her heart pounding in her chest. She couldn't remember ever having felt so alive, apart from when she was kissing Silas. She was free. *I've no idea where this will lead, but it's okay. I know that I will be alright, I will be able to figure it out.* Her father's voice cut through her thoughts.

"You always were such a gullible chit, Ophelia. Just like that imbecile of farmhand you spent the summer mooning over." His bulk no longer threatened, but he loomed toward her like a buzzard over a kill.

Ophelia felt sick to her stomach. She thought of Silas and his mother, of his worry over her well-being. She felt embarrassed that Silas had ever thought she might be capable of her father's kind of cruelty.

"He was probably halfway to France before it occurred to him that I could put his ridiculous mother out on her ear regardless of our agreement." The word twisted poisonously in his mouth. "Pah, the muttonhead," he spat. "And you, my dear daughter, are cut from the same cloth, all wide eyes and best foot forward, but no idea of what it takes to survive. You think you've a hope of making your way in the world alone? More fool, you."

"I am making my way in the world. I have been working for more than a year, and the work here means more than anything you could comprehend. These people are my family more than you have ever been. How you threatened the Larkes is unforgivable, I didn't think even you could be so cruel," Ophelia said, throat tight.

"They have been tenants for generations . . ." She just shook her head, speechless with anger.

"I tire of this, Ophelia. Fathers own their daughters until they pass them on to husbands, and I find I still have need of you."

She bit her lip to keep from screaming. The taste of iron centred her. "I'm not surprised you think that way, but I no longer consider myself your chattel, so you'll have to sell something else if you need the money."

She turned away from her father, hands shaking with adrenaline and found Bess was standing in the space between the shed and the house, Hannah beside her. Bess lifted a hand to her mouth at Merritt's cursing and Hannah, disgust written all over her face, threw an arm around the other woman's shoulders, patting brusquely. She gave a sharp nod of her chin to Ophelia. *You can deal with this*, it said. *You are capable.* She nodded back to her friend and then looked to the groom, whose eyes were like saucers in his pale face. She could hear her father getting louder behind her.

"Damn you, Ophelia! Don't walk away from me!"

He grabbed for the reins, yanking when the horse shied away from him.

"There's no need for that, now," came Mrs. Darling's voice from the doorway of the house. "If you've something to say to one of my farmers, you may say it politely or not at all." She hardly raised her voice, but it carried, firm and clear, over Merritt's angry scolding. He froze, and Ophelia saw a horrible, familiar look come over his face. Derision, disbelief at being called out, by a woman, no less.

"Do you address me, madam?" he said, icily.

Mrs. Darling looked around, amused. "Indeed. You and your man here are the only strangers on my property at the moment. As I said, if you've come to make a scene about the women working my land, you'll find the esteemed committee member for the War Ag down in the village, in the pub more'n likely," she finished under her breath. "You can lodge a complaint with 'im."

"You've no right to prevent me from taking my property with me."

"Oh, your property, eh?" Mrs. Darling's mouth curved in a dangerous smile.

"With me now, Ophelia," her father commanded, failing to meet Mrs. Darling's eyes.

"I'm not coming with you, Father. Not now. Not ever." Ophelia stepped closer to Mrs. Darling, Bess and Hannah tightening in at her back. She could feel them all around her, a wall of affection and strength. She had never felt so safe in all her life.

"She's no more your property than mine, sir. That is, not at all. Now take yourself off 'afore I have to call for the constable."

"This is not the end, Ophelia. Don't think you've gotten away with anything."

It is the end.

Her father motioned to his groom, who gave Blackwood a leg up, before swinging up into his own saddle. The horses swung in a circle in the farmyard, Merritt already raising his crop and bringing it down on the bay's rump. It kicked out an elegant hind leg and shot forward, the group disappearing in a cloud of dust. Ophelia let out a shaky breath. He had always been a bully and had gotten away with it because she hadn't stood up to him. The realization was like the wind being knocked out of her; she had always had this power within her.

* * *

THE HUGE BAY was on top of him before he realized what was happening, and Silas only had time to leap into the verge before the horses thundered by. A crouched figure gripped onto the back of the first horse, the second, ridden by a man who shouted, "Pardon!" as they passed. Standing one foot on the lane, one in the grass, Silas sucked in a breath. He adjusted the hoe he was carrying back from the smith's and continued up the lane to the house.

"'S okay, dove," came Mrs. Darling's voice from the yard.

Silas couldn't see anyone yet, but the low murmur of voices layered over each other in concern reached him. His heart thumped unsteadily in his chest and he hurried the last few steps. Ophelia faced away from him, head tucked against Bess's chest as she leaned close to her friend. Bess's arms circled her protectively, and both Hannah and Mrs. Darling were speaking lowly over their heads. He only caught snippets carried on the air; "no right" and "ignorant" and "safe here." His brain emptied of all thought, save one. *Ophelia was hurt.* He dropped the hoe with a thud and when they all turned their heads at the noise, he saw her face. The streaks of tears were visible on her cheeks, but her eyes were sharp and her chin set in the determined way he had come to love.

"Fee?"

"You're back," she cried and listed out of Bess's arms toward him.

Without thinking, he caught her to him and smoothed a hand down her hair to her back. He felt her arms come about his waist and clutch him tightly. He bent his head to take a deep breath against her hair. She smelt of sun, notes of perspiration, and grass rising as he breathed her in.

"What's happened?"

"My father's just been," Ophelia said against his chest. Her voice was low and tired. "He was shouting about failing my family and the estate. I think he truly expected to cow me into leaving."

"Good God, your father is a . . ." Silas faltered, not able to find the words to properly express his anger.

"He was awful, Silas. About wanting me to return to run the house for him, and you and your family."

"Shh, shh, shh, he's gone now, Fee."

Mrs. Darling caught his eye over Ophelia's head and said, "Let's have a cuppa and catch our breath. Like many a man his age, your father has no end of bluster. I think we all need a moment after that performance."

Ophelia let herself be led into the house and Silas trailed after them, wondering how he had managed to stop one wave of Merritt's cruelty only to be swamped by another.

CHAPTER 35

The letter came two weeks later on a day heavy with the heat of impending summer, the blue banner of the sky limitless above them as Ophelia and Silas ran the mower over the first hay field. The wheat fell in long, golden rows behind them, the birds swooping down to scavenge loosened grains or the rodents startled from their shelter. It was hot work, and dusty, but the horses pulled the machinery steadily along, and before the sun was directly overhead, they had cleared a third of the field.

"Hallo!" Mrs. Darling shouted from the gate, brandishing a water jug and a packet of sandwiches.

Ophelia steered Samson and Delilah gratefully toward the row of beeches and came to a halt near the gate.

"Ta," said Silas, scooting off his seat on the reaper and reaching for the proffered jug. He took a quick swig and passed it to Ophelia.

"There's something else," said Mrs. Darling. "This came for you today."

Ophelia took the letter, her stomach falling at the sight of the Blackwood seal affixed to the seam of the envelope. She slid it open.

"... *badly injured in a fall from his horse.*" She swallowed, something like bile rising in her throat. *"No suffering, never regained consciousness..."* She felt herself let her arm fall, the letter hanging from her fingers.

"Fee—"

"I suspected bad news—"

Mrs. Darling and Silas spoke over each other.

"My father is dead." The words sounded hollow in her ears, her mouth dry. "It seems he fell during a ride. He never awoke." She couldn't find it in herself to feel sad, exactly, but she felt suddenly alone in the world. Then Silas's hand was on her shoulder, running down her arm to catch her hand.

"I'm so sorry, Fee. Maybe sit down a minute?" He gestured to the stile in the fence, leading her gently toward it.

Her head felt muzzy, and she wanted to push everything away and keep mowing the field. It was inconvenient to have to think of her father when they had only a week before the War Ag committee member returned to inspect their progress. Ophelia didn't think she could bear if they were judged lacking.

"Damn it," she whispered into her clenched fists. "Damn it all."

Silas and Mrs. Darling looked at each other. "Perhaps it's best to bring the horses in now. The rest of the field'll wait until tomorrow," said Mrs. Darling.

"No, certainly not," Ophelia said, more sharply than she intended. "Only we've the inspection in no time at all, and I know we can get enough in if we just keep on it."

"Suit yourself," said Mrs. Darling, sanguine. "Everyone takes this kind of news in their own stride. When my husband died, I put my head down and I'm sure I didn't look up for a decade." When Ophelia said nothing, she nodded. "I'll let you get on then. See you both for supper."

Silas passed her half a sandwich and led her by the hand to sit on the ground. He didn't press, but she knew he was waiting for her to say something. Finding no words, she bit into the sandwich and felt the brightness of the raspberry jam and cheddar cheese on her tongue.

"I'm so sorry about your father, love," he said quietly, his half of the sandwich sitting on his thigh, still in the wax paper. "No matter what they were to us in life, there is nothing like losing a parent."

Ophelia nodded and couldn't help but think of Silas losing his own father, the stories he had shared, the love he had felt in his father's presence. There was nothing like that with her own father; he had provided the essentials to keep a child alive, but nothing to nurture or care for one. He had viewed his daughter as a possession, a means to an end. There was nothing to feel for him, as far as she was concerned. She wanted to go back and take up the reins again, to forget all about her father and his venomous words, to pretend that nothing but this farm, these people, mattered. But that wasn't true, and she knew it.

He dipped his head and covered her hand with his own. The grass under her palm was cool and she let herself feel the texture of both it, and the comforting weight of Silas's large hand on hers.

"You seem exhausted, love. I know you want to finish the day, but would you let me get you home?"

Ophelia nodded, suddenly wrung completely out.

It seemed the whole house waited for them; Mrs. Darling stood in the farmyard, Hannah and Bess on the bench next to her. Mrs. Darling shaded her eyes as they approached and called them all into the house. Hannah slid the cat in her arms to the ground and unfolded herself gracefully.

"What's the news?" she asked quietly.

Bess slid her arm through Ophelia's. "Are you okay?" she asked, scanning Ophelia's face.

Silas hung back, letting the women enter first, and Ophelia heard the thump of his boots when he removed them.

"My father's been killed in an accident. I've received a letter from Mrs. Greene, the housekeeper, explaining it all."

"Bloody hell, Ophelia. I'm awfully sorry," Hannah said, squeezing her hand.

"Will you have to go back, then?" Bess wanted to know.

"I don't want to, but I think I must," Ophelia said, leaning into her friend's shoulder. "There's no one else to deal with the estate, nor get the staff situated elsewhere. I can't just leave them to fend for themselves. I won't know for sure until I can speak with a solicitor about the will. I'm hoping Mr. Bone might be willing to help me."

Both women nodded. "Be sure to give a good reference, that'll be the most help to them," Hannah said. "Everything hinges on the reference when you're in service."

Ophelia nodded and folded into a chair at the table and felt her farm family close around her. Mrs. Darling poured tea into cups, Hannah pushed a cup each toward her and Bess, and she heard Silas rustling around in the pantry. Returning to the estate was the last thing she wanted to do, and it wasn't only the harvest that weighed on her mind; she and Silas were . . . well, she wasn't actually sure what they were or what they might be. It felt like the wrong time to be going though.

When all five of them had discussed how the work might continue in Ophelia's absence and worried through things she might face at her father's house, the other women retired to bed. In the dark kitchen, Silas rose and stood behind her chair.

"I wish I didn't have to go back to the estate," she into the dark room. "I'd like to let him vanish without a single thought . . . but I've accused him of ignoring the people and the estate, and it would be wrong of me to do the same thing. As far as I know, I am all that remains of our family, and I think that might mean that I will inherit the estate," she said, the thought so absurd she wanted to laugh. "What am I supposed to do with that now, Silas?"

"It feels like a right bloody mess at the moment," Silas said soothingly, his strong fingers pressing into the knots of her shoulders. "I suppose there is more to it than I understand, but we can figure it out."

She nodded, miserable. It felt strange and empty to be utterly alone, the only one left from her small, unhappy family.

She rested her head back against Silas and let the sadness wash over her.

"Would you like me to come with you, Fee?"

She wanted to say yes, but knew she couldn't. "I want you to come, but it's more important that you stay to meet the War Ag requirements, Silas. We only have a few weeks until the inspection, and I can't even think about leaving Mrs. Darling without your help. Promise me you'll stay?"

"I promise, but I'm worried sick about you going on your own, Fee."

"I'll be fine, Silas. It's only the estate, not the other side of the world, and without my father, there's no threat to me. But I will write, I promise. I should be there tomorrow night, and I will send word when I have a sense of how long it all might take. A fortnight, I should think."

"Thank you." He pressed a kiss to the top of her head. "I miss you already," he whispered against her hair, before leaving through the kitchen door.

Ophelia sat looking across the table at the stove, not seeing the bright embers fade to ash, while her tea grew cold in the cup. She wanted to soak up every second she could of this house, the farm. She was afraid to leave Mrs. Darling's farm, worried that it was the talisman that prevented her from being swallowed up by the estate. She felt safe here and didn't want to give that up to face her father's mess. Finally, hours later, she stood, legs stiff, chest tight, and instead of climbing the stairs, crept to Silas's room in the barn. She shed her uniform and climbed under the eiderdown. He hugged her to his warm body, chest to back, and she fell asleep to the sound of his breath in her hair.

CHAPTER 36

The first days of Ophelia's absence were hard enough, but by the time the second week was crawling toward him, Silas felt he might go mad. He missed her at all hours of the day, inconveniently; the sound of the horses in their traces reminded him of her capability, the empty chair at meals, her conversation, the Ophelia-scented spot on his pillow, her body under his. It was all a bloody disaster. Her letters had come, just as she promised, but they spoke mostly of the tangle of the estate. Her father had gambled away much of the land, and the estate was in significant debt. She wrote that Mr. Bone was looking through her father and mother's wills and had promised to have news within a few days. Silas hoped that at least that part of her family might be straightforward.

A new letter sat waiting for him when he returned for lunch from the field where he was repairing fences. His heart lifted to see Ophelia's handwriting and he broke the seal quickly.

Dear Silas,

I received your letter by the afternoon post the day before last and have been carrying it with me so that I might reread it at my leisure. It seems to me that if you are unable to make a living farming, there is good potential for you as a romantic novelist; your words made me positively shiver. I miss you more than I thought possible; everything here reminds me of you and what you sacrificed for my sake. I wish we could take one of our old walks and talk everything through. I await word from Mr. Bone, but in the meantime, Mrs. Greene and I are packing up the house and putting aside anything that might be of value to be sold. It is a sobering thing to be here again under these circumstances, and I can't help but wish that this house, the land, might be put to better use than it has been under my father. I will write as soon as I hear from Mr. Bone.

Yours, yours, yours,
Ophelia

PS: Give my love to Bess, Hannah, and Mrs. Darling.

HE TUCKED it into the pocket of his trousers, sliding the slim paper down against his thigh so it wouldn't slip out while he was working. Finishing the last bite of his bread, he was rising from the table when Bess and Hannah came into the kitchen. They clattered about pouring tea, cutting bread and cheese, settling themselves at the table.

"Any letter today?" Hannah asked. "You and Ophelia are surely keeping the Royal Mail in business lately."

Bess and Silas laughed. "One from her today, as it happens."

"How are things progressing with the estate?" Bess asked.

"About the same, it seems. She and Mrs. Greene are making headway and there's no word from Mr. Bone yet. She said she misses you all," he added. "It's hard for her to be there alone, all those bad memories."

"I know Ophelia a little now, and she's not one to shirk her duties," said Bess.

"There's more than just her father's death in those buildings," said Hannah. "She'll be properly closing the door on her old life, if I had to guess."

Silas nodded, trying to understand the shorthand that seemed to pass between the friends. He should have understood from their conversations that Ophelia would want to finish this off neatly; it was not only the bad memories of her father there, but also her mother's legacy. He had thought that he might take on the burdens of her life for her; take on her father, protect her from what Merritt was capable of doing to hurt her, but she didn't need him to shield her from her life. Ophelia needed him to support her in it, to take the journey with her, not instead of her. He wanted to tell her that he understood now, and that he could see that he needed her beside him, too. The war and his injury had shattered his confidence, made him doubt what he had to offer, but in his time on the farm, he had realized that he could be flexible, could adopt new ways of thinking, understand his role as a man differently.

"You're right, Hannah," he said, something coalescing in his mind. "And I want to be there with her when she opens the door to her new one."

"Course you do." Hannah's smile was crooked and kind. "Been wondering when you'd realize it."

"You could be there and back in two days, so the inspection could still go as planned. If we keep the horses fed and watered while you're away, we could pick up again as soon as you're back," Bess offered.

"Thank you both so much."

"We're happy to." She lifted her teacup to Silas in a mock salute and winked.

He laughed and returned the gesture. "Best speak with Mrs. D. about this, then."

***

THE FOLLOWING MORNING, they all breakfasted together, reminding each other of any tasks that needed looking to while both he and Ophelia were away. Mrs. Darling seemed as excited and nervous as he felt and kept assuring herself that he had everything he needed. Silas returned to the house from his room with his satchel to find Hannah standing at the kitchen door. She had an odd look on her face.

"What is it, Hann—" he began.

"I don't know if you've need of a token," Hannah blurted, cheeks pink, "but I thought this might be useful." She pushed a thin silver band into Silas's hand. "'Twas mine when I were in the movement in London, and I thought Ophelia might appreciate the sentiment. Only if you feel the same, o' course," she added hastily.

Silas looked at the slender band in his palm, noticing an inscription on the inside of the metal. Lifting it, he made out "deeds not words" in minute script. He looked up to Hannah's face, stern, but also expectant, with a softness in her eyes that he was beginning to notice more often.

"It's lovely, Hannah . . . I don't know what to say. Are you sure you're willing to part with it?"

"I'm sure," she said, pressing his hand closed around it. "Ophelia is lucky to be loved by you, for you do love her, don't you?" She waved her hand when his face heated. "It's none of my business, really, but it was a new beginning for me when I got this ring, perhaps it can be the same for the two of you?"

He thought about this silver encircling Ophelia's finger, about what it meant to belong to another person, how one might ask another to share themselves, their future, their body. He wondered if a ring like this, given in friendship, could be a token of something new, not a marriage born of the past? It occurred to him that he might offer his protection not to provision a house or shield

Ophelia from strife, but to provide room for her to be herself, to discover all she could be in a world that wanted to infringe on her with demands and expectations. Perhaps, he could be her champion instead of her husband. Silas wondered what she imagined their future might look like without the bonds of marriage. He tended to be more comfortable with known situations, boundaries he could see, and this was one more instance where Ophelia was asking him to step out into the void with her. To his surprise, he found himself excited to ask her what she saw for them. He felt himself smiling, a bloom of warmth spreading through his chest.

"Thank you," he said with a laugh. He grasped her strong hand in his and squeezed. "Thank you, Hannah."

She nodded, smiling broadly. "You're a good man, Silas Larke. To be sure, men are not of interest to me generally, but in you I begin to see the appeal."

Silas slipped the ring in his waistcoat pocket, picked up his case, and nodding to Hannah, hurried out the door. He could hear Mrs. Darling and Bess calling "Good luck!" as he headed down the drive.

CHAPTER 37

It took a good part of the day to reach Wood Grange and the sun was sitting low in the sky as Silas headed along the long drive up to the estate house. His body sparked with nervous energy, the long train ride not having dissipated any worries he had about speaking with Ophelia. He moved steadily onward, passing along hedgerows and fields as familiar as the back of his own hands. The ancient oak that marked the turn past his family's house and down toward the big house loomed ahead, and Silas felt grateful he had seen his mother so recently. The weight of the tenancy had been a heavy one, and it felt wonderful to know that Samuel and his mother were tucked into their house, safe and secure as they should be. He couldn't wait to be able to visit them again without the spectre of Blackwood hanging over them.

Right now, he needed to find Ophelia and tell her that he loved her. The words he had been turning over in his mind the entire train journey ricocheted around his chest like caged birds. This desperate aching need to be near her, to watch her work and laugh, to touch her whenever she was within reach. It seemed so obvious now; how could he have mistaken it for anything else? He laughed aloud, his voice ringing in the country afternoon, and did an awkward little jig step, his body suddenly impossibly light. Passing under the oak, he lengthened his stride, covering the distance to the main house as quickly as possible. He arrived at the front door slightly out of breath and thinking it unlikely any of the staff was still about, turned toward the high green hedge that enclosed the kitchen garden at the side of the house. The wooden plank door in the hedge opened on silent hinges, but when he let go of the handle and stepped through, the door swung wide and crashed into a stack of terra-cotta pots, toppling them with a smash. A shriek drew his attention. On the bench under a window, nearly hidden by the wisteria slowly taking over the first floor of the house, was Ophelia, her knees still drawn up to avoid being hit by the avalanche of pots. She looked horrified, her cheeks hot, her eyes reddened.

"Fee?" Silas stammered, caught off guard. Relief crashed through his body and it took every ounce of restraint not to crush her to him.

"Silas!" she cried in surprise and bolted up from her seat on the bench.

"I know you don't need me here, but I had to see you, Fee," he said, still trying to find his bearings. Words rising to his lips almost faster than he could think them through. "The longer you were gone, the less I could bear that you were facing this task without knowing..."

She walked toward him. "Without knowing what?"

He tried to recover some of his composure, but his heart was banging at his ribs and he didn't think he had ever seen anything as beautiful as Ophelia standing in this abandoned kitchen garden. She had disposed of her WLA uniform and wore a grey pinstriped skirt he recognized from before. An embroidered shawl hung loose around her shoulders, a whitework blouse buttoned primly up the side of her elegant neck. He wanted to reach out and touch her cheek so badly his fingers itched. The stood awkwardly for a moment before Silas remembered what he had come to say.

"I've had almost a fortnight to think and I realized how wrong I've been; I haven't been able to let go of the idea of protecting you, clung too hard to what's past. I was afraid this injury had broken me, that I couldn't protect you, and what good was I then? It blinded me to what I can offer; companionship, a champion in equality, a promise to withstand the storms beside you. I can shield your dreams, help you with the privilege of this body, scarred as it is. Until women's bodies and minds command the same respect as men's, I will use mine in your stead."

Silas took a deep breath and met Ophelia's eyes. She was watching him, taking everything in, her grey eyes cloudy and uncertain.

"The thing is, Fee . . . I don't care about the land, certainly not the way I care for you. I'll walk away and not look back, we can start somewhere new . . . anywhere you choose. You are everything to me. I love you."

He felt her gasp and then her hands were reaching for him, and she was looking at him, surprise and joy warring in her eyes.

"This summer you taught me we can make anything we want, a family, a farm, a partnership, or nothing at all but two bodies pressed together for a space of hours."

"Silas," Ophelia breathed, tears pooling in her eyes. A silvery trail snaked down one cheek and slid into the crook of her smile. "Say it again. Say it all again." She laughed and reached for the collar of his coat to pull him toward her. "I don't want what your parents or mine had, and you're right that I don't wish you to live like a shadow, hovering around me in case something goes wrong. It will, probably many, many times and all I want is you right beside me, facing it all together."

Silas leaned forward, his mouth millimetres from Ophelia's,

feeling the warmth of their breath mingling between their mouths. "I can do that. I *want* that," he whispered.

She let go of his lapel to reach a hand up to his face, pushing a few strands of hair back off his forehead, then running her palm down the plane of his cheek and along his jaw. He growled in satisfaction, wanting to push into her cupped hand like a house cat.

"Come here," she said and pulled him to her, arms surprising and strong around his back.

Silas laughed and wrapped both arms around her, feeling his blood leap at the long, lithe body pressed eagerly against his.

"God, but I love you, Silas Larke. Thank you for coming all this way to tell me," she said with a glorious smile.

"I'd go to the ends of the earth, Fee. Truly."

"I know, but luckily you only had to go across Somerset." And then she pressed up on her toes and kissed him.

CHAPTER 38

Ophelia smiled against Silas's lips and pulled her arms tighter around his broad back. He felt heavenly; warm and solid, the linen of his shirt and waistcoat rumpled from travel, his cheek against her hair rough with a day's stubble. It all spoke to the rush in which he had left the farm, a rush to find *her*, and Ophelia couldn't help the flush of happiness that unwound in her chest. She slid her arms farther up Silas's back to loop them around his neck and deepened their kiss. He sighed into her mouth and tightened his grip on her, lifting her right off her feet. She liked the feeling of weightlessness and wriggled against him, trying to get even closer. Silas drew back, his eyes impossibly dark green.

"God's sake, woman, I love you, but I'll not ravish you in public," he said.

"As it happens, I know this place quite well. There's a nice quiet spot just back here," she said, looking back at him with what she hoped was a saucy smile.

The kitchen garden had an air of elegant abandonment; the leafy structure of boxwood and yew topiary still visible among perennials gone to seed, the fruit trees left unpruned. But the sturdy oak bench still sat by the back door, and it was here that Ophelia guided him. Silas sat down, taking in the garden, and she knew he was seeing the bones still there under the overgrown shrubs and bolting perennials. He turned to her and she squeezed his hand. She looked down at their hands twined on his thigh, the woollen fabric pulled tight against the muscles of his leg. He rubbed his thumb down the length of hers sending a flash of desire through her.

"How have you found it, being back here?"

The damp of the garden bench wound through the thin layers of her skirts and Ophelia missed the feeling of her legs in trousers, missed the movement available in her WLA uniform. She felt smaller and more vulnerable in these clothes.

"It is hard," she admitted. "After we finished packing up the things that might be sold, I suggested Mrs. Greene take a week or so to visit family. I paid her as much as I could to cover her time away, but there's not really much to pay her with, honestly."

She twisted a finger in the volume of her skirts.

"It seems my father has gambled away a good deal of what was valuable. I've had letters from Mr. Bone in the last day or two laying out a way forward. It seems I am to inherit the estate, well the house and the grounds, at least, and he thinks that selling some parcels of land will be enough to cover the cost to get the house going again."

"Ah, Jesus, Fee. I'm sorry about the way your father left things."

"Me, too," she said. "Makes me feel uncertain all over, perhaps I'm not equal to what I've chosen to do? Taking on the estate was not what I envisioned when I left."

It was hard to admit that she wasn't sure she could live independently as she hoped, to admit she was glad of his help, his company.

Silas squeezed her hand and spreading her fingers out over his thigh, threaded her fingers with his, making a fist. "You are living independently, have already been doing it. A death is no small thing to face on one's own, nor is resolving a will, especially one that has what I imagine are tangled legal dealings, but you will handle it with grace, as you do all things. And," he said more slowly, "if you want, I will be here with you."

"Yes," she said, then more firmly, "I thought I needed to do this alone to prove that I am independent, but I was wrong. I do want your support and I'm finally realizing those things aren't mutually exclusive. I don't feel much love for my father, but closing up the house, selling the few belongings my mother collected, that feels lonely. I'm so glad you've come."

He nodded and squeezed her hand again. She pressed her thigh closer to his, wanting to feel the warm strength of him, the steadiness of his presence. She could count on him, he had told her so much with words and deeds.

"What you said before, about loving me . . . do you think you might still feel that way in the future? What I mean to say is . . ." He was watching her with those deep green eyes, golden at the edges, somehow soft and sharp all at the same time. She forged on. "I mean, could you love me, stay with me knowing that I may never want to be married? That I might always want to work on a farm or at some other vocation?"

To her surprise, Silas came to his knees in front of her, hands resting splayed over the fabric pulled tight across his thighs. For a breathless second, he knelt with head bowed, wheaten strands falling forward, then he looked up at her. His green eyes were anguished and she felt herself falling into their stormy depths, felt her fingers itch to caress the pale skin taut over his high cheekbones. Ophelia watched Silas's mouth work for a moment, forming and then abandoning words. He blew out a long breath.

"My love, my Fee. I have been wrong about so many things,

worrying about my place in the world after war and in suffrage, not able to see the truth you've found in it, afraid to imagine a different way of seeing the world, afraid of what I might lose." His hands flexed on his thighs and he sat back, shaking his head. "I thought this place, this land was important, was the thing that made my parents work, made their marriage a thing of joy, but living at the farm with you and seeing you working with the WLA, Mrs. Darling, the horses even . . . it's not the land, but the people who make a place whole. You could be in the Arctic or a desert and if I were with you, it would be home. You are my home, I don't want to be anywhere you are not . . . ever." He paused and she pressed her fingers to her lips to keep from breaking the spell he cast. "Whatever future you want to build, I want to help. It doesn't matter to me if it means marriage or not, something others recognise or not . . . I want *you*, Fee, and I'll take you anyway you come. To hell with everything else."

A robin swept down from the stone wall at the far end of the garden and Ophelia blinked, her vision marbled with tears. She slithered off the bench and landed awkwardly in Silas's lap, straddling his knees. He cupped her face in his hands. They were warm and rough against her cheeks, along the line of her jaw, and she felt the damp of her tears gathering in his palms. Stroking his thumbs across her cheekbones, he regarded her seriously, waiting.

"To hell with everything else . . ." she echoed, Silas's words still spinning around her head. Another stroke of his thumbs across her cheeks, the gentle pressure of his firm, blunt fingertips at the back of her head. "I want . . ." She paused and ran her hands up Silas's chest, hooking her fingers under the lapels of his waistcoat, possibility and hope igniting within her. "I want us . . . I don't know what to ask for yet, I only know I want to try to be equals, going forward together, side by side. Could you want that, too?"

"Yes," he breathed, his forehead sinking to rest against hers.

"Yes." He angled her chin with his hands to press a kiss to her lips, soft and chaste. "Yes."

Ophelia pressed her lips together, relishing the taste of Silas that lingered there. Lifting her chin, she pressed a kiss of her own to his mouth. Watching his eyelids flutter closed, she said, "I've been thinking over Bone's letters the last few days, trying to see a way forward and I keep wondering what if we didn't leave here, but we did something different, made something better with the estate, with the land? Something of our own."

The words hung for a moment between them, then Silas kissed each of her eyelids whispering, "Yes."

"Silas?" Ophelia said.

"Hmm?"

"Make love to me?"

He didn't answer, just hauled her farther up onto his thighs, one large hand possessively spread over her backside, the other threading through her hair, loosening it from its chignon. Having freed most of the dark hair from its pins, he lifted a handful and ran it across his lips and cheek. "Like satin," he growled. "God, I've missed you."

Ophelia laughed. "It feels like we've been apart a year."

"True," he said, his voice rough as gravel. "And every moment hellish."

She squeezed her thighs together, giddy with surprise and desire, drunk on the possibility of she and Silas for real, and felt a slow heat kindle as the muscles of her legs contracted around Silas's. He growled again and dropping his handful of hair, dipped his head to cover her mouth with his. His fingers flexed against the curve of her bottom, each fingertip a point of fire through her layers of skirts and petticoats. Ophelia scooted closer to him, settling herself on what she could feel was an already firm erection. The rasp of Silas's woollen trousers against the skin of her inner thighs sent a flood of warmth to her centre, and she sighed at the press of his lips against hers. His tongue flickered against the seam of her mouth, teasing at the corner, and Ophelia opened, sliding her own tongue against his, slick and warm. Silas's arm tightened across her back and he deepened the kiss, teeth and lips sliding over each other in a desperate bid to come closer. Ophelia rocked against him, her hands skimming up his back to wrap around his neck, one sliding into the silk of his hair. His hand had begun to fiddle at the buttons down the side of her neck.

"Fee," Silas hissed, pulling back from the kiss to the press his face into her neck. "Ah, God, I love you."

"Mhmm," she murmured letting her head fall back so that Silas could work his way along her now exposed neck, teeth careful against her skin. Everywhere he nipped, he soothed with a soft kiss, raising the tiny hairs all over her body and drawing her nipples to aching points. He peeled back the sides of her blouse as far as they would go, revealing her right collarbone, and ran the tip of his tongue along the ridge, licking into the hollow at the base of her throat and pressing an open-mouthed kiss there. A hot, white star burst in Ophelia's chest sending tendrils of light and heat along her limbs. She wanted Silas's mouth everywhere at once, wanted to press herself as close as possible to his quiet strength, which she could feel vibrating like an animal at the end of its leash. She gently closed the fingers of the hand in his hair at the nape of his neck, pulling just enough to elicit a grunt of pleasure from him. He raised his head from her chest, eyes all dark pupil, lips damp and swollen.

"Too many clothes," Ophelia said, breath choppy, letting go of Silas's hair to pull her blouse loose from her waistband. She raised her hands so that he could release the buttons at her wrists, then lifted the shirt over her head, laughing out a screech when a button tangled in her hair, pulling sharply at her scalp.

"Sorry, love, just a moment," Silas soothed, his large hands delicately undoing the tangle and tossing the blouse onto the bench behind her.

Ophelia flexed her shoulders and reached for Silas, who ran a hand up the outside of her arms, then placed a firm kiss to the ball of each shoulder. "I love this," he said, lips against the muscles of her shoulder. "And this." He ran his tongue down the line of her bicep, lifting up her hand so he could press his lips to the sensitive flesh on the inside of her arm. Ophelia sucked in a breath and began to pull her arm back. "Don't ever hide this strength, Fee," he said. "You're glowing with it, a glorious goddess."

The words ran like warm honey through her and she relaxed her arm, allowing him to kiss his way back up to her shoulder. With her free hand, she began loosening the buttons on his waistcoat, desperate for the feel of his skin.

"I don't love this," he growled running his finger along the line of her corset, hooking one into the laces. "Makes it hard to touch you." His eyes were hooded and dark, and anticipation shivered through Ophelia.

"Well, sir," she said, smiling at his playful frown, "you'll need to help me with that," and began to turn in his arms. Before the words were entirely out, Silas had shifted her to her knees in front of him, and his broad chest against her back, placed her hands on the bench in front of them.

"Silas," she said on a reedy breath, lust and excitement careening through her body. Everything she touched felt electric, the rough wood under her hands, the band of her corset now cutting into the flesh of her breasts as they rose and fell, the fabric of her skirts bunched around her legs and under her knees, the scratchy heat of Silas's trousers moving against the backs of her calves as he knelt between her legs. His breath at her ear moved the hair against her neck and she shivered.

"May I continue?" he rasped out, his voice catching on every nerve ending in her body. It was all she could do to nod. "Say it aloud, Fee, so I know."

"Continue . . ." she whispered, "please . . . Silas."

His name seemed to unlock him and he moved quickly, hands undoing the knotted cord, his fingers dancing along the length of her spine, pulling at the laces until she felt the corset loosen. Silas pressed a kiss between her shoulder blades and pulled her upright.

"You're the most beautiful package I've ever opened," he murmured against her back. "I can't wait to see what's inside." Then he reached around her with both arms and gently unhooked the metal clasps holding the top of the corset closed. Ophelia leaned back against him and arched her back, enjoying the brush of her chemise against her unbound breasts. Silas slipped a hand inside the open corset and peeled it away from her body, laying it on top of her blouse. Then he cupped one breast in each hand, testing their weight, rubbing a thumb across each nipple.

"Oh, I—" Ophelia began, then lost her train of thought when Silas rolled each nipple between thumb and forefinger with surprising expertise. Pain and pleasure collided, stealing through her body to pool low in her belly, hot and sweet.

"Sweet, strong girl," Silas rumbled, lips brushing along her shoulders to the soft spot where her neck met her shoulder. "*My strong girl*," he said sucking gently at the crook of her neck. Ophelia shivered at the possessive, wondering if she liked it entirely too much. But then Silas whispered "strong" again as he ran his hands down her back to the bulk of her skirts and she knew she liked that part even more.

* * *

SILAS COULDN'T SEEM to pull enough air into his lungs, every breath came fast and hard, and he felt a twinge of hysteria flickering at the edge of his awareness. He focused on his hands, watched their tanned backs move to fan over the curves of Ophelia's waist, watched his fingers curl into the firm flesh of her hips through the fabric of her skirts. *This isn't helping*, he thought, as desire threatened to swamp him. His cock and his heart seem to pulse in time and it was all he could do to stop himself from rushing to bury himself in Ophelia's wet heat. *Be a bloody gentleman.* But he wasn't, couldn't be when this woman was involved. Her back flexed in front of him, the sinews of muscle along her spine and shoulders bunching and releasing as she swayed, pressing her arse into his groin, her hands grasping at the wooden bench in front of her, a soft moan on what he imagined were parted lips.

"Christ above," he muttered. "Fee . . ."

Silas reached down, sliding his hands under the pinstriped fabric, skimmed up the outside of her legs, the mass of her skirts bunching up at his elbows. He felt the soft cotton of her stockings at her ankles, the wrinkle of fabric at Ophelia's bent knees, then, under the legs of her pantaloons, the warm satin of her bare thigh. "Jesus," he growled and sat back on his heels.

Ophelia panted and whimpered in front of him, her bottom swaying, back arching in a criminally tempting manner. She turned to look over her shoulder and Silas feared he would come in his trousers at the haze of desire and anticipation he saw in her eyes. She reached behind her and under her skirts to squeeze one of his hands currently tracing lazy circles on her downy thigh.

"I want—" he began. "Need to see you, love."

Watcing him over her shoulder, she nodded eagerly. "I wish you would," she whispered and pushed backward against his hands.

His mind scrambled and the hysteria threatened again, so he flexed his palms against Ophelia's warm skin and felt her muscular thighs tense as she widened their stance. Silas pushed her skirts up to her waist, making sure they didn't crowd her, and then he wanted to pinch himself because he was rewarded with the most lust-addling image he could have ever conjured. Demure pantaloons, rucked up her legs, exposing stockings straining at the clasp of her garters, the garters themselves pulled snug against the curve of her arse, the split in the pantaloons revealing the high, hard moons of her backside and between them, a slice of her dark curls and wet sex.

"Silas?" Her voice wavered between desire and uncertainty and he answered quickly.

"Yes, love, I'm here." He ran a finger over the curve of one buttock, gentle, reverent. "Just cannot think for your beauty at the moment..."

She laughed, low and throaty, and he wanted to hear it every day for the rest of his life. He thought about all the things he had always considered important; duty, land, family, and knew he would burn them all to the ground to keep this woman. He leaned forward to kiss her behind the ear, ran his tongue around the tip of the soft lobe.

"My glorious, glorious, Fee. I'm going to lose my mind if I don't touch you... May I?"

She nodded, and he felt her back under his chest, rising and falling with shuddering breaths. Sitting back on his heels again, he swept a hand up the back of her thigh, sliding his fingers along the slit of her drawers, tracing the curve of her bottom, feeling a shiver of anticipation rise across her skin.

"Please," Ophelia mumbled, dropping her head between her outstretched arms. "Please."

Grasping the curve of her hip, Silas ran a finger along the seam of her vulva, the lips slippery and soft, so bloody soft. Ophelia's back sagged and he tightened his grip on her hip to hold her. Front to back, he ran one, then two fingers along her sex, slowly pressing against her hot flesh.

"Talk to me, Fee," he gasped, his cock impossibly hard at Ophelia's writhing and gasping. "I want to hear your voice, love."

"That's good," she ground out. "Your fingers, it feels so good."

And then she was pushing back into his hand so that his fingers parted her lips and on the next swipe he sank a finger inside her. Just like the previous times, it was nothing he could ever describe and his mind reeled. He never wanted to not be surrounded by Ophelia, the wet heat of her body, her hoarse cry wavering in the quiet of the garden. However she imagined their future, he wanted to be there beside her when she made her mark on the world, celebrating her every chance he had.

CHAPTER 39

*B*irdsong lingered in the air, damp seeped from the ground up into the fabric pleated under her knees, and Silas muttered beautiful, filthy praise behind her, half curse, half song. She gave herself over entirely to sensation, let his voice, stone-rough, lick over her skin like she hoped his tongue would soon enough. His fingers were thick and blunt inside her, stroking, coaxing her toward a familiar peak, and she found herself grinding back into him, seeking purchase, the apex of her thighs already slippery with desire. His hand on her hip was almost painful, fingers flexing with each caress.

Looking over her shoulder, she watched Silas. His neck was taut, the corded muscles standing out along the tanned column, and his hair, thrown into disarray when they kissed, hung in loose golden tendrils over his brow. But it was his eyes that she could not look away from. Pupils dark as pitch, they were wild and hungry, focused entirely on her reactions as he explored her. She whimpered at the intensity of his attention and his eyes snapped to hers. If she hadn't trusted him implicitly, the ferocity of his stare might have frightened her. As it was, she felt a flood of desire between her legs and an answering groan from Silas.

"My God, woman, you'll kill me with your beauty . . . sweet, Fee." His smile was crooked and lupine, his voice low, eyes softening. "And I'll not utter a word of complaint."

Ophelia suddenly couldn't stand the distance between them a moment longer. She wanted Silas's warm skin under her hands, wanted him inside her, filling the aching void that grew with every stroke of his fingers. She had spent so long feeling wrong, that there was no place for her. Too much, too awkward, all wrong for her world, but in this moment, with Silas, she felt just right, fit perfectly. She knew, for perhaps the first time, that she could call this pleasure to herself, revel in a man whose own fulfilment was predicated on hers. And she found she didn't want to wait any longer, had put off claiming herself for too long. So she said out loud what she had only imagined in her head.

"I want . . ." she said, and straightening and pressing her back to Silas's chest, she reached for his hand, stilled by her movement.

"Anything . . . tell me, love."

"Give me your hand for a minute," she said. He slid his fingers from inside her and she felt her own wetness on them when she coasted his hand across her hip, over the softness of her belly, to the apex of her thighs. "Here."

"Show me again," Silas said, nuzzling the nape of her neck.

Ophelia fitted her smaller hand over his, her fingers guiding him in long, slow circles over herself. Ever the quick learner, he paid attention to each small change in pressure, every place that made her shudder.

"Brilliant woman," he murmured. "Sweetest"—a nip at her neck—"most radiant"—he pressed a kiss to her shoulder—"Ophelia." He slid his free hand from her hip to cup her breast, lifting and kneading.

Ophelia pressed her fingers against his, against her, harder, faster until their hands moved as one, frenzied and uncoordinated. Silas was breathing heavy against her ear, his erection hard at her backside, thrusting against her in time to their hands under her skirts. Desire wound tight as a noose around her, blacking out the edges of her vision. She felt held, cradled by Silas's attention, seen in a way she hadn't known was possible. Of all the things she had wanted for herself, taken steps toward, she hadn't really understood how finding pleasure in her own body would illuminate everything else. Now, hovering on the edge of her orgasm, she felt completely free. Flying into something entirely new, Silas at her side, urging her on.

"Let me feel you come, Fee . . . please," he ground out, pressing open-mouthed kisses behind her ear, breath hot and sharp.

"Mhmm, just like that," she whispered, turning her face back to him, feeling her breath catch as every muscle in her body tightened, her thighs shuddering with the effort it took to stay upright. Silas tightened his arm around her waist, holding her steady as he worked her toward the inevitable release. It came hard and slow, pulsing through every nerve ending, pleasure so bright and sharp it verged on pain, and she cried out, a low keening wail that he swallowed with a clumsy kiss. His lips were gentle, coaxing yet more pleasure from her, his fingers slowing, but not stopping as the orgasm rippled through her. Her hand on his was limp, but he didn't need her instruction anymore, had learned what drew pleasure from her like song from an instrument. His fingers were wet with her, slippery on her clit, and he whispered words of praise when she bucked against his fingers. Words like "more" and "wet" and "beautiful" and "please." She spun out into the pleasure of her orgasm and he caught her, held her while she returned to her body, kissing her softly at the temple, brushing her hair back from her sweaty brow.

Ophelia slumped back against Silas, fully sitting in his lap, her body boneless and sated, quivers still running like electric current under her skin. Of all the ways Ophelia had allowed herself to think of making love to Silas, it had never once occurred to her that it might find her bent over a bench in a dilapidated garden. Now that she was here though, his fingers working their steady magic between her legs, her heartbeat pounding in her ears, breaths dragging out of her too-tight chest, she couldn't imagine anything else.

"Silas," was all she said, turning in his arms, while they scrambled up to the bench, laughing at their stiff knees, her skirts in disarray, Silas's movements hobbled by a distractingly large erection. He adjusted his trousers to sit and pulled her to sit astride his legs, bare legs dangling on either side of his. Ophelia reached out to stroke his length through the fabric.

"May I?" she asked, hand at the buttons of his fly.

The column of his throat worked and he nodded, eyes on hers. She licked over the dry pad of her bottom lip and Silas's eyes followed the movement, a starving man at a banquet.

"That's mine to lick," he said, hoarsely, tracing her bottom lip with a rough thumb. Then leaning forward, he caught it between his teeth, nipping gently. Ophelia's hands were clumsy at his groin, fingers catching and losing the buttons as his teeth worried her lip and he licked into her panting mouth.

"Shall I help you with that?" he asked, winking at her.

She laughed and nodded, leaning back to make room for him. Trousers undone, Ophelia parted the fabric, humming a satisfied noise at the sight of his cock, the solid length rising from the shadows of smalls and trousers, the smooth, flushed head, only just contained by his foreskin, already beaded with moisture. She stroked gently along one side and down the other, still surprised at the satiny give of his skin there. She liked how it moved over his rigid length, almost as slippery in her hand as she was between her legs. Silas groaned her name, running a hand along the outside of her leg and up to her hip.

"You like that, hmm?" she said, curious and proud of drawing out his pleasure.

"So much . . . so fucking much, Fee," he said, jaw clenched.

She stroked him again. Down. And up. Watching his face, beautiful and tense, his hands gripping the edge of the bench. And then her hand on him, the way he had begun tiny thrusts up into her fist, his leg muscles moving under her. She rocked into him, echoing his movements and his eyes snapped to hers, their mossy depths taking her breath away. She couldn't imagine loving anything more than the sight of Silas abandoned to pleasure, all the lines of worry and care gone slack, a sheen of perspiration across his sharp cheekbones, his lips swollen from kissing, her name falling like a mantra from his mouth.

"Silas," she said, not slowing her hand. When he met her eyes she lost her train of thought for a moment. "Inside me . . . I want you inside me again."

"Ah, Christ, Fee," he growled. "Yes . . . yes . . . I'm half wild with wanting you."

He moved so quickly she squealed, hands on her hips raising her over him, taking himself in hand once she was steady, one hand on his shoulder.

"Take your time, love. Go as slowly as you like, I'll hold as still as I'm able." He looked up into her face, smiling softly, pupils blown wide, and she found herself teary, overwhelmed with the gift of him. "Fee, what's wrong? Have I hurt you?" he asked, brows drawing together.

"No, not at all." She sniffed. "Just the opposite, you are exquisite, wonderful in ways I never imagined. I can't quite believe you are to be mine." She blinked down at him, feeling the warm mass of his shoulder under her hand, the lean length of his thighs against the insides of her knees, and knew she was home.

"I *am* quite wonderful," Silas said with a wolfish grin. "Not as patient as I ought to be, though," he said, mouthing her nipple through the thin lawn of her chemise, the head of his cock notching at her entrance.

"Oh," said Ophelia. "Oh . . . oh."

She exhaled and let herself sink down onto him. Silas groaned low in his throat, stroking her cheek and bending his head to kiss along the neckline of her chemise. She rose up a little, drawing another groan from him, then sank down, taking his full length inside her. Silas began thrusting and Ophelia experimented with canting her hips against him, felt her muscles already beginning to clench around his cock. Tilting her hips again she found her rhythm, nudging her clit against him with every thrust, and then she was coming again, head thrown back, hands clutching him to her. The climax shuddered through her, spooled out along each limb in fiery, golden tendrils. Silas crooned her name, still thrusting, holding her hips hard now as he chased his own pleasure. Her body milked him, every thrust sending echoes of pleasure through her until he stilled and pulled free from her, stroking himself twice, and spending across her bare legs. Their breath mingled between them, ragged and sharp. Silas lifted his face to hers, pressing kisses along her jaw. She pressed her mouth to his, nibbling at his full top lip, licking her tongue into the wet warmth of him.

"Thank you," they said over each other, colour high on their cheeks.

Silas's arms came swiftly around Ophelia and he lifted her onto her feet, tenderly straightening her skirts and putting her chemise to rights. "I love you, Ophelia Blackwood," he said solemnly, brushing her hair back from her face before tidying his shirt and waistcoat. She could only bury her face in his chest, the wobbly happiness she felt inside too big to put into words.

CHAPTER 40

They organised themselves as best they could, covering Ophelia's damp skirts with her shawl and buttoning Silas's coat so that his wrinkled trousers were less evident. They lingered in the garden, neither wanting to break the spell of the afternoon. Silas felt like a zeppelin had inflated in his chest, buoyant and giddy, able to face anything if it meant doing so with Ophelia by his side. He felt in the pocket of his jacket, finding the cool loop of silver still waiting there, and he knew there was one final thing to do before they tackled things in the house.

"Fee?" he began. "There's something I've been wanting to ask you, or rather to give you." She turned to him, her face still flushed, eyes bright and sharp as a bird's, an edge of wariness suddenly there. He hurried to continue before he lost the thread of his thoughts. "I was wrong about so many things before, even this," he said, fishing the ring from his pocket. "I brought this for you, a token of what we might make together, a promise more than an agreement." She stared at the band in the palm of his large hand and he could see that she recognised it as Hannah's. "Hannah gave it to me, thought it might be the right thing for our fresh start, but the more I think of it, the more I realise that it's me who needs to wear it, to remember 'deeds not words.' I see now that you've always known that, haven't you, love? You've been fighting for it your whole life, and I've only just joined you." Silas slipped the band onto his pinkie finger, flexed his hand experimentally, and then held it out to her. "A reminder to myself that what we choose together is more important than anything the world demands of us. Always."

He wasn't sure what she would say, had only really realised what he was going to say as he said it. It felt right, though. He watched her looking at the band on his finger, saw recognition and a flash of hope. A soft smile played on her lips, almost more for herself than to him. He was so glad he had slid the ring onto his own finger, recognized in the moment that his own fear had made it hard to hear. He knew that so many people tossed around a great many words, but did very little to make them concrete. Perhaps this small gesture could be the beginning of many things. Changes he would make, ones they would make together. He wanted to be Ophelia's champion, to protect her, but he saw now that she didn't need him to do that. She was capable of anything she put her mind to, but she wanted someone, *him*, to walk with her, to choose a path together. That he could do, *that* he would move mountains to do.

* * *

THE SLIM SILVER band glinted against Silas's hand, his skin tanned by the sun and work out of doors. Ophelia took in the lines across his outstretched palm, the long lines of his strong fingers, the corded muscles of his arm disappearing up into his sleeve. She thought of the disastrous marriage proposals her father had tried to engineer, of how he had wanted to negotiate the price of having her off his hands, a bit of extra baggage he was happy to be rid of. She thought of Silas, standing where her father had almost taken everything, of what it had meant to him to leave for war, to lose this connection to his family, how he had stripped himself bare for her. All he offered her now was himself, untethered by land or obligation, willing to walk into a future of their own making because he loved her.

She looked up from his hand to his broad face, eyes searching hers, his mobile mouth still, drawn a little tight with concern. He waited for her answer, patient, and her heart clenched with love. She wanted to tell him how joy rocketed around her, fireworks on Bonfire Night, sun dancing on the water's surface, larks in a wide blue sky, but all that came from her lips was, "You are the very best of everything, Silas Larke, and I love you beyond words."

He stood stock still for a moment then grasped her hand, and pulling her into his chest, swung her around, whooping until tears rolled down her cheeks and her head swam dizzily.

"My God, I love you, you magnificent woman!" he said, laughing. "I want to shout it from the top of a tower, take out an ad in the *Times*—no—send it by Morse code around the world!"

He let her go and she slipped down his front, clothing catching between them. She reached up to cup his face in her hands, feeling the rough and soft of his cheeks under her fingers.

"For the first time in so long, I am excited for the future," she said, softly. "For our future."

"Let's not linger then," Silas said. "We could stay with my mother for a night or two, until you've finished up at the house. When you're ready we'll return to Mrs. Darling's?"

"Mhmm, I would like to see your mother again, and Samuel. I am a little anxious to get back to the farm though; I've my WLA work term to complete and Mrs. Darling'll still need our help to fulfill the required yield. After that, I guess it's up to us where we want to go." She slid her hand into his, squeezing gently. "I need to lock the doors before we go to your mother's, and I'd like to bring a painting with me . . . it's of my mother, and I want to have her with me."

Silas nodded. "We'll keep her with you always."

* * *

ONE CARPET BAG, one painting wrapped in burlap. That was what her life at Wood Grange amounted to in physical belongings. She should have felt weighted down by the prospect of her father's debts, the health of the estate, but Ophelia felt lighter than she could ever remember. She felt a steady confidence in Mr. Bone's work with the will; for the first time, it felt like there was possibility about the estate, instead of defeat. Silas's feet crunched along the gravel drive next to hers, and she couldn't wait to crowd around Mrs. Darling's table for tea. It wasn't that she thought everything would be perfect from now on; she knew that the future would bring its share of challenges. The farm was still in danger of being repossessed, Silas might be called to the front once his leg was fully healed, she had no idea what she might do for work after the WLA finished with her, and she wasn't naïve enough to believe that she and Silas could live outside the boundaries of polite society without consequence, but right now all those seemed surmountable. Silas loved her, and the brilliant joy of that eclipsed everything else at the moment. They would find a way; she was confident of that.

Swinging her arms, Silas's hand in hers, Ophelia turned for one last look at the house.

"I'll never be able to think of that garden the same way again," Silas said in a theatrical aside, eyes mischievous.

Ophelia laughed and pulled him down for a kiss. "I hope not," she said.

They walked slowly up to Silas's childhood home hand in hand, the light of evening falling, birdsong all around them. When they reached the door and knocked, Mrs. Larke threw both the door and her arms open with a happy cheer, bundling them inside for dinner and a visit.

CHAPTER 41

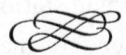

Ophelia slept on the train the next day, her head lolling against Silas's shoulder as they rolled through the Somerset countryside. She hadn't intended to, they had so much to discuss and work through, but exhaustion caught up with her and dragged her under. Silas's warm bulk and the clattering of the train tracks lulled her, taking the edge of panic off all the new information circling her mind. Silas nudged her awake on the approach to the station.

"We're almost home now, Fee. Time to wake up."

He squeezed her hand gently, but didn't kiss her, though she could tell he was thinking about it by the way his eyes lingered over her lips. She wished they were alone so that he might soothe her nerves with the brush of his lips, tell her everything would be alright with a flick of his tongue. But that would have to be for later. For now, they needed to get back to Mrs. Darling's and finish the haying. She thought about Wood Grange, about her father dying alone in the house, truly an island now that she knew the extent of his financial mismanagement. It was incredible what a life of entitlement did for you, she thought. To be utterly at the end of one's resources and still acting as though you had the upper hand. She was incredulous and surprisingly sad. Not for her father, really, but for a person so corroded by vice and their own malice.

The blast of the train whistle cut through her thoughts, steam billowing outside the windows. She and Silas stood, he handed down her satchel, and tucking her mother's portrait under his arm, led her to the doorway. The small station platform was quiet, only a porter and a couple of passengers making their way to the exit. Outside, waiting in the late afternoon light, was the local trap, the driver lounging against his seat, cap pulled low over his eyes.

"The Darling farm, please," said Silas.

"Right away, guv," he said, straightening, and reaching down to take their belongings.

Silas handed Ophelia up into the back seat and slid in beside her. They pulled out of the train station and jogged down the high street, making their way past the church hall and out into the country lanes. Ophelia felt the press of Silas's thigh down the length of hers, muscular and firm through the layers of their clothes. He smiled at her, and she was sure that he felt as comforted by her presence as she did by his. He kissed her then, chaste and quick, but she felt the promise of everything to come and couldn't help throwing her arms around his neck, pressing her nose into the perfect warm skin of his neck. "I love you," she whispered and felt his lips move against her hair.

"I love you."

CHAPTER 42

There was utter chaos when they arrived back at the farm; as if some semaphore had sent word of their happy reunion ahead. Bess hurtled out of the house, clasping Ophelia and Silas in a warm hug.

"I'm so glad you're both back," she said into their shoulders.

"Glad to be home," Silas had said with a laugh. "How've things been here? No more news from the inspector, I hope?"

"Nah, he's stayed away, though we've just received notice of his visit in two weeks," said Hannah from the kitchen doorway. "Glad to see you both back," she had added and shot Ophelia a look that said "we'll talk later."

Mrs. Darling hustled them all inside and pushing Silas and Ophelia into their chairs at the table, began pouring tea and passing out plates laden with scones. She placed a jar of plum jam and the butter dish on the table, saying, "'Tis good to 'ave you all back where ye belong. Eat up now, we've a mountain of work to make up for."

Ophelia didn't think she had ever felt more at home or happier at the prospect of work. Mrs. Darling had patted her hand across the table and began to fill her in on the drying wheat she and Silas had cut from the first field. After eating, they all walked down to check on the harvest, and Ophelia had been relieved to see it standing tall, moving gently in the breeze, the green heads beginning to swell after three months of growth. She tried to remember what the field had been like when Silas first joined them, all rubble and weeds, and how they had fought off the birds and waited out the weather so that they might now look out over this promise of a harvest. She reached for Silas's hand and slid her fingers into his. Back at the barn, she greeted Samson and Delilah.

"Hello again, fellow," she had murmured to Samson over his stall door. He flicked an ear, hearing her, but not lifting his head from his pile of hay. His heavy jaw worked as he took in mouthful after mouthful, tail swishing away a fly every so often. She opened the door and went to stand next to him, petting his warm flank and down his thick neck. Samson stamped a hoof but kept eating, and Ophelia lowered her head to his warm side and let herself relax into his steady bulk. The horse's solid body tethered her to her own, to this farm and these people, and she was more grateful for that than she expected. After checking on Delilah, she returned to the house to unpack and trade her skirts for her uniform once again.

That evening after chores had been done and animals tucked away, they all gathered in the living room to talk over the last few days. Ophelia and Silas shared the outline of what had happened at Wood Grange, leaving out their promises to each other, though Ophelia saw Hannah taking in her ring on Silas's finger. She would share that later, she thought, when it didn't feel quite so private. Silas rose to bring the teapot and refill everyone's cups while Bess shared the news from dairy and Hannah read aloud from the latest edition of *The Landswoman*. Silas, having filled cups and replenished the biscuit supply, settled himself back on to the settee next to Ophelia.

"So what is that you think you'll do about the estate then?" Hannah asked.

"I'm not entirely sure yet," Ophelia admitted. "Mr. Bone is finalizing the will, so for the moment I've closed the house up. Silas's mother and Samuel will continue on with their farm as usual, and I suppose when I hear from Mr. Bone I will have to make some kind of decision."

"That's a great deal to consider on your own, Ophelia," said Mrs. Darling, soberly. "Though I have had words with him in the past, I'm awfully glad you have Casper to guide you. He is honest, above all else."

"When all this is over, the WLA, the war"—Bess gestured, encompassing it all—"perhaps you could go back to live there? Seems a shame for it to lay empty."

"I don't think I would ever live at the house again," Ophelia said after a pause, thinking aloud more than speaking. "I don't know that it was ever really my home . . ." The others waited for her to finish. She turned to Silas, aware that they hadn't had a chance to discuss this aspect of things. "Do you think we might live in one of the smaller houses? I mean, would you like to, could you see yourself being happy there?"

He took her hand and smoothed it over his knee, tracing each finger there. "I think it would be perfect. I'd live under a toadstool if it meant I could be with you." Then whispering "excuse me, ladies" to the others, he cupped Ophelia's face in his hands and kissed her, his mouth moving over hers possessively, perfectly.

Bess whooped and Hannah whistled, while Mrs. Darling laughed and herded them out of the room. Alone again at last, Ophelia sighed into his mouth and Silas deepened the kiss, drawing her into his lap. Outside the sitting room window, a perfect indigo evening rose against a sliver of summer moon, neither of which they saw.

*　*　*

The following week passed in a steady rhythm of much work and little rest, bringing them to the end of June. Ophelia had received a letter from Mr. Bone and sat lost in thought, paper on the table in front of her.

"What are you mulling over, Fee?" Silas asked, coming in from the yard.

"Just trying to understand what inheriting this actually means . . . for us, of course, but also for the estate. It seems unreal, honestly. I mean, I knew that my father was entirely too free with money, but I had no idea that he had beggared the coffers so entirely. The house can't be sold, but I suppose I might rent it out. There's a new society that I've read about that cares for ancient houses, maintains them. Perhaps I might put it into their care?"

He was quiet for a long moment, looking out of the window. "What you said when we were there, about making something better, what did you mean? What would you do if you could make Wood Grange into anything you wanted? Or would you still walk away from it all, as you intended?"

Ophelia rubbed her fingers over the creases in the paper and thought about his question. What would she like to do? What had she always wanted to do and had that changed since joining the WLA? Since falling in love with Silas? Since meeting Hannah and Mrs. Darling and Bess?

"When I started my training at the WLA, I was rubbish . . . no, truly," she said when Silas tried to interrupt and correct her. "I was, but I am not anymore and that is because I had a place to learn and women to teach me, show me. Mrs. Darling, and even Hannah and Bess, let me stumble, but made me get up and keep going. I think if I could do anything with the estate, I would make a place for women to learn to farm, to cultivate gardens, not just arrange flowers. A place where they could learn all the things that men know from experience and education and sharing information. Somewhere that they are taken seriously and not treated as anomalies or unnatural creatures infringing on men's work." She took a deep breath, realising she was just getting started, the thought of what she was saying lighting her up inside. "The estate could be a place where students might billet if they didn't have the support of their families, a safe place where they could learn in community and be with other women, and perhaps men, who shared their commitment to equality and education. Imagine what it could mean to communities all over the country if there were qualified farmers who wanted to stay in their villages and make a living from the land? I know it would be complicated for women to acquire farms or to convince family members of their merit, but the chance to be educated would be such a magnificent start, don't you think?"

Silas was smiling at her, happiness and pride sparking in his eyes. "It's bloody brilliant, Fee. Yes. Yes, to all of it."

It felt right, already half-formed in her mind. Excitement thrilled through her at the possibilities.

She laughed, then sobered. "But what about what your plans, Silas? Have you an idea of what you would truly like to do?"

"This country has wallowed about under the old guard for far too long, and I'm a product of that as much as anyone," he said, gesturing to his leg. "I've had my fill of destruction. I want to build something new, something good . . . now that I've seen my family settled, I'm not sure exactly what that is. I would like to do something for the men that I met in convalescence or for men like me, coming home to a life they don't recognize. It would have meant a great deal to me to have had someone to speak with when I returned."

Ophelia felt her heart clench at the thought of Silas, alone and injured, unsure of what his future might hold. "That's a brilliant idea, Silas. I'm so sorry you were alone during that time."

He kissed the top of her head. "I wouldn't change it for anything; after all it brought me here... to you."

Ophelia and Silas looked at each other and smiling, Silas said, "Tell them what you're thinking of, Fee."

That night at dinner, Ophelia broached her idea for the estate with the other women. Describing it a second time hadn't been as hard as she had expected, and Ophelia had the strange feeling that voicing her idea was slowly giving it solidity, the first steps to making it a reality. She was beginning to see how it all might work in her head, could almost imagine the halls of the house echoing with the sound of many feet, the gardens alive again. Mrs. Greene had done an admirable job of keeping the house habitable in the face of her father's miserly allowance, but it was clear the building was not truly being used. To have so much land and living space laying fallow seemed the height of waste, especially in the face of so much sacrifice by so many. Making the house productive was the only way that Ophelia could see to make things right. She outlined her idea for an agricultural college, a place where women might study and be welcome even without the support, financial or otherwise, of their families. Hannah immediately expressed interest, suggesting there might be classes in basic chemistry or soil cultivation, then more cautiously mentioning the possibility of teaching self-defence or a woman's rights under the law. Ophelia nodded, feeling buoyant with possibility. *This might really work. With help, I might really make something of this.*

* * *

THE WHEAT WAS COMING WAIST-HIGH, the whiskers of its heads scratching at the backs of Ophelia's hands as she stood just inside the planted edge of the field. The abandoned piece of land was hardly recognizable now; the brambles and weeds nowhere in evidence, the uneven ground now almost flat, the dark earth barely visible under the haze of new wheat. They had lost a fair amount of the new crop to birds, but with reseeding and fabric streamers tied to poles throughout the field, they had managed to shepherd most of it to this moment. Ophelia turned at the sound of voices coming up behind her. Mrs. Darling, Silas at her elbow, and the whippet-lean figure of the War Ag inspector crested the edge of the makeshift field. Hannah and Bess followed at a distance, arms linked, heads bowed in conversation.

When they had received notice of the committee's plan to inspect their work, Ophelia had wanted to check the field herself before they arrived. Standing there this morning, the sun warm on her back, the long list of farm work still to be done after this meeting, and the knowledge that they would face this inspection together, filled her with a sense of calm purpose. She knew they had met this challenge, that *she* had met this challenge. There was, of course, still the matter of getting the increased yield cut and threshed, but she knew that they would face that when they came to it. Kissing Silas in the kitchen hallway before she headed to the field, he had said, "We couldn't have done it without your work, Fee. You've proved yourself up to the task, over and over. I'm so proud of you."

"I have, haven't I?" she said, feeling herself pinken slightly, shy to take the compliment. "I've finally found my place, I think . . . with you, with this work."

She thought of his words again, watching the breeze move through the wheat, listening to the voices draw closer, and knew she was home. It wasn't a place, she realized, but inside herself.

They passed the inspection. Mrs. Darling would keep her land. They all whooped and laughed after the dour inspector had taken his leave, Silas swinging Mrs. Darling about in a dizzy waltz. Ophelia smiled until her cheeks hurt and thought she had never imagined happiness could look like this.

EPILOGUE

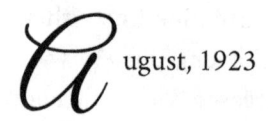

August, 1923

OPHELIA WOKE SLOWLY, taking in the room through heavy-lidded eyes. There was a comfortable ache in her shoulders and an even more comfortable one between her legs. She rolled over in the bed, stretching out an arm across the pillows. Silas's mussed hair was fanned out, his mouth slightly slack, breathing sleepy. Ophelia ran a finger over the dark arch of his brow and his long lashes fluttered against his cheek, giving her a glimpse of his green eyes. Sun pooled at the foot of their bed, shining through the window overlooking the garden, and Ophelia scooted over, nuzzling up to Silas and kissing the tip of his nose.

"Wake up, sleepy," she said. "Time to start the day."

He groaned softly and snaked an arm around her waist to draw her tight against him. "I hardly slept a wink last night," he growled, running a hand up her thigh and squeezing her bare bottom.

It was true, they had stayed up far too late making love, and in between, talking about their plans for the estate. There was so much to do this year; repairs on outbuildings, new gardens to be dug, courses to be developed and taught, and all of it to be accomplished on a relatively modest budget. The thought of it cooled Ophelia's ardour a little, though not so much that she didn't relish taking advantage of the few spare minutes they still had. She slid beneath the linen sheet, running her hands down Silas's chest, stopping to scrape over a nipple, then over the drum of his belly and the smooth bones of his hips, to take his thick stand in her hand. He groaned and gave himself over to her, letting her have her way before grasping her hips and sliding under her. She rose over him, smiling, and let herself sink down to the hilt. The house woke slowly around them as they rocked into each other, finding their rhythm, calling out their pleasure, kissing each other awake.

"I feel I might never get used to this," Silas said, gently wiping Ophelia's sticky stomach and thighs, then his own. "To fall asleep with you in my arms, to wake with you here still feels unreal."

The silver band on Silas's little finger caught her eye as he tended to her and she was struck again, as she was so many times a day, with love for this man. She marvelled at how entirely improbable their second chance was, what a gift it was to be loved by Silas and to love him, to imagine an old age with him.

"I love you," she said, stilling his hand and running her fingertip over the band on his finger. "You are everything in the world to me, Silas."

"And you are to me, Fee, have always been everything, from the very first." He brushed a stray hair away from her face and leaned in to kiss her, his weight on the mattress tipping her toward him. He gathered her to him, washcloth forgotten, and deepened the kiss. "My moon"—a kiss to her chin—"my stars"—a kiss to her collarbone—"my whole universe," he finished with a long swipe of tongue around her exposed nipple. She moaned as they tumbled back into the sheets and Silas rose up above her, eyes dark and promising.

Later, they lay perfectly sated, curled around each other in the shambles of their bed, listening to the sounds of the morning outside the house. Not wanting to ever leave Silas's arms, but knowing they were already late, Ophelia slid from the bed and went to the window, the bedsheet wound around her. Looking out she could see Wood Grange a little ways down the lane, its honey stone beginning to glow in the early morning light. Figures moved across her vision and she knew everyone would be getting ready for the day, could already see groups of students making their way down the lane past the farmhouse.

After tackling negotiations with the estate lawyers and Mr. Bone, she and Silas had agreed to rent the lands around the estate to fund the cost of turning Wood Grange into an agricultural college for women who wanted to make their livelihood as farmers or gardeners. The end of the war and the return of men to their jobs meant that many women who had enjoyed the freedom of employment now found themselves being pushed back into a domestic sphere they were happy to have left. So many wanted the chance to be educated and supported in a field of their choosing that enrolment had been so successful in the first year that they had had to recruit more instructors and convert some more of the outbuildings into classrooms and accommodations. Ophelia still wanted to pinch herself when she walked among the test gardens, through a classroom where students were learning about stock breeding or animal husbandry, or when she heard women's voices raised in eager discussion. She had created a place for women to come together, to learn, to expand their horizons, to test their mettle in an industry built for men. Knowing that she and Silas had built it together, through discussion and partnership was a joy she hardly knew how to express. They had taken the sorrow of the estate and Merritt's malice and alchemized it into something rich and filled with community. Besides she and Silas's still undefined partnership, it was Ophelia's proudest accomplishment. She was drawn from her thoughts by Silas at her shoulder.

"Some tea, love," he said, pressing a kiss to her shoulder and a cup and saucer into her hand.

"Thank you," she said. "How lucky I am to have you."

"Luck has bloody little to do with it, my sweet," he said, eyeing her backside like a vaudeville villain. "Both brilliant and beautiful . . . you'll never be rid of me." He waggled his eyebrows playfully. She swatted at him, laughing, and went to dress.

***

WOOD GRANGE WAS ALREADY BUSTLING with activity when Ophelia made her way through the door. Mrs. Greene strode through from the kitchen with the week's menu and shopping list under one arm, and a tea tray balanced in the opposite hand.

"Oh, Ophelia, thank goodness you're 'ere. I've a mountain of things to discuss with you. There's a letter here from Mrs. Darling, too."

"Right away, Mrs. Greene," she said, looking forward to reading Mrs. Darling's news. After the signing of the armistice and the disbanding of the WLA workforce, Mrs. Darling had continued on without her billets but wrote Ophelia weekly and visited when she could. Ophelia took the papers from the housekeeper and made her way to the dining room, now set to accommodate the many students, instructors, and employees of the Wood Grange Agricultural College for Women.

"Will Mr. Larke be joining us for breakfast?" Mrs. Greene asked.

"Mhmm," said Ophelia, already opening Mrs. Darling's letter. "Silas is just behind me. He was just making some notes in the library."

Silas's own experience of returning injured had been positive and productive, but many fellow soldiers were not so lucky, finding themselves alone, even shunned for wounds that were not so easily healed with a victory parade and a medal of honour. It was newly being called shell shock, but there was a great deal of misinformation and not much help for men trying to navigate life after the front. Having found a home with Ophelia and purpose in their work, he had been speaking with her about compiling ideas on how to offer other men the same chance.

Ophelia couldn't quite believe that it was her lot to be surrounded by friends who believed in her so deeply, who gave her the freedom and support to live so exquisitely full a life. Hannah had taken up the lease on a small cottage near the estate and was Ophelia's constant companion on long rambling walks through the woods. She introduced the women of the college to subjects as wide ranging as fixing farm machinery and basic soil analysis, to birth control and self-defence. Ophelia was grateful for her wry wit and her dedication to the students. It had been Hannah who had buoyed Ophelia through times of worry and indecision, insisting that educating any woman who desired it, showing them that they were capable of more than they were told, was the best way to ensure that fewer women would fall prey to family tyrants like Ophelia's father or unscrupulous employers looking to take advantage of their staff. Bess had taken rooms in Banbury and continued running Mr. Bone's dairy, in which they had become partners, renaming it Wiley & Bone Dairy. She wrote often of new techniques she was trying and ideas for maintaining consistent production. In her last letter, she had mentioned someone with whom she had been walking out. Ophelia looked forward to the next time Bess could make the trip to the estate.

Sitting down at the long table in what had always been the formal dining room, Ophelia reached for her teacup and looked down the table. They all gathered each morning to share a meal and go over the day's tasks, a habit they had acquired at Mrs. Darling's and never really shaken. Hannah and Mrs. Greene talked quietly while they ate. Silas appeared and folded his long legs into the chair next to Ophelia's, sliding his hand under the table to run a finger down her leg from thigh to knee. She sucked in a breath, trying not to draw attention to herself. Silas smiled at her, love and lust mingling in his eyes, making Ophelia truly lightheaded. It was all she could do not to demand he take her home and back to bed immediately.

"Something the matter, love?"

"Nothing a quick lunch meeting won't solve," she said, running her own hand down his arm to his lap. He grunted softly and captured her hand in his own.

"I am entirely at your disposal, my lady," he said lowly, brushing his lips across her knuckles.

Ophelia laughed aloud, at the improbable, wonderful life she and Silas were building, at the joy of being surrounded by strong women who were loved by gentle men, and most of all, at the wonder of finding oneself at long last.

ACKNOWLEDGMENTS

Dear Reader,

Firstly, thank you with my whole heart for reading Out with Lanterns. This book is the book of my heart, and I am so grateful that it is out in the world, and that you saw fit to add it to your shelves.

I came to romance late and have been making up for lost time ever since. In 2020, through a random series of recommendations and articles, I ordered Evie Dunmore's Bringing Down the Duke, and dear reader, it changed my life. Not in a graceful, tender way, but in a brick-through-the-window way, laying bare a bunch of my own literary snobberies and preconceived notions. I was hilariously unprepared for the power of a book that could highlight the fundamental similarities of the current and historical states of feminism, construct an argument for enfranchisement for all, highlight in glorious prose the radical importance of female desire, and a fulfilling happily ever after for everyone. It literally knocked me on my ass. Dunmore was quickly followed by a deep dive into Sarah MacLean's entire backlist, and then onto Tessa Dare and Eva Leigh. As my reading continued, so did my understanding of what romance could really do, how subversive and powerful it is as a genre. KJ Charles, Alexis Hall, Courtney Milan, Olivia Waite, Cat Sebastian, Joanna Lowell, Adriana Herrera, Sherry Thomas, E.E. Ottoman, Jane Hadley, Louise Mayberry, Elizabeth Hoyt, and so many others continue to engage and educate me, and I am grateful for every one of their books, and to the community of readers, reviewers, podcasters, and writers that make up Romancelandia. It is a place I have come to love dearly.

My own novel came to me in fits and starts and would not be in your hands if not for endless support from so many. George and the women of Calliope's – I am so grateful for all our Sundays. Jen Prokop – for unstinting encouragement and straight talk during developmental edits. My beloved Procrastination of Romantics – I'd be lost without you all. I'm so glad I get to talk books and life with you every day. Kaitlin Slowik – you are a genius editor and I'm so grateful for your work on this book. And truly saving the best for last, my family, for being my biggest cheerleaders from before the very first words, for always believing I could finish it and put it out in the world, and for never letting me think that no one would read it. I love you more than I can ever adequately express.

Hillary

AUTHOR'S NOTE

June 2025

Dear Reader,
    I think I might have always loved the idea of the Edwardian era – tea parties in sprawling gardens, lawn and lace whitework dresses, the kind of effortless elegance reflected in the Gibson Girl sketches. In my youth, it seemed idyllic, full of ease. Of course, the reality is much more complicated than any of those original attractions, and as a woman coming to my author's journey in the second half of my life, I find I am even more interested in the juxtaposition of the last endless summer feeling memorialized in so many period dramas with the realities of the era – labour unrest, huge wealth disparities, violent agitation for equality, the waning of the Victorian colonial project.

    It turns out that the twist of brutal and beautiful was the place that I found Ophelia Blackwood, a woman born into fortunate circumstances who longs for something more than what she understands society means to offer her. I wanted to find out what a woman in her circumstances would do with the chance to build an entirely different life for herself – what she would take to instinctively and what she would need to learn about herself, about other women, about the world. I wondered about a question I come back to regularly – what does it mean to be a feminist and believe in a happy ending? Are love and independence mutually exclusive? Now, I write romance novels, so I hope you know there will always be a happy ending, but I still think the question of how Ophelia and Silas get there is a glorious one to explore.

I didn't set out to write Silas as a man who had no growing to do, nor as an alpha male in need of reformation, but I wondered how he might arrive at the same questions that Ophelia faces from a significantly different angle. He is an injured man in a world that is unprepared to treat or even truly understand the physical and mental devastation wrought by the Great War, a man that has understood love as caretaking, providing for others, but is faced with a woman who wants none of that from him. How would he envision a happy ending and what would it look like for him to learn a new way to love Ophelia?

Farm work and billeting in essentially a stranger's house pushed Ophelia entirely out of her comfort zone and allowed me to create a world removed from ballrooms and lavish dresses. In war time, some of the smaller aspects of social rigidity fall away in the face of the immediate challenge of survival. I loved the chance to have Ophelia learn more about herself through the relationship she begins to develop with her own body, its physical limitations, but also the strength she didn't know she was capable of. I imagined her understanding of her physicality changing drastically that first year on Mrs. Darling's farm, and consequently when Silas arrives, her ability to speak to her own desires, to relish them, exists in a way that it hadn't when they knew each other on her father's estate.

AUTHOR'S NOTE

I love historical romance for the myriad ways it gives us to talk about our current situations, to look at how to make different decisions than those made in the past, and, vitally, to tell the stories of marginalized and queer people living happy, fulfilling lives, as they have always done. It is thrilling to contribute, in my own tiny way, to the larger conversations that are happening in historical romance.

And now, onto a few history notes for those interested in the concrete details! Out with Lanterns is set during a time period I am fascinated with, but that I know may be slightly unfamiliar to some readers. The Edwardian era is made up of the years of Edward VII's reign, 1901 to 1910, and often extended to 1914, and the early years of George V's reign. Much like the Regency, the 'cultural' Edwardian era covers more years than the number of actual years assigned it. Generally, it was a time of great social upheaval and is known for being a period where wealth disparity was at one of its all-time highs. Paradoxically, it is also seen as the last golden summer before the destruction and terror of the First World War. This is largely a nostalgic gloss looking back from the 1920's when the relatively quiet, steady era could be seen set between the prosperity and colonial activities of the Victoria era and the horror of WWI.

Demands for better working conditions were coming from a more politically educated and active working class, fueling, in turn, the growing strength of trade unions, and the significant rise in the Labour movement. This dissatisfaction brought a Liberal government to power in 1906, and over the next decade saw the proposal of bills aimed at regulating work hours, the first steps towards the welfare state with National Insurance, and efforts to reduce the power of the House of Lords, and in 1909, the People's Budget.

Though it was blocked for a year, it was eventually passed and made use of increased taxes on land and high incomes to fund expanded social welfare programmes.

Unfortunately, women's suffrage was not on either the general public's or the Liberals' agenda at this time, though the National Union of Women's Suffrage Societies, formed by the joining of two other groups in 1897, and led by Millicent Fawcett, had already been active for years working to peacefully rally for the right to vote. The Women's Social and Political Union was formed by Emmeline Pankhurst in 1903 with an eye to a more politically active and militant activities to advocate for the right to vote in public elections. Hunger strikes, vocal protests, and acts of violence and vandalism were some of the tactics that Pankhurst and her eldest daughter, Christabel, encouraged in the face of the stultifying lack of progress on the issue. The tactic was divisive, but effective in drawing attention to the suffragette cause. The women, who were derisively labeled suffragettes by the press, embraced the term, even changing the pronunciation to a hard 'g' to emphasize that they would *get* the vote.

The determination with which these early feminists fought for the right to representation was met with horrifying force by police, government, and some of the general public. Jail, force feeding via tube, physical and verbal attacks, and social disgrace were just some of what these women faced. There are some excellent books about the suffragettes, as well as the suffragists, and I encourage you to learn more about these women who fought for our right to vote, knowing that they might not even experience the right themselves. It is a solemn reminder of the urgency to protect the right to vote, to be involved in our governments, and to protect that right for everyone.

AUTHOR'S NOTE

I'm sure that many of you are familiar with the WLA from the second World War, there are more than a few books and films about the women who volunteered during that time, but you might be as surprised as I was to find out that the WLA actually started during the First World War.

In the first years of the war, food shortages were not a concern due to a particularly good harvest in 1914 and 1915, but by 1917 a shortage of farm workers, the threat of a German submarine blockade, and falling wheat yields had the British government trying many tactics to increase food production and stave off potential famine. In January 1917, a Women's Branch was established with the Board of Agriculture with a focus on increasing the number of women working on the land and addressing their training and effectiveness. By March of that year with Miss Meriel Talbot as Director, the Women's Branch became a division of the Food Production Department, and the first appeal was made for women over 18 to apply to join the Women's Land Army. Over 30,000 women applied and by mid-July 2,000 women had been assigned work placements.

A woman who applied to join the WLA would be interviewed to ascertain whether she could be sent straight to a farm (if she had previous agricultural experience) or whether she would be sent to one of the training centres for a four-week course in farm work. Depending on how this went, the woman would be held back or assigned to one of the many farms desperate for labour. It was essential to replace the men on furlough who were soon being recalled to the fighting in Europe.

Predictably, there was a good deal of push back on the idea of women labouring on farms, and not only from farmers themselves, who were loathe to waste time with women who were expected to be squeamish and weak, unfit for farms on every level. Citizens, both men and women, also worried that the harsh conditions and rigorous physical demands of the work would roughen women, that it was unseemly and unladylike to be involved in men's work. The messaging around recruitment walked a tight rope to engage women who were prepared to take on the work, while leaning heavily into the patriotic image of the rose of English womanhood rising to the challenge of the times. Eventually, farmers and skeptics were convinced that women were capable of doing the work, though official recognition of the Land Girls' contribution to both wars did not come until 2008.

Silas would have been one of many farmers who could apply for exemption from being sent overseas due to working in a reserved occupation. There were many caveats to an application for exemption and it became more difficult as the war went on. In my research about reserved occupations, I came across a number of notes in county agricultural meetings that referred to men being denied exemption due to their employers refusing to sign the paperwork for the request. I am not certain how common it was, but it fit into the narrative I was building around Ophelia's father. More research about the convalescent experience of soldiers back in England led me to the practise of employing soldiers on leave or in recovery as farm labourers. There was a massive wheat shortfall in the last years of the war and a corresponding drought of able-bodied men to bring in the harvest, and so the work of the WLA and the other farm labour departments were supplemented with available soldiers home from the front. Silas, injured too badly to immediately return to the fighting, is well enough to help with farm work.

Finally, Mrs. Darling and the WLA women face a number of visits from different War Agricultural Committee members who impress upon them the potential of losing at least part of Mrs. Darling's farm. Again, in my research through various Somerset archives I found notes from committee meetings that included mentions of farms needing to be kept under surveillance and some that were in danger of being commandeered and run under committee supervision. There was immense pressure on farmers to produce enough food for the country during the war and the looming threat of failing to meet that demand would have put even more stress on the women to succeed.

I have focused on Ophelia's experiences once she is billeted at Mrs. Darling's farm and because I write romance, the main thrust of my story is her relationship with Silas and how her growing sense of self confidence through her work affects her approach to a future with him. For books that focus more on the day-to-day life of Land Girls, or for nonfiction titles that outline the history of the Women's Land Army, I am including a bibliography below. Happy reading and researching!

Selected Research Books:

The Women's Land Army: A Portrait, Gill Clarke
We Also Served, Vivien Newman
Women on the Land, Carol Twinch
Women in the Great War, Tanya and Stephen Wynn
The Women's Land Army, Neil R. Storey and Molly Housego
Great War Fashion, Lucy Adlington
www.thewomenslandarmy.co.uk
www.iwm.org.uk

ABOUT THE AUTHOR

Hillary Bowen writes historical romance full of swoon and feminism. She lives on the west coast of Canada with her family, two cats, and a flock of hens. This is her first novel.

If you loved Silas and Ophelia and want to spend a little more time with them, find an extra epilogue here - https://dl.bookfunnel.com/n97yfv453n.

To receive updates on upcoming books, character art, and a free novella coming late fall 2025, subscribe to my newsletter: https://hillarybowen.com/#about.